HUNTED
is the PREY

Donovan Hoult

Publisher:
Inspiring Publishers
P.O. Box 159, Calwell, ACT Australia 2905
Email: publishaspg@gmail.com
http://www.inspiringpublishers.com

National Library of Australia Cataloguing-in-Publication entry

Author: Hoult, Donovan

Title: **Hunted is The Prey**/*Donovan Hoult*.

ISBN: 9781925477542 (pbk)

Subjects: Detective and mystery stories.
        Australian fiction.

1

The kid kicked idly at the gibbers on the dirt road. The parched earth stretched until it shimmered and finally melded into the horizon of heat. The plains spread endlessly with the odd stunted salt bush fighting to maintain its hold on the relentless quest for survival. The black soil plains supported sparse native grass the scavenging merino sheep and nature reduced to sun-burnt stubble.

He watched as the leader of a small bunch of sheep trotted up to a cluster of dried remnants, took a quick nibble at no more than air and quickly moved onto the next. The rest of the flock did exactly the same, each following the leader in turn without variance to the approach. Immediately the rest of the flock got close, the leader would feel threatened it would miss something ahead if it did not keep in the fore, and quickly moved on. It was those few dry grass stems that kept its momentum at a constant trot. Stupid bastards, the kid reflected. Just like bloody humans, all blindly following the leader.

He rubbed the side of his face. It was extremely sore. He brushed his tongue over the broken stubs of his teeth, his tongue blistered and sore from the action, but he kept doing it. Pieces of a broken tooth dislodged and he spat them out along with a stream of salty tasting blood. Christ, he almost had the bastard, but a lump of wood sure stops you when you're least expecting it. The fight had been fair he thought. He had kicked the antagonist twice in the guts and was lining up for the final blow when the shout from behind warned him of the danger. He turned and feinted to one side but the move had been anticipated. The lump of wood caught him across the cheek and side of the mouth. The pain was excruciating as the tears welled up in his eyes and blurred his vision. From that point he had no chance as his antagonist got to his feet and sprayed well aimed punches to his head and eyes. He felt the threshold of oblivion overtaking him as he drifted into the sensory suspension.

"Get out of this shed immediately." The words came slowly through the mist of consciousness. "Go cause trouble in some other gang, but after this I'll make fucking sure you don't get another job in this State."

"I didn't start it." The kid moaned as he staggered to his feet.

"I don't give a stuff who started it," the ganger hissed into his face. "All I know is you're expendable. There are plenty of learners like yourself around. You've put my best shearer out of action with possibly busted ribs and ruptured guts, so get your gear and get off the property now."

The kid remained mute as he tried to regain his sight and senses. All the fight had gone out of him. He was in his first year as a learner shearer. The chance of becoming a gun shearer was his aim since becoming a shedhand, and he had been doing that since he was twelve. His father had made him leave school as soon as he could earn a living. It was no use protesting he wanted to stay and his teacher got nowhere by imploring he was smart and academic and should be given a chance to go on.

His father knew better. "Books won't get you anywhere boy. Get yourself a job and pay your way in life."

The belt over the ear that invariably followed emphasised his father's beliefs. He took his pay off him every week, and then headed for the pub in the nearest town. They were always on the track following the shearing circuit, his father a broken down shearer addicted to alcohol, and living in the past. His mother was a shearing camp cook. She had been easy and slow to realise, and the next thing they were married. They never stopped hating each other from the day the kid arrived, but stayed together because of the blind human trait that something was better than nothing to hang onto.

He took the last beating he was going to take from his father at twelve and walked out with his few possessions. The only person who had seen him leave was Emily, his young sister, the only person in the world he felt he had a bond to, although it was very slight. He had written letters from the various towns he passed through with the shearing gangs and received the occasional reply written in her childish illiterate scrawl. The letters never said much except to outline the drab overbearing existence from which there was no escape.

Then one day he picked up a letter addressed care of the local post office. It was postmarked three months previous. Emily was getting married in two weeks and wanted him to attend. She said she was marrying Andrew Markwell because she was pregnant. He felt sorrow and pain for his sister, and grinned wryly as he screwed it up and tossed it in the bin. Andrew Markwell the poor sap, had been fitted with an action he did not commit. The kid doubted whether Markwell could even get it up. Emily had been screwing around since her father had knocked her off at the age of ten. Someone had given her a belly full of arms and legs, and poor Andrew had been saddled with the result. The kid never replied to the letter. It was a past he wanted to forget. He had not heard anything more about his sister until the day the new gun-shearer joined the gang. A big fellow with a big mouth and even bigger ego. Despite his reputation he was not feeling the best when he rolled up in his battered ute to start. He had been drinking all night and looked it. By the time the ganger rang the bell for the first run he was visibly suffering. His face was florid and eyes puffed as he pulled the first sheep out of the holding pen and picked up the shearing handpiece. Despite his condition and suffering, he was quick and booted the shorn animal down the porthole race into the outside pen, following it with a stream of vomit as he disgorged his early breakfast. The ammonial smell of sheep piss and vomit made him hack and hawk his lungs as he rolled himself an odour killing cigarette. It hung in the corner of his mouth as he stumbled into the pen and dragged out another sheep. The stale smell of rum and other body odours oozed and suppurated from every pore, the lily-white skin glistening with sweat. His black Jackie Howe singlet was a sodden shapeless hanging garment tugging at the shoulder straps. Every time he finished a sheep he would look down the board to see if anyone was ahead of him. Being the new ringer and a highly reputed gun- shearer with a reputation to uphold, everyone was try- ing to take advantage of him, even the learner who was only a sheep behind.

The end of the first hour was torture until finally the bell rang. The ringer spat a great globule of phlegm over the head of the learner as he sat down beside him with his back to a wool bale. He rolled a cigarette and spat out the traces of wool and taste of dung as he licked the gummed surface of the paper. His finger nails were long and broken and black with encrusted filth.

"What's your name kid?" The smile was open and friendly, but the eyes were dark and cold. The learner told him, hoping it would be the end of their conversation.

"You're old man's name Charlie?"

The learner ignored the question. He thought he'd heard the last of his father.

"You've got a sister haven't you? Emily isn't it? You seen her lately?"

The learner sipped his tea and made no reply. He could guess what was coming.

"Great little fuck. She really knows how to perform." The ringer guffawed loudly for the benefit of the whole gang. "I went through her along with the whole bloody gang a few months before she got married. She even took that darkie Harry Smithfield on, so I wouldn't be surprised if that poor bastard of a husband of hers isn't looking at some brown-skinned squealer and wondering how it happened. What's his name? Markwell isn't it? Poor bastard."

The ringer slapped his knee laughing as the rest of the gang joined in his mirth. He failed to notice the learner had got to his feet and was standing over him with the mug of scalding tea in his hand. The gang watched incredulously as the learner poured the liquid over the ringer's balding pate. The man screamed and tried to scramble to his feet, but his shearer's boots slipped on the greasy floor.

The learner's boot caught him in the teeth, shattering what was left of the rotten yellow stumps. The next kick took him in the ear, which immediately erupted into a fountain of blood. He then began to methodically work on the ribs of the rising man. The learner knew it would be no contest if he let him get to his feet. He had to destroy him first. It was then he was hit with the plank of wood. The whole gang watched in silence. They were in sympathy with the learner, but said nothing.

"I'll think of you next time I lay your sister," the ringer grunted with a painful laugh as pulled himself up onto a bale.

He turned when he sensed the movement, but he was already too late as the full force of the punch felled him in an unconscious heap.

The kid tried to hide his pain and drunken gait as he walked over to the quarters and wearily showered and changed. He left his shearing clothes where they fell as he knew he would not be needing them again. The cook watched as he strode into the kitchen and made himself a sandwich of thick roast beef and filled a bottle with water.

"Bye cookie, I'm hitting the road." The cook did not reply but turned to her work as he strode out.

He was about ten kilometres down the track when he heard the fast approaching sound. He turned and recognised the ringer's vehicle and bolted for the washout of a dry creek bed. He heard the shot as he threw himself over the bank. He was winded, but fear overcame his feeling of hurt and distress as he sprinted along the creek bed with his head down. Another shot thudded into the earth in front of him. He felt nauseous as his lungs and heart tried to keep up with his fear. He heard two more shots as he finally collapsed to wait for the inevitable. He could go no further. Then there was a sudden peel of mad laughter as he heard an engine start over his laboured breathing and heaving chest. He listened as the sound of the vehicle receded.

2

He stood at the intersection of the station homestead track and the main road leading to nowhere. Just an endless dirt ribbon stretching out in both directions. There was no point in walking, he was too far from anywhere. A vehicle would come along eventually. He had lost his food and water and realised he was in trouble if he had to wait into the next day. He sat down with his back against the signpost pointing back towards the station as he contemplated his predicament. It was a couple of hours later when he became aware of the sound of an approaching vehicle. He quickly ran to the centre of the road and flagged it down. It slowed in a billowing cloud of bull dust which rolled over it in a choking veil. The driver eyed him up and down.

"Where are you going lad?"

"Anywhere you are."

The driver nodded and motioned for him to get in. "You got no gear?"

"Nah, I'm travelling light."

"Sam Carlin's the name. What's yours?"

"Springer."

"Is that all?"

"What do you mean?"

"Well, is it your Christian or surname?"

"Rupert's my first name, but I don't like it."

"Jesus, no wonder. Fancy saddling someone with a name like that."

The kid's face flared in anger, but Sam just grinned. "Where do you come from?"

"I was born in Winton if that's what you mean. Other than that I'm from anywhere I last found a job."

"Well Winton Springer, for the duration of this journey you've got a new name and who knows where this journey is going to end." Sam proffered his hand and Winton shook it firmly. He instantly took a liking to the man.

"By the look of your face you've been in a bit of an argument."

"Just fell over and got dust in my eyes." Winton self-consciously wiped away the drying blood and grime.

"Do you always piss your pants when you get dust in your eyes?"

Winton looked down at his crotch. The front of his moleskins were discoloured black from the clinging dried earth.

"As I was saying, I was running and tripped."

"No doubt about that boy. I'd say you ran into something that frightened the living crap out of you." Sam turned the windscreen mirror and indicated for Winton to look into it.

They both burst into laughter as Winton could only see two black and purple swollen slits staring back at him.

Sam did not pursue the subject as they chatted idly. The road stretched out before them as the afternoon sun gently lowered into a giant red globe into which they drove.

"What do you do Sam?"

"I'm in the gas and oil business."

"Yeah, I've heard there are drilling rigs out this way. Are they yours?"

Sam nodded. "Yes, I've got a rig working at the moment. I've already got one well just waiting to be hooked into the central pipeline and with any luck the present program should give me another."

"And you're driving this old bucket of bolts? Why haven't you got a plane, or are you frightened of flying?"

Sam laughed. "I do have a plane, but once every year l just start this old girl and drive out into this empty wilderness. It was the first vehicle I bought when I became a wildcatter and I'll never part with her. She's brought me luck so far."

He was left with his thoughts as Winton drifted off to sleep in the glare of the afternoon sun. Sam looked over at him and gauged he would be about the same age as his own son.

Sam had worked as a roughneck on drilling rigs in Texas while he completed a geology degree. The huge shallow depressions of western Queensland reminded him of the structures he had seen in America and Canada. Perhaps they did hold the great shallow oil and gas entrapments he was looking for. The experts said no, the age of the rock was too old to hold anything of significance. Marion's father Durand Hains, was an independent oilman who wanted Sam to join him in the business, but he declined. He wanted to be his own man. And besides he really did not relish the thought of becoming a part of a successful organisation he had not contributed to, and was already supporting a whole host of Durand's relatives and hangers on.

"One more is not going to make the slightest difference," his father-in-law would plead in the familiar Texan drawl. "We are all family, and I like to share it with everyone. Can't take it with me, and now you're one of the family I want you to have a share also."

Sam did not feel part of the family and wanted to go home with his new bride. He wanted to show her the vast expanses of the beautiful country into which he was born. She was more persuasive and pleaded with him to accept her father's offer. The next five years rolled by, and during the brief moments of happiness in their failing love they conceived two children, Martine and Alexander. Sam travelled constantly; one month in Venezuela and the next he would be in Canada or Nigeria slowly expanding the Hains Oil empire. Finally all signs of love or even affection evaporated completely, and the short times at home were merely two people living under the same roof with two children, neither of whom he really knew. They were always civil and respectful of each other, but there it ended. The final break was without recrimination. They sat down and talked about it and he signed over his interest in Hains Oil to the children and bought himself a ticket back to Australia.

3

The truck rolled on across the plains trailing its billow-ing cloud of dust. It was dusk when he swerved to miss the kangaroo, but it changed course and hit the bull bar on the front of the vehicle with a solid thud. Two others followed in quick succession as a group of about twenty or more bounded across in front of him. Sam pulled over and stopped the truck. No sense in driving any further tonight. The roos were attracted by the headlights and rather than pealing off away from the danger, they ran full-tilt across the approaching beams. The result could be highly dangerous, and even fatal if one of the animals came through the windscreen.

"There's another swag in the tray," Sam said as he rolled his out on the ground. He quickly made a fire in the middle of a midden of hastily gathered rocks, and lodged a billy-can of water in one corner. The meal was bread, jam, cold meat and a mug of sweat black tea to wash it down. Sam watched the boy eat ravenously and chuckled inwardly.

"You'll eat all my tucker at that rate boy. I'll have to charge you for it."

Winton shook his head in reply, his mouth stuffed with bread and meat. He grabbed the mug Sam had poured him, and took a swig of the black liquid to wash it down.

13

"I've got a hundred bucks I think. If you like I'll fight you for the lift and food. Every other bastard wants a piece of me."

Sam nodded and studied the boy. The typical country kid brought up the hard way, average height and wiry with not an ounce of fat, the slow movements belying the agility of the brain. He could tell this boy had intellect, but no education.

"I believe you would, but don't you think you're through fighting for one day?"

"I sure as hell am. I'm bushed." Winton took off his boots and climbed into the swag. Within seconds he was asleep, totally exhausted. He awoke to the squeal of a hand pump as Sam filled the truck's tank from a drum on the tray. Dawn was coming up fast with the first dull streaks of light breaking through. His whole face ached from the beating it had taken. Sam could see the boy was in pain, but said nothing as he watched him rekindle the fire. Breakfast consisted of mugs of sweet tea, bread toasted over the coals, and spread with a thick layer of treacle.

"You're in a bit of pain."

"Not as much as the other guy, I'll bet." Winton laughed as he thought of the ringer nursing broken ribs, torn ear and possible broken jaw. He would be off work for weeks.

"What happened?"

"Someone got a little personal so I thought I'd teach him a lesson."

Sam left it at that. "Okay, let's be on our way." He tipped out the contents of the billy, and kicked earth over the dying embers.

The bull dust invaded every crevice as it swirled through the cab in ever cycling turbulence. Noses and eyes became choked. It was early afternoon when Sam spotted the drill rig in the distance. He raised his hand and pointed, but Winton had already seen the unfamiliar object on the horizon minutes earlier. A number of low portable buildings were some distance from the rig. Sam pulled up slowly to minimise the cloud of following dust which just rolled over them, the finer particles suspended in the motionless air. The myriad bush flies immediately appeared, settling on anything showing life. The available moisture from the sweat of the body was what they sought.

Overall the silence was broken by the muted sound of diesel generator providing power for the camp, and the all pervading sound of the high-powered diesel driving the drill rig. The heat was still intense from a cloudless sky. A lone wedge-tail eagle rode the thermals high up, just gliding as it rose and gently dropped, watching for the slightest sign of small game. Lizard, mouse or snake would only have to appear for a fleeting second, and its fate would be sealed by the feathered predator, the largest and most majestic bird in the skies.

A tall gaunt figure wandered out from one of the cabins. He flicked the dog end of cigarette into the dust and ground it out with his foot.

"How's it going Harry?"

"Down five hundred, but a long way to go yet. You brought me a new roughneck, have you?" Harry was looking at Winton as he stepped around the front of the vehicle. "I lost one last week. Just walked off the job, so I'm running a bit shorthanded at the moment."

"This is Winton Springer. I picked him up down the track."

"Did you run over him?" Harry was studying Winton's battered face with obvious disdain as he shook hands. "He even looks like road-kill to me. Do you want a job young fellow?"

"I could certainly do with one, but I've got no gear with me. These are the only clothes I've got."

"There's gear here that'll fit you. The fellow who bolted won't be coming back for it."

"Thanks Harry. Yes, I do need a job and will accept your offer."

The drilling went on around the clock, and except for the tedium of adding a new length of drill rod, the days and nights rolled on. The days were hot, so hot that no metal part could be touched without a gloved hand. The nights were cold and descended to zero with heavy frosts, and similarly nothing could be touched without gloves. To do so would risk the skin being frozen onto the metal.

Winton quickly picked up the parlance and actions of the drillers and within a few weeks had acquitted himself to their satisfaction.

"You're doing a good job lad, keep it up," was Harry's laconic and only comment of encouragement to the new employee.

Winton was able to tell what type of formation they were drilling through just by listening to the acceleration and deceleration of the diesel as the governor cut in and out. The load increased and decreased monotonously as the roller bit gouged its way slowly into the reluctant sedimentary rocks. The work was filthy and hard. The grease combined with the fine dust embedded itself into the very pores of the skin. They all looked as though they had deep suntans, but it was the mixture of dirt forming a dark brown near- impenetrable coating of filth which was impossible to fully scrub off after each shift.

The flies were eternal, crawling into the ears, eyes and mouth where they were spat out or swallowed with a mouthful of tea. It was no use trying to brush them away. It served no purpose. Bread, a thick slice of Spam or corned beef, a quick flick of the hand to get rid of the flies for a second, and then the top half of the sandwich was clamped on. Any flies still trapped went the way of the Spam. Winton had struck some rough tucker in shearing gangs, but this beat everything. It was hard living. He ate while working, a sandwich in one hand, a mug of tea in the other, and two eyes and ears on the rig.

Harry nursed his diesel and fussed constantly over the rig, repeatedly checking oil levels, and temperature and pressure gauges. He studied the drilling sludge that rose out of the hole looking and smelling it for any signs of gas or fluorescence. It was though he did not sleep, his only interest being his beloved rig. His skin was like tanned bullock hide, his eyes fixed in a permanent squint under the remains of a broad-brimmed hat with no crown, on which a yellow hard-hat was perched. The cigarette dangled as a fixed attachment from his lips. His thin wiry shoulders shook violently as he tried to contain the consumptive bouts of coughing brought on by the years of nicotine irritating the tissues of his tortured lungs. The damaged membrane fought for oxygen through the inhaled smoke and fine dust.

Every week Sam would fly in bringing stores and newspapers which Winton read from cover to cover. He quickly gained a good understanding of the finance pages and the stock market, and what he didn't understand he wasted no time in asking Sam what it meant.

"You're not listed on the stock market Sam. Why not?"

"I'm not big enough yet. I'm using my own capital and I've got a few seed-capital investors. We're doing alright to date."

"Yeah, but you're selling gas now and trucking a little oil from your other strike, so why don't you take advantage of that and go public?"

"Because I've been unable to find a broker who'll back me. I've worn out shoe leather banging on broker's doors, but they all say come back when you have a substantial oil or gas hit. The small gas field I've come up with hardly provides living, and doesn't excite the brokers."

"You obviously haven't tried hard enough then."

"What the hell would you know?" Sam flared in annoyance. "Shearer to tool-pusher to financier in less than a couple of months. Lad, you certainly have a big mouth, and a big ego. If you think you can do better, why don't you find a broker who'll take me on?"

Winton was unfazed by the sarcasm, and went back to studying the paper. "I just might, I just might at that. What's in it for me if I do?"

"I'll double your wages, and buy you a new car."

"It would be worth more than that, but I'll accept that for starters," he replied holding out his hand.

Sam laughed as he shook it. "You've got plenty of confidence lad, but I think you've bitten off more than you can chew. We'd have to make something really significant, be it oil or gas to get the market boys interested."

"Bullshit Sam. I've read every report available, and some of these companies must have floated on the strength of their head office being located next to a local drive-in gas station. They've found nothing. At least you're producing."

Winton tossed a newspaper at Sam. "Here read this article and discover how to promote yourself in the oil and gas business."

Sam made to pick it up when a shout came from outside. They were both off and running for the door at the same time. Harry was standing at the wellhead peering at the spinning stem. The high pressure of escaping gas assailed their ears and nostrils. It came bubbling up through the drilling mud bringing the soft flow of fluorescence with it.

"This is more like it boss," Harry commented, his gaze fixed on the mud. "I don't think this is the zone we're looking for, but it certainly looks interesting. Another five hundred and I think we'll be into the real payola."

Sam bent down and scooped up a handful of mud and ran it over the palm of his hand as he turned to Winton.

"What do you say now eh lad? The brokers will listen if this turns into what I think it is. Below this gas layer will be another couple and then an oil entrapment if I'm not mistaken. We'll know in a week or so."

"Why don't you stop while you're ahead Sam? You're taking a risk it may be a dry hole. I say sell the sizzle, not the steak. This should really get the brokers interested."

"Okay, shut her down Harry." Sam gave a derisive laugh as he turned to the driller with a wink. "We're charging into an oil zone and Winton wants to shut her down. What do you think of that?"

"It's your well Sam, I'm only the hired hand," Harry replied as he spat on the ground. "I'm not here to give advice."

Sam had not heard the remark. He was rubbing the mud hard into his hand and chuckling to himself.

"Stop it now Sam or at least slow it down," Winton said quietly, but he knew Sam was not listening. "Get some publicity and make a public offering to float the whole project into a stock exchange listed company. The brokers will raise all the money you want. You've been handed the chance to make it big. Grab it."

Sam turned to him. "I've heard every word you've said, but I believe this time I'm going to hit something really significant. I want to roll the dice."

Sam did not reply as he walked off to a small rise a short distance from the rig. He stood amongst the low scrub and watched the birth of another day. It was a beautiful country and despite its barren unhospitable nature it was full of unseen life. He loved it most when he saw it now with the sharp contrasts between colours of the ancient layers of stratified sandstone and rock formations standing starkly out of the surrounding plains. He reflected on the comfort he could now be enjoying if he had stayed in the States. The comfort of a large Houston home surrounded by a substantial green acreage with mature trees adding charm and grace to the lifestyle he had dismissed. He picked up a handful of the barren earth, and let it trickle through his fingers. There was no turning back. He had sunk every cent into this venture, and although he was partially successful, the success was only minor to what he had left behind.

A breeze brought the aroma of breakfast and his mind snapped back to the present. Winton was frying bacon, eggs and sausages in a large pan. He dished out a plateful before handing it to Sam.

"You're due for a couple of days off, aren't you lad. Do you want to come to town with me? I've got stores and supplies to pick up."

"Sounds great. I'm certainly a starter for that."

$$4$$

Three hours later they pulled up in front of the country hotel.

"Reckon you can stay out of trouble?"

"I'll try Sam."

Sam was soon standing under a shower scrubbing off the in-ground filth in an attempt to remove every trace of grease and diesel fuel. He could not do this at the camp as their water was trucked in, and shower time was strictly limited. Satisfied he had removed as much grime as possible he towelled himself and lay down on the clean sheets. He drifted off to the constant lap-lap of the overhead fan.

It was some hours later when he jolted awake and lay still as his brain assimilated with his surroundings. He wondered what was missing, and then realised there was no steady thump of diesel motors, the overriding constant and dominant sound. Winton was at the bar when he got downstairs. He seemed to be deeply in conversation with the publican, but the conversation died as he came within earshot.

"Hi, I'm Bill Harcourt. Welcome to my hotel. Sam Carlin isn't it?"

Sam nodded and shook the outstretched hand as he stepped up onto the barstool.

"Young fellow here tells me you're drilling for oil and you're going to pull in a gusher?" Harcourt pushed the schooner of beer closer to Sam and looked more intensely at him as if demanding an answer.

"Has he now?" Sam raised the glass and let the astringent taste of the ale assail his palate.

"Well, isn't that true?"

"Might be and might not be. Still early days." Sam pretended not to notice the searching look Harcourt cast at Winton. He tried to change the subject but Harcourt was having none of that, although he realised he would have to use tact and patience to gather the intelligence he was after. He knew everything and everyone's business long before they thought it was in the public domain, and obviously Winton had told him something of real interest. Sam noticed Winton quietly sipped his beer, but stayed out of the conversation. He sensed he was laying the groundwork for some as yet obscure plan.

"How long are you staying around for Sam?"

"We're off again in the morning."

The publican was satisfied with the answer. He would be able to confirm the kid's story in that time. No need to hurry the inquisition now and possibly make an enemy. He would catch the kid later when Carlin wasn't around. He had made a fortune buying, and selling properties, and livestock simply by listening to idle and confidential chatter, and gossip. He paid no attention to the fact he was not the most well liked or respected man in the town, but he knew he was the wealthiest, and intended to capitalise on what the lad had just told him.

"Well, I'll be off on my rounds. Pour yourselves another beer if you want and chalk it on that board. You can settle your bar and food tabs when you leave."

Sam waited until he was out of earshot before hissing a question at Winton. "What the hell did you tell him?"

"Nothing really. I just told him what he wanted to hear. I told him we'd hit gas and the indications we could have a good oil discovery."

"You did bloody what?" Sam choked and thumped his glass down so hard the bar fell silent. It was a good minute before the buzz of conversation started up again. "Why did you spin that line of bullshit?" He glared at his young hired hand who did not look apologetic.

"What's wrong with gilding the lily?"

"Because, it's bullshit and you know it. We don't have an oil discovery as you put it, not yet anyway."

Winton looked into his beer, totally ignoring Sam's outburst. "Don't be so fucking moralistic. It's not bullshit. You've been preaching to me that no one's got faith there's oil out here. You don't build up people's confidence by telling them the gospel truth the whole time. Look at the politicians, they're the biggest bloody liars on earth. Look at the churches trying to sell something that doesn't exist, and if you don't believe, you're damned. Look at the advertisements for women's face creams. Apply this and the ageing will disappear overnight. There aren't any morals, ethics or scruples in this world or any such thing as fair play. You can preach to me all you like, but unless you can sell yourself first, and then the idea there's oil out there, you're going to wind up a loser."

Sam was startled by the tirade. Obviously the kid did more than just read newspapers. He soaked them up and absorbed every detail. He showed a maturity and understanding far beyond his years.

"You may not believe in morals or ethics Winton, but I do and will continue to hold those views and values."

Winton chuckled. "The only moral and ethical human I ever encountered was the priest who used to visit every month, that was until my old man caught him in bed with my mother one afternoon. Essentially there was nothing wrong in my father's eyes as compensation took the form of a carton of beer every month. Ethically the priest was there to counsel my mother, and morally he was making sure she had something to confess. Wake up Sam, you're a geologist, not a salesman. You've got to start standing on a soapbox like all the successful entrepreneurs and hustlers in this business."

Sam broke into a stifled peel of laughter. He was still chuckling and shaking his head as Winton drained his glass and stalked off in annoyance.

5

Winton strolled down the street casually peering in shop windows and enjoying the nearness, and company of other people. A café caught his eye, and he went in. The woman behind the counter was swarthy with rolls of fat bulging in a series of Michelin's from her enormous breasts to her expansive backside. She nodded as he ordered a coffee, and sat down at the furthest table. He was not aware of anyone's presence until the slender hand reached in front of him, and set down the heavy cup.

"Will that be all?"

Winton looked up at the sound of the soft voice with just the faintest hint of accent.

"Hi there. What's your name princess?"

The girl smiled nervously, but ignored his question. "You're new in town aren't you?"

Winton shrugged, and stirred his coffee without taking his eyes off the girl. "I've been here before, but I've never seen you. You've been in hiding, because I never miss noticing a pretty bird."

"You're a shearer, are you?"

Winton laughed. "I used to be, but that seems a long time ago now. I'm on an oil drilling rig at the moment."

Out of the corner of his eye Winton could see the advert for Michelin tires was getting nervous, and ready to interrupt the conversation.

"What time do you knock off work?"

"Not until Mama decides to close the shop, and that could be any time depending on how busy we are. But I can't go out. Mama's very strict, and won't let me go anywhere unless she or Theo go with me?"

"Who's Theo, your boyfriend?"

"He's my uncle. Don't look now, but he's watching us from the kitchen."

"Can't you get out a window? I want to get to know you, and there's not much chance of that with Mama and Theo hovering around."

A look of surprise crossed her face. "I could, but I'd be killed if they found out."

"So be adventurous. You're too beautiful to be locked up all the time. Has anyone told you what a stunner you are?"

He could see that her mind was churning over. No one had ever been this forward before. Several had tried, but the sudden appearance of Theo with a knife in his hand had quickly dampened the interest. Suddenly there was a high pitched demand in a foreign language from Mama, who judged delivery of coffee was taking too long. The girl jumped at the command, and started to move away.

"I'll meet you in the alley two hours after you close," Winton whispered not knowing whether she had heard him. He finished his coffee, and walked over to the counter to pay. Mama took the money, giving him his change without a word. He looked up to see Theo glaring at him with menace written all over his face He was tapping a large carving knife on the side of his grill. It was not an idle or bored gesture.

It was meant with intent, and Winton got the message. He did not look at the girl as he broke into a low whistle and walked out of the café.

It was past midnight as he waited in the shadows. It had been three hours since the café closed and all the lights in the single storey shop and dwelling had long gone out. He was thankful there was no dog as he walked around the back of the premises. Finally he heard a soft rasping sound as the window was slowly pushed up, and first one leg, and then the other appeared over the sill. He quietly helped her down, and was immediately aware of the warmth of her body against his. He held her to the wall, and gently kissed her on the lips and neck. She returned the gesture, and then hurriedly led him out of the alley, and away from the café. The streets were deserted, and dark with only the light from an occasional shop window display casting a dim glow on the drab surroundings. Winton realised they were aimlessly walking back towards the hotel, and as they drew near he steered her around the side to the flight of wooden fire stairs. There was no sound or movement. He knew he and Sam were the only guests, and Sam was at the other end of the long corridor. He quietly opened the door of his room and guided her in. She spun around and clung to him with fear, and excitement.

"Theo will kill you if he finds out," she murmured as he peeled off her coat, pulled her towards him, and ran his hands down her buttocks.

"Just forget about Theo." He nuzzled her neck as he leaned her back on the bed. Their needs were urgent, and animal as they stripped off. The sounds started as guttural murmurings deep in her throat, and then rose to a low wailing as she began to move with him, and dig her fingernails into his back. Orgasm after orgasm racked her body as she clung to his lithe form. It would finish, and they would roll apart exhausted only to be aroused again by their urgent and mutual demands.

It was daylight when Winton awoke. She was gone. He had not heard a thing. A thrill of satisfaction, and conquest went through him as he showered, and went down for breakfast. Sam was nowhere in sight. He checked for his one means of escape and was relieved to see Sam's truck still parked in front of the hotel. After a further hour of waiting he decided to check Sam's room. Maybe he was ill. He knocked, and threw the door open without waiting for a reply, before quickly closing it again. The woman had not paid the slightest attention to the intrusion, but a startled look of annoyance crossed Sam's face.

He had already finished breakfast when Sam finally appeared and sat down. Winton was grinning from ear to ear. "Getting or giving a little lesson in morals were you?" He leaned forward so he could not be overheard by a nearby waitress. "That looked like Harcourt's wife you were in bed with. At least that's what he introduced her to me as when I first walked in yesterday." Sam did not react so Winton baited him again.

"You're a real moralist, you are mate. Did you tell her you still loved her this morning?" He could no suppress his laughter any longer. It was infectious and soon Sam was laughing along with him.

6

It was the following day when they first heard the high revving sound of an aircraft engine above the dull throb of the drill rig. It was coming from the east, and flew directly overhead out of the morning sun. The single engine Maule circled a couple of times and then came into land, the oversized tires easily riding over the grass clumps and gibber strewn plain.

They watched as a solitary figure alighted and walked towards them. He was a technical looking type in immaculate khaki shirt and trousers, with a row of pens in one pocket, signifying he was no local blow-in looking for a friendly face.

"Hi, I'm Bill Waterman." The smile was as broad as the extended hand. "You boys having any luck?"

Sam shook hands but his expression remained deadpan. "What can I do for you?"

"I represent PacOil. I guess you've heard of us?"

Sam nodded, waiting for the reason for the visit to emerge. This was not a social call out of the blue. It was planned, and had a definite objective.

"PacOil's always looking for likely projects. Heard you might be onto something of real interest, so I thought I'd come out and introduce myself and my company. We would be interested in sharing some of the costs of what you've got going here."

Sam stiffened and took the stance of an adversary. "You might be interested, but I'm not."

Waterman was unfazed by the sudden rejection. For an independent to say he wasn't interested in receiving financial help immediately aroused his interest. It confirmed the rumours he'd heard in town.

"We're a big mob Carlin. We could help you."

"I'm not interested at this stage. I'll let you know if that changes."

"You're making a mistake if you don't consider a deal with us. If you're onto something we can make it happen a lot quicker. We've got the financial strength, and know-how, and the contacts to raise capital for you. We'll take some equity of course, but you'll wind up a rich man. Why don't you cash in on what we're offering?"

Sam turned away. "I heard you the first time Waterman. Now if you don't mind, I'm busy. I reiterate, I'm not interested in any proposition you have at this time."

Waterman slowly nodded as though deep in thought. "You sure you've got title to this ground?"

Sam flared, catching the inference of the query. "What do you mean by that?"

"It's just that PacOil has title to most of the area around here, and it wouldn't surprise me if you're not where you think you are."

Sam laughed derisively. "You know very well we have title. You didn't fly out here to offer me a deal if you weren't sure of that."

"Well, it's been nice meeting and talking to you Sam."

They watched as he climbed in, and fired up the engine. With a burst of power he swung the aircraft into the slight wind and took off.

"What do you make of that Sam?" Winton realised his mistake before the words came out of his mouth.

"It's the result of someone dropping his guts in a small country hotel where everyone's ears are big, wouldn't you say?"

"I didn't drop my guts," Winton countered. "I just told them what they wanted to hear, and it looks as though it worked. You're going to accept his proposal aren't you?"

"No I'm not. I've waited long enough to put this licence area together, and I'm not going to share it with anyone, especially the pack of sharks he represents."

"How do you know they're sharks?"

"PacOil is well known. They've never found a thing themselves. They merely prey on small companies, and independent operators like myself. They're bottom feeders. When I bring this well in I'll be talking to people on my terms, and not going cap in hand to the likes of Waterman and PacOil."

"Seems to me you'll go broke before you get around to talking terms to anyone," Winton shot back.

Sam turned on him. "I run this show and I make the decisions. You're beginning to get on my nerves the way you keep trying to tell me what to do. I think it's about time you took your worldly knowledge someplace else."

Winton sat down in the shade of the rig, and idly tracked a pattern with a stick in the dust. "No, I think I'll stick around. I haven't finished learning about the oil and gas business yet Sam."

Two days later Waterman flew low overhead again. Another figure could clearly be seen beside him taking photos.

"What's he doing?" Winton was fascinated.

"Waterman is taking photos so he can count the number of stacked drill rods and from that he can calculate what depth we're at. I think I'll give him a little surprise."

Sam pulled a rifle from behind the seat of the ute and leant against the bonnet for support as he sighted. Waterman flew almost directly overhead, the flaps of the plane fully extended so as to give him minimum speed without stalling. Winton saw his face break into a look of horror as he noticed Sam and the rifle. Waterman gunned the engine just as the shot crashed out momentarily drowning out all other sound. Waterman fought the power of the engine against the drag of the flaps as he wrestled for control in the cloud of a confused, and frightened brain.

"That'll be the last we see of him," Sam guffawed as he watched the plane slowly regain height and disappear.

They were standing on the steps of the post office when Sam drew in his breath as he studied an official looking envelope embossed with the legal firm's logo. He tore it open and read the letter. His face suddenly flushed with anger.

"I hope you're proud of your big mouth now." He pushed the letter into Winton's chest.

PacOil was serving notice Sam was drilling on their licence area, and was being given notice to stop immediately, and hand over all results forthwith. If the order was not complied with, legal proceedings would follow along with a claim for costs and damages. It was all very official looking and stilted in legal jargon.

"How the hell can they do that?"

Sam snatched the letter from Winton's hand and grabbed him by the front of the shirt. "Because you've got a big mouth boy, and they've got more money than me." He thrust Winton violently away. The offside door of the ute flew open as Sam jumped in and reversed out onto the street. It slammed shut as he swung across the street and accelerated away. Winton had been making for the open door, but missed and then desperately jumped for the tray. He got one leg over the side where he hung on grimly until he managed to roll over into the tray of the vehicle. The ride was violent. Sam was a man possessed, completely ignoring Winton's shouts and constant hammerings on the back of the cab. He felt there was not a single part of him that was not bruised when they finally reached the camp. The choking bull dust had completely clogged his nose and his eyes were streaming from the irritation. His hair was a thickly clogged matted mass.

Sam pulled the ute up in a skidding cloud and disappeared into his quarters. Ten minutes later he was back out with a bag in his hand, and heading for the airstrip. He shouted some instructions at the bewildered Harry.

Winton had anticipated the move, and was already sitting in the passenger seat of the Cessna with his few possessions.

"Where do you think you're going?"

Winton spat a glob of mucus and dust through the open window. "Well I figure my education and employment in the oil and gas industry has come to an end. I'm hitching a ride as far as you're going. Don't suppose there's any point in asking for the money you owe me?"

"Not a chance. You've probably cost me a gas field and maybe an oil field with your big mouth."

"I guess I could apologise?"

"Fat lot of good that is. The damage is done."

Winton did not answer. He thought it prudent to remain silent, and wiser to let the attrition of time work the hostility out of Sam's system. Also, he was in a plane being flown by a very angry man. It was last light before they finally landed in Brisbane after two fuel stops.

"I'll pay for the taxi. Where do you want to be dropped off?"

"Knowing you Sam, you won't be staying at an expensive hotel, so I'll stay there until I can sort myself out."

They checked in as complete strangers, but the desk clerk could clearly see there was some connection. He had seen them get out of the same taxi with angry words being vented at the younger man by the older of the two.

Winton did not look up from his plate as Sam strode into the dining room an hour later. All the tables were fully occupied so he either had to sit at Winton's, or walk out. Winton grinned at Sam's discomfort.

"There's a seat here Sam. Join me," Winton said in a loud voice as he pointed with his knife. Before he could decline the waiter was ushering him towards the empty chair, and unfolding the napkin.

"Sit down Sam. The damage is done and you're wasting your time spinning your wheels. If you have clear title there's not much PacOil can do about it. So why get steamed up over something you have no control over at the moment. Tomorrow's another day."

Sam was astounded at Winton's attitude as he made to study the menu. The absolute certainty and gall of his employee was amazing.

"I would like to stay with you Sam, if you'll let me?"

"What makes you think you can possibly help me after all the damage you've caused?"

"No one makes it on their own Sam. We learn something from everyone we meet, and I haven't stopped learning from you yet. I'm like you now, a believer. I believe you're going to make a big strike out there, and I want to be part of it."

Sam did not reply. He was furious and yet he felt a twinge of admiration. Almost anyone else would have accepted being fired, was a clear sign of rejection. Not this one.

He was coming back for more. He had the killer instinct of survival, and the vital ingredient of animal cunning necessary for success. However, deep down in the depths he could not yet tap, he had the premonition of danger. It was Winton's eyes that gave him away. Just the odd look in an unguarded moment when the eyes flashed hard from within the piercing blue.

"Well, how do you propose I solve this one. I've got a meeting with Minerals and Energy in the morning, and then I'll have to get a lawyer to reply to PacOil's claims."

"You have the area under licence, so what's the problem?"

"Sure, but I sense there's more to this. PacOil doesn't have a legitimate claim, and I'm sure they know it, but they can tie me up in court, and drain away every penny I have in legal fees."

"What are you going to do if that's clearly what they intend to do?"

"I'm not going to let them get away with it. I intend to fight them and win."

"Fight them and lose would be more correct," Winton countered.

"What do you mean by that?"

"Just what I said. You've already acknowledged they're bigger than you, and have more money. There's only one thing you can do, and that's join them."

A look of determined anger crossed Sam's face. "To hell with them. I've been working my guts out for years to prove there's commercial oil and gas out there, and I'm not going to let someone else take it from me just because they have money and muscle."

"They're not only using money and muscle Sam. They're using the one faculty that makes us superior to all other living creatures, and that's brains." He let the remark sink in.

Sam Carlin was a fighter. It was in his nature and he preferred to fight rather than compromise.

"You could be right Winton, but my reaction is to fight them, and that's precisely what I'm going to do. There's a right way and wrong way of doing business, and they've resorted to the latter."

"They did make an upfront approach Sam. You didn't even listen to what they had to say. There could have been room for substantial negotiation."

Sam bunched his fist. "Well, they're not going to get away with it."

"My guess is that shiny-arsed paper-shuffler you've got an appointment with in the morning is in PacOil's pocket."

"No, no I don't believe that for a moment."

"Wake up Sam. I was born in this State, and corruption is rife at all levels. That's the name of the game, get yourself set and stuff the other bastard."

"I've got to be able to live with myself," Sam replied firmly.

"Crap. As long as you've got money in the bank, and know there's plenty more of it to be made, you'll soon forget about your fellow man, and a thing called morals I believe you're alluding to."

"You make it sound as though you're not to be trusted your-self?" Sam's eyes narrowed as he waited for the answer. He got it direct and to the point.

"I learned a long time ago Sam to never to bend over in front of anyone with your pants down. You'll get screwed faster than an acolyte in a Greek monastery. I believe I'm honest, but don't tempt me."

Sam nodded slowly. "I'll keep that in mind. You'd better come along with me in the morning. I suppose if you want to learn about this business, you'd better learn every aspect. Maybe I'll also learn something."

7

They were kept waiting for half an hour as clerks went in and out of the director's office, until finally they were ushered in by a cadaverous youth who showed no expression, other than that of total boredom.

Winton mused the person behind the vast desk was about the same age as the surroundings. The gold lettering on the nameplate facing them on his desk was dull and flaking. Evan Glasser looked crusty and was crusty, as he acknowledged them with a cursory glance and waved them to sit down. He finally leant back in his chair.

"And what can I do for you gentlemen?"

"Perhaps you could read this first. It would save a lot of time." Sam handed over the PacOil demand.

Glasser took it, and sucked his teeth while he studied it. Nothing stirred except the ancient wide-blade fan in the ceiling. It hummed quietly while the gentle downdraft did nothing to relieve the intense humidity of the day.

"What's this letter got to do with my department?"

Sam raised his eyes with a twinge of annoyance. "I was hoping you would give me some guidance as to how to restrain this company from claiming my land."

"It's the government's land Mr Carlin, not yours." The eyes fixed him from behind the thick rimmed glasses.

Sam was about to make a rejoinder when he was cut off.

"The government grants licences to companies and individuals, much against my advice and recommendation in the latter case. As long as the fees are paid and the appropriate reports filed, we take no further interest and cannot involve ourselves in any disputes between licence holders."

Glasser began to turn the pages of a file. It was too far away for Sam to read its contents. "Both PacOil and yourself have adjoining licence areas. In fact they have you surrounded. Don't you think it would be easier to work it out with PacOil?"

"But the co-ordinates clearly show we are within our licence boundaries. PacOil has no claim," Sam replied in exasperation.

"I'm sure you think that's the case, but apparently so does PacOil. It's come to my notice you're having a bit of success out there Mr Carlin. The government would certainly like to see any natural resources developed. From what I can ascertain, PacOil is a very good company to deal with."

"But it's my ground." Sam checked himself as he saw the look on Glasser's face. "Okay, it's government ground, but I hold the licence to it. Why should I bow to pressure from a company that has no right to it?"

"Because the government wants new discoveries developed Mr Carlin, and if I perceive this dispute is going to drag on I have the authority to forfeit the licence, and put it up for tender to the highest bidder. If that were to happen you would clearly lose. Do I make myself clear?"

"Perfectly Mr Glasser. I get the inference and message very clearly."

Glasser ignored the tone of the reply. "Very good Mr Carlin. I'm pleased you understand the government's viewpoint. I take it you have accepted my advice and there will be no dispute with PacOil. Life is a compromise Mr Carlin." He did not wait for Sam's reply as he flipped the file shut and stood up to shake their hands. "I'm sorry I could not be of more assistance to you."

Sam sat stunned before he followed Winton's lead and walked out. Winton sucked in his breath. "What did I tell you?"

Glasser looked up sharply as his keen ears caught the remark. Winton glanced back to see him re-opening the file and reaching for his phone.

"He's already on the phone to Waterman I'll bet."

Sam was fuming as they stalked out of the building. "I'm not going to roll over and let that company take what's mine."

"You'll lose Sam. That old sod made that very clear to you, but perhaps you weren't listening. You can't tell me he didn't know the whole story before we walked into the room. You can't fight them Sam. They know you're onto something good and they have infinitely more money than you. And they have that old prick on their side making very veiled, but direct threats. No prizes for guessing who's going to wind up with the area if you fight. Join them and cash in. How do you know what they're going to offer until you've heard the terms? Forget about getting a written legal opinion on your rights. All you do is pay some thieving lawyer for advice you've already received free from Glasser. I suggest you go back and let them come to you. You won't have to wait long, but this time don't try and blow a hole in Waterman's plane."

"Seeing you're so bloody smart, you'd better come back with me. You're a smart young bugger and I see I'll have to keep an eye on you."

Waterman flew in a few days later accompanied by an overweight individual who was obviously the money-bags. They watched him waddle across from the airstrip as he wiped the sweat from his face with a large handkerchief. A shapeless cloth hat did little to shade his florid porcine features from the relentless sun. The sweat-drenched shirt clung to accentuate the successive rolls of over-indulgence. And he was clearly stressed by the heat, and a covering of flies which he tried frantically to swat away.

"Sam, this is my boss Jim Bain."

Sam's initial observations were borne out when he shook the proffered limp and lifeless hand. It was wet, puffy and soft, with no fibre or strength of resolution. The nails were beautifully manicured, and a large diamond ring glistened on his pinkie finger.

"What can I do for you Jim?" Sam wiped his oiled stained hands with a wad of cotton waste.

"I'll come straight to the point Sam. I believe we might be able to get around this legal hassle with a minimum of cost to both sides." Bain fixed Sam with a friendly and unctuous smile. "Of course, if you want to we can fight it out in court, but by the time it gets determined you'll be broke, and the government will confiscate the licence. I'm only patient to a point Sam. Why not see it my way, you have the prospect and we have the money. Why don't we combine our ideals and make a great deal more money?"

"Mr Bain, I've only got a prospect with a good chance of an excellent gas producer. I don't have oil yet, although it's looking good."

"Please call me Jim," Bain replied with a disarming smile. He had established Sam's attitude and measure, and his face took on a benign look as he adjusted to the approach he knew he must adopt if he was to win over this irascible character. "I'm not really interested in whether you have a gusher or not.

All I want is enough promise so I can promote it, and sell it to the investing public."

"I've really got nothing to sell. I've got gas, but it's not enough to really promote at this early stage, is it?"

"On the contrary we have plenty to sell," Bain replied smoothly. "We have an exciting new company with the promise of a commercial oil and gas discovery."

Sam did not like the plural. Bain was already talking as though the deal was done.

"We're a long way from calling it a commercial discovery, be it oil or gas," Sam replied firmly. "I'm not going to mislead anyone into thinking otherwise."

Bain raised his eyes to the heavens. "Sam we're not going to mislead anyone. I'm going to put more money into your pockets than you ever thought possible. Of course, I don't deny I will be making money for my associates and myself."

Sam was instantly on guard. "How much are you intending to make out of it?"

Bain shrugged his shoulders. "Why should you concern yourself with how much I make. If you're satisfied with what you get out of the deal, isn't that the whole point of the exercise?"

"What are my alternatives?" Sam could see the fat man was melting standing in the open under the hot sun, but did not offer to show him into his air conditioned office.

"I hope you understand by now your alternatives and options have been spelled out. However, to answer you question, you have none."

Winton could see Bain was trying to close the deal too quickly. He moved between the two men when he noticed Sam's fists begin to bunch. The fat man was going to be laid flat on his backside in the dirt at any second.

"Obviously Sam wants to think about this Jim. He can't give you an immediate answer and certainly not in the face of your direct threat."

Bain viewed Winton. They had not been introduced, but he could see the young man was a mediating influence attempting to cool Sam's hot blood.

Bain threw his hands wide, relieved the danger had been averted. The sweat was streaming down his fat pudgy neck. "Of course, of course, but we don't have all the time in the world. We have to catch the market while gas and oil are running hot as they are now. We can float this company at a huge premium."

"How about letting Sam think about it overnight. You're welcome to stay here if you like Jim."

Bain looked around at the sparse quarters and tried to hide his disapproval. "Thank you, but we've already made alternative arrangements. We'll come back in the morning to discuss it further." The heat and flies were stressing him. All he wanted to do was get aboard the plane and leave. "And by the way Sam, don't push ahead with that well too quickly. There's nothing like spoiling a good oil prospect by drilling it and finding nothing there. The gas strike will carry a good premium, but if we can allude to oil, the returns will be so much better."

"To put it another way Mr Bain, you suggest we drill for money rather than oil?"

Bain checked himself. "You've got a great prospect here Carlin. Get smart and come in with us. No fun being up to your arse in grease and filth all day, not to mention your bank balance disappearing as fast as that drill rod."

Sam was deep in thought as they watched the Maule kick up a cloud of dust and gibbers as it taxied across the open plain and swung into the slight breeze. The sun was full in Waterman's eyes as he gunned the motor. In what seemed only a few yards it was off, and gently banking towards the north-east as it circled low overhead. Sam could clearly see the diamond sparkling on the fat hand as it waved to them from the cramped confines of the cockpit. The sun was throwing down its fiercest morning heat as the plane gradually disappeared from view.

"The man has a point," Winton ventured. He could read what Sam was thinking. The frustration, long hours, and gamble were beginning to take their toll.

Sam slowly shook his head. "Do you really expect me to get into bed with that fat slug. I was going to hang one on him, that was until you stepped into the breach."

"For an educated man Sam, you're a downright dill at times. So you get two seconds of pleasure by belting him one, and all the time in the world to regret your actions when you lose the licence. The man has offered to make you a pile of money, albeit a little immoral, and you're going to knock him back. I could understand if you were in a position to tell him to go to hell, but you're not."

Sam poked an unyielding finger into Winton's chest. "Listen you, I'm getting bloody sick of your lecturing. I'll make the decisions."

Winton held up his hands in submission. "Okay, okay I'll borrow the ute, head for town tonight, and get out of your sight for a few hours."

"You do that, but make sure you're back at first light," Sam threw over his shoulder as he strode away.

8

Winton started to whistle a tune as he drove past the airport. As he'd hoped, the Maule was parked near the solitary hangar.

Harcourt's face beamed as he checked Winton into his hotel again. "How's the drilling going lad?"

"Very good. I'll catch up with you later after I've had a shower and changed. Say, is Jim Bain staying here?"

"Certainly is. He and Bill Waterman have checked in for a couple of days. Say what's going on?" Harcourt lowered his voice and looked around to see that no one was listening. "That Bain looks like one well-heeled dude. What's the story?"

"Don't know at this stage," Winton lied. "But if I find out I'll let you know."

Harcourt looked perplexed. "But obviously you know him? After all, you asked if he was staying here?"

"So I did." Winton picked up the key and made his way upstairs to his room which was clean, but smelled musty. He threw open the French doors leading onto the balcony and went looking for the bathroom down the hallway. Half an hour under the shower removed much of the embedded grease and dirt. He was padding back along the corridor when he heard the unmistakable tone of Bain's voice coming through the open louvre on top of door of the room next to his. He quietly let himself into his room, slipped into clean clothes, and inched out onto the balcony. He could clearly hear every word through the open French doors of Bain's room.

"Pig headed bastard. He came close to punching me if that kid hadn't stepped in. Is he going to listen to reason? If he doesn't I'm not going to pursue it any further."

"You're not going to give in that easy are you Jim? We've got Glasser on our side, and he'll pull that licence if you say so." Waterman had a note of angst in his voice.

"That's not the solution. We don't have a guarantee if Glasser does pull it and put it up for tender, that our bid will be successful. Someone may be getting the same information and outbid us. No, we've got to convince Carlin to go along with us otherwise I'm out of here. How do people work in those conditions, let alone live in these terrible little towns with no class or comforts?"

Bain threw his bulk onto the bed. The steel frame groaned under the weight, his hand tooled shoes crashing to the floor as he kicked them off. "I didn't come out here to fail. There must be away of getting Carlin to see sense. The man doesn't seem to like money."

"So Glasser is not our ace in the hole?"

"No, it's too late for that. If you're right, Carlin is very close to striking something very significant, and I want part of it. We've got to make the deal too good to refuse. Pity you got him offside."

"Me get him offside," Waterman protested. "You're the one who said get out there, and scare the shit out of him with the threat of legal action."

"Oh, shut up and be constructive." Bain waved his hand with an air of annoyance.

"I think you're worrying too much Jim. I've got a feeling we only have to wait and he'll come to us. Rather than go out again tomorrow, why don't you let him stew for a few days?"

Bain let out a rolling belly laugh of derision. "You'll learn someday Waterman, there's no such thing as waiting when there's money to be made. We might all be dead next week. I want this deal to go ahead."

"Why don't you just buy him out? You've got the money and Carlin must have a price?"

"Whether I've got the money is not the point. Lesson number two Waterman. I'm not greedy. I don't want all the action, and all the risk. I just want a healthy piece of the pie for which I'm willing to pay. Of course, he'll never know I'll make multiples of what he does. He thinks I'm after his company, which as you know, I'm not. I just want to make the lion's share, skim the cream off the top, and let him have his company. What's fairer than that?"

"What about nobbling his operation to slow him down?"

Bain cocked a jaundiced eye at the suggestion. "Do you really believe that's a serious proposal? You couldn't get within earshot of that rig without being spotted, and how would you nobble it as you suggest? I thought you were a practical man, but I've got my doubts."

"Just thinking out loud Jim. I believe we should just bide our time for a few days."

"Don't know how I'm going to sleep in this bed. It's bloody uncomfortable. Ah, come on, let's go down and have a beer. I feel like a long cold one. Maybe, we'll pick up more information about Carlin down there?"

Winton quickly stepped back into his room as heard the bulk of Bain roll off the bed. An idea started to germinate in his mind.

The two men were sitting silently in the corner of the bar milling with patrons when he strolled in half an hour later. He pretended not to notice them, but he knew they had seen him. The overpowering body odour of shearers and rouseabouts filled his nostrils. It brought back memories, but he shut it out of his mind. From what he had learned in the past few days, the only way of making real money was by using the brain. There was no point in using muscle or indulging in physical labour. It was only worth so much because there was plenty of it around, and there were only so many hours in the day you could sell it. The brain, that was an entirely different story. It ticked over constantly and needed no physical exertion to crank it into productivity. He recognised the hard part was making the transition from selling the hands, to selling the brain. Bain used his brain entirely. One had only to glance at his body to realise his brain was the source of his money. The morality of how he acquired that money, he had just witnessed by eavesdropping. The idea of being clean all the time, and not filthy appealed to him. Clothes and nice things attracted him, and he was determined he was going to have them.

Winton picked up his schooner of beer, and moved to a quiet spot not far from Bain and Waterman. He had his plan clearly mapped out as he waited for the inevitable approach. It was no more than a minute.

"Hello there, you're boss didn't introduce us, but I'm Bill Waterman."

"Winton Springer," Winton shook the outstretched hand with a deadpan expression.

Waterman slid into the seat opposite. "You been working for Sam Carlin long?"

Winton nodded without replying or altering his expression. Out of the corner of his eye he saw Bain pick up his beer, and begin sidling towards them. He had sent Waterman to open the conversation and judge whether the prey was hostile. If everything looked amicable it was then safe for the big fish to swim into the centre of the pond. He did not realise he was in fact the target.

"Hi there young fellow, my name's Jim Bain."

Winton shook the lifeless bunch of fat fingers. "Winton Springer. Pleased to meet you Jim."

Bain nodded and sat down, and opened the conversation which had nothing to do with his objective. Finally, he made a move to broach the subject, but Winton anticipated his intent, and quickly took the conversation off on another unrelated tangent. He drained his glass and accepted Waterman's offer of another.

"I think I'll go and eat. A long drive makes me hungry and tired and I would rather we get our business meeting over early." Winton picked up his glass and pushed back his chair.

"Business meeting?" Waterman could not restrain the look of surprise. Bain on the other hand was hearing and understanding perfectly. A broad smile crossed his face. He recognised a smart mind when he saw it in action.

"Yes, a meeting Waterman. Winton has suggested a meeting, and we can't have it here with too many ears pretending not to listen. Why don't we adjourn to the dining room? The dinner is on me."

"It was always going to be," Winton quipped.

The room was almost empty. They found themselves a secluded table. Bain picked up the menu, and screwed up his face in rejection as he studied it. There was nothing apparent or appealing that would excite his large intestine, but it had to be satiated so he quickly chose, and dropped the menu back on the table.

"Looks like a steak with everything. What about you Winton?"

Winton did not answer as he continued to study the menu. It was either chicken or steak, and he pretended to be torn between the two. Finally he tossed the menu back on the table.

"That will do me fine Jim."

"And that makes three." Waterman handed his menu to the hovering waitress. "Also bring us a bottle of your best cabernet sauvignon."

Both men were waiting for Winton to open the conversation, but he said nothing. Finally Bain could not bear the silence any longer.

"Well, Winton you called this meeting. What's on your mind?"

"Simple," Winton replied. "You tell me what you want, and I'll tell you what my end will cost you."

"I don't think you've got much to sell Springer," Waterman bridled. "You're only Carlin's grease monkey. What can you possibly offer that would get Jim interested?"

Winton ignored the remark and looked directly at Bain. "You have a problem. If you intend to get Carlin's co-operation you've got to adopt an alternative approach."

Bain held up his hand as Waterman was about to butt in. "Let the lad finish Bill. Proceed Mr Springer."

"As I was saying, you have a problem. In my short experience in the oil business I would say Sam Carlin has got himself the best bit of dirt in this region. He's getting results, and the strong indications are he'll bring this one in as an oil producer. He's already talking to other people so you can forget about mounting a legal challenge to his tenure," Winton lied smoothly. "Carry on with your legal threats and you'll lose the game. Someone will dive in and fund his defence for a piece of the action and you'll be locked out for all time. You can forget about Glasser being of any assistance. I think his phone records would show he phoned you immediately after Sam and I met him. You know all government phone calls are recorded, don't you? He'd shit himself if he was ever called to testify."

Waterman gagged on his beer while Bain just smiled at the audacity and confidence being demonstrated.

"If I'm not mistaken, the object of this exercise is for everyone to make money, and I believe I'm the only hope of you achieving that aim in regard to this particular project."

Waterman tried to hide his surprise. How did the kid make the connection to Glasser? Bain was grinning broadly as he anticipated what was coming. The kid was too smart.

"We have only a short time in which to achieve our objective." Winton paused to let the statement sink in. "If Sam brings that well in, the game will be over. He'll make a fortune, raise all the money he wants for further drilling, and we'll be looking from the sidelines."

"Tell me what you have in mind Winton? If what you are offering is sound and achievable, I'm all ears."

Winton nodded and outlined his proposal. Half an hour later Bain pulled out his wallet and began peeling off large denomination bills. "You sure you can deliver?" Bain queried as he watched Winton fold the money and stuff it into his shirt pocket.

"If I can't, then you've lost your money," Winton replied with a smirk. "You can put it down to experience, and my inexperience if it fails. However, you liked my proposition, and I can assure you my career in the oil business is only just beginning."

Winton awoke early. He took the wad of notes out from under his pillow and slowly counted them again. He felt sure he would collect the other half when he delivered on his end of the bargain.

He had a giant appetite and treated himself to a full breakfast. Bain and Waterman had flown out at daybreak so he was able to compound his thoughts free of any of Waterman's negative queries. He left the hotel whistling an aimless tune. The first stop was the bank to open an account. He pushed open the door to the empty bank and strolled up to the counter. A drab looking girl looked up from her teller position.

"What can I do for you?" There was no enthusiasm or attempt at greeting in her voice. She recognised Winton as being a shearer. They only had money momentarily before their accounts hovered into the red, so why encourage the business, was the opinion of her boss.

Winton gave what he thought was a disarming smile. The face opposite remained deadpan. The smile had made absolutely no impression.

"I want to open an account."

"Hang on a minute. I'll get Ryan." She turned and ambled off towards a glass partitioned office. She hung over the top and talked in whispers before returning. Ryan followed her out and eyed Winton up and down. The area was full of his type. A shearer, or rouseabout, or some itinerant worker one step in front of his creditors, and possibly the law. Always wanting to open an account with a credit card attached. Both would be maxed out within a matter of weeks. Ryan reached under the counter and flipped a yellow card across.

"Fill this out and sign it. I'll need some ID. Then fill this deposit slip out and we're in business."

When he was finished Winton pushed the completed card across and watched Ryan's incredulous look as he noted the size of the deposit.

"Is that cash?"

"Certainly is." Winton pulled out the wad of $100 notes and counted them off. He noted the immediate change in Ryan's attitude, breaking into a broad welcoming smile as he took the money and certified the count.

"You've made a wise decision Mr Springer. I hope you won't be like the rest of them and blow the lot in a couple of weeks. Had a big win at the races did you?" Ryan knew from long experience the kid certainly looked like a shearer, right down to the cracked and filthy fingernails. But he could not put his finger on it as to what made this one different. He did not have the simplicity and rough exterior of a shearer, or the shiftiness of a criminal type, or the braggart stance of a gambler or chancer. Ryan quickly realised he was not going to get an answer to his question.

"You'll be wanting a credit card with that, will you?"

"No, I just want a bank cheque for half now and the rest can ride."

"Why leave it in a non-interest bearing account? We can offer you a competitive rate." He reached for a fly-specked card showing interest rates.

Winton glanced casually at it. "No thanks. I believe I can do better than that."

Ryan wrote out the bank cheque and then watched as Winton disappeared through the door. He was intrigued as to where the young fellow had got so much money from. No one in town had withdrawn such an amount in recent days, and no one would be wandering around with that much on them.

Ten minutes later Winton was sitting in a comfortable leather chair with a coffee in one hand, and a Tim Tam in the other. He liked the taste of the chocolate. The financial adviser and stockbroker had shown immediate interest when he walked into his office.

Mike Robinson maintained he could smell money the moment it walked through the door, and this young fellow had confirmed that instinct when he started to talk about how much he wanted to invest. His assumptions were confirmed when he noted the amount on the cheque. It was a bank cheque and not some worthless personal scrap of paper. Not much of a commission involved, but it all added up and he was doing very nicely since he had hung out his shingle. The recent and continuing flurry in small cap oil and gas stocks had certainly padded his financial position very nicely. If more of these people would flow through the door he could eventually buy into one of the major main-stream broking firms. Rumours fed the market, and it was only in the major centres the punters were numerous enough and gullible enough to suck up every scrap of gossip and act upon it. He was getting polished at floating his own rumours. He was right on top of the local action with his phone ringing constantly as city associates checked on progress of the multitude of rigs in the district.

Robinson prided himself on the size of the discretionary accounts he handled for a few wealthy clients. He mused that people were absolute fools in their immediate trust of anyone who made them money. It was a strange and innate human fault people possessed. Give them an initial quick profit and the rest was comparatively easy. No round of drinks at the local grazier's club. That was too crass and clumsy. A quiet invitation to his office after business hours, a scotch in the pleasant surroundings of wall charts and computer screens showing graphed price movements, bold pictorials showing stocks of the month and assumptions of progress, were essential selling tools. The investors, not wishing to show their ignorance, their only interest being in how much they stood to make, did not really want to know the finer points of investing.

"You handle that Mike," they would say as they entrusted him again with the proceeds from their latest market success. They just wanted to touch their winnings and then they were quite happy to re-invest in some other stock he recommended. A win in the market and their trust was complete. Discretionary accounts were the lifeblood of his business as he gave the client a read-out every month of their position. If they wanted to cash out, he handled it without question, knowing it would be quickly re-invested on the strength of another hot tip. On top of his usual commission for buying and selling, Robinson was skimming the discretionary accounts as well. Just a percent here and there, nothing greedy or obvious. Life was good for Michael Robinson and here was another one for the plucking, not much of a plucking, but a handy profit all the same and small gains mounted fast. He was showing just the right amount of interest and keenness to his client, being neither effusive nor obsequious, and displaying just the right amount of confidence in recommendations which showed through as professionalism to his clients. It had not taken him long to realise the art was not in being able to sell the client on a particular stock, but to sell himself. Sell yourself and the rest was easy. Robinson had been discussing the market and stocks for some minutes trying to assess just how educated his new client was in that regard.

"You know enough about the market for me to offer you a job if you're interested," he remarked jokingly.

"I may take you up on that someday, but at the moment I've got other things on my mind."

"Well then, let's narrow down a few stocks I think you should invest in."

"I want you to split the cheque between these two." Winton handed over a slip of paper with the names of the two stocks Bain had given him.

Robinson raised his eyebrows. The kid was onto good information as he had heard from his city contacts both stocks were being set for a run by a particular brokerage with a track record for picking obscure stocks and promoting them heavily. First they got the rumour mill running and traded heavily in and out to build up interest, setting themselves and then moving stock into their clients' discretionary accounts for a small profit. If the stock continued to run they were happy with what they made, but if the stock looked as though it was about to slide they would sell all the way down and buy-in again at the bottom of the market. They could not lose because they worked on inside information. A broker could not hope to survive in the market without inside information. It was a crime to trade on inside information, but the whole world revolved around knowing something the client did not, and it would never change.

"And where did you get these tips from, may I ask?" Robinson was intrigued this apparent country hick would have such good information. He had only heard it himself that morning.

"Same place as you. I've got a crystal ball."

Winton had originally asked for double the figure he had finally settled on. Bain had laughed at his audacity as he wrote down the names of two stocks. "If you haven't doubled your money within a month, I'll make up the difference."

At first he thought about ignoring Bain's offer. Why punt on some obscure companies, and lose most or all of his investment? However, he determined Bain had no motive in giving him a bum steer. He decided to follow his advice.

"I'll get you set as soon as I can."

"Would you place the order now please? I want to know the price."

Robinson momentarily lost his air of confidence. He never set a client and then gave them an immediate buying or selling price. He would buy in immediately, but fob the client off on the pretext the order would be executed sometime during the trading day. If the price continued to move up during the day he could buy-in the client at a higher price and sell the original order, claiming the margin for himself. Similarly, it worked on a falling market by selling the client out immediately, and then waiting for the close when he would buy in again, and give the client the lower price. No client ever got the top selling price or the bottom buying price. It was a no-lose situation.

He tapped into his computer under the watchful eye of his new client, realising he would only make his normal brokerage on this transaction. After the usual small talk he confirmed the trade, and handed the buying slip to Winton.

"Sell me out immediately the stocks double." Winton got up, shook hands with the startled broker and walked out.

9

She was behind the counter. There was only the glimmer of acknowledgement with a fleeting smile as he pretended to ignore her. Mama had not noticed him enter, but she was instantly on the alert when he slumped into a chair facing the counter.

Winton watched the girl more intently. Previously he had only one thing on his mind, and she likewise was intent on the urgency of the assignation. He had not really absorbed her features or mannerisms. She was beautiful, the almost jet black hair, the deep caramel coloured eyes and olive skin and body to match. The wogs could certainly punch out good looking women he reflected as he played with the saltshaker and pretended to show no interest in his surroundings. He could feel the front of his jeans tighten as he watched her move towards him and hand him a menu.

"Hi there," she murmured under her breath. The warm smile persisted as she turned her back towards the counter, blocking Mama's view as she wiped down the table.

He grabbed her hand and squeezed it. He could see Mama motionless behind the counter watching every movement and straining to hear any conversation. Uncle suddenly appeared and stood in front of his vat of cooking oil. Winton shuddered as he looked at the slab of dark European contempt glaring at him. He was one mean looking mother with his swarthy almost black complexion and huge hooked nose. He was overweight, and his unwashed greasy black hair hung down over his ears. His arms and wrists were also coated in a thick mass of hair.

"Can you get out tonight?"

"Can't. Theo is taking me to the movies." Her voice was low and barely audible.

"I'll have a burger, fries and a coffee," Winton replied loudly as he handed her the menu. He watched her turn and move away, his eyes and mind glued to her buttocks. He checked his unconscious smile when he realised uncle's eyes were boring into him from the kitchen. The face was rock-hard and cold. Winton stared back with an unwavering look of arrogance. Finally, with a dismissive grunt uncle turned to his grill and threw on the beef pattie for the burger, followed by the sliced bun. She returned and put the coffee down in front of him and averted his gaze.

"I'll wait for you after the movie."

She made no comment or acknowledged she had heard his whispered statement.

Uncle was watching again when she returned with the burger. Despite what he thought uncle may have put in it, it was actually very good. Theo was still glaring when he walked up to the counter and paid.

"That was a great burger. I really enjoyed it." He turned toward uncle Theo with a disarming smile. The compliment was returned with a stony nod.

Winton sat the row behind them in the theatre. He had been watching from across the street, and followed them in behind a small crowd. The theme of the movie passed over him as he studied the back of her lovely head. The curtain came down for interval. She sat motionless, but Theo arose suddenly and walked back and around into Winton's row of seats.

"You looking for trouble mate?"

Winton pulled away. The garlic and smell of cooking oil overpowering. "Not unless you are." He was not going to be intimidated as he replied with a defiant expression.

"What's the interest in my niece?"

"She's beautiful and I like looking at beautiful women that's all." Winton sensed the movement, but did not see the knife until he felt the point of it being pushed into his ribs. The pressure gently increased and he was forced to rise in his seat. The beads of sweat and fear began to break out on his forehead. The bastard was crazy. He should have realised he would be carrying a knife.

"You not so smart now, are you?" Uncle Theo was getting more than a passing pleasure from his actions. "Listen, I give you only one warning."

The knife had broken the skin and the pain was intensifying. The wet feeling was not only sweat. He could feel the blood beginning to ooze from the wound.

"You keep your filthy eyes off her, and don't come into the shop again otherwise I push harder with this knife next time. You understand?"

Winton was speechless as he nodded in shock. The knife was slowly withdrawn, the blood on the blade clearly visible. He felt he had been sandbagged. No one had ever threatened him with a knife before. The danger and fear were very real, and the memory of being shot at flooded back. The blood began to stain the front of his shirt. He used his handkerchief to stem the trickle as he sat motionless. Slowly the shock began to subside as anger took over. Just prior to the curtain going up Theo turned and a broad smile crossed his face as he noted the ashen pallor of his victim.

Winton wondered how many of the local studs had been frightened off by Uncle Theo. No wonder he had found the running so easy. The local lads had obviously had their erections quickly revert to flaccid normality by the show of cold steel and murderous intent. He decided it would be wise to do the same, but as the shock dissipated the determination welled up in him. He was going to defy Uncle Theo just to prove he had not lost his nerve. He could deal with the knife now that he knew it existed.

The movie ended and he waited for them to get up and begin moving towards the aisle. He pulled his jacket over the front of his shirt and timed it to reach the end of his row, and step out into the aisle as they drew level. He was about to step behind them when Theo drew back and motioned him to walk ahead. It was a knowing smile. He was not going to be suckered with a punch in the kidneys from behind. The girl was slightly behind her uncle. Winton caught the imploring look in her eyes. The message was only fleeting, but Theo sensed the contact and gripping her arm, propelled her up the aisle.

He had been sitting in the ute for about two hours down the street from the hotel. The music was country and western as the glow from the radio cast a subdued illumination. He was sure he had read the right message in her eyes. Another hour ticked by and a cold chill of danger began to creep through his bones. He jumped suddenly when he felt the presence of someone at the window. The knife was still clearly in his mind. She smiled at him and then hurried off around the side of the building into the shadow.

The tightness in his crutch became acute as he quietly got out and followed her. She was standing in the darkness and threw her arms around him as he drew level. The blood was pounding through his body and brain as she sought out his lips and pushed her body firmly into him. He began to lead her towards the rear steps of the hotel again.

"No," she whispered. "I think we were seen last night. Someone came into the café this morning and made a joke about me being out late. It took a lot of talking to calm Mama down, but I'm sure Theo didn't believe me. That's why I'm so late. I just had to make sure they were both asleep."

Winton nodded and changed direction as he led her towards the stables at the rear of the hotel. There was the sweet smell of hay as he slowly pulled open the door and pushed her inside. Their needs were identical and urgent. They teased each other with their bodies as they undressed, but the game ended quickly. Her deep throatal cries and whimperings became more and more desperate. Winton's brain was a congealed mass of confused pleasure, ecstasy and nagging fear as he climaxed. The writhing body under him did not stop and continued to thrust upwards. She was the most sensual thing he had ever come across. Jesus, did all wogs act this way? He felt himself growing hard again and returned the responses of the sweating body. There was no stopping her as she closed her eyes and wrapped her legs completely around him. It was this grip that stopped him from reacting fast enough. His brain was electrified with fear as he realised someone had placed a boot level with his face. He threw himself sideways, but it was already too late. He saw Theo's maniacal eyes as the stirrup iron, swung with the full leverage and force of the leather strap, crashed with a glancing blow into the side of his skull. The waves of nausea swept over him as the tidal movement of consciousness drifted in and out in giant surges. Through the veil of mist he could hear the curses being rained down, and waited helpless for the final fatal blow he was sure would follow. The sea became calmer and he became aware of the guttural sounds of an animal grunting. He moved his head and through dazed vision saw two naked bodies. Theo was on top of her thrusting savagely as he talked to her in a language Winton did not understand, although the message was obvious. She raked Theo's back with her long fingernails as she sobbed hysterically, but the loss of thick scrapings of skin made no difference to the intent of her assailant. The curses changed to the rage of conquest as he ejaculated. His frenetic movement slowed for a few seconds and then slowly began to thrust again. She raked his face and went for his eyes, but the bloodied and torn facial skin and blood impaired vision only seemed to increase his lust as he leant back on his hairy-black haunches and delivered a solid open hand slap to her face before backhanding her to the other side. He was leering through his rage.

"Slut, I take you when I want you." He pinned her arms above her head and began to thrust into her again.

Winton rose on one elbow and lashed out with his foot catching Theo on the side of the head. It knocked him sideways and off balance. The girl was out from underneath in an instant.

With an animal cry of rage Theo rose and reached for his jacket, the knife instantly appearing in his hand. He lunged without caution at the still groggy figure on the ground, but Winton's foot crashed into the man's unprotected engorged genitals.

Theo doubled up in pain, but the knife did not leave his hand. The look of excruciating pain was interfaced with madness as the blade began its lunging descent towards Winton's exposed stomach. The stark terror melded into the acceptance of death, as fascinated he watched the blade coming towards him. He was helpless to respond or counter what was about to happen.

At that moment the girl hurled her full weight against her uncle. Before he could throw her off and regain his balance, Winton was on his feet fighting for his life. With all his force he threw a punch at the side of the ugly black head. Theo's eyes rolled drunkenly for a few seconds as he lost orientation. Winton kicked the knife out of the dangling hand and watched it spin across the dirt floor. They both followed it like tigers. Winton got to it first and rolling away, thrust it blindly upwards. He did not feel it hit anything, but the next instant he was being drenched with a gush of hot arterial blood as Theo threw himself backwards grasping the gaping wound in his neck. The carotid artery was severed, and already the glazed look was settling in his eyes as the dying hands tried to stem the flow gushing out through his loosening fingers.

They stood transfixed as they watched the hands slowly fall away and the body slump sideways in the final spasm of death. Winton shuddered as he thought how close he had come to being the lifeless body on the ground. They dressed quickly without speaking. The girl picked up the knife and wiping it clear of blood, closed it and thrust it into her jeans. She gently kissed Winton and ran her fingers along the thick blue contusion on the side of his head. He winced as she touched it and became aware of the intense pain.

"What do we do with him?"

"Leave him," Winton replied without thinking.

The girl shook her head violently. "No, we have to get rid of the body. Mama will know what happened if we leave him here. I couldn't stand the police asking questions. Get your truck." There was no emotion in her voice as she looked down at the cold staring eyes of the bloodied corpse.

Winton stumbled out of stable and ran down the alley. She had opened the stable doors as he returned and reversed the ute in. She was standing over the body with the knife in her hand. He gagged in shock as he saw she had mutilated it.

"What the Christ did you do that for?" He took the knife from her hand and threw it into the back of the vehicle.

"He's been trying to screw me since the day he moved in after my father died. He's not really my uncle, just a distant relation who was pressuring Mama to let him marry me and take me back to Greece. You've just released me from Hell." She threw her arms around his neck and kissed him passionately and hard. The eyes were beautiful, and yet clinical and calculating.

"Come on, give me a hand." Winton broke away and reached under the armpits to lift the body. He motioned for her to grab the feet. He felt revolted as the head rolled to one side and the congealing blood oozed over his arm. They heaved the body into the tray and covered it with sacks. Winton picked up a broom and brushed earth and hay over the blood which was soaking into the layered dirt and dust. It was the best he could do and hoped no one would visit the long-abandoned stables. He waited for her to get into the cab, but she stood aside as he kicked the motor into life.

"What are you going to do?"

"There's a train due in about an hour. That'll give me time to pack a few things and get out of this town." She stepped forward and kissed him gently on the cheek. "Thank you," she murmured.

"I won't see you again then? Say, what is your name?"

"I don't want to see you again, and likewise you don't want to see me either so we don't need to know each other's names. It's better that way. I'll always remember you though." He watched as she disappeared into the shadows.

Winton slipped the ute into gear and slowly idled out of the driveway. The street was deserted as he drove away. An hour out of town he turned off into a dry creek bed and followed its banks until he found a large sandy hollow partially filled with water. He retrieved a shovel from the tray and dug a hole nearby deep enough so the corpse would not be dug up by pigs or dingoes. He dragged the body into the hole and threw the sacks and shirt-wrapped genitals in on top to cover the dead face that stared back at him. He quickly shovelled sand to fill in the grave.

It was still dark as he washed down the tray and inside of the vehicle with the stinking brackish water until he was sure the last trace of blood had been erased. He stripped and inspected his clothes for blood. There appeared to be none, but as an added precaution he waded into the water and washed them and himself thoroughly. Why wouldn't she tell him her name, not that it mattered? The desire had been strictly mutual and animal.

10

The first shards of dawn were appearing as he pulled up in front of the camp. He sat there for a few moments collecting his thoughts. The next part was the hardest. It would be the beginning of his fortune, or the end of his dreams.

Sam was cooking breakfast when he strode in. He looked up from the frypan and grinned. "Get the dirty water off your chest, did you?"

Winton nodded and slumped into a chair. He greedily accepted the plate of bacon and eggs shoved in front of him and devoured it without a word. He finally looked up to see Sam staring at him intensely.

"You sure worked up an appetite lad. What have you been up to? By the look of your face you've been in a bit of biff again."

Winton ignored the question as he pushed the empty plate away. "How's the drilling going?"

Sam sighed. "Haven't made a lot of progress."

Winton could see the man was tired both mentally and physically. The stress was beginning to take its toll.

Harry stomped into the hut and nodded at Winton. He, on the other hand was showing no signs of fatigue. The hardened leathery face was completely expressionless. He was used to long hours nurturing his beloved rig listening for trouble and keeping an eye on the spinning drill stem as it slowly ground its way into the resisting strata. Harry was standing talking to Sam as he held a bacon sandwich in one hand and a coffee in the other when he suddenly cocked his head sideways, spun around and rushed out. He had heard the sudden acceleration of the main diesel engine and the sound of tortured metal.

Sam stood at the doorway with a look of despair written all over his face. This was the third breakdown in as many days. The rig was old, but had served him well to this point. Purchasing a new rig was out of the question. The constant attention to this bastard piece of mechanics with its ongoing mechanical faults was beginning to gnaw at his reasoning. He cursed Harry's supposed inattention had cost him time and money for replacement parts he could not afford, and mounting labour costs for staff standing around while repairs were effected.

Harry had said nothing as he shut the rig down and reached for his tools to take the shattered gearbox apart. He knew where the problem lay. It was an instinct borne of years on drill rigs. It was no use raving and cursing, the damage was done and the object was to fix it and get the rig moving again. He worked all day and into the night replacing the bearings and putting the gearbox back together. The whole scene was flooded with light from the powerful arc lamps surrounding the rig.

"We may as well pull the rods and have a look at that bit," Sam remarked as Harry finally finished and declared the rig ready to start again. There was no thought of waiting for daylight as the rig worked around the clock. He sent Winton up the drill mast to guide the rods into the racks as they were winched out of the well. It was a long, slow, laborious and filthy job as the drilling mud, oil and grease penetrated his leather gloves and covered his arms and clothing. Despite the cold of the dawn he broke into a sweat every time his mind drifted back to the girl and Theo. It was late morning before the rods were drawn and a new bit attached. The whole process was then reversed as they began to feed the rods back down. As each length of rod reached the drill collar it was held fast by the locking stem vice as the next length was lowered and screwed into place. The heat of the day was intense and Winton's aching joints protested every movement. He was not thinking, but just reacting mechanically, as the throb of the diesel pounded into his addled brain. Finally, the last rod was locked into place and they commenced drilling ahead again.

Winton began to step down when his foot slipped on a grease encrusted rung and he felt himself falling. A desperate lunge with one hand broke the momentum and he arrested his fall with the other. He clung there for long seconds unable to move contemplating the long fall to the platform below. His feet found the rungs again and he slowly felt his way down making sure his foot had found a rung before letting go with his hands. He knew his job was done for the time being. Harry always took the shift after the rods had been pulled. He stripped off and showered before throwing himself down on his bunk exhausted. What a hell of a way to make a living. This life was not for him, but he would have to be patient for a few more days. If his plan did not work he had no intention of staying. It was late afternoon before he awoke and made his way over to the rig. Sam was there with Harry. He had no idea when Harry took a rest or slept, but he could tell he had been there for some time judging by the pile of cigarette butts at his feet. He constantly rolled a cigarette and put it into the corner of his mouth where it would sit slowly burning until he finally spat it out and rolled another in his grease encrusted hands. He appeared to live on nicotine as Winton had never seen him eat a full meal. His dry wizened frame was as tough as an ironbark tree. He finally broke away and headed for his room satisfied the steady beat of the diesel and the even hum of the drill stem signified they were drilling through a constant sedimentary horizon. It was safe to close his eyes for a few hours.

"This is one tough game." Winton turned to Sam as they watched the spinning stem. "How much further until we hit the pay zone?"

"Don't really know, but if we don't hit it in another five hundred we'll have to cap it as a gas producer rather than the oil strike I was aiming for."

"Have you thought anymore about Bain's offer?"

The answer was curt. "I don't want to get mixed up with people like Bain. I set out to find oil and that's what I'm going to do."

"Or until your money runs out."

Sam ignored the barb. "People like Bain are parasites. We're worlds apart in our thinking and objectives and I can't ever see myself getting into bed with the likes of him."

"Some people are as thick as two short planks." Winton murmured to himself under his breath.

"You say something?' Sam had clearly heard the remark.

"No, just thinking out loud. What are you going to do about the legal action?"

"Nothing. I'm sure our fat friend is bluffing."

"Wouldn't it make a whole lot of sense to join him and cut your losses before this hole turns out to be a duster?"

"I know what you're inferring, but the answer's still no. I've studied this particular formation and I'm quite certain I'm going to get an oil entrapment. It may not be big, but it will prove my theory."

"How many of these wildcat holes can you afford to drill?"

"Before I run out of money?"

Winton nodded. He was drawing Sam into an area he had never been able to penetrate before; his solvency. He waited silently for Sam to answer.

"I've got to find it in this hole. A good gas strike would relieve some of the pressure, but I'm really after oil. I just need a little luck on my side and then I can farm this whole field out to a major company who will finance and develop the discovery. I've no need, nor am I desperate enough to strike a deal with the vermin in this world.".

"So, I'll be out of a job if you're lucky?"

"Not necessarily. Companies are always looking for good staff with drilling experience. You've been performing very well so I'd have no hesitation in recommending you to anyone. If I strike it lucky I'll give you a bonus of a couple of grand. That should keep you going for awhile."

I want more than that, Winton thought wryly. This was the one big chance for him to make it and Bain was his meal ticket. He tried to steer the conversation around to Bain again, but Sam cut him off and changed the subject.

Winton was nervous, but determined as his shift approached. He was quickly becoming an accomplished driller and tonight he intended to put his plan into action. He had to be careful as at anytime Harry could suddenly appear out of nowhere. Winton had watched him as the older man literally sniffed the air as though it would give him an indication of any impending mechanical disaster. He caressed various parts of the rig, his hand like a stethoscope on the beating heart of the machine. He would stand in one spot for minutes staring at the ground, lost deep in thought. He never spoke to anyone during his inspections, and disappeared as quickly as he came.

Winton was two hours into his shift when he made his move. The diesel seemed to run for an age before it finally started to splutter and then abruptly stop. Harry and Sam were on the scene almost immediately.

"What happened? Sam demanded.

"I've no idea Sam. It just suddenly cut out."

Harry was studying the temperature and pressure gauges. The radiator temperature had risen past the red line with the oil temperature firmly into the danger zone. He pulled out the engine dip-stick and ran it over the palm of his hand. He held it up for Sam to see the tell tale globules of water in the milky fluid.

"Must be a cracked head, or cylinder," he grunted. "There's a lot of water in the oil."

Sam swung on Winton. "What the hell have you been doing? It should have been obvious there was something wrong if you'd been paying attention. How long are we going to be out of action for Harry?"

"As long as it takes to replace the head, if indeed that is the problem."

Winton smiled inwardly as Sam broke out into a torrent of obscenities. He was stretched to the limit. The costs were starting to really bite and the mental stress was relentless.

Suddenly Harry stopped what he was doing, got up and strode off towards the equipment shed. He came out holding a large oil container. He picked up a stick and dipped it into the can, repeating the action of rubbing the oil over his palm. He cursed. It was his fault. He had topped up the engine oil before handing over to Winton, but had not checked if contaminants such as water, were present. He scratched his face lost in thought. He was sure he had opened a new container which would have been free of contaminants.

To Sam, the actions were self explanatory as he had been keenly following the sequence of events and the look of devastation on Harry's face. There was no point in discussing it further or blaming Harry.

The next day during Winton's shift another accident happened. The reduction gearbox on the rig seized without warning. The drill head suddenly stopped turning in a clatter of tortured metal as the clutch seized and started to burn. The thick acrid blue smoke spread quickly as Winton threw the machine into neutral and shut it down. It took Harry only moments to see the cause of the problem.

"Oh shit, the drain plug has worked loose. Couldn't you see the oil coming out?" It was the first time Winton had ever seen Harry's face take on a look of anger.

"It's dark Harry. I didn't notice a thing."

"I'm afraid this gearbox is stuffed boss." Harry turned to Sam with a look of exasperation.

"Jesus Harry, You're supposed to be the fucking mechanic. And yet you let something like this happen. I pay you to look after this machinery." Sam turned his back and stormed off.

Harry did not reply, but remained silent lost in thought. It was as though someone had a hand in these so-called accidents, but he could not think of anyone with a reason or grudge to do so.

The final accident happened within days. It was moonless and dark when the whole drill string had been pulled to replace the roller bit. Winton had the first length with bit attached locked in place over the hole when they heard the yell from above. It was more a screamed warning rather than a yell of danger. The roughneck at the top of the mast had slipped and lost the grip on the brake holding the length. The section of pipe came hurtling down as Winton threw himself out of danger. The descending pipe was transformed into an unstoppable lethal force as it hit the collar of the first section which Winton thought he had tightly clamped.

Sam attempted to throw a chain around the descending section. It gripped before jerking him off his feet as the two sections started to slide down the hole. At the moment it would have torn his arm from his shoulder the chain whipped around viciously and flung him clear. He was hurled to one side and his shoulder crashed into the guardrail of the platform. An explosion of blinding light seared through his skull as the shoulder muscles and tendons tore and dislocated his arm. He threw out his other hand to catch the rail, but missed and fell over the edge.

Winton knew from the solid meaty thud that Sam was seriously hurt. Harry quickly went to work feeling for broken bones and peeling back the eyelids of the unconscious man.

"He's concussed so we might have to take him into town to the doctor. Get his feet lad and we'll put him on his bunk."

Winton began to lift, but quickly lowered the body when a guttural cry emanated from deep within the injured man's throat. Harry pushed him aside and propped up the prone form. With a sudden jerk and twist he set the dislocated shoulder back in place. Years in the outback, hundreds of miles from the nearest doctor or medical facility had qualified him to deal with sprains, reset broken bones and dislocations and deal logically with any medical emergency.

"He's going to be in a lot of pain from that shoulder when he comes to." Harry gently lifted Sam under the armpits and nodded for Winton to take his feet. They carried him over and put him on his bunk where Harry rechecked for broken bones. He gently poked and pushed with the skill of a surgeon. The calloused hands had the gentle touch of an expert.

"Well, you didn't have anything to do with this accident lad."

Winton looked up in shock. "What do you mean by that remark?"

"Perhaps nothing lad, but there have been some strange things going on that can't be explained. All I know is they happened on your shift and I was beginning to suspect you, but I couldn't understand your motive. Now this has happened and it's clearly not your fault."

"Thanks very bloody much," Winton retorted indignantly.

"Don't push your luck with me lad. It was on your shift when the water in the sump caused that breakdown, and then there was the gearbox sump plug coming loose. I'm too careful for that. Take real care lad, because if anything else should go wrong when you're around, I will start asking more serious questions. You're up to something, but I can't fathom out what your motive is at this stage."

Winton clenched his fists in anger, but stopped when he noted the steely look from Harry. "And don't even think about it lad. I could break you in two in a moment."

Sam started to regain consciousness half an hour later and cried out in pain as he attempted to sit up.

"You've got a couple of busted ribs and you dislocated your shoulder. I've reset it for you, but you'll be in a lot of pain." Harry assisted him into a sitting position. "You're going to be out of action for awhile."

"Can't you strap me up?" Sam was in agony.

"I could do, but I don't think it will make the slightest bit of difference. Strapped or not, it will take the same time, and you'll be in pain for a week or more."

Sam's breathing came in shallow gasps as the pain increased. Harry handed him a mug of tea laced with rum and gave him a handful of aspirin.

"Swallow the lot and then rest."

"What the hell happened anyway. How did that pipe break loose?" Sam demanded of Winton between clenched teeth.

Winton did not answer. He was still in shock from the near miss, but in a way elated the way things were turning out.

"It was not Winton's fault Sam," Harry interjected. "It was mine and I take full responsibility. "I was pushing things too hard wanting to get started again. Billy's okay. A fall from up there would have killed him. He claimed he lost his footing."

Sam looked at the ceiling and grimaced in pain. "Did we loose it?"

Harry nodded. "You guessed it boss. Straight down the bloody hole. We've got fishing gear, but I think it's too deep to recover."

Sam knew that fishing for lost gear down a hole was entirely in the lap of the gods. You could strike it lucky on the first probe, or it might take a week or it might just prove to be an impossible task.

"What's our alternative?"

"Too early to tell. I'll have a go at recovering it, other than that I can put a wedge in as far down as possible and try a step-out hole. Might be quicker and cheaper to start a new hole altogether. Anyhow, I'll try probing for a couple of days and then we can decide what to do."

Sam nodded in misery and resignation. This was just about the last straw. If the stem could not be recovered it would just about mean the end of the road as he mentally calculated what it had cost him to date and what the delay would cost. Wildcatting was a crap shoot, sudden death on one roll of the dice. Only one in twenty made it and those statistics were based on success ratios in the U.S. The chances of him bring-ing in a successful oil discovery were multiples of that figure.

The wildcatters in the panhandle of America had a great deal of geological information accumulated over a hundred or more years of drilling. He had nothing when he started except his own interpretation of previous limited drilling for gas and some crude seismic profiles shot by the government many years before. Ignorance was blinding. The only thought on his mind was this well would strike oil, or at the very least a large gas show. Nothing else mattered, but the first doubts of failure were beginning to creep into his thinking. The series of accidents and breakdowns over the past week he had not factored in, nor allowed for in his budget.

Over the next few days Harry attempted to recover the drill stem with a crude fishing tool he had improvised, but every time the diesel took the strain to pull the stem clear, the line parted.

"Shut it down Harry." Sam leaned against the rig. Although his damaged arm was in a sling, he clutched it to his body with his other hand to relieve the pressure and pain of his ribs. He talked in short bursts in between the bouts of pain brought on by movement. "We'll pack it up and plug the hole."

Harry shook his head. "No Sam, don't quit now. It's just that we haven't got the right gear. I might be able to borrow some from another company. There are other rigs working within a hundred kilometres of here, and one of them is sure to have what we're after."

"Tell me what you need and I'll go get it," Winton suddenly chipped in. "I'd like a break from this godforsaken place anyway."

He knew Harry would accept the offer and Sam was in no condition physically or mentally to stand the continuous jolting over bush tracks and unmade roads.

11

Bain was sitting in a squatter's chair on the wide upper veranda of the hotel studying the occasional passing traffic. His look of complete boredom broke into a broad grin as he saw Winton pull in and climb out of the cab of the ute. He rose and bustled his fat bulk downstairs with Waterman in tow.

"Well, how did our little business arrangement work out?"

"The turkey's ready for the plucking." Winton adopted an off-hand look of complete confidence. "I told you I'd deliver the goods."

Bain stuck out his hand. "Well done my young friend. If you have indeed achieved it, I can promise you a long and lucrative business relationship. I think I might fly out and call on your Sam Carlin today."

"Hell no," Winton protested. "He'd smell a rat if you suddenly turned up. It wouldn't take him long to realise there was something going on involving me."

"I want to get on with this. If he strikes oil our deal is off. He'll be able to raise all the money he wants."

Winton held up his hand and laughed. He explained the purpose of his visit to town. Bain became alarmed and turned to Waterman who had been reading his thoughts.

"Don't worry about that Jim. There won't be any fishing gear available. I'll see to that."

Bain looked relieved as he mopped his brow with a hand towel. His light linen suit was looking crumpled and stained.

"Well, you won't get the gear you're after lad, so there's no use in chasing all over the country for it. Why don't you join as for a drink?"

"I will later Jim, but right now I want to clean up and then I want to see my broker. I'm hoping my investments are showing a tidy profit."

"If you put your money into the stocks I tipped, you've doubled your money."

An hour later Winton was in Mike Robinson's office seated on the soft leather lounge. He liked the comfort, it had the feeling of security and money.

Robinson was beaming. "You did okay with your two punts."

"I'm not a punter Mike." Winton adopted the cocky air of indifference. "I only bet on sure things."

"Want to let it ride, or do you want to cash in?"

"I thought I told you to sell when the stock doubled?"

Robinson opened his mouth to explain he'd forgotten the instruction, but Winton cut him off. "Cash me out, and put the lot on this stock." He handed over the slip of paper Bain had given him earlier.

Robinson looked at the name. It was a company he was aware of, but knew nothing about. "I'd like to know where you get your information from. Putting everything on the nose is gambling, not investing."

"So I like a little gambling along with my investing, and no I can't tell you where I get the information from."

Robinson showed him to the door trying to draw him out as to his background and where he was getting his information from. Who was feeding this grease-monkey the tips?

Winton ignored him as he shook his outstretched hand and strode off down the footpath followed by Robinson's steady gaze. His elation turned to disquiet as he realised he was passing the police station. He tried to appear nonchalant and not quicken his pace. He was nearly clear when he heard the shout from behind. He slowly turned on his heel and smiled dumbly at the beckoning cop.

"I've been looking for you lad. Come inside." It was not a polite request, but a firm demand as Winton followed him in with as much innocence and confusion as he could muster. His brain was racing. The heavily built cop showed him into a dark office smelling of dry wood and piles of papers.

"Sit down." He indicated the chair on the other side of the desk. "What's your name?" The voice was rough and demanding. It gave no quarter, the questions were to be answered, and answered immediately. The face remained expressionless, but the penetrating eyes were glued to Winton for any sign of unease or facial twinges that would provide clues of evasiveness or guilt. This form of interrogation was highly effective. Frighten shit out of them in the first minute, and they could not think straight after that. The lies were easily trapped, and the truth filtered. Any smart-arsed answers, or refusal to answer was quickly dealt with by a journey to the cells where a few open slaps to the face or an unexpected blow to the solar plexus invariably produced results. He could tell from long experience who was lying, or who was attempting to shield the true perpetrator of a crime. Hit them hard and fast before they had time to dream up an excuse or alibi.

Winton's eyes were unmoving as he gave the cop his name. He managed to keep any trace of fear or guilt out of his expression or voice, but his brain was spinning.

"Been in trouble with the law?"

"Never."

"You know Louise or Theo Zuckas?"

Winton looked puzzled. "No, should I?"

"I'll ask the questions Springer. You just answer them. It's known Theo Zuckas threatened you in the theatre. It was reported you were sitting behind Zuckas and when you left, you had blood on your shirt. Zuckas was known to have threatened a couple of the town lads with a knife. He had a go at you, didn't he?"

Winton nodded. He did not think anyone had witnessed the theatre incident, but then again everyone notices everything in a small town.

"Yeah, some wog did rough me up a little, but he never told me his name."

The face staring at him looked meaner. "You were trying to screw his niece?"

Winton laughed and shook his head. There was no use feigning complete ignorance of what the cop was driving at. "I did have the idea of getting into her nickers, but the action in the theatre soon cooled me of that idea. The bastard is mad. He'll kill someone if he keeps that up."

"He wounded you. Why didn't you report it? I don't like people who carry knives and cut people up."

Winton shrugged. "He scared the shit out of me at the time. No real damage done except to my ego."

"And you didn't see her again after that?"

Winton shook his head. It was the crucial question. It they had been seen together the game was over. He did not fancy being slapped around by this mean looking bastard. He waited, fully expecting the cop to stand up and grab him by the shirt front and shake the truth out of him. Instead he remained seated, studying the face for any signs of hesitancy. His years in the force had built up a sixth sense when it came to dealing with the local ferals, as he called them.

"I'm going to ask you one last time. Did you see Louise or Theo Zuckas after that night?"

Winton remained impassive. "I've already told you. I didn't see either of them after the incident in the theatre. I wasn't going to argue with that gorilla again. Anyway, what's this enquiry about, and what's it got to do with me?"

"They've both disappeared."

"They might have shot through together," Winton ventured. "She was one stunning looking bird. Maybe Uncle Theo and her just hit it off and decided to get out of town."

The cop never took his eyes off Winton's face. "Every stud in town was trying to lay her, but without success it would seem. They all got a warning like you did. She was promised to some Greek I heard. One of those arranged marriages and it was uncle's job to ensure she arrived at the altar with everything intact."

"Maybe Uncle Theo wanted to pick the cherry before it got overripe?"

The cop's face suddenly cracked as he broke into a thin laugh. The mood had changed. Winton could see he was in the clear for now.

"I can't help you any further. Can I go now?"

The cop nodded without getting up. "If you hear anything, you make sure you get back to me and if I find out you've been lying, I'll come after you real heavy."

Winton expressed just the right amount of fright and concern as he got up to leave. "I'll do that." He felt the eyes boring into him as he walked out the door. His knees were like two jellied pinions trying to co-ordinate and support his weight. He had a nauseous feeling of relief as he unconsciously walked towards the café. He checked and made to turn around as though lost in thought. His downcast eyes caught a glimpse of the uniform. The cop was standing on the veranda watching his every movement. He turned around, and told himself not to alter course as he once again moved towards the café. He went in and sighed with relief when he saw there was no sign of Mama. He ordered a coffee from the stranger behind the counter, drank it slowly and then left.

12

Winton heard the sound he had been waiting for droning slowly from the north-east. The Maule threw up its intense cloud of choking dust as it taxied up close to the rig. He noted Sam did not look half as hostile when Bain stumbled out of the aircraft.

"I hear you've been having a bit of trouble?" Bain tried to keep a concerned tone of voice as he shook Sam's hand.

"You can say we're having more than our fair share," Sam replied flatly. "Winton tells me you have the recovery gear I'm after, so let's cut to the chase and discuss terms. How much will you rent it to me for?"

Bain shook his head with concern. "It's not for rent. Didn't Winton tell you that?"

"Don't be unreasonable," Sam implored. "We only want to fish the drill stem out and I'll pay you a fair price. We'll be on our way again in a day or so with the gear you have."

Waterman shook his head as he took the cue. "And what about the next hold up, and the next breakdown, and the next after that. By the look of it you haven't made much progress since we were here last."

Bain took up the attack with a soft tone. "Why don't you come in with us Carlin. You can't sustain any more stoppages, and you're as good as finished if you don't retrieve that rod. Look at you, injured and out of money. You've got an excellent piece of ground. Why don't you let me handle it from here? I'll undertake the complete financing."

Sam stared into his mug of tea. "What's in it for you?"

"Fifty percent of the action." Bain held up his hands as Sam tossed his tea into the ground in disgust. "Just before you reject it, think about it. I'll take over the financing from this moment. All you have to do is supervise."

"And, if it's a dry hole? A duster?"

Bain's eyes lit up behind his heavy lashes. "Let's just say I'm confident I'm backing the right horse. Anyhow, let me worry about that. I'll take the loss if I'm wrong. I'm going to get you underway again, and in the meantime I'm going to prepare Roma Oil for a float onto the stock market. How do you like the name? I've registered it already."

Sam nodded. "And my end is fifty percent and you pick up the tab from now. Is that correct?"

"That's the deal." Bain could see the prospect was hooked. It was now just a matter of closing the sale and obtaining a signature. "And I guarantee Roma Oil will be on the lists within a month."

"In effect, you'll wind up with control of the company?"

Bain had anticipated the question. "Effectively yes, but you will have complete managerial control. I can assure you Sam, I'm only a short-term player. The stock will come on at a premium, and that's where I abandon ship and gradually sell out. That's how I make my money. You'll then be in effect the largest shareholder, and retain control if you don't sell out."

Winton could see Sam was agonising as he chewed it over in his mind. He finally stuck out his hand. "You've got a deal Bain."

Winton let out his breath as he turned to hide the look of triumph on his face. It had been easier than he first thought possible. Continue to play your cards right Winton Springer and the oil business held a bright future, he murmured to himself. He had noted Bain's style. Why be a front runner trying to grab all the attention? Stay behind the scenes like Bain and pick up a healthy percentage. No point in being the greediest hog in the mud patch. Spread the risk, and give everyone a share of the upside. He had observed how the stress and strain had affected Sam as he tried to keep all the balls in the air at the same time.

Bain was all business the moment the handshake was completed. He penned up a memorandum on a sheet of paper before handing it to Sam.

"The legals will follow, but that's the guts of it so we can get the show on the road." Bain handed across his pen.

Sam scanned the page and signed it before handing it back.

"Believe me Sam, you've made the right move." Bain folded the paper and put it into his pocket. "Waterman here will get you all the fishing gear you need and anything else you may require. You rest and get those ribs healed. I've got to get back to Sydney to get my public relations crowd involved. They'll get the press and brokers organised and get them up here on a junket. A few of them know what a drilling rig looks like, but oil's the buzz word at the moment, and we'll soon educate the ignorant. A little here and there in the right pockets and Roma Oil will list at a fat premium, I can guarantee you that."

Winton could see the immediate change in Sam's demeanour. His face and manner lost the signs of stress.

The proper equipment was flown in and the drill stem fished back to the surface after two days of probing. Winton was amazed at Bain's professional approach. He flew in with the formal agreement, and draft prospectus for Sam to sign off on.

"I'm flying in a group of press and stockbrokers next week to drum up the publicity."

"Is that really necessary?"

"Sam, unless you beat the drum loudly, no one will flock to your tent to see what's going on. I learnt it from my father who used to run a boxing troupe at country fairs and rodeos. Until he got on his box and started shouting and banging his drum, the punters took no notice. But once he started making a noise about how good his boxers were, all the half- pissed local young studs wanted to test their pugilistic skills against them. The same applies to this project. Get the press and brokers involved and they sell it to the public and clients."

"I wouldn't know how to do that Jim," Sam protested.

"I don't expect you to. All I want you to do is look intelligent and stick strictly to drilling topics. I'll be at your side to handle any of the facetious questions that will surely be tossed at you."

"Facetious questions? What do you mean by that?"

"Oh, I won't go into that now, but just remember what I said. Don't get sidetracked by topics you don't understand."

Sam made to interject again, but Bain cut him off. "I've arranged for a slap-up day. Full catering and beer and wines laid on. It should be very interesting."

The two Beech King Air's landed on the hastily graded dirt strip. Winton watched in amazement as Bain hosted the deplaning passengers with consummate skill. He quickly intervened if he saw Sam being waylaid by a journalist or broker. He listened to every question and quickly butted in if he saw Sam was out of his depth, or chopped him off if he thought he was giving too candid an answer.

"I think what Mr Carlin is saying is this well will be successful, and then it's just a matter of further drilling to see how big the discovery might be. He's already into a big gas intersection." He ushered his partner away from what he could see was going to be an interrogation rather than an idle question.

"That's bullshit Jim. There's absolutely no guarantee this well will be successful," Sam hissed.

"You don't understand Sam. You may think some of these guys are just making conversation with you to while away the day. Some of them are, but there are some very smart guys here and you've got to be on your mettle the whole time. Just don't get out of my sight."

Bain was ebullient and expansive. The mood was catching as the barbecue, beer and wine flowed under the shade of large marquees. Bain had thought of everything.

"Ah, come with me Sam. I want you to see how this game is played." He grabbed him by the arm and guided him towards a journalist. "Sam, this in Dave Croft of the Investors Chronicle."

The quick introduction over, Bain would immediately launch into business. "Dave, have you found enough of interest to write about?"

"I think I have Jim."

"Good for you. I'll put you down for twenty thousand then?" Croft did not answer, but nodded as Bain smiled and led Sam away.

"What the hell was that all about?"

"I just gave him twenty thousand shares. He'll give us a good write up. Some of these guys are not paid enough to resist the temptation. I've got to be careful, but I've got certain of these people in my pocket. They know Roma is going to come on at a substantial premium, and they'll cash in immediately. Money for old rope."

"You mean some of these guys can be bought?"

Bain laughed. "Keep your voice down Sam. There are a lot of ears here and not all of them are exactly friendly with me. But to answer your question, the whole world can be bought, so don't think any different."

"I don't go along with that."

Bain turned on him with an amused look. "I bought you didn't I? Now before you profess righteous indignation there's one person here I want you to steer clear of unless you're with me. If only I could get Peter O'Grady, the greasy red-headed little schmuck on side, we'd be oversubscribed twice over."

Winton watched from the sidelines as Bain worked the crowd. He could see Sam was completely out of his depth, but his partner ensured he never left his side. There was more to promoting and floating an oil company other than finding oil. The name of the game was promotion and selling. Without Bain, Sam would not have stood a chance of remaining solvent.

Sam pondered whether it was just fate Bain had arrived on the scene. He was puzzled how Bain knew the right moment to strike. His timing was impeccable as he was at his lowest ebb when the fat man suddenly appeared and made the offer. He could not put it out of his mind somewhere in the background he sensed Winton's involvement. The lad possessed animal cunning. It was the cunning of someone who fought for survival from an early age.

"Sam Carlin?"

Sam had not noticed Bain had drifted away button-holing his chosen targets when he was jolted from his thoughts by the short figure standing in front of him. The red curly hair was completely unkempt. The stubble on his chin gave him an unwashed appearance. The linen suit was crumpled and dirty and it was not the dirt from today's surrounds; it was the accumulation of many days or even weeks. The shirt matched the colour of the suit, although it would have originally been a shade of white. Sam reflected nothing could be done to improve the man's appearance. His figure was such that it would not matter how he dressed, or how fashionably, he would always look like a bundle of last week's washing before being tossed into the machine.

O'Grady had a tick which made his head twitch to one side every so often. There was a cynical look in his dull looking eyes and the cynicism was honed by the number of beers he had already consumed.

"Peter O'Grady's the name. I suppose Jim's already warned you about me?"

"I don't know what you're talking about." Sam eyed the journalist coldly.

"Well, if he hasn't, he's been doing a good job of shielding you from me. I know what he's up to buying various guys off. It's his usual game. I've been waiting to get you by yourself without Jim shooting me a line of shit."

"You know Jim that well?"

"Jim it aint." O'Grady chuckled. "Aaron is his real name. Circumcised up to his belly button. Absolutely transparent of course. Thinks he can buy everyone he comes into contact with. Has he bought you Carlin?"

O'Grady took a sip of his beer and went on without waiting for a reply. "Tell me about yourself Carlin. What are the chances of hitting a gusher, or is this just another of Jim's ramps. Get the brokers hyped up, pay-off the complying media, get the gullible public in a frenzy, and then float the whole thing and shoot through with a huge profit."

O'Grady belched and reached around for another beer from a passing tray. "Not that I'm totally opposed to the concept, but I like to know in advance what I'm dealing with."

Sam tensed, immediately on guard. "I'm a geologist Mr O'Grady. I don't know anything about ramping companies as you put it. I'm only interested in making a commercial discovery and I believe there will be plenty of them in this country in the short term."

O'Grady's eyes glinted. Either Carlin was totally ignorant of what Bain was really up to, or Bain had told him to be careful when speaking to him. "Ah, it's wonderful to meet an honest person Carlin. I had the same ideals once. I was going to change the whole world by revealing the truth. Tell people the truth and they would be eternally in my debt. That was of course, before I heard the words vested interest, insider trading and profit, and realised the greed for money is the driving force that corrupts all men. Of course, there are degrees of corruption, but it eventually gets everyone. Without it there is no life."

"You have a very perverse philosophy on life."

O'Grady's intense gaze was penetrating. "Don't you have the same philosophy Carlin?"

"No, I don't. I believe in what I'm doing. If I strike oil I don't deny money will follow, but at the moment I'm only intent on bringing this well in."

"I'm pleased to hear that. I thought I was out here to interview another rogue and thief in the same mould as Jim. I guess I'm wrong this time. Why don't you show me around and explain what you're about?"

No one noticed them wander off as Sam was engrossed in explaining the complexities of an oil rig and his theory on the prospects of an oil discovery. O'Grady appeared to be engrossed and was not lost for questions. Behind the supposed façade of cynicism and appearance of shambled alcoholism was a very sharp and enquiring mind. Sam was not lulled into a false sense of security that his inquisitor was perhaps also a little corrupt and wanted to confirm his suspicions that Sam was likewise. Bain's warning was at the back of his mind. Despite O'Grady's professed interest Sam remained on guard, not diverting from only commenting on oil and gas exploration. Out of the corner of his eye he saw Bain hurrying towards them. He was hot and agitated.

"I've been looking all over for you Sam." He glanced nervously at the journalist. "Hello there Peter, I'm glad to see you accepted our invitation."

"Wouldn't have missed it for anything Jim. I don't get paid much, so a trip in the country with all expenses paid is very appealing."

"I hope you're going to write something nice about us."

"Jim, you know my attitude towards you and the scams you keep perpetrating. I would never write anything nice about you. I was fascinated by Sam here and the human interest story associated with his background. I accepted your invitation to check him out and I believe he does appear genuine. Too bad he's mixed up with you."

O'Grady was enjoying the discomfort he was causing, but kept his voice low. Bain remained impassive with a large grin on his face while Sam, about to protest his indignation, felt Jim put a restraining hand on his arm.

"I think Carlin was heading for insolvency before you came on the scene Jim." O'Grady drained his glass. "I'm off for another beer. By the way Jim, while we're out of earshot, put me down for twenty thousand on the usual terms. I'm not going to mention the float in my column, but I'll put it around it's got the right smell about it. It's not up to my standard to give it the seal of good housekeeping, but I won't knock it. I take it the terms are acceptable?" He raised an enquiring brow, but Bain was already nodding agreement.

"Thank the Messiah for that." Bain started mopping his brow and neck with an oversize handkerchief as they watched the little man walk off.

"Thank who for what?" Sam demanded. "What the hell is going on? That little slug is crooked."

Bain grabbed Sam by the shoulder to calm him down. "I can tell you one thing Sam, you've made the grade with him. He's convinced you're genuine in your aims and beliefs, and will accept twenty thousand shares not to tip a bucket of effluent over us. The way he'd been dodging me, I thought we were going to get the thumbs down completely."

Sam was shaking his head in disbelief. "He's just as corrupt as some of those others you've been paying off today."

"Yes, yes, Sam I know he's corrupt, but there are degrees of corruption, and we all practice it in various forms according to our level of moral values."

Sam was beginning to laugh. "Jesus Jim, how do you live with yourself?"

Bain ignored the question. "There's honest corruption. That's the category he puts himself into because he's not going to mention us in his column because he's convinced I'm a crook. But he will accept twenty thousand shares to mention it around his broking mates as a good punt. And there's the dishonest corruption like the certain other media representatives I've approached today. They will accept the shares and also give the company the thumbs up in their publications. Tell me, what did you two discuss?"

Sam told him what had transpired.

"Yes, I can see it now. You came across as being honest and hardworking and completely naïve and therefore trustworthy.

He won't wind up with egg on his face. A lot of mining and oil floats that hit the market have absolutely nothing except some bullshit written up by an independent expert as required under the rules. The directors don't have any intention of drilling for anything. They sit back on the money pile and stash money into anything in which they have a vested interest. Make big loans to themselves at no interest that never get repaid, and have half a dozen ghost staff on their payroll to give themselves spending money."

"You sound as though you have first hand knowledge of this?"

Bain laughed. "You could say I have a very good knowledge of what goes on, but I promised O'Grady this was not the case with Roma. That's the only reason he agreed to come out here. Just verbally mentioning the company to all his contacts is going to mean success, but the ultimate goal would be to get it mentioned in his column. But that is a very rare event indeed, very rare. I would say an impossibility. He likes the money I pass to him under the table, but doesn't want any taint he's associated with me. He's a complete hypocrite, but I've got to live with it. We'll still have a substantial over-subscription and we should be thankful, but if he did write us up the stock would come on at a significant premium. In any event, Roma Oil is on the way Sam. You've cracked the toughest nut and you did it without my help."

"But you've just given him twenty thousand shares. Why don't you blackmail the bastard into giving us a full write up?" It was Winton, the silent witnessing shadow attached in the background, all during the discussions with O'Grady and Bain.

Bain choked back a laugh as a look of derision crossed his face. "You've got a lot to learn lad, but I'll tell you why I can't blackmail him, as you put it and that's because there's no trail linking the shares to him. Don't worry, I would if I could, but he's too smart for that. The stock is never registered in his name and therefore he's never listed as a seller. I pay for them and sell them on the opening day of listing. I meet him in a bar and give him a bundle of cash and that's about it. Very hard to blackmail someone if there's no money trail. Besides why resort to that and burn your bridges forever? We both understand the rules, he gets what he wants and so do I. The arrangement has worked well for a number of years and I can see no reason not to prolong it."

"And he doesn't even mention the company in his column?" Winton was incredulous. "And what's this about selling shares on the first day. Why do that? The company has a bright future."

Bain rolled his eyes to the heavens. "Winton, that's where the profits are made. Stagging, or selling on the opening is the name of the game as far as I'm concerned. I'm not in it for the long term. I like to take my money and wait for the next opportunity. Don't be under the illusion I'm married to the company, or any company. I'm only in this business to make money. I'm not interested in getting mixed up in the politics or the day to day running of a company. Sam has nothing to fear in regard to that. Do you understand where I'm coming from?"

Winton nodded. "Yes, I accept that. Are you sure Roma is going to come on at a premium?"

"It will come on above the issue price, but at how much of a premium is in the lap of the god's and depends on how much publicity I can generate in the meantime."

"So it could bomb?"

"I don't back losers. At the moment the market is caught up in the hysteria of finding oil and will bet on two flies crawling up the wall. I don't intend to disillusion them about the prospects of Roma being successful. So why don't we share the enthusiasm with the investing public. Get them keen and get plenty of publicity. Look at this bunch. They all appear to be very positive and they'll go back and spruik it to their friends and clients. That's the whole purpose of this junket." Bain spread his hands around to encompass the gathering. "Spread the word. Tell the whole world Roma is about to strike oil and the investors will come running with their wallets open."

"Any chance of getting an allocation of shares for myself?"

"Sure lad. You can have as many shares as you like as long as you pay for them. I've already paid you for your assistance to date. That was the deal. You have nothing to offer at this stage so you don't get a free ride like O'Grady."

Winton had been calculating his available funds and the profit he stood to make if the stock listed at anything like the premium Bain was hinting at.

Bain looked around at the milling media, stock analysts and brokers. "Well, I suppose I'd better get this mob back to town. Food and drink's all gone and there's nothing more they can learn out here. I've got a big reception for them tonight so there'll be a few sore heads in the morning."

"Can I come along with you Jim? Do you mind Sam?"

Sam was in a happy and expansive mood now the burden of stress had been lifted. "No, by all means. I've got to go in tomorrow for stores so I can bring you back."

Winton followed Bain up the stairs and dropped in beside him at the very front of the plane.

"You may have to move from there lad. There's a particular broker I want to chat to on the way back and he'll be joining me at any moment."

"Sure Jim, but I would like to discuss a little business with you if I may?"

Bain was not surprised by the request, or the direct frontal approach. He was getting used to Springer's style and determination.

"You wanted to talk to me Jim?" The broker was looking down at Winton expecting him to give up his seat.

"Give me five minutes Bill. I've got something to discuss with Winton here and then I'm free."

The broker gave Winton a dark look as he moved further down the plane.

"Now, what's on your mind?"

"You say O'Grady never mentions you in his column, and has never written up any company you've promoted."

Bain nodded. "That's correct, but don't think for a moment you could change that habit. I've tried, but no amount of money will budge him."

"What would it be worth if I could change his mind?"

"I'd give you a hundred thousand shares," Bain replied laughing. "But my shares are safe, because you'll never pull it off."

Winton made to stand up. "I'm going to hold you to that." Bain was still chuckling to himself as he shook the outstretched hand.

O'Grady was sitting by himself. Winton sat down beside him. He had a premonition and started to work on it. As long as business was not discussed the journalist was happy to talk, and it soon became apparent to Winton his premonition was correct. Everyone had a weak spot and he quickly determined what O'Grady's was.

13

Robinson invited him to lunch at the Graziers Club. He was determined to find out the source of Winton's information.

"You're more than a hundred grand ahead. Do you want to let it ride or have you got another stock you want me to buy?"

Winton eyed the broker. "It's been good for both of us hasn't it? I've no doubt you've been piggy-backing on my tips."

Robinson laughed. "Of course. You've been getting terrific information from somewhere, so I thought I may as well get onboard."

"How would you like to make a real killing?"

"I'm all ears."

"I can put you in on the ground floor of a new float my boss Sam Carlin and Jim Bain are putting together. It will come on at a big premium."

Robinson tried to hide his excitement as he nodded as though deep in thought. Jim Bain was legendary for hustling stocks. He worked purely on inside information, a crime in itself, but he had never been charged, not yet anyway. He listened as Winton outlined the proposal and terms.

"You say you have enough pull to get me a large allocation of shares?"

"Yes, I believe I do, but if I don't get them I'm the loser under the terms I'm proposing. What have you got to lose?"

"Just explain your end of the deal again?" Robinson was running it over in his mind and wondering how hard a bargain he could drive.

"I want twenty five percent of the net profit, free and carried."

Robinson was shaking his head. "I don't like the sound of that. I'm putting up all the money and taking all the risk. Anyway, why should I deal with you? I'll no doubt be able to get a sizable allocation."

"Bullshit. We both know you're bluffing. Remember, this is a Jim Bain float and he doesn't deal with small country town brokers. There's no leverage in that. He wants the city boys involved, the brokers and hustlers who can hype the story and maintain the momentum. Any stock that comes your way won't be enough to buy a bus ticket to the next town."

"And you reckon you can guarantee me a large allocation?" Robinson was incredulous, but there was something about this roughneck suggesting he could deliver what he claimed.

"Okay, your end of the deal is ten percent. I'll put up the money."

"Go screw," Winton replied with finality. "I'll find someone else who wants to make big bucks. I don't think it'll be too hard." He made to get up, but Robinson raised his hand for him to sit down. His mind was racing. Springer was no ignorant country hustler. He was alert with a maturity borne of the constant awareness of survival, a quick learner with a knowledge of stocks and the stock market, way beyond his years. If he could deliver and Bain was up to his usual tricks, the stock would come on at three or four times the issue price. It was a chance too good to miss, and as Springer was saying, there appeared to be no downside. He envied his broker colleagues in Sydney and Melbourne who waited like vultures to take large allocations into their house accounts, a proportion of which were stagged on the first day of trading, or sold into favoured client's discretionary accounts. A Jim Bain promotion was not to be missed, despite the odium of the man and his dealings. It was all a vicious game, the broker maintaining an air of utter probity and respectability, while behind the scenes reaping huge profits from dubious companies and promotions. No company could obtain listing unless it was promoted by this elite band of licensed thieves. Robinson grinned to himself at the irony. It was a crime to deal in inside information, but no broker could succeed without it. It was a licence to print money. Here was a chance to make enough money to move to the big time and buy into one of that elite band. He always managed to get a few shares in every float through his contacts with the city brokerage firms. Nice pickings, but that was all it ever was, just pickings. It was nothing like the deal that Winton was offering him now.

"Alright, you've got a deal, but only if you deliver the allocation of shares you claim you can, and only if the stock lists at a one hundred percent premium to the issue price." Robinson was attempting to keep the excitement out of his voice.

"Agreed." Winton held out his hand.

"You seem sure of yourself. You're also very trusting. How do you know I'll keep my end of the bargain?" Robinson tried to bite back the words as he made the comment in jest. The look on Winton's face did not require the question to be answered.

"Okay, let's assume you can deliver the allocation I want, the thing that intrigues me is how you can be sure the stock will list at more than a hundred percent premium?"

"It will actually be multiples of that," Winton replied without a moment's hesitation. "What if Peter O'Grady was to write it up in his column?"

"I read his column in the Financial Daily and I've never seen him ever say anything favourable about a resource stock. Are you telling me Roma Oil is going to be a first?"

"I have the feeling this time it will be different. By the way, have you ever met O'Grady?"

Robinson shook his head and then looked around in amazement as Winton beckoned to the journalist as walked in. O'Grady nodded at Robinson as they were introduced and sat down. The man had cleaned himself up, but a flab of lifeless flesh protruded through where a shirt button was missing above the waistline. He had changed his suit, but it still had the dishevelled appearance of being stuffed, rather than folded into a bag. He belched and scratched the belly flesh. Robinson was repulsed by the exhalation of sour alcohol as he slowly began to move his chair back.

"And what do you do for a living Robinson?" O'Grady reached over and filled a glass from their bottle of wine.

"I'm a stockbroker." Robinson replied with the assurance the mention of his profession would command a measure of respect and awe.

"Oh, a member of that tribe of incestuous thieves are you?"

Robinson winced inwardly and was about to say something when he caught the look in Winton's eye which said *'stay where you are and take whatever he dishes out.'*

It was an exercise in extreme self-control.

"No, I'm not a thief Mr O'Grady and I reject your personal opinion of the broking fraternity. I would suggest journalists would have a more unsavoury reputation."

"Don't be so bloody touchy. This is a nice drop of wine. Order another would you Springer and I'll have a rare steak seeing you invited me to lunch. I see you two have already eaten." He turned to Robinson again. "I'm always a bit rude when I'm out of my comfort zone in one of these decrepit little towns. People don't live in these places, they merely exist."

"What are you going to say about Roma Oil? Something good I hope. The company will certainly bring progress to this area."

O'Grady looked up from his glass. "What do you mean by progress?"

"This will bring money into this town," Robinson blustered. "And lord knows we need it after the prolonged drought. The grazing industry is on hard times with falling cattle prices combined with the cost of trucking in feed."

"The grazing industry's a disaster from what I can see." O'Grady was enjoying the broker's obvious discomfort. "It's not my game to bring so-called prosperity to an area by writing crap. I won't be writing anything about Roma Oil. All these penny stocks are ramps for promoters like Jim Bain. They don't give a fuck about prosperity, other than their own."

Robinson bit his lip as he was about to make a caustic reply. He stood up to leave. "I'll be getting back to the office. Nice meeting you Mr O'Grady." He felt a little smug, but disappointed. Springer would probably get him his promised allocation of shares, but he could not see how he would be getting his twenty five percent commission if the stock did not list at the premium he had indicated. He could see O'Grady was not going to deliver it for him.

O'Grady dismissed him with a grunt and turned to Winton. "And now, what about our little arrangement?"

Robinson caught the question as he was walking away. He paused and turned to see Winton give him a knowing nod.

"See you tomorrow Mike."

The night was chilly as Winton guided the girl towards the rear of the hotel. She had cost him fifty plus two flagons of cheap port.

"What's your name honey?"

"Maggie," she replied as a sudden breeze made her shudder and pull the thread-bare woollen cardigan around her shoulders. Winton knew she would have nothing on beneath the thin cotton dress. The small breasts were well formed and prominent. Her features were fine, courtesy of a white stockman somewhere in her ancestry, and the legs and buttocks shapely with the blooming of puberty. She was no virgin having lost that to a relation or had it sold for a bottle of cheap wine, port or sherry. Winton felt a stirring in his crotch. He felt horny and was inclined to take his pleasure before completing the delivery. He refrained, not out of sensitivity for the girl, as she had been bought for the night and was his, but for the revulsion at what he was doing.

The hotel was quiet as he hurried her up the back stairs onto the landing and thrust her into the shadows as he opened the door and checked the hallway. It was clear and he grabbed the girl and propelled her towards a room at the far end. They were level with a doorway when it suddenly swung open.

O'Grady looked stunned as he eyed the girl up and down. "How old is she? She's not jail bait is she?"

"You said you wanted a young one, and this is the best I could do."

Without a word O'Grady pulled the girl in and quietly shut the door in Winton's face.

Winton whistled softly as he went back to his room. He checked over the camera again and tested the flash. He laughed to himself as contemplated who was going to get the biggest surprise, O'Grady when the flash lit up his orgy, or Robinson and Bain when the read the glowing write-ups in O'Grady's column.

Winton turned out the light and opened the French doors onto the outside balcony. He padded softly towards O'Grady's room. He was surprised to see the light still on and the French doors and curtains partially open. O'Grady was obviously not concerned with privacy. He cautiously looked into the room and made to pull back when he saw the girl had her head to one side and was looking directly at him, her eyes expressionless. He watched fascinated as the formless frame of nude flesh covered her small figure. The bed sagged with each grunt and then sprang back into shape as the downward inertia was arrested. Christ, the bastard was insatiable Winton mused as he slowly pushed open the glass panelled door. It grated, but O'Grady was oblivious to the sound drowned out by his laboured efforts. He suddenly grunted and rolled the girl onto her front. Winton caught the imploring look of fear and torture on her face as he entered her again. The girl moaned and buried her face in the pillow as he slowly and rhythmically worked his way inside her. O'Grady's face changed to complete serenity. It was obvious this was the position he preferred and confirmed Winton's suspicions. He had offered him a boy, but O'Grady had declined knowing Winton could easily broadcast his true preference. On the other hand, no one would care about his supposed heterosexual deviations.

Winton had guessed correctly. It was all falling into place as planned. He stepped into the room at the precise moment O'Grady closed his eyes in preliminary orgasm, his head turned to the ceiling, his back concave with ramrod straight arms supporting his weight as he thrust down and forwards.

The flash lit the room for a split second as Winton pressed the shutter again to catch O'Grady staring at him in shock and then pure fury. The flash went off again capturing the expression and moment. Winton did not expect him to move so fast, as suddenly the jellied heap of flesh propelled himself at him, his outstretched hands reaching desperately for the camera. Winton sidestepped and brought his foot up into the the exposed genitals. O'Grady staggered back and folded in a cry of pain as his head connected with the steel bed frame. He was unconscious as he hit floor, his arms and legs splayed out like Michelangelo's Vitruvian man.

Winton stood over him and took another photo. The bloody contusion on the forehead began to ooze. He leaned down and checked the wound. Nothing serious, but it would be a nasty reminder for the next week or so. The girl needed no encouragement to get out of the room. She had already thrown on her thin shift and was bolting for the door, but not before grabbing money laying on the dresser O'Grady was obviously going to pay her. She spotted his wallet and made to pick it up, but Winton was faster and indicated with a wave of his arm for her to go as he took hold of it. He shut the door after her and turning to the inert figure, lifted him under the armpits and up onto the bed. He would have trouble walking. Winton chuckled as he observed the already inflamed testicles. He tossed a sheet over the prone figure and sat down to wait. Minutes later O'Grady stirred, and the groans of pain became more deep-seated and tortured as he drifted back into consciousness.

Winton pushed his chair back out of reach. If he was going to be attacked again he wanted plenty of space to move. O'Grady's eyes slowly focused on Winton as he leaned over the side of the bed and retched. Blood from his head wound trickled down into the sickly stream as O'Grady spat, trying to clear his mouth of the acid taste.

"I'll kill you for this." He groaned and threw himself back on the pillow. One hand explored his devastated organs as he rolled and started to get out of the bed. Winton quickly rose and held him down.

"You're in no condition to kill anyone at the moment. Just lay back and rest."

"There are police in this town. I'm going to lay charges you arsehole." O'Grady gasped between spasms of pain.

Winton picked up his camera and made to leave. "You're right, but you're the one who will be up on a charge. That kid wasn't even fifteen. You're in deep, deep shit if you lay a complaint, and don't be surprised if the girl's parents don't shake you down for compensation."

"She's a slut and you procured her, so you're in it up to your neck also."

"True, but it's against the law to screw minors, sluts or not. It's a criminal offence, and you'll be doing a stretch in rock college if this ever goes public."

Fear began to creep into O'Grady's eyes. "What the fuck do you want?"

"That's better. Now we can talk business." Winton pulled his chair up to the base of the bed and looked straight into the frightened eyes. "I want your complete co-operation in regard to Roma Oil. I'll see you get well paid for it. Let's say the deal is you get the profit from fifty thousand shares sold on the first day of trading. No money up front, entirely a gift from me. All you have to do is make some very favourable comments in your column."

O'Grady lurched forward, but the pain was too intense and he collapsed backwards. "Go screw yourself." The tears of pain and frustration welled up in his eyes.

"You're the one who's going to get screwed O'Grady. I've got photos of you in a couple of very compromising positions which the law will take a very dim view of. Of course, the second position, which was most interesting, is the one that's going to see you destroyed if it gets out. Chock a block up the rear of a minor with a look of sheer ecstasy on your face is really damning, don't you think? Your days as a journalist with enormous influence would be numbered."

"You're equally to blame," O'Grady blustered. "You procured her."

Winton laughed out loud. "But I don't have a reputation to lose. You're clearly the person in the pictures having all the fun. However, you never know, the editors might let you write your column from jail. I don't think you'd fare to well in prison anyway. Once the lads in there know you're a rock-spider you'll be on the receiving end of some rough treatment."

O'Grady let out an anguished cry of defeat and sagged back on the bed. "Tell me what you want."

"Just as I said, nothing more than a glowing appraisal of your trip out here, and your conclusions on Roma Oil. If I don't see a positive report in your next column, your editor and the police will have photos on their desks courtesy of an anonymous source. I need you because I want to make a pile of money, and I think you should have a share. I realise the deal is not exactly to your liking, but life's a compromise. You don't have any choice, and the sooner you come to terms with that, the better."

O'Grady murmured his agreement and watched as Winton smiled and disappeared through the veranda door. Springer was the most cold and calculating person he had ever met. And to think he was going to sling him an extra twenty for procuring the girl. Instead, Springer had planned all along to take him to the cleaners. He shuddered as the full horror of it hit him. If those photos got out he would be serving time. Springer had purposely set him up with a juvenile. He slammed his fists into mattress as he sobbed in frustration at his stupidity.

Winton was having breakfast when Bain hurried in and sat down. He was clearly agitated, but Winton gave no sign he had noticed.

"What happened to O'Grady?"

Winton shrugged his shoulders. "Haven't a clue. I haven't seen him this morning."

"Don't give me that rubbish. You do know something about what happened. We had to get a doctor to him last night. Jesus, someone really did a number on him. His nuts are as big as golf balls. Doc says he'll be in bed for a few days."

"I'll go and see him." Winton stood up but Bain restrained him.

"I wouldn't if I were you. He keeps muttering your name, and how he's going to lay a complaint of assault with the police." Bain's face suddenly turned angry. "By the saints lad, if you had anything to do with it, and O'Grady decides to tip a bucket of shit on Roma Oil, you've had it with me. I'm not letting some roughneck beat up my meal ticket without some consequences."

"Don't get so bloody upset. C'mon, let's go and see what he's beefing about. If he tells me to my face I had anything to do with it, I'll gladly get out of town." Winton offered up a silent prayer as they climbed the stairs and entered O'Grady's darkened room. The man was awake, but only just with his eyes rolled back in the sockets. He was plainly dosed up with painkillers.

"Jim tells me you're not feeling too well?" Winton wore an expression of concern as he leaned forward to block Bain's line of sight, and the look of molten hatred in O'Grady's eyes as he focused on his assailant. "Jim seems to think I may have something to do with your present condition?"

O'Grady looked into the ice-blue eyes and the barely concealed abyss of cynicism. It was clear who was in complete control with insurmountable power, so there was no point in making an issue of it. Any retaliation would destroy them both.

"No, Winton had nothing to do with it Jim. I don't know how you ever got that impression. It must have been the painkillers and sleeping tablets the doc gave me. I am still somewhat delirious."

Bain could see O'Grady was lying. Winton was the direct cause of his injuries, and he was intrigued how he could control the country's most influential financial journalist. O'Grady had been breathing fire and revenge when he first saw him, and the doctor had described the condition of his genitals. Winton's appearance had now reduced him to a flabby nervous heap, his denial an obvious and blatant reversal of the truth. What hold did Winton have over him? There had to be something very compelling, whatever it was?

He watched as Winton's expression changed from one of tension to a broad compassionate smile. "I'm glad to hear that O'Grady. I'm relieved that misconception has been cleared up, as I'm sure neither of us wants to waste any time lodging complaints with the law. It would simply be a waste of time, wouldn't it?" Winton was nodding his head inciting subliminal agreement. "You must agree Sam Carlin has a first class project, and you're keen to assist by explaining the economic benefits. Jim and I are certainly looking forward to a positive report in your column."

O'Grady had the look of complete defeat as he reluctantly gave a shallow nod. He spoke slowly. "Yes, I'll be giving Sam and Roma Oil positive coverage. Carlin is the type of entrepreneur who makes this country great, an adventurer with the true pioneering spirit. He is one of a breed who creates the opportunities and wealth of a nation. Every successful person has someone in the background who's helped them towards success. I can see Springer, that you have been of great assistance to Carlin, and I cannot see him failing with someone like you behind the scenes. Sam doesn't realise what a compelling asset he has in you."

Bain was startled by the remarks. Gone were the incendiary accusations threatening to bring the whole house down an hour previously. "What do you mean by a compelling asset?"

"Just a slip of the tongue," O'Grady waved away the question. "And now I need to rest." Bain drifted out of the door lost in thought while Winton lingered at the foot of the bed.

O'Grady beckoned for him to come closer so Bain could not hear. "You might have beaten me this time Springer, but keep it in mind that I'm going to cut your balls out, not just kick them out, someday."

Winton smiled. "I've got absolutely no doubt you'll look for every opportunity to do that, but I have the advantage. You start putting any shit on me and some very compromising photos are suddenly going to see the light of day. I'm holding all the aces O'Grady, but I'm not going to shaft you. It's still fifty thousand shares stagged on the market opening and paid to you in cash."

14

The Porsche tooled through the drizzling rain. It was early evening and heavily overcast. The long drive had dulled his senses, but now he was back in the city his full faculties returned. The city appeared dormant, but underneath it was vibrant and alive. It excited him.

The form next to him was curled up with her head snuggled into a cushion against the passenger window. She had slept nearly the whole way from the ski fields as he drove oblivious to the incessant sweep of the wiper blades and muted music playing. The exhilaration and speed of the Porsche lured him into a false sense of security as he overtook slower vehicles with a burst of power. His inattention had been suddenly jolted by his heart responding to a burst of adrenalin and fear as he rounded a bend and saw the semi-trailer jack-knifed across the road. He had no chance of stopping in time. Brakes, gear change and accelerator were fluid, automatic and defensive as he threw the small coupe onto the gravel verge and around the nose of the stalled truck. He felt the wild slide start to evolve as he applied opposite lock, and a wall of mud and stones spewed over the windscreen.

Jo choked a scream and threw her hands across her face as she awoke and sensing the danger, braced her body for an unseen impact. Winton was driving blind. He knew he was clear of the truck, but what was in front of him that he could not see? Through the wall of mud he glimpsed a car coming towards him on the same side of the road. The Porsche gained grip on the bitumen, fishtailed as he dropped it down a gear and applied opposite lock and power to correct the slide. He snaked around the oncoming vehicle, but did not look back as he heard the crunch as it slid into the side of the truck.

"Ooh, that was fun," Jo purred with relief . "Are you going to stop and see what happened to that car? They could be injured?"

Winton shook his head. "None of my business. I don't want to hang around for hours explaining to the cops what happened. The truck caused it, so he can explain."

"They might have your plate number. Isn't it a crime to leave the scene of an accident?"

"I believe it is, but I didn't see a thing. Did you?"

"No, I suppose not." Jo shrugged as she put her head in the cushion again and dropped off to sleep.

No wonder she was tired, he reflected as he cast a quick look at her. He was tired also and that had nearly resulted in an horrific accident. It was pure luck there was enough room between the front of the truck and the steep embankment for him to slip through.

The lady was pure gelignite, insatiable and demanding both in her skiing prowess and in bed. She was no amateur in either field. There was only a numb feeling in his groin. He felt as though he had no male appendages at all. Through the Cross tunnel and down towards Rushcutters Bay, and then a burst of power up the hill towards Darling Point.

Jo had come awake as she felt the changes in momentum and recognised her surroundings. "Drop me off at my apartment darling. I've got to be in the office early and want to look the best." She stroked the inside of his thigh. The message was clear. However, although the appendages were still in place, the electrical current from the cerebral source to the vital organ was barely perceptible. All he had thought about on the drive back was a soft bed and a good night's sleep, but here she was tempting him to ignite the detonator to the explosives again. He still had some cocaine if she was that insatiable. Go out in one big explosion. Instant self-destruct. To hell with the board meeting in the morning he pondered as he pulled up in front of her apartment block. They got out and he followed her. She took her bag from him as she used her security pass and pushed open the foyer door. She gave him a quick kiss on the cheek as she turned towards the lifts.

"Thank you for a wonderful weekend. I hope you enjoyed it too?"

Winton watched as the door closed and gave a sigh of relief. He simply was not up to another night of Jo Delaney. She was one classy lady with it all going for her. Looks, ability, poise, maturity and experience, but then she would have to be if she was Miles Morgan's personal secretary.

Morgan was the principal of Morgan Corporation, a fast growing merchant bank with an incredible success and earnings record in the oil and gas business, or so it would seem. Morgan Corp had never drilled a well or owned any oil or gas producing assets, but it had the uncanny ability to seize control of small companies just as they were on the verge of a commercial discovery. Morgan would gain control, sell the assets to larger predators to cover his investment while retaining a healthy royalty stream from subsequent production. Morgan believed in drilling for cash and not oil or gas. Let the wildcatters take all the risks while all he had to do was sit and wait and pounce when the inside information he paid for, delivered the results. His contacts and networking skills were vast and finely tuned. He entertained lavishly all the while gaining confidential information from directors and their wives as the bonhomie flowed, the talk grew louder and idle gossip turned into the intelligence that was his life's blood. Morgan was never without a glass in hand at these events, but he never finished the contents. Information was priceless and far outweighed the cost of a glass of the finest champagne.

Jo's unit was exclusive and too expensive for an ordinary working secretary. Morgan was obviously picking up the tab, but the word was it ended there. There was no romantic connection. Morgan was well known for paying the highest and getting the best and Jo Delaney was the best. Winton had met her at a cocktail party three weeks before. It was not a chance meeting. He already knew his target and he had delved thoroughly into her background. Her qualifications startled him. Why was she working as a personal assistant when she could be earning multiples in the commercial world outside Morgan Corporation? Something just did not ring true, but he was not concerned at this stage. His motive for going after Jo Delaney was purely commercial. He wanted to establish a clandestine link into Morgan's operation to see how it really ticked. He found Jo Delaney was two people. One the sophisticated secretary able to discourse on any subject, whether it be politics, economics, finance, business structures, banking, or the stock market. She never argued or showed any trace of arrogance or superior knowledge of a specific topic when included in a discussion within a business group. She sold herself with charm and reasoning, and soon her would-be detractors realised they were not dealing with a female they could ignore.

The other person in her makeup was the female, the primordial female with a rapacious appetite to express her sexuality in all its forms. She had the complete suite of animal instincts to lure and torture and then figuratively kill. She was the most amoral being he had ever met as the educated veil dropped away and her sexual demands dominated. She was a whore in bed, but what a whore.

The car still smelt of her when he got back in. He thrust it into gear, slipped the clutch and accelerated away, the power transferred smoothly to the road with a sharp squeal of rubber. If that was the calibre of person Morgan hired, there was no stopping the expansion of Morgan Corp. Everything Miles Morgan touched turned into money. He was a superlative net-worker who maintained top analysts tuned into the commercial nerve of the city. They sucked in and dismantled the rumours into fact and various shades of fiction offered to entice Morgan Corp to invest. Morgan gave the impression of being distracted as though lost in a time-warp somewhere, but hidden was the razor-sharp mind and mental calculator that could instantly smell money. Fools were not suffered. They did not exist in his rarefied atmosphere as they were invariably dismissed with a polite but thinly disguised contemptuous rejection. Morgan was a trader, not an accumulator and everything was for sale if the price was right. Nothing was retained if someone was prepared to pay more money for the privilege of owning it. Morgan had got his start as the legal and financial advisor to a small oil exploration company. Richard Agnelli knew Morgan had access to considerable funds, and made the mistake of placing a large parcel of his company's stock with him in order to raise working capital and block any predatory takeover. Agnelli Oil was a prime target for a company with adjoining ground where a significant discovery had been made. They wanted the Agnelli licence areas, but were rebuffed by Agnelli himself. Unbeknown to him, Morgan approached through a contact suggesting he might be able to deliver control. A deal was struck and a takeover bid made. Along with the stock Agnelli had placed in Morgan's hands, and a mysterious Singapore based company which had been slowly buying Agnelli stock, control was delivered to the predator. Richard Agnelli knew who had orchestrated the manoeuvre, but could only lament his stupidity. He was found sitting in his car in a remote location with the shotgun between his legs and the barrels pointed at where his mouth and head used to be.

Winton had absorbed every scrap of information he could about Morgan. The secrets of the way the man operated and thought, engrossed him. Winton had been a director of Roma Oil for some years, but he wanted more. He wanted absolute power, and recognition and the money that went with it. He ran the car down into the underground car park and caught the lift to his penthouse. He showered and then turned on the television, but after a few minutes realised he was not watching it. His mind was a long way off.

15

The board meeting had been set for eight. Sam was excited and the atmosphere charged. Winton had no idea of what Sam was about to announce, but he knew it would be important.

"Gentlemen, I want to discuss our entry into offshore oil and gas exploration." He let the statement hang in the air as he strode to a large map at the end of the room and stabbed at Western Australia. "It's a vast area of opportunity."

"Dominated by a couple of majors and way out of our league," Winton interjected. "Big gas plays. Don't you think we'd be getting in over our head?"

"I've given it a lot of thought and if we're to keep growing we need to look for new opportunities. I know it will be expensive and we certainly can't afford to take all the risk ourselves, but I think we can lay-off a lot of that risk by first acquiring a licence area, and then attracting a joint-venture partner."

"That's deep water drilling Sam. It will cost us a fortune." Winton was annoyed he had not been informed of Sam's intentions before the board meeting. Sam knew he was opposed to the expense involved in offshore drilling and was attempting to temper that opposition by bringing it up at a board meeting. Sam had deliberately snookered him.

"Where did you get this idea from Sam and how long have you been working on it, because this is the first I've heard of it."

Sam did not reply as he picked up a phone and talked to his secretary. "I want you all to meet someone." He replaced the receiver and walking over to open the boardroom door. "Gentlemen, I would like you to meet Dr Harry Taylor." Sam introduced him to each board member.

The deep drawl of Texas was balanced and methodical as the scientist began to explain his theory regarding the oil and gas entrapments off the coastline of that State.

"We are all aware big gas strikes have been made and will continue to be made offshore, but I'm not referring to what they're focussing on. I've spent years in this area before returning to the States, but the potential for close onshore discoveries along this coast line has always remained in the back of my mind. I believe the potential has been overlooked, particularly in the Rowley Basin."

"And so you think the basin extends offshore?" Winton was becoming mildly interested.

"Correct. The basin most certainly does extend offshore."

"And why do you think we'll be more successful?"

Taylor ignored Winton's question. He had already sensed where the opposition to his proposal was going to come from.

"Gentlemen, there are certain things I will not divulge at this stage as to why I think the area has great potential. However, what I can tell you is with only a couple of exceptions, both the off and onshore programs over the years have all come up with pockets of oil and gas, but not enough to be deemed commercial or be other than of academic interest. Have any of you heard of fraccing?" Taylor looked around the room at the deadpan expressions.

Winton nodded. "I think it was first used on the Barrow Island discovery years ago."

"It's advanced a long way since then," Taylor replied. "You're going to hear about it a lot in the coming years. It's a process whereby oil and gas can be released from tight strata formations previously thought to be uneconomic. It's only in recent years directional drilling has been developed to the stage where a well does not have to be drilled vertically, but can be drilled horizontally for anything up to five kilometres. In other words, drill down until you intersect the oil or gas zone and then chock the drill stem and bit into a horizontal plane so it follows the oil or gas bearing layer. Whereas normally the gas or oil was confined to say a one hundred metre column as it was penetrated vertically, you can now fan out in all directions for up to a five kilometre radius. Then comes the science of fraccing where high pressure water and chemicals are injected to facture the rock along the length of the hole. This releases vast quantities of oil equivalent and gas which previously could not be recovered by the usual method of drilling a vertical hole through the section. Fraccing changes the picture completely. With the latest technology previously uneconomic discoveries can now be made economic."

"Surely, the likes of Woodside and Shell must be aware of this technology?"

"They certainly are." Taylor addressed the director who had made the observation. "But they are big companies with big fish to fry. They just wouldn't be interested in going back over old ground unless they could see a big payday in the offing, but that doesn't preclude a small company like Roma recovering significant quantities of oil and gas and making the whole exercise extremely profitable."

"How do you intend to proceed?"

Sam smiled to himself as he could see by Winton's question and expression, he was falling in behind Taylor's thinking.

"I have my contacts in a certain major company which currently holds inshore licence areas. However, my source was told to complete a report recommending what areas could be dropped as being of no commercial significance to the company. He's not divulging any proprietary information. He's made his report and the board has resolved to act on it. The licence will come up for tender again once relinquished, but I don't think any of the smaller companies are going to be very interested simply because it looks very unattractive. Small companies are also tightening their belts at the moment, but the real key to this proposition is that I've been involved in this coastline for more than thirty years and believe I know where the bodies are buried so to speak. There's no need for us to conduct any expensive seismic surveys. Those have already been done over the years and its all on record. I will re-process some of that data using algorithms I've developed, but basically all the work is complete. I don't have to drill any wildcat holes. I can simply locate one of the previous holes and go straight to what I'm looking for. It may cost a few hundred thousand to take up the licence, but that budget would be well within Roma's means." Taylor turned to Sam. "And I've already discussed this project with Sam and he agrees it's of real interest to Roma."

"I imagine your fees will be considerable? You don't look as though you come cheap?" Winton was annoyed he had not been taken into Sam's confidence. What was the reason?

"Roma will only pay my expenses and a small retainer."

"Now for the sting in the tail," Winton quipped. "What's the rest of the deal?"

"I will take it from here Harry." Sam got to his feet. "Dr Taylor will work on a carried interest in the project. Two percent of net. If we find nothing that's precisely what he gets. The field must be commercial, but that can be spread over a number of close vicinity discoveries. The same deal applies to a major gas discovery. The point of this meeting is not to really hammer out the fine detail, but to get the board's opinion of whether we're interested in principle, or we tell Dr Taylor to take his proposal somewhere else. It's as simple as that. Do any of you have any concerns or objections?"

"And Roma gets a complete exclusive to you and your technology? You're not shopping it around are you?"

"Roma has an exclusive deal Mr Springer."

"It's Winton."

"Okay Winton. Yes, it is an exclusive deal. I've not approached anyone else and I'll give you a day or two to think about it."

"On that basis I have no concerns and I believe Sam, you can put it to the vote."

Harry Taylor nodded as he looked around at the board room noting the individual expressions. There did not appear to be a single dissenting look.

"You have unanimous agreement." Sam rose and held out his hand to the Texan. "Winton will lodge applications as soon as any areas become vacant."

The meeting over, Sam sat staring out over the harbour as he took a folded sheet of paper out of his pocket and began to read. The directors and Taylor left, but Winton remained.

"Where did you get Taylor from, or did he just spring out of the woodwork? And why didn't you tell me about this beforehand? You set me up Sam. I'm the managing director of this company, and yet you went right over my head. Why?" He could see Sam was lost in thought, but it was obviously a cheerful thought by the look on his face.

Sam looked up, carefully folding the paper. "Oh, he was recommended to me by someone I knew long ago. Someone I thought had forgotten I existed. In answer to your next question, I didn't tell you about it because I knew there would be a blazing row in view of your negative attitude towards offshore drilling. Okay, I suckered you, but make no apologies. You're happy now aren't you?"

"You're an old fox Sam. You've obviously been working with Taylor and his theories for some time now?" Winton was intrigued by the contents of the folded paper Sam kept tapping in the palm of his hand. His mind and attention was clearly somewhere else.

"I'm going to take a holiday Winton. A couple of the weeks in America. I've made the arrangements and I leave in the morning. The company is under your control until I get back. Why don't you get some grease on your hands and do a tour of the rigs? You're getting soft in that chair of yours. Get out there and get the feel of where it all began. Where I started it."

Sam did not notice the sudden flash of annoyance on Winton's face. "I'll do that Sam. I'll go and take a look at where you started it, all by yourself. You're right, it's about time I got grease on my hands again."

The sarcasm went right over Sam's head. "Good, well let's go to Luciano's for lunch."

Luciano's was packed with the usual brokers, lawyers, financiers, bankers, chancers, hustlers, fringe money men and entrepreneurs who kept the fibre of the city resonating. Rumour and counter rumour ebbed and flowed with every entrant through the door being instantly noticed. Someone was always looking for someone, but the topic of conversation was always, and only about money. The serious ones deep in conversation broke into a practised set greeting and effusive smile when recognised by friend or acquaintance. There was not a long face in the place. All were winners and all had learnt the axiom of the money world and success; keep smiling and beaming success. To admit you were not doing so well, or times were tough meant the rumour mill went into overdrive. Phones would ring and credit positions examined with any exposed position being firmly closed off. There was no compassion considered or quarter given. Profit was the sole motive. Compassion was an exterior expression to hide the interior calculation of what could be gained from some unfortunate's diminished position. All the while the sharks swam lazily around just observing and feeding at their leisure. The barracudas darted in and out of the pack picking off the strays and watching their tails unless they should swim too close to the sharks.

Winton chuckled to himself when he caught sight of Jim Bain. There was one category he had omitted, the gropers. They were the huge fish who swam just outside their lairs, ingesting with a single gulp anything that came within reach of their cavernous maw. After ingesting the prey they shat out the liquefied and calcified excrement.

Jim waved as he caught Winton's eye. He was holding forth in a very distinguished gathering of gropers, obviously working on some new deal. Winton could relate to Jim despite his gross appearance, and despite his mistrust and loathing, he greatly admired the man. He possessed flair and an understanding of how to operate and flourish in a dangerous environment. They had made a fortune together, and Sam had never found out about their original association. They remained in very close contact, each feeding on the other for snippets and verification of information. They had only ever had one argument and Winton remembered and cherished it as a lesson well learnt.

He had queried how much Jim stood to make out of a deal he had cooked up. It seemed a long time ago.

"I'm not happy with what I'm making out of the deal Jim. It was my idea and I want more."

"Were you happy with your end of it at the time?"

"Sure Jim, I was quite happy, but…"

The fat financier had leaned across and gently patted Winton's cheek with a bejewelled hand. "Well, if you were happy at the time, why the fuck are you trying to change the rules now? Don't come to me and complain a month after we shook hands."

The logic was simple and direct. From that day on the rules of the game were firmly understood. Once the terms had been set and understood, they could not be changed.

Luciano showed Sam and Winton to a table. With a flourish he produced menus and wine list while unfolding the napkins with a practised flourish.

Sam glanced at the menu before handing it back. "A Chivas on the rocks to start with, followed by a rare filet, a salad and a bottle of St Henri."

"And the same for me." Winton handed the menu back without opening it. It was obvious the restaurateur had heard Winton's order, but was already moving away without acknowledgement. It was as though Winton did not exist.

"Ignorant bastard," Winton murmured. "I would like to kick his ignorant dago arse someday."

"Well, what's got into you today Mr Springer?" Sam was eyeing his confederate with amusement. "Cheer up, the boss is going on holiday. I don't want you kicking the backside of my favourite mine-host while I'm away."

"What are you really going to the States for?"

Sam sipped the scotch the waiter had placed before him. "As I said Winton, I'm going to take a holiday. Look up a bit of the past you might say." He was about to go on when the voice beside him broke his train of thought.

"Hey Sam, you look happy today. Brought in another oil well have you?"

It was Miles Morgan. Luciano was clucking impatiently a few feet away waiting for Morgan to follow him to his reserved table. The table was exclusive to Morgan. It did not matter if he failed to show up for lunch or was out of town, the table always remained empty and exclusive. Winton had tried to calculate what it was costing him, but the king needed a throne from where to hold court, so the throne remained exclusive. He appeared to have modelled himself on Ivan Boesky, the infamous share trader who reserved an exclusive front window table at the Algonquin Hotel in Times Square in the 1980's. That was before he landed in jail for manipulating stocks. Miles Morgan relied exclusively on inside information. So far he had not been caught.

"I'm finally taking a holiday Miles," Sam replied warmly. Winton knew Sam despised Morgan, but today everyone appeared to be his friend. "I'm off to the States for a couple of weeks."

Morgan laughed, gently patting Sam on the shoulder. "I don't recall you ever taking a holiday. Well, enjoy yourself. Winton, maybe we could get together and you could sell me Roma while Sam's away. Then we could make it into a real oil company."

Winton made to reply, but Morgan had turned his back and was following Luciano. The remark had not been made casually. It had meaning and purpose. Sam appeared to have ignored it, but Winton was deep in thought as his gaze followed the man.

Morgan sat in solitude, but was not alone. No one walked past his table without acknowledgement or greeting. Morgan was holding court and he enjoyed the status of a high profile achiever with a razor sharp grasp of business in all its facets. Morgan was in the barracuda class, Winton reflected. No one could match his analysis of a business opportunity. There was no apparent chink in his armour because he never allowed anyone to get close enough to observe and expose his weaknesses. It was the domineering strength of absolute control and certainty that generated the aura of mystery and supremacy. The tip of his personal wealth was barely visible except for his waterfront mansion on Sydney harbour and his chauffeured Benz. His private life remained private behind a pair of heavy electronically monitored gates. It was impossible to get a true picture of the conglomerate worth of his empire. Even trained market analysts found it hard to keep track of the takeovers and cross shareholdings within his group structure. Winton suspected Morgan was hiding behind a very thin opaque glass wall, liable to shatter if one of the balls he was juggling should bounce into it.

Sam Carlin, on the other hand, held nothing back. He had built his empire on solid ground. His methods were slower, but surer. His asset to debt ratio demonstrated Roma Oil was well cashed up and able to meet any commitment. The company remained steady, aided by foreign capital looking for a safe investment when other stocks were on a downward trend.

Morgan on the other hand had the complete flair and panache of an entrepreneur. The man's sole existence was a public relations exercise in selling himself and his companies. The style and charm of the man was evident from the first handshake, but Winton noted he was highly selective, and only talked to people who could advance his cause. He never wasted his time with idle chatter or with people of no consequence.

"I don't know what makes that man tick," Sam said as he cut into his steak. "He appears to be very successful, but I have my doubts."

"He sure knows how to project himself. He has a big following and seems to be able to raise money easily when he wants to finance a deal."

"I wouldn't put a cent into any company he's involved with and I advise you to take my advice. Anyway, I guess you've already worked that one out for yourself?" Sam suddenly put down his glass and tossed his napkin on the table. "I'm going to leave you to it Winton. My apologies, but I've got a few things to do before I leave tomorrow."

Winton had been toying with his wine glass and made to rise.

"No, you stay and finish that excellent bottle of wine. I don't like to see anything wasted, not at the prices Luciano charges." Winton was puzzled as he watched him thread his way out. He leaned back in his chair pondering the reason for Sam's sudden decision to take a holiday. Who was he going to see?

The waiter reached for the bottle and topped up his glass. "Mr Morgan would like you to join him sir."

Winton turned slowly and looked at Morgan who was signalling to join him. He picked up his glass and walked across.

"What's on your mind Miles?" Winton sat down opposite knowing full well he was being observed by a restaurant pretending not to notice Morgan had a guest and of particular interest, the identity of the guest.

"How would you like to join Morgan Corporation?"

Winton slowly shook his head. "Why should I join you? I've got everything I want now."

"No you haven't Springer. I've been observing you for some time. You're hanging onto the coattails of Sam Carlin. He's stifling you and all you're ever going to get are the crumbs. Why not make a fortune? Put Roma together with my group."

"Roma Oil is a public company. Why don't you make a bid if you're that keen to get control?"

"That would be too expensive and take too long. Besides you never win battles by charging at the enemy head on. The Light Brigade made that mistake at Crimea. I prefer conquest by stealth with the assistance of insider information, and that's where you come into the picture."

"I'm flattered to think you've been observing me." Winton gave an amused shrug. "I really don't think I can assist you with whatever you have planned. I don't like the odour of your whole modus. I'd prefer to stay clear of you."

He could see from the sudden flash of anger he had struck a nerve. Morgan could not handle rejection. For a second the patina of supreme self-confidence developed a hair-line crack. Nerves had a way of unconsciously manifesting themselves. Morgan quickly regained his composure and broke into a broad grin, but his hands twitched as he tried to regain total control.

"That remark was uncalled for Springer. I learned long ago never to burn your bridges."

"Why should I help you to take over Roma Oil and destroy Sam in the process?"

"Simple really. You have nothing at the moment except a secure position, a healthy salary complete with all expenses, and very little else. You probably do hold Roma stock, but the register shows nothing substantial in your name, and you hold nothing through companies that have you listed as a director. You could hold some through a nominee account, but I doubt that. You have stock options which tie you to Carlin and Roma. You have a degree of wealth in real estate, but nothing like you could achieve when you join me."

"I won't be joining you, but what would you pay if I did agree?" Winton was astounded at the effrontery of the man. He had obviously been waiting for the opportunity to approach him.

"I don't want you to work for me. I want you to work with me. There is a subtle difference, you know."

"I'm listening, but what are you really after before I tell you to go to hell?"

"I want inside information about Roma Oil. I want to know about any oil or gas strikes before they're announced. I want to know about agreements and disagreements. I want to know when Sam Carlin scratches his butt. I want to know everything before it happens. Do you get my drift?"

Winton started a low belly laugh, and then spluttered as he tried to hide his mirth. "Christ, you don't want much do you? You're unreal Morgan. But tell me before I break up completely, what's my end?"

Morgan's eyes were suddenly like ice. "Same sort of deal you've had with Jim Bain for years. You've been supplying him with inside information, and now I want you to supply me."

Winton felt cold warning prickles at the base of his brain. What did he know and where was this leading? He sensed Morgan had a hand of high cards.

"Jim's a friend. We discuss business all the time, but he's not party to inside information."

A derisive sneer began to form at the corners of Morgan's mouth. "Robinson's just a friend as well, is he? Amazing how those two stick to you like glue. I can see you're losing some of that cocky air Springer, so I'll deflate your balloon a little more. I know about your connection with Delta Oil of Vancouver, and I know about your bank accounts in the Channel Isles and Hong Kong. I hope you've been declaring the income and paying taxes. It's a criminal offence to defraud the commonwealth by hiding income offshore. However, as a man of integrity and honesty I'm quite sure you're completely clean in that area. I'm correct in assuming that, aren't I?" Morgan could see he had struck a nerve. "Oh, the fact is I have a lot of information on you that you're not aware of. I believe I could destroy you by whispering in Carlin's ear or writing an anonymous letter to the tax boys. I know about the deal you had with Bain to promote the listing of Roma all those years ago. Probably doesn't mean much now as you certainly saved Sam's backside, but I'm sure it would raise doubt about your integrity if he became aware. Trust is everything and I could let drop about a few other shady capers you've been mixed up in over the years."

The eyes never left Winton's face as he looked for the signs of nervousness. There was nothing as Winton eyed him coldly. Underneath he was frozen with shock.

Morgan pressed on with his attack. "You never take holidays and if I was Carlin I would be suspicious of that. The loyal servant never leaving his post. In my considered opinion the only reason for that is something is being hidden. If it came out it would blow you away."

Winton's mind was racing. It was obvious Jim had supplied him with some of the information, but that was of no consequence and could easily be laughed off. It was too long ago. But who had tipped him off to the offshore bank accounts and the connection with Delta?

Morgan had chosen his moment well to strike. He hunted with a stacked deck. "You've been screwing Carlin and Roma for years Springer. I don't have the full story, but I have enough to finish you, or at the very least make it very unpleasant. Of course, if I get what I want there's no need for this to go any further. Nothing personal you realise, just purely business."

"You're barking up the wrong tree Morgan. I've already stated my position."

"Don't be a fool Springer. Your assistance will reap you a fortune." Morgan knew he was hitting the mark hard and he was determined to press the advantage. Winton had made no move to leave the table. That was not the normal reaction of someone wrongly accused. "In fact you'll receive a handsome reward for your information and it certainly won't visibly harm Sam. Roma will grow quicker under my control and I don't deny I want Morgan Corp to grow a little quicker with your assistance"

"And gradually build up a big shareholding in the company before making a takeover bid when you have all the inside information I'm supposed to supply you with. You stand to make millions out of that arrangement."

"You're getting the picture," Morgan beamed. "It will be so much easier with you supplying me with a constant stream of information. Play the game right and I'll see you get the president's chair when I take over."

"I don't need your assistance to get there Morgan."

"Oh, but you do Springer. You see Sam Carlin is not going to release control until he's breathed his last and the moment that happens the sharks will move in and you'll be out of a job. How much better it would be for you to co-operate with me and be assured of running the company and covering up any little scams you may have going Sam isn't aware of. You don't have the financial muscle or clout to raise money to gain control, but I do. You have to lay the groundwork now if you want a large slice of Roma. Sure, you're squirreling money away in overseas accounts, money that could not be accounted for if there was a forensic investigation of how you acquired it. I'm not really interested in what you've got going on the side. It's peanuts compared to what you can make if you join me. Roma holds the best ground and the best prospects and the cash flow will be enormous within the next five years. Don't you think you're entitled to a larger share than you've got now? Sam will toss you crumbs by way of stock options, but that will never amount to anywhere near control, and I'm sure that's what's in the back of your mind. Carlin is standing in your way. He's strong now and has you snookered in regard to your ambitions, but it's amazing how quickly people begin to lose their grip when something unforseen, like sickness, happens. As Sam gets older he will find it harder and harder to retain control. Roma will offer too much of a target for a larger predator. You've got to plan for succession now and not wait to be seen as an also ran when the brawling starts. You and I working as a team can ensure Sam doesn't wakeup until it's too late he's been outsmarted. Let's face it, we don't need money in our old age. We want it now."

Winton had taken in every word of the self-evident truth and silently agreed, but did not show it.

"I think I've heard enough Morgan. However, I'll never co-operate with you." Winton made the statement with force and conviction, but in the pit of his gut he felt sick with the knowledge this man knew so much about his affairs.

"There's no such word as never, Springer. Think it over. You've got a few weeks before Sam gets back from the States."

How long had Morgan been hatching this plot? A deep revulsion was overridden by a deep respect for the man's direct frontal attack. He stood and turned to walk away.

"Remember. You've got until Carlin gets back, otherwise I'll destroy you Springer."

Jim Bain had his rubbery lips around a piece of prime rib as Winton drew level with his table. It was obvious he had been closely watching the encounter with Morgan and noted the strained look on Winton's face when he got up from the table. In fact the whole restaurant would have noticed the encounter. They could not hear what Morgan was saying, but from the determined look on his face and the expression of the person doing the listening, some strong points were being made.

Winton's expression changed in an instant as he broke into a broad smile.

"How's business Jim?"

Bain quickly brushed his lips with his napkin and picked up his wine glass. "Can't complain. Still managing to put a little aside for my old age." He lowered his voice and signalled for Winton to bend down so he could not be overheard. "Might have a little business proposition for you in a week or two, so don't go spending up big until you hear from me. What did Morgan want?"

"What does he ever want? Information, that's all. I told him to read the newspapers."

"From where I'm sitting it looked as though you were in serious discussion."

Winton ignored the remark and laughed as he made to straighten up. "I'm interested in any deal you've got cooking. How much am I in for?"

"A couple of hundred grand should buy you a piece of the action."

Winton patted the fat man on the shoulder. "I'm in. Let me know when you're ready to roll."

Bain returned to his steak with renewed appetite. A cloud had suddenly lifted. He felt very uneasy when he saw Morgan in such a concerted conversation with Springer. He knew he had often divulged too much to Morgan during the course of their secret meetings. However, his philosophy had always been that to receive, you first had to give, even if the giving might be a little generous at times. Bain was aware if he personally was the subject of what Morgan was telling him, Winton would not be able to mask it. However, from the warmth of Winton's greeting he knew he was not what was on Morgan's mind. It was simple logic, but a logic that never failed him. He believed firmly in the adage that the study of mankind was mankind. When people were angry they were revengeful and wanted to express it immediately. Similarly, if they had heard something disparaging it would show.

Winton glanced back as Luciano opened the door with a beaming flourish. Morgan was leaning back smiling directly at him. It was a knowing smile of complete confidence.

The knock on the door was quiet and persistent. He realised the tapping had been going on in his subconscious for some time. He had not heard the entrance foyer security intercom. He was mystified and a little alarmed his privacy was being invaded. How had the person got up to his secured penthouse floor? He turned the television down and walked out into the hallway in his stockinged feet. The carpet felt lush and therapeutic. Likewise, the sight when he opened the door was also lush and therapeutic. Jo Delaney was leaning against the doorway smiling sensuously.

"What took you so long lover? I was starting to worry. You haven't phoned me lately." The tone of her voice shot through him in a carnal surge. "You going to invite me in?"

"If you're alone. How did you get into the building?"

"I just followed a charming old man in and yes, I am alone. What do you mean by that wisecrack?"

"I just thought you might have Morgan hidden around the corner. Did he send you here?"

Winton caught the open-hand slap a fraction from his face and pulled her into the room as he kicked the door shut. She was springing at him again, the feline flash of anger clearly visible. He grabbed both her arms and as the fight went out of her, let her sink to the carpet. He leaned down and pulled her to her feet.

"And now, if you prefer to leave I'll show you to the door." Winton's reaction was a fraction too slow and the nails got through. The skin did not break but he could feel them grazing the side of his face. He grabbed the thrashing hand and lunged to control the other. The action took him off balance and the next instant he had fallen on top of her. He quickly pinned both arms behind her head and threw more weight on her as he sensed her bringing her knee up into his crotch.

"You fight dirty." Impulsively he leaned forward and kissed her slowly and deliberately. He wondered if she was going to retaliate, but the response was immediate and urgent. She thrust gently at him and he made the mistake of thinking it was a signal of submission. A fraction of a second after he let her arms go they were hurtling towards his face again. He sprang back in a straddling position and grabbing both arms, pulled her to her feet. Before she realised what was happening he had thrown her over his shoulder in a fireman's lift and carried her into the bedroom. She made no further resistance as he tossed her down and began to gently undress her. He kissed her breasts, gently rolling his tongue around her areola as they grew hard and erect. Her eyes closed as he kissed her naked form. She felt for him, but he gently pushed her hand away and felt the crescendo of preliminary orgasm begin to subside. The female aroma drew him in as he nestled his face into the soft pit of her stomach. He plucked at the soft downy hair as he worked lower. He smelt the moisture and gently worked over the exposed lips of her femininity. She arched upwards as he flicked his tongue around the distended clitoris. The animal cries started low in her throat and became more urgent and louder. Her undulating thrusts in response to the teasing excitement increased as he sucked it with extreme lightness. She clutched his head and forced it down. Winton suddenly ceased and rolled over on an elbow.

"You bastard," she murmured as she dropped her hands to her genitals and slowly began to massage.

"Didn't your mother warn you about that?"

"Oh God Winton, please, please." The moans were coming from deep down in her consciousness while her eyes rolled back in a glazed narcosis. She was completely drugged by her own surging hormones.

Winton lifted her gently and thrust a pillow under her buttocks. Her eyes focussed on his engorged penis as she smelt the odour of the male emissions. Her nostrils flared as he tantalised her until they were both at the finite point of exquisite pleasure before thrusting gently into her. Their orgasms were immediate and prolonged and he felt the masochistic sensation of pain as she dug her fingernails into his buttocks. He felt her rolling series of orgasms begin to subside as the guttural demands slowed and the thrusting of her pelvis ebbed. The last rays of evening light fled the room as they curled into each others arms. A spontaneous telepathy woke them during the night and their bodies drove at one another before parting in exhaustion.

16

R obinson poured Winton a shot of single-malt and watched him savour it.

"That really is a lovely scotch. Not drinking the cheap stuff any longer?"

"I keep the Ballantine's for the clients," Robinson chuckled. "They don't know what a fine scotch is, so why educate them?"

Winton observed Robinson had lost all the trappings of the country broker hungry for business. Here was a man with the solid look of establishment about him. He was a leading city broker who thrived on inside information and manipulation of the market.

"And what news do you bring Winton? I haven't seen you up here in ages?"

"Nothing really Mike. I don't get mixed up in the buying and selling of speculative stocks any longer. Roma Oil is my whole life."

Robinson guffawed. "I don't believe that. I know you too well and you'll always play the market if there's a buck to be made. Bain and you are always up to your necks in some deal."

"You've never been left out of one of our deals have you?"

Robinson screwed up his nose and raised a brow. "No, I haven't, but my complaint is you never let me in early enough.

136

That's where the real profits are made. Your latest venture sounds interesting."

"Does it?"

"C'mon Winton, don't fence with me. Jim phoned about it yesterday. I must say, you two cook up some brilliant ideas."

"And what did he tell you?"

A look of doubt crossed the broker's face. He had the sudden feeling Winton did not know what he was referring to. Had he betrayed a confidence? Could it be that Bain was cutting him out of this deal?

Winton caught the look of uncertainty. "I just don't know what deal you're referring to. We're always working on several at any one time."

"Australco Oil. Morgan will have apoplexy when he finds out one of his own companies is going to be hijacked from right under his nose. I've got to hand it to you two."

"Oh, that one." Winton laughed with the look of complete assurance. "I've been out in the field for a couple of weeks and haven't caught up with him. Why don't you fill me in on progress?"

Robinson hesitated. He was concerned he had already overstepped the mark and said too much. "You're on the level with me aren't you Winton?"

"Pick up the phone and talk to him," Winton indicated. "He'll confirm I'm in on all his deals. We go back a long way. You know that."

Robinson squirmed uneasily in his chair.

"Come on Mike, stop horsing around. Do you want me to phone him to confirm it?"

"Okay, okay." Robinson drained his glass and poured each of them another shot. The effects of the alcohol began to ease the uncertainty. "As you know Australco is controlled by Morgan through a couple of offshore entities. He uses it as a cash-cow trading the stock up on rumours he floats, and then shorting it on the way down. He can't lose although he's about to be caught out. The punters are mugs really. It never ceases to amaze me how they come back to be milked time after time."

"I didn't think Morgan had such control of Australco?"

Robinson took a long draft of his scotch and leaned back in his expensive leather captain's chair. He was in command of his success. "No, he's got a couple of stooges running it, but he holds the whip hand. He calls it his pin-money company and I know personally he's made a fortune out of it over the past few years. Only, here's the rub." Robinson leaned forward, dropping the level of his voice as though someone might be listening through the walls. He had not noticed Winton momentarily raise his eyebrows as his alert antenna switched on. "The company is about to become legitimate and Morgan doesn't know a thing about it."

"Legitimate. What do you mean by that?"

"It appears the two Morgan installed to run the company aren't as stupid or compliant as he's taken them for. They have some political clout and influence in this part of the world, or should I say particularly in this State."

"And what are they going to do that's so dynamic?" Winton was trying to appear nonchalant.

The broker raised his glass towards Winton. "What would you say is the most prospective offshore area in Australia today. Very shallow water and very protected."

Winton was dumbstruck. How had Taylor's proposal leaked out so quickly. Was Taylor up to something or had one of the Roma board members leaked the confidential information to one of his golfing buddies? And then it struck him like a thunderbolt as the word *protected* flashed in his brain.

"You're not talking about the Barrier Reef are you?"

"Close, but not the actual reef."

Winton laughed. "Australco is whistling into the wind if it thinks it will get permission to drill anywhere near the reef. It's a national park and a recognised world icon."

"I'm not talking about Australia. The project is in New Guinea waters right on the edge of the reef."

"It's not worth the hassle. The scream will go up from the greens and environment nutcases and the Australian government will be forced to lean on New Guinea. Whoever came up with this one has bitten off more than they can chew."

"I'm aware of all that, but Bain believes it's all arranged and they'll get away with it."

Winton sank back in his chair deep in thought. The idea was utterly preposterous, but he could envisage the faint possibility of it happening. "How did Bain get to know of this?"

Robinson chuckled. "Apparently, about three months ago a friend of Jim's was up on the reef holidaying. Naturally, although he was there to relax he still had his ears open just in case there was a little business to be had. He got talking to a stranger in the bar who turned out to be working on one of those scientific research vessels often in that part of the world. What followed was the old story. The character swills a few drinks and gets friendlier and starts to relate an interesting yarn about the vessel not being what it was supposed to be. Marine research vessel it was not. Seismic research vessel it was. They've already run thousands of kilometres of seismic profiles over an area just north of the reef, but abutting right up to it. When Jim heard about this he immediately checked the vessel out. It was registered in Hong Kong to a company by the name of Eastern Research and Marine, one of C.T.Yong's enterprises. Yong is one of the largest oil tanker operators throughout the East with extensive oil interests in Indonesia. Not the sort of man to be interested in researching fishing you would think?"

"Fishing is big business. There are millions of mouths in Asia to feed."

"Ah, hah, that maybe the case, but in this particular instance it had nothing to do with fish. Jim approached me to quietly ferret out through my government sources whether there was anything going on behind the scenes up there in regard to oil or gas. The result as you can guess, was a fat nothing. But one interesting fact did arise and that was one of C.T.Yong's sons is a lecturer in geophysics at the Townsville university. His specialty is oil and gas."

Winton raised an eyebrow but showed no emotion. "Keep going."

"Yong the younger is a very good friend of Struan McIlwraith and Dudley Jardine, the chairman and managing director respectively of Australco."

"And where do McIlwraith and Jardine fit into the picture?"

"They have considerable behind the scenes influence with the present government. Big fund raisers for the Party, excellent connections, or so it would seem. Morgan signed them up as directors when he put Australco together. He wanted their names and prestige and influence to pull in the punters. They thought they were getting involved with a legitimate exploration company, but soon discovered they were being used as front men for some of Morgan's questionable deals. Consequently it leaked out to Bain they want to clean up the company by taking control and removing Morgan. When Bain knew enough to be dangerous, he decided to front the pair. I'd love to have been a fly on the wall at that meeting. At first they both denied any knowledge of what Bain was talking about and tried to stonewall him. However, as you know, Jim is not a man to be fobbed off."

Winton was listening, but was mystified why Bain had not already brought him into his confidence. Was this the deal he was referring to in the restaurant? He had been cut out of several of his deals in the past year. Winton did not always tell him what he was up to either and he knew Jim had got wind of a couple of extremely lucrative plays he had been involved in. Was this Jim's way of hitting back?

"Bain played the ace when he saw he wasn't getting anywhere. He suggested seeing they were denying there was any truth in the rumour, he would discuss it with Morgan and get his reaction. Apparently McIlwraith nearly fainted on the spot and Jardine was equally afflicted and poured himself a double brandy. They both panicked and from then on it was a downhill run. After swearing Jim to the darkest Masonic secrecy and offering him a piece of the action, they divulged the whole plan. They really spilled their guts. Here's the most thrilling piece of information though, the piece that guarantees the success of the whole plan. Take a guess who's smoothing the way for an area just outside the reef boundary to be drilled?"

"Wouldn't have a clue."

"Stillmore."

Winton sat bolt upright. "Jesus man. Are you talking about Arthur Stillmore, the Premier of the State. Is this a joke?"

Robinson held up his hand to stop him. "Sometime in the next month or so Stillmore is going to announce the State government will part finance a seismic study to be undertaken by Australco covering the northern edges of the reef in conjunction with the New Guinea government. The study is outside the boundaries of the national park. It will be a five year program to get an idea of the potential of the area. The man who'll be in charge of the program is Alex Yong, a person above reproach and someone both the government and the people can trust as being purely a disinterested academic with no thought of monetary gain. Yong will advise both governments as to the potential of a commercial oil or gas strike. It's all just a red herring of course to divert the attention of the conservationists and the other ratbags who think they run the country. Stillmore wants the area drilled as quickly as possible if Yong comes up trumps. Apparently, it's looking good from the data already gathered."

"The Federal government won't allow it."

"They won't have a lot of say as the area is just within the territorial sea boundaries between Australia and New Guinea. And the New Guinea government is so corrupt they'll just thumb their noses at Canberra."

"What's in it for Stillmore?"

"I was wondering when you would ask me that. He's guaranteed a big fat payoff in the form of a couple of million shares placed in an offshore nominee account just for assisting the deal. Of course he justifies it by saying if oil or gas is found it will inevitably be piped onshore to be processed in Queensland, the financial affairs of which are nearest to his heart."

"From what you're saying, drilling must be imminent?"

"It is, but it's been kept very quiet. A floating rig is already on its way from Singapore and they should spud the first hole early next month. Yong has resigned his post at the university and will operate from New Guinea. An oil or gas strike will put paid to any opposition from the Feds in Canberra. The howl from big money and the politicians on both sides of the Torres Strait will drown out the conservationists. Potentially, massive profits for Australco as it will be granted an exclusive twenty year licence for the whole area. Australco can drill right up to the very boundary of the reef with impunity. It can carve up the area under the deal with New Guinea and sell off concessions. Imagine the scramble by the major oil companies to get involved. Australco's stock will go through the roof."

"So Morgan doesn't know about it. McLlwraith and Jardine get control and Stillmore get's a big payday. Who does he know in New Guinea to keep this whole thing quiet?"

"Stillmore is somehow connected to Marcus Komale, the Natural Resources Minister in New Guinea, and as you know that whole bunch is corrupt."

"How have McIlwraith and Jardine been keeping it quiet?"

"By only dealing with the top man, Stillmore himself who has the direct conduit to Komale. How come you know nothing about it, if I do? Are you levelling with me about being in on it?" The broker trailed off as he witnessed the smirk and slight shake of Winton's head.

"No, Jim hasn't invited me in, but thanks to you I am now. I just can't believe that the State's number one citizen is party to this."

Robinson was shaken. "I hope you're not going to say anything to Jim, are you? It would completely stuff our relationship. I get a heap of business from that man and don't want to jeopardise it."

"Your secret is safe with me Mike. I'll deal myself in. How much of Australco do we own?"

"Aha." Robinson beamed a sigh of relief at Winton's reaction. "That's where Jim showed his brilliance. The entire game would have been screwed if he hadn't arrived on the scene and taken control. McIlwraith and Jardine had been acquiring stock slowly over the past six months. Morgan has run his holding down to less than ten percent so he's got no control and is in a particularly vulnerable position at the moment. He must be using the proceeds to finance some other deal, but it won't be long before he puts another project into the company and takes its stock for another ride in the elevator. The risk the duo face is the more loose stock they mop up, the more the price will start to rise and that's just what they don't want. Morgan will wonder what's going on and start to make enquiries. Jim has finally convinced them they have the power to tell Morgan to go to hell. Up until now they've been terrified of him, but Jim has psyched them into believing they can beat the man at his own game. A week before the announcement of the new concessions they're going to call a board meeting to increase the capital of the company with a big placement of stock. I'm handling the issue and expect to make a fat fee, so I'm very happy."

"And who in fact is getting the stock?" Winton's mind was racing.

"It's all being placed in one hit offshore in Hong Kong and no prizes for guessing who'll get the lion's share along with Jim. C.T. Yong is down for fifty percent for providing all the initial finance and the drill ship. The rest of the parcel will be dealt out at Jim's direction and I've no doubt all into offshore or nominee accounts. I'm going to subscribe for as many as I can get."

Winton shrugged his shoulders. "What's Stillmore's end."

"The proceeds of two million shares, fully paid for by Bain and C.T."

"Don't you think Stillmore's getting too much?"

"Doesn't concern me Winton. As long as I don't have to help pay for them I don't care what they give him. As far as I'm concerned, as long as everyone is allowed to drink at the trough and I get a piece of the action, it's none of my business what C.T. and Stillmore receive."

Robinson was not looking at Winton as he mentally calculated the profits and waved his glass around in excitement.

"Can you imagine what the stock will do when the news finally sinks in. They'll double or triple as soon as the announcement's made, and it's all blue sky from then on."

Winton tried to introduce a note of caution. "I'd be careful. If the Federal government puts the heavies on New Guinea by threatening to curtail vital aid the country is always in need of, you might see the whole scheme blown apart overnight."

Robinson laughed and shook his head. "It's all a matter of timing. Those wankers in Canberra won't know what's happening until the horse has bolted. First they'll have to discuss the proposal with New Guinea and apply pressure, and they won't be able to do that overnight. By the time they've worked out which way is up, I'll have sold out. Anyway the drift I get is Stillmore has already run the idea of a five year seismic study past Canberra and they've raised no objections. Five years will give them plenty of time to assess the implications, so why worry now, is their attitude. They're in for one hell of a shock."

"Yes, I can believe that, but I wouldn't count on them sitting around knitting when they finally get wind of it."

"By the time they wake up the rig will be sitting over the hole and drilling ahead. Too late to stop it then, and if they get oil or gas the objections will be overruled. I reckon the market will go mad when this gets out. Who'd bet on racehorses if they knew the truth about this game?"

"This is really going to stir Morgan up. It'll be akin to poking a wasp's nest." Why didn't Bain want him in on the deal? There's plenty of fat for everyone to share. He had told Robinson, so why not him? "Why do they want control of Australco? Why not tell Morgan and take a part of the action?"

"That's part of Jim's agreement with McIlwraith and Jardine. Jim's financing them into taking their share of the placement and hiding it offshore. They don't trust Morgan. He would simply push them to one side. They both hate his guts and want him out of the company and the placement will really dilute his shareholding. Any influence or control he thought he had would be gone. They stand to inherit control of one of the hottest stocks on the market."

"I wouldn't like to be in their shoes if he hears about it prior to the stock being issued."

"Well, nobody is likely to tell him unless you do. You will keep it under your hat won't you?"

Winton knew Robinson was studying his expression intently as he put the question.

"He's no friend of mine."

"That's what I thought. I told Jim that...." His voiced trailed off as he realised he was saying too much.

"What did you tell Bain?"

"Jim said you'd now taken to lunching with Morgan," the broker replied nervously. "I told him that didn't mean anything. It doesn't, does it? Jesus, have I shot my mouth off?"

"Calm down Mike. I'm the only person who knows you've told me anything and I'm not going to blow the whistle. I can assure you I'm in on the play. Bain didn't mention the company, but he did tell me to put a couple of hundred grand aside and for that figure it would have to be Australco he's lining me up for. And as for dining with Morgan." Winton eyed him coldly. "I'll talk to anyone. That doesn't mean I sleep with them."

"That's precisely what I said to him," Robinson hurriedly countered. He suddenly leaned over and picked up an aviation magazine which he thrust at Winton. "Hey, what do you think of this beauty. Twin engines, six seats and cruises at three-twenty knots."

"Nice, very nice Mike. Spending your money before you've got it is somewhat imprudent I would think. I hope you get to fly it." He closed the magazine without really looking at it and tossed it back on the desk. "Well, I must be going."

Robinson jumped up and followed him out to the lift. "You,.. you won't mention our discussion to Jim, will you?"

Winton patted the broker on the arm as the lift doors opened. "No, we're all in this to make money, not enemies."

Robinson's face broke into a relieved smile. "Looks like we're onto something really big. Just like old times. It seems only yesterday you walked into my office with the arse out of your pants wanting to buy your first stock. We're a winning combination."

"Yes, we are." Winton smiled reassuringly as he shook the extended hand.

His facial expression turned to stone the moment the doors closed. Robinson was obviously the person who had told Morgan about his offshore bank accounts, money from his trading activities transferred directly from Robinson's trust accounts to the offshore tax havens. Winton was determined Robinson's big mouth and indiscretions would cost him dearly. It was obvious Bain intended cutting him out of the Australco deal, or at best only throwing him a few crumbs. Bain always took him into his confidence well in advance, but on this occasion nothing had been said except for the comment in the restaurant. There would have to be a few scores settled in the near future and the groundwork and rules firmly established for any future dealings.

17

Sam Carlin was at peace with the world as he came through Customs and out into the foyer of the terminal. He kept walking with determination and not looking for anyone as he headed out for a taxi. Winton weaved his way through the waiting throng and tugged at his sleeve.

"What's the hurry Sam?"

"Hello my boy. I'm not in a hurry. Just lost in my thoughts. Have been since I left Dallas."

"Did you have a good holiday?"

"Marvellous, couldn't have wished for a more relaxing and enjoyable time."

"I'm over in the car park." They walked along with Sam enquiring about business. Winton tossed Sam's bag in the back seat of the Porsche.

"Bloody awful car these," Sam remarked as he lowered himself in. "Built for a young man, not an old fellow like me."

Winton quickly pulled into the traffic and accelerated away. He cast a glance at Sam. "Tell me what you're looking so happy about? I thought the end of a holiday always brought people down to earth again with the gloomy thought of having to get back on the treadmill?"

"She's coming out Winton. She's agreed to work for Roma Oil."

"Who the hell is she?"

"Martine. Marty my daughter."

The Porsche pulled to a rubber tearing stop centimetres from the rear of the stationary car. Winton's knuckles were white as he gripped the wheel.

"What were you thinking of? You almost drove into the back of that car. Didn't you see the light was red?" Sam was looking straight ahead and did not notice the shock on Winton's face. "I've always said you drive too fast. Now slow it down."

Winton eased the car back into gear and moved off without comment. The incident was forgotten after another hundred metres as Sam remembered what he was about to say before the near accident.

"I also caught up with Alexander. Too much like me that boy. Has a mind of his own. I don't see how we could ever work together, but says he may come out for a year or so to get some experience in oil exploration here. I hope he does. Roma would be a complete team of Carlin's then." Sam glanced across and caught the look of surprise on Winton's face.

"What's the matter? Aren't you feeling well?"

"You never told me you had any family." Winton could feel the bottom dropping out of his world. The team was Carlin and Springer and that's how he wanted it to remain, that was until it became just Springer.

"No, I didn't because I didn't think it important. It just never entered my mind, I've been so busy over the years. They were teenagers when I left Marion. I didn't want any friction over who had control of their upbringing, and they naturally looked to their mother as I was always away somewhere chasing oil and gas projects around the world. Anyway, her father was wealthy so I didn't have to worry about their welfare."

"What made you go looking for them if you were that estranged?"

"Harry Taylor took me to lunch after we accepted his drilling proposal. We talked and I could see he had something on his mind. He kept steering the conversation back to Marion and the kids, so I told him to come clean. He then gave me a letter from Marty. He'd promised not to give it to me if he thought I didn't want to see her again. A lot of water had gone under the bridge, and she thought I might have married again and would rather just forget about the past. I didn't say anything to anyone as to why I was going to the States for a holiday because I wasn't sure what the reception would be."

"How did she know Taylor?"

"Taylor worked for Marty's grandfather, Durand Hains of the Hains Oil group. Durand and I got along okay, but there were too many in the Hains' extended family all working for the company so I decided to return to Australia. I just didn't fit in. Apparently Marty has been keeping tabs on me for years, but was just too scared to approach."

"When's she arriving?"

"She's just finishing up with Hains Oil and will be out early next month. You'll like her Winton. She's a real stunner and she really knows the oil and gas business."

"And Alex?"

"He's an unknown quantity. Could turn up next week, next month or next year. I just left the invitation open. He may not even bother. His grandfather left him a slice of Hains Oil so he doesn't have to bother about working too hard. I've been a lousy father to him so I won't hold it against him if he just ignores me."

"Is your ex wife still alive?"

"No, Marion passed away a couple of years ago."

Winton nodded, but said nothing. Sam noticed the silence and was puzzled until the implications of what he had been saying dawned on him.

"Hey, snap out of it. You're not going to be told to move over. There'll be no nepotism in Roma Oil. You're still the top man and my right arm. I've told you that many times."

Winton was unconvinced. It was like any cancer, creeping and insidious and he felt the disease was about to claim him as a victim. "That's reassuring Sam." He tried to keep the trace of sarcasm and doubt out of his voice.

"Now look here Winton. I realise I should have mentioned Marty and Alex well before this, but it just didn't occur to me. I didn't know whether I had a family, or how they'd react. I was the one who abandoned them. My God, I've a lot to answer for, but I'm not going to shove you aside just because I've found my family again."

Winton could sense Sam was fighting within himself, determining whether or not to tell him something. Finally he breathed out heavily.

"I suppose now is a good time as any to tell you Winton, but in my Will I've made over a block of Roma stock to you. Not enough to control the company, but still a very sizable interest. You won't ever have to worry about money as long as you keep Roma on an even keel and paying dividends."

"That's very kind of you Sam. I really appreciate the gesture," Winton lied. He felt no guilt. His only feeling was one of self-preservation.

"I will never disadvantage you in any way and I want you to believe it. I feel you are more of a son to me than my own son. Naturally, I feel a strong paternal love for him, but he had no part in building Roma Oil."

Winton was about to say something, but held it back. We built it together, he was thinking. Without me you would have failed.

"We've been together for too many years to distrust one another now. I want you to believe me when I say your position is not under threat. Marty is purely moving in on the financial side of the company and will have nothing to do with the primary business decisions, although she can offer advice. It's about time we streamlined our computer systems and undertook a complete stock-take of every nut and bolt."

"Marty suggested that?"

"Yes, she did. When I explained how we were integrated from top to bottom she suggested she could improve it and save a heap of money while doing so."

"Our systems are in excellent shape Sam." Winton displayed no sign of the alarm he was experiencing.

"Maybe so, but let's see what she recommends when she comes on board. She wants six months to complete a study and we can either accept or reject the recommendations. She's highly qualified as a forensic accountant and knows this business inside out. I can't wait to see what she comes up with."

"What about Alex? What are his qualifications?"

"He's an oil engineer, about your age, very well qualified and someone who also knows his business. Look Winton, I can sense you're worried, but I can assure you the top position is yours and always will be. If Alex decides to join us, he won't be immediately elected to the board. If he wants to stay, he'll have to work his way up as I'm not just going to hand him the silver spoon."

Sam paused and sucked in a long breath. "I'm a very happy and contented man now I've found my family and business is going so well, so I may as well tell you the whole story. I'm going to make over a quarter each of my stock holding to Marty, Alex and yourself. I'll hold the remaining twenty five percent in the meantime. I've not decided whether it will be split between the three of you or give it solely to you on my demise." Sam let the statement sink in. He watched for any reaction, but none was visible.

"So you see Winton, you will have effective control of Roma once I drop off the perch. Don't do anything to betray my faith in you. I'm not being generous. I appreciate loyalty and this is my way of repaying that loyalty."

"I can't express my gratitude enough Sam."

"You don't have to, you've earned it. All you've got to do is keep the company growing and expanding, and of course look after the interests of Marty and Alex. That's all I ask."

"I don't think that request will be too hard to comply with." Winton was elated and yet disappointed. Elated Sam had divulged he was to receive a quarter of Sam's controlling shareholding, but disappointed he was not to receive more. After all, was he not solely responsible for getting Roma launched?

"You know Winton, the trip made me realise there's been a terrible emptiness in my life. All the time I've been pursuing something intangible and yet all the time it has been there right in front of me to reach out and touch. Marion was a good wife, loving and loyal, but I was too busy to reciprocate. It's strange how you always hurt the ones you love most. She put up with my unstable wanderings and actions without a murmur and I just walked out of her life without a backward glance." Sam went silent and stared out unseeing at the passing buildings. "I shudder when I look back on it now. I haven't been a father at all. I plan to make amends from now on."

"You're getting maudlin Sam. They both obviously think a lot of you. Well, Marty must if she's packing her bags now and

Alex doesn't sound as though he holds a grudge. They've had a good life by the sound of it, so they can't blame you for too much."

Winton was reflecting on his own childhood of poverty, neglect and abuse. Marty and Alex had it easy whereas he had to fight every step of the way. The thrill of the hunt was in his blood. How to outsmart the next man was an inherent instinct for progression and survival.

"Yes, I suppose you're right." Sam nodded in agreement. "I checked out Harry Taylor while there. I spoke to Rick McCarroll of McCarroll Oil. They're getting into deepwater drilling in the Gulf of Mexico. McCarroll said Taylor is a highly respected oil man who knows all about offshore drilling. The technology to drill in deep water is getting more sophisticated every day and Rick certified Taylor knows what he's up to. We had a long talk about fraccing, which you know is standard procedure to tap into those shale oil deposits in the States."

"While you were away Sam, those two areas onshore and off-shore in the Rowley Basin were relinquished and I immediately applied. If my inside informants have it right, there were only two applications, ours and one other."

"Who's the other one?"

"I've got no idea as my informant wouldn't, or couldn't tell me. I didn't want to press the issue and lose an excellent contact."

"Well, we'll just have to settle for what we get. It will be interesting to see who the other party is when the successful bidders are revealed. I still can't believe our luck having Taylor fall into our lap like that. If he and Marty hadn't known each other he could have easily sold the concept to another company. We were certainly very lucky."

"It certainly looks that way Sam. Let's see if Taylor can deliver."

"Don't forget. I want to know the identity of the other bidder, and if it's an offshore company I want it thoroughly investigated as to who's behind it."

"Why's that so important?"

"I want to make sure Taylor's not mixed up with it. I can't believe he would be, but you never know."

"Other than identifying the company, it may be impossible to really find out who controls it."

"It could be, it could be Winton, but I would like to know if someone like Morgan, or some other undesirable, is lurking in the background. If they turn out to be genuine I want you to approach them and see if they're interested in a joint exploration program. You should be able to find out whether they're awake to Taylor's model or they're opportunists who've grabbed the licence with the idea of selling it on."

"What's the problem with that?"

"We do all the work, make a discovery and they just hang onto our coat-tails," Sam countered, clearly irritated. "I've noticed it's happened several times over the years on other licence areas we've applied for. Suddenly, a foreign registered company is in the mix, and we've had to buy them out at a substantial premium. It may be a coincidence, but I find it very odd. Haven't you ever given it any thought?"

"To be honest it's never crossed my mind because I just accept it as a cost of doing business."

"Well, start thinking about it. We've paid out tens of millions over the years buying out licence areas close to our discoveries from companies based in Bermuda, Hong Kong and Singapore. I wonder if there's not some thread of connection. It should have occurred to me to hire someone to investigate if there are any links, and to whom."

Out of his peripheral vision, Winton could feel Sam glancing across at him, but there was no trace of accusation in his voice. It was as though his eyes were disconnected from his thought process.

"Might be an idea Sam. I'll make some inquiries and see if I can't get the name of some expert in that field to start the ball rolling. I should have paid more attention, but it has never occurred to me someone within Roma might be involved, if that's what you're implying?"

"I don't believe anyone is, but you never know. Yes, I will leave you to follow that up. I don't suspect anyone, but it does sound odd the moment we make a move, someone has been thinking along similar lines."

18

Winton had his feet up on his desk looking out over the harbour when the intercom buzzed. He was irritated after giving instructions he was not taking any calls for an hour. He had just put the phone down to a contact in Hong Kong. He pushed the intercom and was about to reprimand his secretary, but she got in first.

"There's a Mr Bain on the line for you. He has phoned several times in the last half hour, and is now insisting on waiting until you're free. Will you take the call?"

Winton picked up the phone. "Yes, Jim what's so urgent?"

The voice at the other end was flat and menacing. "It's Miles speaking Springer. I thought it more appropriate if I said it was Bain calling."

"What do you want Morgan?"

"Don't adopt that tone with me Springer. You and I have a bit of business to discuss. Why don't we have lunch?"

"I find dining with you particularly odious Morgan and certainly not good for my image." Winton caught the audible sound of a breath being drawn in.

"Very well then, we'll make it at my city apartment at eight this evening and you'd better be there Springer or else your image will take on a different hue."

"Oh, has your wife thrown you out?"

"I only invite friends to my home. My apartment is where I conduct business, and this is business Springer."

The elevator doors opened directly into the exclusive penthouse foyer. Morgan was waiting for him drink in hand.

"And right on time. Please come in."

Morgan's apartment was an extension of himself, ultra modern, tasteful and very expensive. The impressionists were evident with a small Picasso taking pride of place. It was quite obviously an original, otherwise it would not be there. A striking salmon-coloured pure silk Qum carpet covered the entrance foyer, the hunting scene depicted, intricate and quite exquisite. A golden Tabriz runner led the way from the foyer to the lounge.

"Can I offer you a drink?"

Winton nodded as he followed his host in. There was nothing that gave away the occupant's interests or occupation. No books, no photos, no memorabilia of any kind. He handed Winton a scotch on ice and settled himself into one of the soft leather armchairs. "And what have you got to tell me?"

Winton slowly swirled the liquor in the crystal tumbler. The ice even took on an aura of expense as the scotch ran over the facets and glowed a rich amber.

"I don't think I've got much to tell you at all Miles."

Morgan's eyes rose with a trace of frustration. It was only for a second and then they lowered, overtaken by a flat smile.

"Well let's approach it from a different angle then. My intelligence tells me you've got a new oil specialist working for you, by the name of Taylor."

"That's no secret. You'll have to do better than that."

"I'm working on it, but my contacts tell me the man is an expert on offshore exploration. Now why don't you tell me about Taylor and what he's up to?"

Winton wondered how much Morgan actually knew. Obviously he did not know what Taylor was proposing, otherwise there would be no point in this meeting.

"You're right Morgan, we do have Taylor working for us and he is an expert in offshore oil and gas, but that's all I know. He was hired by Sam and there's nothing extraordinary about his appointment as we've been looking to get into some offshore licence areas for some time. Personally, I'm against it as being too costly for a company our size, but Sam calls the shots so I've just got to accept it."

"I don't buy that Springer. I've already checked him out. Taylor is renowned as an expert who doesn't work for wages. He works for a modest retainer and a percentage of whatever he comes up with. He's one of the smartest and wealthiest consultant's in the business. Carlin didn't hire him on the off-chance he might produce something interesting. Taylor's too professional for that. No, he's put up a specific proposal and Carlin bought it. Now why don't we cut out the bullshit and fencing and tell me what's going on?"

"What guarantees do I have anything I tell you remains confidential?"

Morgan smiled thinly. "You don't have any, other than my word if you co-operate the information will remain with me. I put great store on my word Springer. I maybe known as a sharp operator, but no one can point a finger at me and accuse me of breaking my bond. Look at it this way. I'm hardly going to say anything to Carlin while you're giving me the inside running, and when I take over Roma Oil you won't have to worry as you'll be working for me."

"I thought you said I would be working with you, not for you?"

"In my book they're one and the same."

Winton began to laugh at the audacity of the man. "I didn't come here to tell you anything. I don't care if you tell Sam about a couple of foreign bank accounts. Everyone, has something hidden offshore if they've got any brains, and no one other than my bank knows how much is in those accounts." He put down his glass and stood up.

Morgan remained motionless. "Is that your final word?"

"It is." Winton started to walk towards the lift. "Your bluff won't work Miles. Thanks for the drink, but I'm out of here."

Morgan pulled a slip of paper out of his pocket and carefully studied it. "You're correct of course Springer. Countless people have foreign bank accounts, but few would have accounts with balances such as yours do."

Winton stopped. There was something about the sheet of paper and Morgan's tone that stopped him in his tracks.

Morgan held out the paper. "Those are the closing balances as of last week in your accounts in Bermuda, the Turks and Caicos and Hong Kong. I don't think you could convince Sam you have accumulated that type of money by banking your pay packet, or they're the result of a little share trading on the side. I believe the taxation people might be very interested and start asking some awkward questions. However, that's only an assumption on my part as being the honest citizen you are, I've no doubt you've paid all your taxes. On the other hand, if you haven't you'd be no doubt subject to a tax audit and unpaid taxes along with penalties would just about knock out your entire net worth. Your days at the helm of Roma would then be numbered. Sam Carlin couldn't afford to have his chief executive branded as a tax cheat, could he?"

Winton felt his entire body go cold as he looked at the account balances. It was incredible Morgan could have obtained such confidential information about his finances. His mind jumped to Jo Delaney. She was the only person who had ever been inside his apartment for more than a few hours. He remembered leaving her sleeping the morning he took off on his field trip after Sam left for the States. It could not be her, as his computer was password protected and encrypted. It was way beyond her capabilities of cracking the code and hacking into it. The safe was well hidden. It would take an expert hours to find it and it was on a time lock. It contained his bank records and other personal information. But it had to be her.

"Jo Delaney gave you access to this information, didn't she?"

Morgan shrugged. "No use denying it. Yes, she did get into your computer and into your safe. Josephine Delaney has a Masters in Pure Mathematics and Information Technology from the University College of London. Your security measures didn't stand a chance. I met her at a conference in London when she was between jobs. We were just chatting over dinner and a bottle of wine one evening when your name came up. I knew nothing about her background at the time other than she'd been freelancing for various of the major London banks building fire-walls to protect access to their computers. In jest, I said I would give anything to get into yours. She asked me what it was worth to do just that. I made her a substantial offer, not thinking for a moment she'd accept. Needless to say she realised you'd immediately tumble to how I was getting my information once I showed you this readout, so she decided to go back to London. She left yesterday. What a brain. She sure rattled your rocks, didn't she Springer? You thought you were screwing her, but it was the other way around, wasn't it? Your ego has taken an almighty hit."

"She certainly had me fooled." Winton was stunned as he sank back into a chair. How could he have been so blind and stupid?

"Now let's get down to business. You are vital to me if I'm going to take over Roma and I plan to do that this year. You've got plenty of time to plan your future and by the look of those bank balances you're not going to be poverty stricken in the event you decide not to work for me. However, you can't refuse as an anonymous letter to the tax boys would clean you out as well as landing you in jail for a stretch. Get it through your head Springer, I own you."

Morgan got up and refilled Winton's glass before handing it to him. "What do you say?"

"You don't think I'm going to hand over information for nothing, do you?" His mind was racing as he looked for a solution. Morgan had him in check with checkmate a mere move away.

"A hundred grand a month starting from now. You nominate where you want it paid, Bermuda, Turks and Caicos, Hong Kong or wherever."

Winton slowly twirled the glass as he thought. His days were numbered with Roma Oil. Morgan would wipe him the moment he gained control and he had no choice, but to comply with his demands. It was time for him to cash in.

"Okay, but I want a retainer of a year in advance tomorrow and then I'll tell you what Taylor's up to. If my information satisfies you, and I'm sure it will, I want five million on the barrel head, and an irrevocable line of credit for another five for ninety days."

Morgan leaned back into the chair and laughed. "You're being ridiculous Springer. No information is worth that much. You don't seem to understand I've got you by the balls."

"You may have, but my information is going to cost you. I guarantee it's worth multiples of what I've just asked. You play along and I'll give you a bonus that will make this the best deal you've ever closed."

"What do you need that amount of money for? You've got enough to cover that in your accounts now."

"I'm just like you Morgan, a greedy bastard and like you I never use my own money. I always use someone else's and take a percentage."

"You think your information is that good?"

"The information is both mind blowing and impeccable."

"It's offshore?"

"You're fishing Morgan. It's both on and offshore, but where exactly, is information you'll have to pay for."

"What's the other five mill for?"

"That's my business, but I reiterate it will be the best deal you've ever made. You're going to laugh all the way to the bank when I tell you."

"Ninety days?"

"At the outside." Winton replied without emotion.

"What's the security?"

"My backside. C'mon Morgan I don't play losers. You hold all the high cards. You've already said you own me and I'm not contesting that. One word to the revenue authorities and I'm history."

"I want a lien on any stock you purchase because that's what you must want the money for. Your backside I don't care to own."

"You accept my backside as collateral, otherwise there's no deal." Winton swirled the dregs of his drink. It looked anaemic as the ice melted and diluted the colour. He was thinking very clearly and deliberately. The trap was being carefully set and he wanted to make sure the bait was irresistible before drifting it in front of his target. He let Morgan linger while he got up and reached for the crystal decanter. Morgan had style he reflected, as he poured himself a good measure from one of a trio of beautifully cut crystal decanters housed in an ebony tantalus, richly worked with inlaid silver.

"Let's close the deal Morgan. My conditions are you transfer the first twelve months by not later than close of business tomorrow. My guess is that if you read O'Grady's column tomorrow morning you will start to get the drift and that's what the first twelve months will buy you an option over, the fifty percent of the licence area Roma lost out on. In addition, you will pay a twenty five percent commission when you flip the option on, as you most surely will. I'll meet you here tomorrow night to give you the complete picture. I guarantee you'll be more than happy to part with five mill and extend the credit for another five. In return you'll receive ownership of an offshore company with an exciting project you can cash in immediately, or go with the flow. Either way you can't lose."

Morgan slowly arose, his mind churning the downside. "I accept, but I'm warning you the information better be worth it. I'm handing over a lot of money to a crook."

"It takes one to know one," Winton replied with a smile. "As I said Morgan, I don't back losers. You'll realise you got the information cheap when it becomes obvious what I'm giving you."

19

"Hello O'Grady. Can I buy you a beer?"

The journalist looked up from the paper he was reading and squinted at Winton. "Oh, it's the motherfucker himself. I thought I was the one who always did the paying?"

"This time, it's on me." Winton pulled another bar stool closer to O'Grady and signalled to the barmaid.

"You're a bit out of your territory aren't you Springer. Don't you know this is the low end of town. Come up to get laid did you?"

"No, it's not my end of town. I came to see you." Winton raised his glass in salute before he took a sip. "How's the finance journalism these days?"

"I manage okay Springer. I still get some good information and it keeps me employed."

"What have you done with all the money you've made over the years O'Grady?"

"Wives, horses and drink in that order. All very expensive hobbies."

Winton studied the man. The body was emaciated and his clothes unkempt. The appearance was that of a down-and-out rather than one of the most respected finance journalists with enormous influence and power in the finance world.

"Rumour has it you and Miles Morgan are holding hands these days. You leaving the Roma camp or has Sam Carlin finally woken up to what a degenerate, thieving, devious arsehole you really are?"

"What the hell's wrong with you O'Grady? I made you a pile of money when I put you into Roma, and now you're trying to kick me to death."

"There's a little matter of some photos of a particular situation which could send me to jail even now, if they ever came to light. Have you come to blackmail me again?"

It was on the tip of his tongue to tell O'Grady the photos did not exist. He had thrown the camera away years ago. He realised the torment the journalist must have been enduring and was still enduring since that incident.

"I've never threatened to use those photos again and never will. I got what I wanted and you made a pile of money. What are you bitching about now?"

O'Grady turned and pointed an accusing finger at him. "There are two people in this world I'd like to see screwed. One's a crook who knows he's a crook, but the world doesn't know. That's you Springer and the other's a crook who flaunts it before the world and that's your buddy Morgan."

Winton shook his head. "You must be real lonely O'Grady. Is that all you can do? Go around hating people? Man, you've got a giant sized chip on your shoulder and it's eating you up."

"You're correct Springer. I do hate myself, but beside myself I only hate you. I despise and detest Morgan, but I don't hate him as he hasn't done anything to me personally. You're number one on my shit-list for that reason, but Morgan is running a close second in my book."

Winton chuckled as he shook his head. "Don't tell me Morgan has something on you as well? Did he catch you with a boy?"

O'Grady reddened, but ignored the question.

"You can forget about getting back at me O'Grady. My business dealings are clean and you can't prove otherwise. You start printing any innuendo or detraction and I'll hit you with a criminal defamation action. As for Morgan, he can look after himself. I don't think you'll have much success at bringing him down on your own though."

O'Grady leaned closer. The jowls hung down like flabby pendulums, the soft belly hidden beneath the folds of an oversize shirt. The muscle tone of the abused form had long since eroded into an amorphous shape of living tissue, gelatinous and fluid. "The mighty fall hardest." His breath stank of stale beer.

"How about we make a trade then O'Grady? You continue to keep off my back and I'll feed you Morgan's head on a plate."

Although possessing a liver pickled by alcohol, O'Grady was the consummate newsman. His faculties were still sharp as he cocked a jaundiced eye. "And what are you offering me I don't already know Springer? There are no secrets in this city I don't know about, so you must know something that will stand examination and is not just mere rumour?"

"Agreed, but you only know scraps O'Grady. You don't know the full picture and you can't print rumours without leaving yourself open to legal action. What if I give you something that will blow Morgan's world apart?"

"It would have to be good. In fact it would have to be so bloody good so as to withstand any scrutiny."

"It is, and the ramifications would be devastating if it was leaked. He wouldn't survive the fallout."

O'Grady's jowls twitched in anticipation as he unconsciously scratched his belly. "Tell me more."

"Hang about a second. We haven't established the terms. I'm going to give you an exclusive, so naturally I want something in return."

"And what might that be?"

"Nothing for me personally, but I think it's about time you started to write something positive about Roma Oil again."

"Roma's dull. There's no speculation in it at all. Nothing for the punters. It's moved into the area of respectability, with the exception of your involvement Springer, so what more can I say about it?"

"You could drop a hint something big could be about to happen."

"About what?"

"How about the rumour the company is about to move into highly prospective offshore oil areas. This is an area no one's cottoned onto before. It will really catch the market's attention."

"That's interesting. Offshore where?"

"I'll keep that confidential for the moment, but I can tell you Sam's got a hot-shot American oil geologist running the program. The guy is so sure of himself he's in for a piece of the action if he's successful. He receives nothing if it turns out to be a dud."

O'Grady was nodding his head. Winton could see he had the journalist hooked.

"Okay, if I go along with this, when do you deliver Morgan?"

"Be patient. It could be sometime in the next month. It's all a matter of timing, but I can assure you I won't be holding back. In the meantime you start plugging Roma and I'll deliver my part of it."

"I'm interested Springer. Now if you don't mind, I must be off. Wouldn't do my image any good to be seen talking at length with you."

Winton ignored the insult as the hand reached out for the change on the bar. He did not protest as O'Grady crumpled the notes around the loose coins and shoved them into his pocket. It was worth the fifty bucks Winton had put on the bar for the drinks as he watched the journalist slide off the stool and wander off.

Winton was sitting back reading a report, when the door flung open and Sam burst in. His face was florid and enraged. He was waving the half screwed-up finance pages in his hand. "Have you seen this?"

Winton feigned ignorance. He had got up early to get the first edition and noted with satisfaction O'Grady had delivered. He had been waiting for Sam's reaction.

"No, what?"

"This column by O'Grady."

"Haven't seen the finance pages yet Sam. I've been too busy. What's he on about?"

"We have a leak, or he has our phones tapped. Where did the guy get this information from?" Sam tossed the paper in front of Winton and fell into a chair. He sprang up again and crashed his hand onto the paper. "How did he get hold of this information? I want to know and I want to know quickly."

Winton ignored the outburst as he calmly straightened the paper and began to read. He read slowly, his facial expression demonstrating the desired concern for effect. "We do have a leak, don't we?"

"Precisely. I would trust anyone in that boardroom and they were the only ones who knew about it and Taylor of course, but why would he say anything. It wouldn't make sense."

"Maybe it didn't come from a board member, but from the notes taken at the meeting. Perhaps it's one of our geological staff?"

Sam was baffled. "What are you getting at?"

"Nothing conclusive Sam and I'm not pointing the bone, but have you considered you may have wounded someone's professional pride by taking Taylor on? Our own staff wouldn't be feeling too secure in view of the fact they had overlooked what Taylor spotted. After all, it's been sitting right under their noses for sometime. Board members don't necessarily spread rumours. It could have been the secretary at the meeting talking to another staff member whose lover happens to be on the exploration staff. Who knows, there are any number of possibilities, but I can guarantee no one is going to own up to it."

Sam's eyes narrowed. "I've left a message for O'Grady to phone me. I want to know who gave him the information."

"Don't be so gullible Sam." Winton adopted a worried expression. "And don't take the call if he calls back. Believe me, by phoning him you've already confirmed there's some truth in the article. I can just see his follow up column tomorrow: *What is Sam Carlin not telling his shareholders?*'" Winton extended the headline in the air with his hands. "Ignore it and forget about contacting the man. Let's analyse the situation. What damage has the article actually done?"

"You positively amaze me sometimes Winton. You appear awfully laid back about O'Grady tipping off the world we're looking offshore. It won't take too long for a few of the smarties to put it all together."

"But we've been awarded half the areas applied for, so it's now on record. I can't see the problem. O'Grady may have picked up the information from someone in the government agency. I thought we might have been in the pack with a lot of other companies applying for the areas, but there were only the two applications and we were successful with ours."

"You still haven't found anything out about the other company?"

"No, but my bet is it's not involved with Morgan, if that's what you're worried about."

Sam's memory was suddenly jogged and he looked up. "What's this I hear about you and Morgan dining together?"

"Sam, don't throw aimless punches. There's no need for that type of comment. You were also at that lunch. It was the day before you left for the States. You had left the restaurant and Morgan asked me to join him. Nothing of any importance was discussed, except he did offer me a job."

"Not much chance of you accepting I would imagine?"

"No Sam, there's not." Winton noted the expression of concern mingled with the jest of the question. "Be logical. I'm hardly going to sell this company down the drain. I'm part of this company and always will be, so you can take that look off your face."

Sam nodded. "You're right. It's just I don't know what to believe at the moment. What if Morgan is behind the other company? What would Taylor do if he was offered a better deal to change sides?"

"I don't think Taylor is that kind of person. He's already struck a deal with you Sam and I can't see him suddenly wanting out."

Winton reached over and picked up the buzzing phone. It was Maria Stenner, Sam's secretary. "Mr Springer, Miles Morgan is on the line for Mr Carlin."

Winton studied Sam's face as he took the phone and grunted a greeting. His mood and facial expression changed as he listened. The blood started to pump, the carotid artery standing out like a thick cord embedded in his neck. A vein on the side of his temple stood out ugly and proud under the increasing pressure. The strain on his heart was enormous as the adrenalin diluted the flow and set the organ into a stampede. Sam's arm started to shake as the ramifications of what he was hearing flowed through his brain.

"Well Miles, it looks as though you had some inside information. You've had a win and I wish you well. I won't give you my answer now. I'll need to think about it." The voice was controlled and rock steady and in complete contrast to the physical reaction Winton was witnessing. He could not catch any of what Morgan was saying, but did catch the occasional peel of laughter. Sam listened further for about a minute and then slowly handed the receiver back to Winton with a vacant stare.

"No need to tell you what that was about."

"No, but I did catch Taylor's name. Was Morgan the other applicant?"

"No, but he's secured an option to buy it from the successful party. Yes, and he was delighted with O'Grady's column this morning. The long and short of it is he wants to come up with a deal to join our two areas together. He wants a large cash payment for the privilege and won't approach Taylor to change camps if I agree. He's not interested in putting in his own money to drill. He wants to sit on the sidelines and sell to us, or the highest bidder. He couldn't help rub it in by saying I should really increase security as it appeared we had a leak."

Sam was rambling onto himself, clearly in a state of shock. Winton got up and poured a double brandy. The hand came out and mechanically took it. It went down in one swallow.

"Well, I suppose that's life. You get the good days and the bad days." He put down the glass, and stood up with a look of determination as he tried to wipe the phone call from his mind. He turned and took a step, before pitching forward on the carpet.

20

Bain sipped his wine delicately. No brain befuddling reds for him. He enjoyed the finer more subtle texture of the whites. The dry crispness of the Marlborough Sauvignon Blanc prepared his palate for the excellent piece of fish he was toying with.

"How is he?"

"Mild stroke they think," Winton replied as he nosed his glass of red. It was gutsy and full-bodied. "He's still undergoing tests. It could have been the brandy I gave him. He downed it in one go, and then sprang to his feet. He went out like a light. I can tell you, it scared the daylights out of me."

"I thought a stiff brandy was supposed to be just the thing for someone in shock?"

"Apparently not when you're in a state of agitation as well. I thought he was dead. I really did."

Bain stuffed a piece of succulent fish into his mouth and smacked his rubber lips with satisfaction. "Let's hope everything's okay. However, Sam's tough and I think it will take more than a stroke to finally knock him over. How do you think Morgan got onto Taylor's project?"

Another morsel of moist white flesh was fed between the puffy lips. He put the cutlery down, and patted them gently with the immaculate white napkin. His eyes were fixed on Winton.

"Now hold on a minute Jim. If you're suggesting......."

Bain held up his pudgy hand. "It was only a rhetorical question. No need to get upset about it. I'm not accusing you of anything."

Bain had a way of making Winton feel uneasy. It was as though there was a telepathic path between the two brains borne of long association.

"You didn't ask the question Jim. You inferred it. We've known each other for a long time. What's on your mind?"

"It could be a coincidence Morgan has acquired an option from the other successful applicant for those licences, but I think it goes deeper than that. I'm not suggesting it was you, but it was certainly your style."

Bain watched for the effect of the statement. It was Winton's style, but for what gain? Surely, there would be no point in selling out to Morgan. He was a piranha. He would pick his bones clean without a second thought.

"It might be my style Jim, but I'm not responsible. I'm upset we didn't get the whole area, but it hasn't had the same devastating effect on me as it has on Sam. I don't think it was co-incidence Morgan beat us to the punch. I think we have a leak within our staff, or it could be a board member. My first thought was Morgan had bought Taylor with a better offer, but then I dismissed the idea. It just doesn't match Taylor's style. I think the problem may be with our chief geologist, Harold Atkinson. He would have been party to all Taylor's data once the board approved the project. He's the only person I can put in the frame, but that's pure supposition."

Bain nodded. "I heard a whisper a while ago Atkinson was thinking of joining Morgan."

Winton raised an eyebrow. "You did? When was that?"

"Atkinson met Morgan recently. That I do know."

"How do you know that?"

"Shall we say a certain friend of mine works for Morgan. Poor-love starved thing. I help her out now and again with her immediate needs. She feeds me with little snippets as a sign of gratitude." Bain pushed his plate aside with studied effect, savouring the impatient look on Winton's face. "Lovely bit of fish that. Luciano certainly know how to prepare it, or rather his chefs do."

Bain poured himself the remainder of the wine as he sucked his teeth, gleaning the last succulent morsel of the meal. "This not so young lady, who shall remain nameless, maintains Atkinson has visited Morgan on a couple of occasions. Now, unless you can give an official reason why Roma's chief oil man would be visiting Morgan, I can only assume Morgan has been making overtures, or Atkinson was asking for a job. Maybe he was selling information. Who knows?"

"Are you sure your lady friend has identified the right person?"

"Absolutely certain. Morgan is extremely thorough and records every meeting and phone call. The record is then typed up and no prizes for guessing who the typist is. I don't think you need any more proof than that. Why don't you confront the man with it?"

Winton was deep in thought. "Thanks for the information. It looks as though you've fingered our leak. Is that all you were able to find out from her?"

"That's all I have at the moment. I will of course get more, but the lady is most demanding during our brief encounters and we don't discuss business, although I do reward her handsomely for her information." Bain's fat belly was undulating with mirth as he talked. "You could say it's one of those compulsory chores. In my business I've got to have good information. By keeping the lady happy once a month, I can keep abreast of what Morgan's up to."

Winton was revolted, and yet fascinated by the thought of Bain indulging in a sexual pursuit.

"I've made several worthwhile and highly profitable sallies into Morgan's companies and all the leads have come through my friend, so keeping her satisfied is a small price to pay. However, it does become wearing at times."

"You haven't let me in on any of those deals." Winton took advantage of a lapse in Bain's concentration. "I thought we were going to keep each other posted on good investments?"

"Pure oversight on my part," Bain lied without hesitation. "Naturally, I would have told you, but they were only small deals that had to be decided on the spur of the moment. Into the stock that afternoon and out that night in London. Pure arbitrage plays."

Winton could see Bain was on the run and trying to cover up his mistake. He had been caught out by carnal meanderings rather than keeping his mind sharply focussed at all times. Bain tried to hide his feelings of guilt by smacking his lips as he savoured the last of his wine. There was just not enough profit to be shared. He inwardly cursed himself for not being more careful. It was the wine. It always loosened his inhibitions and his tongue. Potentially it was a costly flaw and one which he would have to watch in the company of Winton Springer.

"The profits were only small Winton. Sweet, but small and hardly what you'd be interested in. They just meet the day to day living expenses and nothing more." He was looking at Winton with an air of honesty and openness. Winton's cold stare did not rattle him. "I'll certainly tip you off if something really worthwhile comes along. I know you're only interested in deals with a bit of size to them."

"I'd appreciate that Jim. Which reminds me. What about the deal you mentioned last time I was in here?"

"I mentioned a deal?" Bain feigned a look of surprise. "I can't think what I would have been referring to. Are you sure I mentioned something?"

"The day before Sam went to the States. You were sitting at this very table and you told me to get my money ready."

"You have the advantage of me. I can't recall saying that."

Winton pressed on. He was not going to let Bain off that easily. "I'd been having lunch with Sam when he suddenly decided he had to organise a few things before he departed for the U.S. Morgan called me over, and it was after I left him you mentioned it to me. Was it something to do with one of Morgan's companies?"

"No, no." The denial was too quick. "I haven't had any news of what Morgan's been up to for some time." Bain glanced at his watch. "If you'll excuse me Winton I have to get up to the hospital to see Sam. It's the only time I have available. I've got a very busy program this week." He pushed back his chair and stood to leave. "If whatever I had in mind comes back to me, I'll let you know immediately. For the life of me though, I can't think what it could be."

Winton nodded and watched him hurry off. It was more of a scurry as he dropped the bill and a fist of notes on Luciano's desk and fled without waiting for the usual effusive and unctuous goodbyes from the restaurateur. Luciano was concerned as he looked at the empty entrance where the formalities of obsequious grovelling took place. The happiness of Bain's large intestine was of paramount importance to him. Concern showed on his face, as losing Bain's patronage would mean the loss of all Bain's acquaintances. Wringing his hands he hurried over to the table and peered at Bain's empty plate. "Did something upset Mr Bain?"

"Complained of stomach pains. Said something about this place was giving him the shits."

The coarse blunt statement jerked the restaurateur up straight. With a toss of his head he hurried off. The insult would not be forgotten. Winton grinned as he watched the departing back, and reached for his wine as he became lost in thought. So, Bain was not going to tell him about Australco for fear it would filter back to Morgan. He dismissed the idea. It was not that. Bain could not help himself, and would have made some obscure comment. He would not have been able to contain himself as he strived to be first with rumour prior to it becoming general knowledge. Bain always ensured he was set in the market before he leaked good or adverse news about a company. He maintained an aura of mystique as to where he got his inside information from. Winton was inwardly seething at the man's duplicity. It was a clear case of porky pig not being satisfied with his share of the contents of the trough. Whatever it was, Bain did not want to share it. Winton suddenly felt relieved. There was no duplicity on his part. He could go ahead with a clear conscience now Jim had declared his hand and cut him out of the action. There could be no recriminations on Bain's part. The instant it happened, Bain would know who pulled the lever to spring the trap, but it would be far too late to avoid the disaster.

21

Sam was propped up in the hospital bed, the look of frustration clearly visible.

"Hi Sam, how's it going?"

"I'm going to throttle the next person who asks me that."

Winton laughed. He could see the boredom of the immobility was eating at the man.

"The rest will do you good. Has Bain been up annoying you?"

"Why would he waste his time with me?"

"I thought he would have at least paid you a quick courtesy call, or sent you a bunch of roses with a get-well card."

Winton sat down in a chair beside the bed. "You gave me one hell of a scare Sam. I thought I'd killed you with that brandy."

"You can't kill me that easy. I just want to get out of this miserable place."

"Everything's under control at Roma. Just take it easy for a few days and do as the medicos tell you."

"I'm signing out of here tomorrow morning. I'm sick of being told what to do. Stick this in your mouth, pee into this, roll over sir while I wash your arse. A man loses all dignity in this place. I repeat, there's nothing wrong with me and I'm getting out of here in the morning. Do you know some fool even phoned Marty. I'll lay odds it was Stenner."

"Well, Maria Stenner's been with you for a long time Sam. She was obviously worried."

"Marty's on her way out here. Probably thinks she'll be just in time for the funeral. Maria had no right to contact her. Causing a flap over nothing."

"It wasn't nothing Sam. The docs say you suffered a mild stroke, and if you carry on like this you'll have another. As it is, you're going to be popping pills from now on."

Sam eyed him fiercely. "Who told you that? They haven't told me anything."

"I shouldn't have said anything either. For God's sake calm down and see reason. If you don't, I reckon they'll sedate you. This is a hospital and you're not the only patient, so just shut up and take their advice."

Sam cast a critical eye around the ward. "Look at this place. It's a death house. A man pays private insurance for a private room, and then gets thrown in with this lot. Gallstones, hernias and haemorrhoids about sums them up. Christ, it's depressing."

"You're in for two or three more days, so you'd better get used to it. You've had a warning to take it easy, otherwise the next time you won't be in front of the hearse, you'll be riding in the back."

Sam sighed and leaned back on the pillow. He stared at the ceiling as if in a mesmerised act of relaxing. His clenched fists slowly opened as they lost their tension.

"I don't want her to see me like this Winton. I wanted to be at the airport to meet her. I don't want her to see a crock lying in a hospital bed. I just can't stand people worrying about me."

Winton stood up and patted Sam on the shoulder. "You take it easy. I don't believe Marty will be worried about your surroundings. She'll be overjoyed to see you're not a basket case. You just look your best for when she arrives."

Winton parked his car in the two minute zone and hurried into the terminal. He was late. It had been a long night and the alarm in his brain had not gone off as it usually did. He glanced at the exits to Customs. Weary passengers from many flights were flooding into the arrivals hall. He recognised her immediately from the photo Sam had shown him. There was no mistaking Marty Carlin as she pushed the luggage trolley before her. The aggressive, quick witted Carlin characteristics were obvious. Sparkling hazel eyes, a beautiful soft skin tone that immediately attracted and beguiled. She was clearly Sam Carlin's daughter. The thick black curly hair was the only contrast. It was close cropped and spherical. Winton watched her as she slowly made her way through the throng, fascinated by her aura of complete control and confidence. She was a lady who knew where she was going in life, despite the rigours of a thirteen hour flight from Los Angeles.

"Marty Carlin?" She was level with him when he stretched out his hand to stop her trolley. "I'm Winton Springer."

The smile was immediate and genuine. "I'm so pleased to meet you Winton. Dad told me so much about you. All good of course," she said laughing. Sudden concern crossed her face.

"How is he?"

"He's fine, but will be hospitalised for a few more days which doesn't sit well with him at all. He's not a model patient."

The look of relief spread across her face. "Oh, that's a load off my mind. I didn't know what to expect. Can we go see him now?"

"Sure can. I knew that's what you'd want to do."

The parking ticket had been thrust under the wiper blade of the Porsche. Winton folded it and shoved it in his pocket. The parking attendant stood a little distance away tapping his book on his hand waiting for the next victim.

"You've got them here too, I see. He's got a face only a mother could love."

Winton was more intent on the length of the leg that slid into the seat as he held the door open, rather than acknowledging the remark.

"I'll drop you at the hospital. I guess you'll want to be alone with Sam for awhile, so I won't stick around."

"Yes, I'll stay for an hour or so. I'm here for good Winton. I was only two weeks off finishing up at home anyway when I got the call about Dad. I was marking time. I'd handed over my responsibilities, and the goodbyes were getting tiresome."

"That's great to hear. I'm sure it will buck him up no end. He's really excited you know. He's been impossible since he returned from visiting you. He hasn't stopped talking about you. If you can get him to slow down and relax I'm sure he'll be back to normal in no time."

"What brought the stroke on?"

"Harry Taylor had me apply for a couple of permit areas he'd recommended. Unfortunately we only got one of the permits. We lost the other to an unrelated offshore entity based in some tax haven who did a deal with a local bandit by the name of Miles Morgan. Morgan phoned Sam to gloat and that's when Sam keeled over right before my eyes. I believe someone within Roma tipped off Morgan about Taylor's recommendation."

"Give me the background on this?"

Winton started at the beginning and explained the whole lead-up to Sam's stroke.

"This Morgan character sounds as though he lives on the very edge?"

"He does. He's barely clean in the eyes of the authorities, but a real bad arse behind the scenes."

"Who's the mole in Roma?"

"Mole?"

"Yes, the person who tipped off Morgan?"

"It's one of two people. It's either Harry Taylor or Harold Atkinson the chief geologist."

The fiery challenge in defence was immediate. "I can assure you Taylor would not stoop to that level of deceit. I can personally vouch for his integrity."

"Don't get so uptight Marty. You're sounding just like your old man. I was just giving you the two suspects. Okay, it looks as though Taylor is clean, so that just leaves Atkinson."

"What are we going to do about him?"

Winton caught the plural. As he guessed, straight into the driving seat. He got the uneasy feeling he was being questioned by the next head of Roma Oil. Cool, efficient, calculating, clearly alert and eager to grasp any situation. The long flight appeared to have had no debilitating effect on her.

"I think I'll confront him at our next board meeting."

"You have the evidence?"

"I don't have any conclusive proof, but I can certainly insinuate enough to put the skids under him."

Marty went quiet as she considered his remark. "And what do you do in your spare time for thrills?"

"I fly aeroplanes, ski in the winter and scuba dive in the spring and summer."

"That's interesting. Do you surf as well? All Australians surf, don't they?"

Winton laughed. "No, I don't surf. Never took it up and I'm too old to learn now. What do you do for kicks?"

"I'm just a plain old fashioned girl. My work is my hobby and I follow the arts. I enjoy the theatre, but I haven't got around to outdoor sports much. My specialty is......"

"Budgeting and cost control. I know."

Marty looked hurt for a few seconds, and then burst out laughing when she caught the mocking look in his eyes.

"You guessed exactly what I was going to say. I really am very boring. I haven't done very much in life except work and haunt the galleries of Europe when I'm on vacation."

"Well, you can laugh at yourself and that's a good start. For a moment there I was beginning to think you had balls."

Marty looked puzzled. "Is that what I think you mean, or is it some obscure local terminology I'm not aware of?"

"You had it right first time. It means the steroid female. Sterile if you like, with balls between her legs. The archetypal female company executive fighting her way to the top."

"You're very direct Winton Springer."

"Always have been. You are either male or female in this world. There are no shades or variations in my thinking. I adore women and I particularly love women who are feminine."

"I read you loud and clear. Does that mean you disapprove of my professional calling?"

"Hell no, I was only expanding on the remark that for a moment there I..."

Marty finished the sentence dryly. "Thought I had balls."

"I can see there's no chance of that," Winton laughed. "You're too good looking. Sam said you were a stunner and I totally agree with him. How come you're still single? I take it you haven't been married?"

"Haven't been married and haven't met anyone I was particularly interested in."

Marty unconsciously began to preen herself. The dress was straightened and the fingers went quickly through her hair.

"Would you eventually like to run an oil company?"

"I think I'd enjoy it, but why do you ask?"

Winton shrugged. "Just gauging a reaction I suppose."

"You practice psychoanalysis on the side, do you?"

"No, I just open my big mouth too much at times."

"You have analysed me then?"

"Not yet," Winton grinned. "It will take more time."

"I think you're full of crap."

Winton jerked his head around to catch the expression on her face.

"See, you've got me being crude and direct now."

"Let's call a truce until dinner this evening. If you're in the mood and not too tired, we'll carry it on then."

"I would love that. Perhaps you could fill me in more on the background of Roma Oil, the people and personalities is what I'm interested in. I've heard all about the corporate set-up already."

Winton raised an eyebrow in mock horror. "My nights are purely for seduction. Business is never discussed with beautiful women, and never with the boss's daughter."

"Not so quick Mr Springer." Marty was enjoying the charade. "I'll begin to think you're making advances if you keep that up."

"Well, why don't I hide my true intentions and talk about business while subtly leading into the topic of seduction?"

"Done."

Winton pulled up in front of the hospital. "I'll drop your bags out to Roma. Here's the address," Winton scrawled it on the back of his business card. "It's only a couple of kilometres from here. I'll pick you up at eight."

"I'll look forward to it." With a wave and toss of her curly hair she disappeared into the entrance.

"How is he?"

"Depressed, but the doctor said it was normal for a stroke victim to swing between the highs and lows." Marty played with the remnant salt on the edge of her margarita glass. "I'm thankful it was only a mild stroke, but he's had a warning. Any stress could bring on another. I can't see him taking it easy or retiring though. Can you?"

Winton shook his head. "Sam Carlin is the type of person who always wants to be in the driver's seat. It's not that he doesn't trust anyone else. It's just that he sees no point in retiring."

"He's very depressed about losing half those Rowley areas. He's bitterly disappointed to think one of his own staff has been tipping off the competition. He feels Morgan has acquired something by deception, something he's not entitled to."

"It's true Morgan's got under our guard, but I would suggest we see if we can't do a deal with him. Anything Morgan has is for sale. He's not in anything for the long haul."

Winton stopped when he noted the sparkle had gone out of her eyes and she looked dull and tired. Jet lag combined with the worry of her father's health had taken their toll. He put his hand on hers.

"Don't worry about Sam. He's a fighter and he'll recover. Let me take you home. "I don't think tonight's the night to talk about business."

"How about seduction?"

"A question posed with very unconvincing enthusiasm. You need a good night's sleep to let your time clock catch up with your body and brain." Winton stood and took her arm.

The night was warm with a gentle breeze. "I think the margarita went to my head," Marty said as he opened the door of the Porsche for her. Neither spoke as Winton headed for Point Piper. Twin yellow lights signalled the entrance to the driveway. Besides the company, the colonial era manor was Sam's personal status symbol. Except for a butler and housekeeper, he lived alone. Winton did not like the place, it was far too big for one man to live in. The grounds were spacious and went right to the harbour edge. A yacht rose and fell with the gentle swell at the end of the pier. Sam Carlin had all the trappings of wealth in line with the dictates of the society in which he lived.

Winton pulled into the driveway and nudged the dozing form beside him. Not quite as stunning as Jo Delaney, but a stunner nonetheless. Why wasn't she married? What a waste if she had an alternate preference.

"Hey, wake up Cinders, you're home."

Fred the butler hurried down the steps and opened the door of the car. Marty mumbled an unintelligible thankyou and stepped out. Winton waved to her and was about to drive off when she walked around to his window.

"Thanks Winton. I'm sorry I was so dull tonight, but would you call a board meeting for late tomorrow. I think we should sort this Atkinson fellow out and see if he's the one who sold out to Morgan."

She did not notice the flash of anger cross Winton's face as he nodded and drove off. She's got balls he muttered as he swung out of the driveway and accelerated away. She had only been in town five minutes and was already stepping into her father's shoes.

The phone was ringing when he opened the door of his apartment. He strode over and picked it up.

"Hello Springer." There was no mistaking Miles Morgan's voice. "I've arranged your money and it's on deposit with Shergold, the merchant bankers. How's Sam by the way?"

Winton could not keep the sarcastic tone out of his voice. "Are you really that interested?"

"Not really, but one doesn't enjoy hearing a business associate has suffered a stroke. It's a little close to home, and makes one realise one's own mortality. Will he be out of action long?" Morgan did not wait for an answer as he hurried on. "We'll just have to get together now you're running the show."

"It's only temporary. Sam will be back on deck in a matter of days."

"I'm told his daughter has arrived. You'll have to watch your step Springer. You might get pushed down the ladder a rung or two. Nepotism runs deep you know. On a more serious note I believe I'm entitled to know what you're setting up for my next five million."

"Listen Morgan, I'm tired so I'll be direct. We made a deal on which I've delivered the first part. You hold an option over the offfshore company that controls half the project resulting in Sam's stroke. We settled on the terms and I've arranged for Roma to willingly take it off your hands for $15 million, minus my commission of $3.75 million. Sam want's you out of his hair. Result? You walk away with $11.25 mill. Now I want two tranches of $5mill for the next part if the exercise where you'll make multiples of what I've already made you if you don't stuff it up. Now, if you want to make a real killing you'll do it my way or not at all. It cannot be rushed, and I'm not going to divulge at what stage it's at now, other than to say it's a company I've got in my sights."

"No need to get upset Springer. You really are a brilliant criminal. Goodbye."

He knew Morgan would have his analysts working overtime trying to identify the company he was going to manipulate. He grinned as he envisaged them pulling their hair out in frustration by the end of the week. There would be no clear trend in any stock, just the usual buying and selling patterns. The timing would have to be impeccable if he was to make the money he planned to. He made a mental note to check with Robinson in the morning and apply pressure and maybe a little blackmail to get the information he wanted. He was to have lunch with O'Grady during the week. The thought of it repulsed him. Slowly the bits would come together. Morgan, Bain and Robinson would be severely mauled before the month was out. Depending on his level of greed, Morgan could well be wiped out. As for Roma and Marty Carlin? Winton drifted off to sleep with the dark haired girl's image in his mind.

<h1 style="text-align:center">22</h1>

Winton strode through the foyer and into his office without a sideways glance at the receptionist who was on the phone. She looked up too late as she tried to attract his attention. He was standing leaning over his desk scanning a report when he became aware of another presence slumped in a lounge chair in the far corner. Irritated by an uninvited intrusion he turned to confront the stranger.

"Who the hell are you? How dare you just walk in?"

The figure rose out of the armchair as Winton's brain snapped a warning.

"Alex Carlin. I only got in a couple of hours ago. I must have dozed off. I hope I haven't got anyone into trouble by letting me in here?"

Winton's demeanour changed as he advanced around the desk offering his hand. "I'm glad to meet you Alex. Your father will certainly be pleased you've come."

Winton noted they were about the same age. He had very few of Sam's features except the firm handshake.

"How is the old man?"

"As of this morning he's doing fine. He'll be out of action for a time though."

"Hells bells, Marty led me to believe he was about to croak."

"You seem to have a singular disregard for the health of your father."

Alex snorted. "I don't see why I should be overly concerned about him. He never bothered about me. Marty said I should get out here although she didn't know at the time how bad his stroke was. Now, when I get here you're telling me he's almost a picture of health."

Winton could sense he was going to have another problem in the form of a Carlin to deal with. Maybe this one would just go away without making too much trouble.

"He's not okay, but he's not as bad as first thought. Time and rest will have him back at work before long."

"Yeah, I suppose Marty panicked. Typical broad."

"You consider you've wasted your time in coming then?"

Alex broke into a laugh and spread his arms to indicate the office. "Hell no. Now I've seen it, this place really impresses me. I just might take him up on his offer to come and work for the company. Who knows, I might get to fill his shoes, that's if sis doesn't beat me to the top job." He cast his eyes around the office, taking in the various pieces of sculpture and oil paintings. "Yes, you know I might like it here after all."

Alex sat and threw one leg over the arm of the chair, the expensively tooled Texan boot positioned so Winton could not fail to see it. "Tell me about Roma Oil."

Winton's dislike was increasing by the second. "I thought Sam would have already given you the full history?"

"I didn't pay much attention," Alex replied with a grin. "I thought he was just running some wildcat outfit struggling to pay wages. By the look of this, the old boy has been holding out on me."

"What would you like to know about the company?"

"The most obvious, market capitalisation, cash flow, profitability, producing fields, prospects, and of course your ambitions for this organisation."

"I'm here to stay and grow with the company. The rest of the information you can read in the company's annual report. No secrets. Roma Oil is a public company."

"I only spent a couple of hours with the old man when he was over. I was just too busy, but he did mention you. You're the one he picked up on some dirt track years ago, aren't you?"

Winton laughed to hide his disdain. "Yes, that's about the size of it. The dirt track seems a long time ago, but it was as your father said, a dirt track."

It was not the reaction Alex expected. He had intended to rile the man to see how short his fuse was. Winton continued to smile pleasantly as he gave a brief rundown on the company's history and present position. He tossed over the company's annual report bound with a full glossy photographic cover depicting various scenes of the group operations.

Alex quickly flicked it open and thumbed through until he came to the financial accounts. "Quite a nice little money machine. Not big by our standards, but a really nice little earner. How much of the group does Sam own?"

"There's a list of the twenty largest shareholders in there somewhere. You'll note Sam has a very big position. It could certainly be called a controlling interest."

Alex drummed his fingers on the patterned boot. "Do you think I could fit into this outfit?"

Winton could see where the question was leading, but decided to play along. "I can't see why not, but I would prefer you took that up with Sam."

"Marty appears to have just slotted in. Maybe I could do the same. Mind you, he thinks the world shines out of her butt. So you think he could find me a position if I decided to stay?"

"Why don't you get a feel for the company before you apply? Look us over for awhile. Get out in the field and see what we're doing." Winton had the distinct feeling the prodigal son was not going to fit in with his father. Very soon he would be fitting Sam with a Zimmer frame, and pushing him out of the scene if he was ever allowed to join the company. Sam would quickly wake up here was the son and heir looking to take over in a hurry. It just would not work.

"I should really get out to the old man's place and crash out for the rest of the day. That's one tiring flight."

"When are you going to see Sam?"

"I'll do that first thing in the morning, now I know there's no emergency."

Marty Carlin swept into the room with an armful of papers. She walked right up to Winton's desk without noticing her brother.

"High sis."

A broad grin of happiness crossed her face as she put down the papers and embraced her brother.

"I see you're running the place already." Alex indicated the papers she had put down.

"Now don't be nasty little brother. You know I enjoy my work and I love doing things efficiently. I'm thrilled you've come. I bet Dad was happy to see you."

"I haven't seen him yet, but from what Winton tells me he'll survive so there's no rush. I want to get some sleep first. I'll see him tomorrow sometime."

"Well, make sure you do," she admonished. "Is this a flying visit or are you going to take up Dad's invitation to stay and get involved?"

"I don't know yet sis. I might stay if Dad offers me a decent position, but otherwise I'll head back to the States. It's all up in the air."

"The chairman's job is vacant for a week until Dad gets back. Why don't you take that? You'd probably fill that with ease. Your head's big enough, although I don't know about the shoes."

"Don't be a bitch Marty," Alex replied with a smile. "And knowing you, you're already trying to run the place."

Marty's nostrils flared. "Dad invited me here to do a specific job, which I'm doing. You, on the other hand are likely to blow through as quickly as you blew in."

Winton could sense the banter was taking on an edge that would test the sibling bond. "Steady on you two. I don't want any blood spilt in my office and I certainly don't want to be party to any arguments in which I've no direct interest."

Alex grabbed his sister by the shoulders and kissed her on each cheek. "The man's right sis. Let's talk about it over lunch. We can stab each other with the fish knives."

"Agreed, why don't the three of us go for lunch?"

"I won't join you Marty. We've got the board meeting this afternoon and I want to prepare a few things. You two go and enjoy yourselves. If you'd like to sit in on the meeting Alex, you're welcome."

Winton assumed Sam's chair and sat at the head of the board-room table. Marty commandeered the seat next to him, shuffling the board members out of their usual positions. Winton formally introduced Marty and then Alex who was sitting just inside the doorway, but not at the table.

"Board members, this meeting has been called to address a serious security breach within the company which I believe had a direct bearing on the reason for Sam's stroke. As you know we have lost half of the Rowley licence area to Morgan Corporation. It would appear someone in this room, or someone connected is responsible for the security breach."

There was an immediate undertone of protest as Winton's eyes flicked from one board member to the next. He noted Atkinson sat quietly staring down at the table.

"I can see I've touched a nerve and each of you is taking it as a serious affront to your integrity, but someone within this room is lacking that attribute." Winton's gaze fixed on the side of Atkinson's lowered head. The room went quiet as the other board members followed the gaze. "Could you throw any light on this Mr Atkinson?"

For a moment the man looked as though he was going to suffer a similar fate to Sam. The facial veins burst into life with colour. His jaw tensed in defiance as he clenched his hands.

"You're not suggesting I had anything to do with this are you Springer? Be careful, I will take legal action if you impugn my integrity with unfounded accusations or statements."

Winton's attitude did not change. Deep down he was revelling in the man's discomfort. "I didn't accuse you of anything Mr Atkinson. I merely asked if you could throw any light on it."

The rest of the board made no move or sound. They could sense a sacrifice was about to be offered up to the gods of quilt. They knew Winton too well not to realise he would not be asking the questions if he did not already know the answers. They had all been informed why the board meeting had been called at such short notice. It was obvious Winton was sure of the identity of the guilty party.

"What the hell are you getting at Springer?" Atkinson was on his feet and glaring at his accuser. A fine line of spittle was dribbling from the corner of his mouth. They could see the man was losing control.

"Have you been in contact with Miles Morgan or anyone from his companies in the past month or so?" Winton idly tapped his pen on his pad as he waited for an answer.

"I, I have seen Morgan on occasions. Naturally I talk to him when we meet…" Atkinson's voice trailed off. "This is preposterous. You are suggesting I told Morgan about the Rowley project?"

"I reiterate Atkinson, I'm not accusing you of anything. I'm simply asking if you had any dealings with Morgan, and I don't mean just idle chats in the street."

Atkinson slumped back into his chair as the colour drained from his face. He was about to face his executioner. "I have had a meeting with him."

"Only one meeting?"

"No, I've had several meetings with him. He made several approaches through intermediaries, and then he phoned me at home one evening. I met him a couple of times out of town. He made me a very appealing offer, but I was not completely ignorant of what he was really after. I broke off contact immediately Taylor's project was confirmed by the board. I thought it was the most exciting project I'd heard of and wanted to be part of it." Atkinson looked around to judge the reaction of his peers. They could not meet his gaze, and their silence was the acceptance of his guilt. The only sound was the tapping of Winton's pen.

Alex ran his fingers through his sandy hair in anticipation of what was about to happen. Winton Springer was one of the coolest customers he had ever met. It was the cold penetrating eyes that bored into the man's soul and exposed his guilt. He could see he was getting pleasure out of Atkinson's discomfort. Atkinson lifted his chin and looked around the room.

"I am of course, being judged guilty by association. The association was as I've stated. Morgan offered me a job which

I did seriously consider, but rejected. At no time have I ever discussed any confidential information in regard to this company and that includes the Rowley project. I don't accept the burden of blame for the loss of part of the licence area to Morgan falls on my shoulders. I realise now I'm to be the scapegoat for someone else's treachery. I don't know who that person is, but someone within this company or room is directly or indirectly responsible and I don't wish to be associated as long as that person is present. I therefore submit my resignation to take immediate effect. I will leave the premises just as soon as I've collected my personal effects."

Atkinson strode from the room. The silence continued as each man contemplated their position. The verdict was clearly guilty as accused. The man had not bothered to defend himself with any force or conviction.

"There being no further business, I declare this meeting closed." Winton snapped his folder shut. "Off the record, does anyone want to discuss this further?" He looked at each director in turn, but none spoke. Winton heaved a silent sigh of relief as the directors filed out. It had been easier than expected.

"You really did a number on him," Alex remarked as Winton walked past. "No evidence, no hearing, no trial, just the sound of the corporate axe falling."

Winton pulled up short. He was a study in self-control, but inwardly he was seething at the remark. "I did not do a number on him as you term it. He convicted himself out of his own mouth. Did you think otherwise?"

Alex slowly stroked his chin as he contemplated the question. "Seemed to me as though he might have known something about it, but I'm not sure he's the guilty party. You sure as hell sprung it on him. He didn't stand a chance. It wouldn't have mattered if he was innocent in my opinion. I think you decided to throw him to the wolves and that was it. I don't think there was any fairness in what you did." Alex expected a hostile retaliation, but the reply was firm and level toned.

"I'm in the business of business Alex, not compassion. Roma is an oil company with thousands of shareholders who put their faith in the belief the board of the company is beyond reproach. What do you think would happen to this company if it was revealed it has serious governance problems, the directors are incompetent and dishonesty is acceptable? Poor management, corrupt board. The rot always sets in at the top, never at the bottom. Unless management can provide leadership, the cancer spreads quickly to every facet of the operation. Cut it out and cut it out quickly, is the only way to deal with such a situation. I have to make hard decisions at times. I admit to you I may have made a mistake, but I don't think so. The evidence was too compelling."

Alex stood his ground. "You admit now you could have made a mistake. Why didn't you give the man the benefit of the doubt? You crucified him."

"And how would you have handled it?"

"I would have pulled him in for a one-on-one meeting and asked him to explain himself. You would have had a clearer understanding of his actions and either asked him to resign or fired him. I don't think there was any call for him to be exposed to such humiliation as has just been the case."

Winton nodded. "We differ in our approach, but I believe in the direct approach and I wouldn't expect anything different if I was in his shoes. You see Alex, the buck stops with the person who has the responsibility. Atkinson was the chief geologist and it was his department. That's where the ball stops bouncing in my opinion and I'm sure Sam would not disagree with me."

23

"Miles, I thought we might have lunch tomorrow out of town somewhere. I'm about to enact the second phase. Pick me up at the Wentworth at midday and don't phone me back. Just be there." He grinned as he disconnected from Morgan's message bank.

Winton had been waiting for about five minutes when the white Mercedes coupe pulled up. He slipped in quickly and the vehicle accelerated silently away.

"You look jumpy Springer. The dark glasses don't hide your face very well."

"I just like to be prudent," Winton replied leaning back in the seat. "You aren't exactly the most desirable person to be seen with."

Morgan's features tightened, but he said nothing.

"I have a reputation to uphold Morgan and I don't particularly want to be recognised as one of your drinking buddies. Guilt by association is a hard stigma to remove."

"I find your tone particularly offensive Springer."

"I didn't start it, but let's call a truce for today." Morgan nodded as Winton leaned back in the seat and pretended to watch the passing scenery. He was really studying Morgan and noted the man appeared to be edgy and nervous. It was clear Morgan wanted him to start the conversation as to the purpose of the lunch, but Winton was adept at playing the waiting game. Just a micron behind the hard business exterior, super confidence and overbearing air of superiority, Miles Morgan was a shell, a bundle of nerves treading a tightrope. The tightrope was his group of interrelated companies. The juggling of shareholders funds, concealed loans, the bolstering of non-existent assets, blatant insider trading through foreign accounts, the rigging of the market and the siphoning off of funds into overseas accounts, were all part of the game of tightrope walking.

Winton closed his eyes. A small grin crossed the corners of his mouth. He had learned more about Miles Morgan in the last few minutes than he ever thought possible. He could read the signs of stress. The unconscious opening and closing of his hands on the wheel. The muttered curses as another motorist blocked his progress for a few seconds. The sudden stabbing of the brake and then accelerator. He wanted to get to his destination as quickly as possible to learn what Winton had to tell him. It spelt money and he needed money. He always needed money. Morgan Corp was a conglomerate with a huge appetite. Stop the wheels turning and the illusion of continuing unabated progress and growth would collapse. Shareholders funds financed his stock- rigging forays into the market. Activity and apparent progress were the two requirements the market lived on. The company had always to be seen doing something and creating news was integral to his operation. Morgan came across as being dynamic and forceful. At least that's what his highly paid public relations consultants were commissioned to project.

"Bad news about Atkinson."

Winton did not open his eyes. "Yes, it was."

"It was suicide wasn't it?"

"It looks that way Miles."

"A bit too much for him to take I suppose. It would have been devastating, and totally humiliating for a man to get fired at that age."

"He wasn't fired. He resigned."

"Either way, and I'm not questioning the method, but the fact is he got the chop is the way I see it. He walks out of his office and instead of catching the train home, he steps in front of it. What a hell of a way to go. I couldn't think of anything worse. Imagine getting chewed up by a succession of train wheels."

"After the first set he wouldn't know a thing about it," Winton replied without compassion. "Shock shuts the nervous system down immediately. I once saw a fellow gutted when the rim of a truck tire he was changing exploded off. Pure negligence on his part. His guts and shit were hanging out. It took him an hour to die. He was lucid the whole time and said he couldn't feel any pain."

"You're the one who should have jumped under the train, not Atkinson. Don't you feel any responsibility for his death?"

Winton opened one eye and fixed it on Morgan. "A man dies how he wants to. If he's bent on suicide, that's his decision. I didn't force him to resign, but he was on the scrapheap anyway. He was getting past his use-by date and he made the mistake of talking to you. Don't get moralistic with me. If you want to start laying the blame, perhaps you should start with yourself. You're the one who's blackmailing me. You had as much to do with Atkinson's death as I did."

Morgan's hands clenched the wheel tightly. "He came and saw me the day he died you know. I could see he was depressed, but didn't realise he was going to top himself."

Winton snorted. "You don't have an atom of compassion in you Morgan, so don't hand me that crap."

"He told me he'd resigned from Roma and asked me whether the position I'd offered was still open. He of course, was no use to me by then. You'd already delivered."

"And I'll deliver on this one. Anyway, I wouldn't lose too much sleep over Atkinson. If a person can't handle rejection, who are we to stand in the way of his future actions?"

"Christ, you're a cool bastard Springer. You have no feelings, no pity whatsoever."

Winton pulled himself upright in the seat. "The difference between you and I Morgan is I do things and accept the consequences. I'm totally pragmatic, but you live in the world of delusion. You delude yourself you're impregnable, a fortress that cannot be breached. You're as fallible as everyone else Miles. It's a weakness you should work on."

"I've got a clear conscience. I had no part in the death of that man."

"Once again you're deluding yourself Miles. You're responsible, just as much as I am. Remember that. You were the catalyst that set the whole chain reaction in motion. Don't hand me any bunkum about having no part in it."

"I'm beginning to think you're capable of anything. Does anything ever weigh on your conscience?"

"It's a rough world Miles. If you don't like playing the game you can hop off the hamster wheel just as Atkinson did."

Morgan swung the car into the driveway of the restaurant. The loose gravel showered up as the vehicle lost traction. The correction was hesitant as Morgan regained control and swung into a vacant space.

"I thought you were going to slide into that wall and bend your lovely car. Not losing your cool are you Miles?"

"Why don't we switch off the sarcasm over lunch. We must have something important to discuss."

Winton sat under the umbrella and watched the Hawkesbury River flow torpidly far below, the brown silt-laden streams flowed from each bend as the sluggish force plucked at the banks of the fertile citrus-covered river flats. Sandstone escarpments stood proud of the surrounding stunted eucalypts which clung desperately to life. Black trunks marked the path of last season's bush fires. The blue haze hung in the valleys, as the combination of heat and vapour from the eucalypts combined to form the thick atmosphere of summer. A gentle breeze wafted across the polished hardwood floor, fluttering the edges of the umbrella as though moved by some unseen hand.

Morgan emerged from the rest room a changed man, his hair neatly combed and his tie straightened. The air of confidence had returned. "And now Springer, shall we get down to business? Tell me what you have for me?"

It was amazing how people went about regaining their self assurance, Winton pondered. In Morgan's case it was obviously a piss and pomade.

"How much Australco stock do you control?"

Morgan was not expecting such a question, and was caught off guard while he thought of an answer. "I have absolute control."

"Bullshit. You have less than ten percent and even that figure is too high I wager. Let's skip the make believe and get down to facts." The cold blue eyes were fixed on Morgan. Their intensity made him nervous.

"As you say, less than ten percent. I've been looking around for a good investment to give the stock another run. I've been letting it idle along, but I should get down to giving it another push. Why, what do you have in mind?"

"I don't have anything in mind, but I think your two friends McIlwraith and Jardine do."

"Those two fuckwits wouldn't know which way was up," Morgan exploded in indignation. "They're only a couple of stooges I hired to give the company an air of respectability. They're both no more than a couple of window dressers."

"I wouldn't be too sure of that Miles. They're starting to grow up a little from what I've heard. They don't want to be manipulated by you any longer."

Morgan pushed his drink aside and leaned closer. "Just before I hear what you have to say, you'd better tell me what you stand to gain out of this information. Is this the reason for the next ten mill, or do I have to pay extra for what I'm about to hear. I want all the ground rules out in the open and agreed to now."

"I want you off my back Morgan. You've already made a motza when the Rowley deal goes through, as I can assure you it will, and now I'm going to give you information that will not only make you a fortune, but save a company about to be stolen from under your nose. I don't want to hear from you again after this. I will have delivered and kept my side of the deal. If you try and blackmail me again I'll personally shove a shotgun up your arse and pull both triggers. You yourself said I was capable of anything. Do you understand?"

"Perfectly," Morgan nodded. "You have my word on that." He was in no doubt his dining companion would carry out the threat, or have someone do it for him.

"Australco is about to granted exploration licences covering areas adjoining the boundaries of the Barrier Reef in the Coral Sea."

Morgan shook his head in amusement. "It's my turn to say bullshit to you Springer. You've been listening to too many rumours. You're way off beam on that one."

"Laugh all you want Miles, but it will be to your expense if you don't take it seriously." Winton let the comment soak in as he sipped his beer. "Those two hate your guts. They have political clout you're not aware of, and I can assure you they're about to be granted the licences. What's more the seismic has already been run and the first hole as good as sited."

"I don't believe it." Morgan looked stunned and the assertiveness had gone out of his voice. "If anything like that was happening I'd know about it. Those two lack the balls to do anything behind my back."

Winton leaned casually back in his chair. He could see that the tell-tale traces of belief were beginning to override doubt. "Look Morgan, if you're going to sit there and argue the toss I don't think there's much point in continuing the discussion. If, on the other hand you drop the charade of knowing everything that goes on with Australco, and want to make money as well as saving your company, I think you'd better take notice."

Morgan nodded in submission. "Proceed, but I just can't imagine how those two could have engineered licence approval."

"They may look stupid in your eyes Morgan, but they don't lack cunning and connections. It's the old story of who and what you know, and those two are in bed with the powers that be, both here and in New Guinea. Believe me, those two have some impeccable connections that go right to the top in Queensland."

"You're not talking about Arthur Stillmore, are you?" Morgan was stunned, his mouth wide open. "If what you say is true, the world has been passing me by. Stillmore you say? That pair have really been working behind my back. But how did Stillmore engineer this?"

"Stillmore was born in New Guinea. His old man was a coffee planter so he knows the ropes and has all the political contacts. No doubt money has been passed under the table for that government to agree. This is Stillmore's final term in office, but before he goes he wants to line his pockets. Along with his other wheeling and dealing, parliamentary pension and fringe benefits, the greedy sod wants to make sure he has plenty for his old age."

"But, he's really in the clear. There's no connection between the granting of licences by the New Guinea government and himself. Where does he get his corner of the action?"

"Australco. He's been set up with an offshore company by McIlwraith and Jardine, and they're going to issue him with a bundle of stock."

Morgan flared. "Greedy old bastard. He runs the police and with that comes, gambling, horse racing, drugs and all the attendant vice the cops get up to. He also holds down the oil and gas portfolios. And he's made a fortune handing out coal concessions to all his mates."

Winton was amused by the man's outburst of indignation. "I take it from that statement you wouldn't avail yourself of the opportunities if you were in his position? Who are you trying to fool Morgan? You're just as crooked as him, and so is the rest of the population given half a chance. That's the problem with this country. Everyone howls down the success story as being something sinister, when they're really howling at themselves for not thinking of it first. I say good luck to Stillmore. Individual entrepreneurs, rogues if you like, but they're the ones who create the wealth and excitement."

"Ever thought about running for office yourself?" It was Morgan's turn to be amused. "That was quite a speech. Mind you, it's not one that would win many votes. It needs polishing."

Winton ignored the remark. "McIlwraith and Jardine are stalwart party supporters. They put the proposal to Stillmore and convinced him they could piss you off the scene. They needed a good prospect and in return for a large political donation, and a share of the pie they managed to get Stillmore to use his influence to gain the licences. You'll be out on your arse Morgan."

"May I ask how you know all this?"

Winton shook his head. "I'm not going to divulge that, but you can rest easy the information is from an impeccable source."

"You say seismic lines have already been run and a drill site selected. How have they managed to keep that quiet for so long, I wonder?"

Winton was inwardly revelling as he watched Morgan's facial expressions of doubt and acceptance at what he was hearing.

"Ever heard of C.T.Yong?"

Morgan pondered the question. "Yes, Hong Kong Chinese, oil tankers, construction and banks. What has he got to do with this?"

"He's connected. I won't tell how, but it should be sufficient to indicate this is no idle bit of gossip I've picked up. It's real and there's big money involved."

"But how did they think they could possibly keep it from me?"

"They're not going to, but it's all a matter of timing and that's what they're working on at the moment."

"I think I'd better hurry back and secure my piece of the action."

Winton held up his hand. "Once again, it's all a matter of timing. You could easily screw it up by moving too fast. Why not let them do all the work and then step in and take your share? The whole thing will be too far advanced for them to do anything else but agree."

"Hell man. I could quite easily be left out in the cold with the backside out of my pants. How do I know I can trust you anyway?"

"You have to date, so what's changed? There's no need to tell you what I just have. I could have sat on the sidelines, and made a bundle without risking you coming along and lousing it all up."

The meals came and Morgan watched impatiently as the waiter poured the sauce over the rack of lamb. He eyed the meal, but had suddenly lost his appetite. The thought of coming within an ace of being made to look a complete fool sickened him. He quaffed down a glass of red wine without tasting it before pouring himself another.

Winton was already through his first chop and wiping the fatty juices from his chin. He was relishing Morgan's discomfort. The blow to the man's ego was enormous. The fact an outsider was telling him the most intimate details of what was being hatched behind his back was deeply disturbing. Morgan pushed his plate aside in deep thought as he searched for a plan of action.

"Am I to assume Bain and his mates know about this already?"

Winton slowly wiped his mouth with the napkin and lingered as he tasted the wine. "He may, or may not, but you know what Bain's like. His intelligence network is extremely good. Far better than yours Miles. However, he's said nothing to me, and the stock hasn't moved much, so I don't believe he's cottoned onto what's afoot. I can assure you, I didn't get the information from him." Winton told the half truth easily and smoothly.

"One of my stock analysts did warn me about a sustained buying pattern emerging in the stock price, now I come to think of it." Morgan was dredging his memory. "That was a couple of weeks ago when a parcel of a million shares was crossed. I take it that was you Springer?"

Winton kept a straight face and said nothing.

"You've played the game with perfection Springer, now what is the rest of the plan?"

Winton knew he had the fish on the line. A little bit of jiggling for the bait to be swallowed and then the long slow pull in.

"I wonder how those two have been getting themselves set? I think I'd better have my fellow check the volumes going through the market in the last few months. They may already have control." Morgan scrolled for a number on his phone.

"Forget it Miles, you're panicking. They've bought a few no doubt, but that's not what they're up to."

"You can be calm Springer, but it's not your company or your money at stake. I want to know the answers to a few questions now."

"As I said, don't panic and put your phone away. Do you really think I'd be sitting here if I didn't have the whole game plan in place?"

Morgan was poised on the edge of his chair. All composure was melting away as he mind churned. "Tell me how you're going to solve it then?"

"McIlwraith and partners are going to make a fortune out of this scheme," Winton said as he picked up his wine glass. "They're not interested in making a few hundred grand buying on the open market as I've done. They're going for the big time, the big lick. They're going to call a board meeting and verify a placement of a couple of hundred million shares to raise working capital. A week or so later the company will announce it's been granted preliminary licence to run seismic profiles over parts of the sensitive area abutting the reef. Canberra won't take any notice, and neither will the Greens or the other save-the-earth crackpots. As we all know running seismic profiles takes time and even longer before a commitment to drill is made, which could be years away. There'll be a brief flurry before the market goes back to sleep again. However, certain people will be in the know, and the rumour mill will commence if Bain is involved. And then bingo comes the announcement a rig is on site and about to commence drilling. As you know Miles, the experts have been predicting for years there's a basin of oil under the area, and the only reason its been kept under wraps is due to the Federal Government threatening to withdraw vital ongoing aid if the New Guinea authorities don't play ball. The stock will double or triple overnight."

"So who's in line to take up the stock?"

"It's being made to a group of foreign investors through off-shore nominee companies and no prizes for guessing C.T.Yong is behind those entities. Companies have been trying unsuc-cessfully for years to gain access to the Coral Sea right on the fringes of the Barrier Reef, but now the game's about to change."

"How do I get back into the game and take control?"

"It's quite simple really. You're going to show your hand and make a deal with them on the day before the next board meet-ing. What alternative do McIlwraith and company have? If they tell you to go to hell, you blow the whistle to the press, then bang goes their whole scheme. If on the other hand they agree to your demand, which I guarantee they will, you wind up with any percentage of the stock you nominate. You will have made a killing."

Morgan mulled over the strategy. "That's good thinking. I will enjoy regaining absolute control of a company I created. I don't create things to have them taken away."

"You didn't create this Miles. You nearly fucked it up. I could have easily taken it from you. A couple of minutes ago you were in a cold sweat, and now you're back in the driver's seat. You owe me one."

"The money I'm lending you is going towards taking a share of the placement, isn't it?"

"Maybe, but I'm not greedy. I've picked up a bundle of stock options already in London so I'll make a tidy profit."

Morgan played with the stem of the wineglass as he slowly thought through the facets of what Winton had told him. Finally, he nodded and smiled thinly.

Winton could read the man's mind. He was going to raise every penny he could, both by bleeding his related companies for cash and liquidating any asset positions.

"You know Springer, I think it will be very easy to muscle in on this. I'll be able to demand what I want. All I've got to do is make sure Stillmore gets his share as he's the only person who could screw it up. The rest can go to hell."

"Successful people don't operate like that Miles. Let everyone have a drink at the water hole. It's only pigs that put both trotters in the trough." The remark went right over Morgan's head. His mind was elsewhere.

"Springer, you are one of the smartest and most amoral operators I've ever met. You're completely crooked, but I can see the money I've advanced is safe. Why don't you join me? We could go a long way together."

Winton gave a wry smile. "You've made mention of that before, but I don't think so. I'm quite happy where I am. Roma suits me. Not as dynamic, and not as exciting as it would be working with you, but I know where my next meal's coming from. I have no desire to change horses at this stage."

"You intend to wait and take over from Sam, don't you?"

"It has crossed my mind. After all I did help him start the company."

"You're wasting your time Springer. Sam will still be holding the reins when they stick him in the cremator. And when he goes his daughter will step into the driving seat, and you'll be out in the cold. Of course, you could put your cock into the cash register by marrying her."

"It doesn't concern me if I don't get the top job. I get along with Marty just fine, and she'll need help in running the company. It's growing all the time. Not as fast as you'd like, but it's okay for me."

"You don't fool me for a moment Springer. You play it low key, but it's really not your style. I can read you, because in many ways you're just the same as me. You're heading for control and won't be happy until you achieve it. You may be able to work with Marty, but what about that brother of hers? You don't stand a chance if he suddenly gets ambitious."

"I can't see him sticking around. I get the feeling the sibling rivalry is very intense, and he'll head back to the States."

"You're dreaming. You'll be answering to him in a couple of years, if not sooner. Sam will be over the moon the prodigal son has returned to the fold, and will give him anything to make sure he stays."

Winton shrugged, giving the impression he wasn't concerned. He was well aware the prediction would prove correct. Alex was a thorn that had to be eased out or become the victim of a more drastic departure.

"When is Sam due to be released?"

"He'll be out of hospital next week and it looks as though he's going to heed medical advice and take it easy for awhile. Marty is interviewing nurses to live in and look after him. He needs someone to make sure he takes all the pills and potions and he also needs someone to keep an eye on him at night in case he suffers another seizure. He's already protesting he doesn't need any help, but Marty is insisting on it. I think underneath it all, he's enjoying her attention."

Morgan had ceased to listen. He was sitting back in his chair staring vacantly down at the river. He suddenly glanced at the bill and kicked back his chair.

"Let's get out of here. I've got a lot of things I want to do. I suppose the lunch is on me?"

"Good information always costs." Winton got up and sauntered out to the car as Morgan went inside to pay. He was sure it was all going to fall into place exactly as planned.

24

Marty bounced into the office with a broad grin across her face. Winton looked up and smiled. "How's Sam, but by the look of your expression there's no need to ask?"

"You're right. Dad is coming along nicely and it looks as though I've found a nurse for him. He raised hell about the cost of the old vampires, as he refers to them. I thought the appropriate one would be a clinical type who would not accept any nonsense, but father had other ideas. If he was going to agree to a nurse he wanted someone who would keep his blood running. I'd been trying for days without success to comply with his request, but they're either far too young, or too old in his opinion. Alex finally took over the job, and like father like son, he came up with someone they both took a liking to."

Winton nodded and returned to the report he was reading. "What's her name?"

"Louise Zuckas. Very efficient with a lot of experience at looking after stroke victims, and very attractive."

Somewhere in the back of his mind he heard the faint sound of a bell. He dredged his memory, but there was nothing to associate the name with anyone he knew. Still, the resonance continued.

"I'm organising a little welcome home party for him next week. Just a couple of hours to show his friends and business acquaintances he's alive and well. You're expected to attend."

"I'll be there. Do you have any other instructions for me?"

An annoyed expression crossed Marty's brow. "Are you implying something by that remark?"

"Keep your nickers on lady." Winton held up his hands in resignation. "I merely implied Sam may have conveyed instructions. After all, it's only natural for you to be seeing more of him. I've just been so busy of late."

"You resent my actions though, don't you?"

"Too be honest Marty, yes I do. I'm the managing director of this company, and I would like everything brought to my notice first. I don't mind you reporting directly to Sam, but I don't want information second hand."

He held up a folder he had been studying. "For instance, I see we are going to carry out a study into our computer systems which I feel will mean a large upheaval in the accounting and operating side of the business. Who approved this?"

Marty tossed her head. The tight black curls merely bobbed momentarily before settling stiffly back into place. The lips pouted as the eyes took on a defiant look. She was the image of her father.

"I'm in control of the accounting side of this company as you are well aware. Our computers and systems are out of date. They need a total upgrade along with the software running on them."

Winton smashed his open hand on the desk. The look of outrage removed the look of defiance in Marty's eyes. "I can assure you Martine Carlin that any such action will not be cleared by me until I have a full report and it's presented to the whole board. You're talking about major capital expenditure, and I'm not sure this company is ready for that. We're getting along just fine, but if you can present a strong written case I'm prepared to go along with it."

"I don't see any need for that. I've already cleared it with Dad. He agrees the company should move into the twenty first century. You really should move with the times."

Winton could feel the slow but steady erosion starting to emerge. One gently lapping wave at a time and then the inevitable force of the full flood tide. "I repeat, I want a complete proposal of the advantages and the cost and I want to know how many staff will be affected and at what cost."

"It will mean less staff, a substantial cost saving and a completely streamlined system," Marty replied tartly. "The company is in the dark ages at present. I bet I can cover the outlay through operating savings in one year."

"Good, convince me and you have my backing." He tossed the folder back across his desk.

Marty was tapping a pencil on her teeth as she studied Winton's expression. Her nerves were taught and the look of disdain clearly visible. Sam had told her to proceed with the planned upgrade as long as she first cleared it with Winton. She had proceeded in the belief he would automatically agree as she had raised the matter on a number of occasions. She was shocked at his reaction, but she also realised she did not have the influence to pick a fight just yet. He had the complete faith and trust of her father and she recognised now was not the time to test the strength of the family bond as opposed to Sam and Winton's long association. She was puzzled however, as to why he had acted with such hostility. Why? Was there a more sinister motive? She dismissed it from her thoughts. Obviously, Winton was buying time so that when the complete proposal was put before the board he would be able to present it with authority, and confidently answer any of the detailed questions that were sure to follow. She felt a surge of admiration for him. It was no wonder her father felt so highly of him. Yet, there was something about him that struck an odd note. It was as though he was expecting some unknown person to suddenly tap him on the shoulder. Marty could not quite put a designation on the train of thought running through her head.

"Okay boss, you'll have a full proposal on your desk by the end of the week. You can study it, and then I'll be quite happy to run through it with you so you're entirely conversant before you present it to the board."

"That's exactly what I want Marty. This company has been run along the lines of an established chain of command and I don't want to see that disrupted."

Secretly within, Winton heaved a sigh of relief. He thought for a moment Marty was going to pull familial rank and ride right over the top of him. She had signalled by the defiant look in her eyes she was going to challenge, but suddenly came the capitulation and agreement to his terms. She had raised the issue previously, but he had always fobbed her off by saying they must get around to looking at it with no fixed time line set. He had no doubt her proposal would be of considerable benefit to the company, but it was not going to be of benefit to him. He wanted to delay it as long as possible, at least until the trail became cold.

"Do computers scare you?"

"It's natural to resist change Marty. Scared of the unknown you might say, and I don't want to put my head on the chopping block by introducing new systems before the implications are completely understood. I prefer change to happen slowly. Sudden and erratic behaviour are not my style."

"Don't you think you were a bit sudden and erratic with Atkinson?"

"That case was an exception. I didn't know he was going to throw himself in front of a train. He cost the company half of a major project, which I'm negotiating to buy back from Morgan at some cost. Atkinson was a continuing risk to security. The damage he caused was irreparable, and his actions were a direct cause of Sam's stroke. I know I was shooting in the dark a bit, but he did convict himself out of his own mouth. His subsequent actions were entirely his decision."

"They could have been the actions of a very confused and depressed man. After all, he suddenly lost everything. Strange things happen when the mind snaps. I'm not entirely convinced he was guilty."

"If not Atkinson, who else do you have in mind as the guilty party?"

"Oh, no one. There obviously was a security leak, but I have no idea who else could be in the spotlight."

"What does Alex think?"

"He hasn't discussed it with me, but I think he's shocked about what happened."

Marty caught his enquiring look. "You're wondering whether he's going to stay, aren't you?"

"You've taken the words right out of my mouth. He's well qualified as an oil engineer, but I don't know whether he's particularly interested in going out into the field to start at ground zero. And I've no doubt he would be asking himself the question of where he would fit in here?"

"Let's hope for the both of us he goes back to the States," Marty replied with a knowing grin. "Well, I'll be off. I've got a report to write up."

Winton pulled up on the gravel driveway behind a stream of expensive cars. "Well, brace yourself Miss Carlin because you're on show. They'll all want to see and meet Sam Carlin's daughter."

"I didn't go to any trouble for them," Marty replied too quickly.

"Rubbish, you've been to the hairdresser and you're obviously wearing a new number. You look absolutely ravishing."

"I must say I do feel on top of the world, but I don't know why I went to all that trouble for a few drinks in the garden."

"That's easy to explain. You're hoping to meet some blindingly handsome man who will leap into your life."

"I think you fit the bill very nicely Winton. It's a pity you're my boss. Now introduce me to some of the more interesting people here."

Winton gave a wry grin as he got out and went around to open her door. How was he going to handle this? The signal was unmistakable, but it was moving too fast. He could feel the first flicker of the flames of danger.

All eyes were fixed on Marty as they moved from one group to the next. She was not fazed by the attention and handled the situation with grace and confidence.

Tables had been set up under the wide pergola shaded by a giant flowering jacaranda. The mauve petals of the fallen blossom formed a carpet under the spreading canopy. Catering staff hovered among the guests offering flutes of champagne and trays of hors d'oeuvres. As if on cue the crowd turned to face the glass terrace doors leading out onto the garden. The gentle handclapping started when Sam raised his cane in acknowledgement. In the background, partially hidden by the doors stood a woman dressed in a simple black dress. Winton noted Sam looked well, and except for the cane there was no exterior evidence of the stroke.

"Thank you all for coming. You thought you'd see an old cripple confined to a wheel chair, but I'll be back in a week or so to haunt you. I would like to thank the doctors and nurses who are present and for the attention they gave me. I know I wasn't an easy patient, but I don't like hospitals or being ill for that matter. I would like to thank all my staff who kept Roma Oil running. Just goes to show I'm superfluous around the place anyway. Once again, thank you all."

Winton was clapping along with the rest of the guests when the woman in black stepped out of the shadows and closer to Sam. He stopped clapping and his expression froze in the shock of recognition. They had never exchanged names, but the sign *"Zuckas Café"* on the window of an outback burger joint flashed into his latent memory, along with the confrontation with the cop. He was unaware Marty was watching him intently.

"What's up Winton? You look as though someone just walked over your grave?"

Winton recovered in an instant, but his smile was tissue thin. "Nothing Marty, nothing. I thought for a moment I might know Sam's nurse, but I realise she bears a strong resemblance to someone I used to know. It's a long time ago."

"Let me introduce you." Marty took his arm and lead him towards the terrace. Louise Zuckas is a lovely person and an excellent nurse. Dad thinks the world of her."

"A little later Marty." Winton disengaged himself. "I've got some people I have to talk to before they leave."

Marty nodded and walked over to her father. "You look good Dad," she said kissing him on the cheek.

"I'm on top of the world and ready to get back to work."

"Louise is looking after you I trust?"

"Perfectly. Alex made a wonderful choice."

Marty was about to leave when Alex joined the group. "Hi everyone. You're looking great Dad."

"I believe you know Winton?" Marty was looking directly at Louise. It was not a question, but an accusation.

"I know the name of course. Mr Carlin mentions him often, but I don't believe I've ever met him."

"He's our one and only managing director," Alex interjected as he looked around the grounds. "He was here a minute ago. I'll be glad when you're back on deck again Pop."

"Why, are you finding it hard to get along with him?"

"No, not really, but I can see he's one mean mother under it all. He hides it well, but there's another side to that guy. I may ask him for a job, but I reckon he'd want to bury me in some outback project, and that isn't for me."

"It would do you good. Learn the company from the bottom up."

"Well Dad." Alex wrapped his arm around his father's shoulders. "I don't want to work for Roma under those terms. I only came out to see you and I can't say I'm really impressed with this country. On the other hand, if I was offered something more befitting the boss's son, I might be enticed into staying."

"You've made up your mind to go back then?"

"I didn't say that Dad. I'm still considering my options." Alex was under the impression his father was accepting his banter with good humour, but Marty could see it was just the opposite. It was as though Sam was seeing his son in his true light for the first time and did not like what he saw.

"Son, I can assure you whatever position Winton offers you, is the one you'll have to accept. I've no intention of interfering with his decisions, so if you don't like it, you're free to leave at anytime. However, if you decide to stay I would be overjoyed."

Sam did not catch the *good on you Dad'* look in Marty's eyes. Alex looked sickly as he slowly withdrew his arm. The rebuke had been stinging and delivered with Sam Carlin bluntness.

"Hey, don't take me too seriously Dad. I was only joking." The lie sounded very hollow. Alex was confused and off guard. The reaction had been the complete opposite to what he expected.

"I hope you were only joking Alex, because don't make the mistake of putting yourself between myself and Winton before you've earned the right to do so." There was no malice in Sam's tone, only a plea for understanding. It had taken a lifetime to regain his family and he did not want to see it come apart over such a petty discussion.

"Sure Dad. I think I'll get a drink and mingle with the crowd."

"I hope he doesn't leave. I want him here, but I'm not going to buy him," Sam murmured as he watched his son walk away.

"You've laid down the ground rules Dad. If he doesn't accept them, then that's his problem. I'm glad you said something, because I couldn't work with him with the attitude he's just displayed. Don't make the mistake of giving into him."

Sam nodded and sighed as he moved out onto the lawn. "Where's Winton? I want a word with him."

"Down by the boatshed I think."

"Would you go and get him for me please Marty?"

Marty was halfway down the path when she saw Winton walking towards her lost in conversation with Jim Bain. She shuddered. She detested the man. He reminded her of a fat garden slug oozing its protective slime as it slid from one plant to the next. She knew Winton had more than a passing friendship with him.

"Dad would like a word with you Winton." She acknowledged Bain with a smile and slight nod.

"Will you excuse me Jim." He took Marty's arm and drew her close to catch her aroma as Bain peeled off and slid towards another group of people.

"Thanks for rescuing me."

Marty looked surprised. "I thought he was a friend of yours?"

"Past tense my dear. He's beginning to get on my nerves. He's like a leech. You don't realise he's there until you suddenly feel itchy and realise he's sucking your blood. I think Bain and I have just about worn out our relationship."

"You've probably been seeing too much of each other," Marty laughed.

"Not really. We used to get on well and it was good for both of us, but he's been reneging on a few deals of late."

"Oh, and what deals are those?"

Winton bit his lip. He had been lost in thought and not paying attention to what he was saying. "Nothing really. Just a loose arrangement we've had for a number of years. Good while it lasted, but it's the old story of one party being a little too greedy. It's nothing that affects Roma."

"There you are Winton. You've been talking to old money-bags I see."

"Just keeping up with the latest scuttlebutt Sam."

"You haven't met my nurse. This is Louise Zuckas."

"Pleased to meet you Louise." Winton shook her hand. The beautiful smooth olive skin was unblemished. The soft brown eyes had a depth of beauty and compassion and lurking enticement. The Mediterranean influence of her forbears was a mélange of all the fine hereditary characteristics of her bloodline. Louise was a strikingly beautiful woman. What had happened in those intervening years?

"And likewise Mr Springer. Sam's told me a lot about you. All good things of course."

"You two look as though you know one another?" Marty was positive there was a connection somewhere in the background.

"Should we?" It was Louise who asked the question. Marty was taken off guard by the ease of the query. There was not the slightest trace of duplicity or sarcasm.

"You'll have to excuse me Louise. I don't know where I got that idea from. It was just that Winton...."

"It's just that I what Marty?" She caught the edge in his voice and looked at them both, confused. There was no doubt in her mind Winton had got a shock when he first saw Louise. She felt sure there was some connection, but their acting was superb if that was the case. Marty made an excuse and moved away to talk to more guests. Sam had been distracted by some of his business colleagues.

"We've finally been introduced," Winton murmured under his breath. "You know, you never did tell me your name?"

"We were both in too much of a hurry. We had more urgent needs at the time and I couldn't see the point." They both tried to hide their mirth.

"You really gave me a shock Louise. Certainly the last person I expected to see on the lawns of a Point Piper mansion nursing an oil magnate."

"You think I should be back in a bush town flipping burgers do you?"

"No, no I didn't mean that. I'm confused and still trying to come to grip with meeting you again in these circumstances."

"Don't you think I was shocked?"

Winton felt Marty's eyes on them and moved to block her view of Louise's expression.

"You certainly hid it well."

"I've been hiding things well for a number of years now. I've never forgotten you Winton. You've never really been out of my thoughts."

Winton's mind flashed back the years to the dry river bed where he buried her uncle. He recalled the countless nights he had lain awake thinking about when the remains would be exposed by the next wet season or dug up by some scavenging dingo. The fear of the law coming to look for him faded with the years, but it was always at the back of his mind.

"You did me a big favour Winton."

"I did?"

Louise nodded. "If you hadn't come along I would have wound up being married to that animal. I'd still be in that café mopping floors, wiping tables, serving coffee and greasy burgers, with a tribe of kids hanging off me. The thought of that hairy gorilla taking his pleasure still revolts me. Yes, you did me a favour."

"Did you ever go back or contact your mother?"

"No." Louise shook her head slowly. "I was tempted once or twice to phone and tell her I was okay, but that would have only led to the fact Theo wasn't with me. All hell would have broken loose then. She really had no time for me. I was the result of one of those forced marriages. My father just took off one day and then Theo entered my life. I don't know whether she's even still alive."

"Would you like me to find out?"

"No, leave it alone. If she's still alive she would have reconciled herself by now, so there's no point in opening up old wounds."

"And you became a nurse?"

"At first I worked in cafes and hotels. Eventually, I got sick of being molested by cooks and pub owners so I went nursing. It was a pleasure to get the smell of grease out of my hair. I finished training in Brisbane and then went to England and Europe for a few years. I thought I'd married a wealthy Greek, and life was good until he got killed in a car accident. I found I didn't inherit anything, except his lecherous brother, so I packed a bag and came home. I took on private nursing."

"And you've got your eye on Sam Carlin?"

"What gives you the right to say that?"

"It's the truth though, isn't it?"

"Why not? He's lonely and he's wealthy and we get on very well, but I don't think for a moment I could force my way into his life."

Winton laughed quietly. "You'll trap him easy Louise. It's quite obvious he's completely infatuated with you."

"I don't think Sam Carlin would walk into a trap. He's far too astute for that. Although I've never known your identity until now, I've heard a lot about Winton Springer while under the roof of this house. And from what I've heard it would appear we're cast in the same mould."

"And what have you heard about me?"

Louise laughed. It was a shrill laugh that attracted attention. He felt the hair on the back of his neck rising. He resented being laughed at.

"I'm not going to betray all the confidences, but you can rest assured your competence and ruthlessness in business come through very loud and clear. Nothing derogatory. Sam admits he would never have made it without you."

Winton felt a warm inner glow. It was the first time he had ever received any feedback as to what Sam thought of him. He suddenly felt threatened and wary.

"And you think I'm going to let you trap him?"

The smile never left the edges of her mouth. "Why don't you mind your own business Winton. We are much alike. Both calculating and avaricious although I think you're a long way ahead of me on the latter point. We both come from similar backgrounds. You helped me out of a dead-end existence, and from what I've heard Sam helped you out of yours. Why don't we just keep going our separate ways and remain friends. I'm no threat to you."

"Yes, you're right Louise. I think we understand each other perfectly."

At that moment Sam moved back from the group he had been talking to. "You're supposed to be looking after me Louise. You've spent far too much time with Winton. The next thing he'll be proposing to you."

"He's not my type Mr Carlin. Although I admit, he's quite enchanting." Louise continued the banter while putting her hand under Sam's elbow in a token gesture of support.

Winton noted he moved her hand onto his forearm and patted it affectionately. He grinned inwardly. He had to admire her style.

"She's rather sweet, don't you think?"

Winton had not noticed Marty appear at his side. The evening was warm and her perfume brought him back to the present.

"You know her don't you? Was she one of your old flames?"

"Let's just say it's a case of déjà vu. We both might have been on this earth before. I've a feeling I've known her a long time, and yet I don't know her at all."

They both watched as Sam and Louise mingled with the guests.

"She's about your age as well Winton. Are you sure she's not some one night stand from a country town of your past?"

Winton laughed and shook his head. "No, I've never met her before. I don't know about you, but I've had enough of this party. Would you like to do something?"

"How about a drive? It's a lovely evening."

25

They did not speak as he tooled the Porsche up through the Cross, over the harbour bridge and then along the northern beaches. On the freeway he suddenly flattened his foot. The tacho bounced into the red and then dropped back as he changed into fifth gear. The trees started to flick by as the speed soared. He dabbed brake and throttle as he changed down for a long sweeping curve and he saw the police car pull out in pursuit. He buried his foot once more and the sound of the pursuing siren diminished as his speed increased. The adrenalin began to spurt into his pounding blood stream. It was the climax of the ultimate sensation. Sex was the primordial animal action, danger was its twin. At first Marty took no notice of the speed. She was lost in a transient world of thoughts as to what she was doing. She was endeavouring to resist the physical attraction to the man sitting beside her, but now it was surging towards her in a wave she could not resist. The traffic was light as the small car swerved in and out, but never diminished it its forward rush. Winton was a study in self-control as he constantly changed gears as his feet danced from clutch to accelerator to brake. The present world suddenly burst back as Marty put her arms out with palms spread, her eyes opened wide in fear as the unavoidable smash unfolded. The thin scream started to emanate deep within her throat as she thrust herself back in the seat. Her outflung grip went to Winton's muscled arm, but there was nothing to hold onto. The flesh was iron hard, giving no grip for her fear-heightened fingers to bite into. Stark terror welled in her eyes and yet she felt a strange conflicting pleasure. The car swerved suddenly and she could feel the surge of acceleration again. The blasting of horns signalled the fury of vehicles he had overtaken and cut off. The sound disappeared almost immediately beneath the scream of the Porsche engine.

"Please slow down Winton. For God's sake please."

He took no notice as he hurled the car into a series of torturous bends. The scream of the tires and engine drummed through the small cab. No other car could do this he reflected as he threw the small projectile into another bend. The Porsche exhilarated him. It was a lethal lightweight aerodynamic wedge of speed and sheer pleasure. It gave the feeling of dicing with death being so close to the ground, his only protection being the lightweight body panels.

He could hear the thin murmurings of fear beside him, but he ignored them. He knew her façade of strength and surety were breaking down as the inner fears took over. The controlled being was falling apart, the mind a scrambled mess of uncoordinated thoughts and actions. The nerve ends were numb with fear and her heart was beginning to lose the rhythmic signals from the brain. Hysteria choked in her throat as she fought to make a scream come out. There was nothing. She could hear nothing, just a strange serenity of total solitude as the landscape flicked past and yet underneath it all she could feel the instincts of desire still clinging. It was several seconds before she realised the car had stopped. Not in a scream of buckling metal, but with a soft swoosh as the front wheels buried in the sand. She could see the crashing surf from atop the small embankment. The surf was the only sound. The motor was dead. She felt her door open.

"Let's go for a swim." He gently helped her out and supported her as she kicked off her shoes and they walked over the dune onto the beach. There was no moon, but the breaking lines of white foam were clearly visible.

"This is a new dress and I've just had my hair done."

"You don't need the dress and your hair will be just fine."

Without a word they peeled off their clothes and ran into the surf. The cold shock of the first breaking wave stunned and brought her back to reality. Winton was already beyond the breaker line stroking strongly for the distant bobbing marker buoy. He did not look back as he instinctively knew she would follow him. Five minutes and he was hanging onto the buoy watching her stroking the last twenty five metres. Her style was not too bad, but a little flowery. The sudden upthrust of the arm and then the gentle pointed slicing motion as the hand and then the arm slid cleanly back into the water. She grasped the other side of the buoy. Winton noted there was only a hint of heavy breathing from the exertion. She was fit and alert in both body and mind.

"You keep yourself in good trim."

"I don't know about that." She gave a toss of her water-laden curls. "I must say this buoy is convenient. I don't think I could have swum much further. What's the buoy here for?"

"It marks the end of the shark net. On the other side and at each end you're liable to get taken." Winton got pleasure out of watching the colour drain from her face. "But I am on the other side. I can't see a net."

"You could be in trouble then. The net is just below your feet or it could have broken away. It happens all the time."

"You're joking aren't you? About the sharks I mean?" Marty could see the evil look of pleasure on Winton's face. "Oh God, stay close to me," she implored as she attempted to look through the black waters beneath.

"No sense in us both being taken. You've got a plumper butt than me and much whiter. It stands out like a beacon, so any shark around will go for you first."

With a final rolling laugh he struck out for the beach. He quickly broke into a racing crawl, the arm fully extended out and the full stroke pulling straight down and then in towards the body. The powerful kick left a churned white wake of foam behind him. Near the shore a wave lifted him bodily as he accelerated to ride its momentum. He surfed the rest of the way until he felt the firm sand beneath his feet before turning to watch her. She was swimming as fast as her lungs would allow her. The style and rhythm were gone as she tried to escape the unseen danger. She did not have the experience to catch a wave as breaker after breaker swept over her. She gasped and sputtered as she tried to keep the biting salt water out of her lungs. Finally she made it to the shore and was stumbling forward when a dumper caught her full in the back. She disappeared under a foaming white mass which tumbled her, knocking all the air out of her lungs. The dumper was suddenly gone, leaving her coughing, gasping and helpless.

"Not very stylish at all." Winton ran down to assist her. "You were fine on the way out, but you sure loused it up on the way back."

Sobs interrupted the lung-fulls of drawn air, as fear and delayed shock took over. "You bastard Winton Springer. I could have been taken by a shark or drowned."

"Not a chance. You were too fast for them," he replied off-handedly. "Now get back into the water and wash all that sand off."

He watched her intently. She was beautiful, positively beautiful. Rounded hips with not the slightest trace of fat or cellulite on the shaped thighs. The breasts firm with the puckish turn up of the nipples, denoting firmness of tissue and muscle, the belly flat and firm. She suddenly dived back into the surf and like a porpoise frolicked through the breakers. By the time she came out Winton was already halfway back to the car. She ran past him and on up the sand. He watched fascinated by her nude form as she bent down quickly, picked up their clothes and continued to run. Then the impact of what she was about to do hit him as he bounded into action. His lungs were gulping in air as he tore at the sand with his clenched toes, attempting to explode and close the distance separating them. He had gained the crest of the dune when he heard the angry burble of the Porsche as it burst into life. The gearbox screeched as the unseen hand tried frantically to engage reverse gear. He was within inches when the car violently reversed and then slewed around out of control. The rear wheels buried in the soft sand and spun as the engine revved at high pitch. Winton jerked open the driver's door. Her look of anger broke into peels of laughter as she could only see his body from the waist down. "Really officer, I'm not drunk. I was only taking this car for a spin. You can put that gun away. It's not loaded is it?" Marty was doubled up with laughter as Winton pulled her out and gently eased the car out of the sand.

"I should leave you here." He grinned as he watched her run around the front of the car and get in. As the rear wheels hit the bitumen he pushed the accelerator to the floor and left two trails of smoking rubber as the car leaped forward.

"Oh, no Winton, not again. I'm too young to die and I haven't got any clothes on." She began to laugh again. "What are you going to tell the cops when they finally pull you over for speeding?"

Winton swung the car into a driveway. "This is as far as we go tonight princess." He cut the engine and leaned over and kissed her gently. Desire swept over her as she returned the kiss and caressed his face. Her other hand dropped to his lap.

"Cut it out," he said brushing it away. "I won't be able to get out of this car if you keep that up."

The house was high on a hill overlooking the beach, the sound of crashing waves incessant as he pushed the sliding doors opening onto the expansive balcony.

"It's beautiful Winton. Is it yours?"

"It's my hideaway." He had bought it from the proceeds of a deal with Bain. No one in the company knew about it. It was his sanctuary. He did not know why he had brought her here and pondered whether it was a mistake. It was a haven where strategies were planned and deals thought out to the final detail, and always in complete solitude. He turned and gently caressed her. Her skin was still taut from the stimulation of the cold surf. She nestled into his body as they kissed.

"You frightened me," she murmured. "You're a crazy driver and you really scared me about the sharks."

He kissed her on the cheeks and tasted her tears. "I got the biggest scare. I thought you were so mad, you were going to drive away without me."

"I wouldn't have gone far."

"You wouldn't?"

She shook her head and gently snuggled into his chest. "I love you Winton. I have since the moment I saw you at the airport. You know my brother warned me about you. He said you were dangerous and only wanted one thing."

"Alex said that?"

She nodded and ran her fingers up and down the small of his back.

"What else did he say about me?"

"Let's forget about him. I'll tell you some other time."

He took her hand and led her towards the bedroom. The ceiling fan slowly rotated the warm air as they made love throughout the night.

The sun had just come up when Marty felt its warm rays through the open balcony door. She reached out, but he was not there. She listened, but there was no sound above the crashing surf. The house was silent. She leapt up and ran out onto the veranda and sighed gently with relief when she saw him walking along the beach below. She smiled with pleasure as she ran her hands over her body. The cold shower invigorated her, the full pressure of the spray made her flesh tingle. She was sitting on the bed brushing her hair when she felt his presence in the room. He leaned down and gently kissed her on the back of the neck.

"How are you this morning lover?"

"You're an animal Winton. I didn't plan on being conquered that quick, but I do love you."

"That's what they all say, but they all fall for my charms and graces when they see what I have to offer."

He saw the brush swinging towards him. He ducked as he threw her arms around her.

"You've got a dirty mind. Oh, no Winton. I'm sore. No." She moaned gently as he pushed her back on the bed and slowly made love to her. She was swollen and tender, but the juices instantly lubricated as they fell into the undulating rhythm of love. He was slow and loving and felt climax after climax rack her body. They finally rolled away from each other in a sweat. Winton showered and went out into kitchen. The chilled orange juice was pure nectar as he gulped down a large glass. She was still lying in the bed staring out at the sea, when he came back with a tray.

"You feel like something to eat?"

"Just a cool drink will do. I'm going to stay here all day."

"Like hell you are. You've got too much work to do."

"Rubbish. Nothing's that important," she said with an impish grin. Why don't we just goof off for the day. We won't be missed."

"You're joking of course. I can read the office headlines now *'managing director and boss's daughter go missing for the day.'"* Winton held up the imaginary newspaper. "The chins will really be wagging. Your father will think I'm after your fortune."

"How do you know he doesn't think that already?"

Winton was struck by the odd question. "Oh, that's interesting. What does he think?"

"Nothing, nothing. It's of no consequence. Not to me anyway. Come here and cuddle me."

She threw her arms wide and they embraced before he picked up his glass and walked out onto the balcony lost in thought. Marty was sound asleep by the time he finished his drink and came back into the room. He shook her, but she moaned and rolled away.

"Good morning Mr Springer." The high note in Maria Stenner's voice was shrill and mocking. It had the trill of *'I know what you've been up to and with whom.'* "There have been a number of calls for you this morning from the same person."

"Who was that?"

"Wouldn't leave his name sir, but he did give the impression he wanted to talk to you urgently."

He knew it could only be Morgan, and Maria would have certainly known that. Morgan the ice-cold business macho who did not realise he was about to lose a fortune.

"Thanks Maria. I don't want any calls in the next hour. I've got some urgent business to attend to."

"Will Miss Carlin be in today sir?"

Winton spun around to snap an answer, but Maria was intent on her computer screen as she typed, oblivious to the look on his face. He muttered a remark.

"What was that sir?" She looked up innocently having caught the full meaning of the remark. She had ears like a cat. It stung her, but she showed no reaction.

Winton leaned back in his chair and tried to think clearly. His brain was going in a dozen different directions. Why had he got mixed up with Marty? He knew why, but she was the last distraction he wanted in his life right now. He got up and poured himself a brandy and threw it down. The raw liquor burnt his throat, but immediately focused his brain to the present. The phone on his desk buzzed. He snatched it up.

"I told you I didn't want any calls."

Maria's voice was flat and calm. "I'm quite aware of that sir, but it's that same gentleman again and he insists on talking to you." The tone in her voice was emphatic. Nothing went on in Roma Oil without her knowing about it. Snippets of conversations overheard on phones and at meetings, luncheons and appointments. They all gave her clues which she pieced together to guess, or arrive at the truth. She never gossiped what she knew, but merely dropped subtle hints she knew it all. She was a powerful assistant to Sam Carlin whom he confided in. She was equally as reliant on him, although Winton was sure there was no romantic attachment. Winton had often searched for a way of getting rid of her, but she was glued to

Sam and an irremovable piece of the company while he was in command.

"Springer speaking."

"Where have you been? I've been trying to get through to you all morning."

"Careful Miles. You sound as though you're panicking about something?"

"Where my money's concerned Springer, I'm always panicky," Morgan snapped back with a hard edge in his voice. "Australco is ten points up this morning and looks very strong. The word's out there's something about to happen. I want to move on those two before it's too late."

"Move, and you'll blow the whole game," Winton replied coolly. He was alert again as he rose to the thrill of the hunt.

"That's okay for you Springer, but if the stock moves too quickly the company will get a query from the Securities Exchange. Those two are then likely to spill the beans and I stand to lose a bundle of money."

Winton chuckled at the man's frailty. Behind the iron hard exterior was a frightened avaricious being afraid of failure. It would be a massive dent to his ego.

"You're not thinking straight Miles. They're not going to say anything before the placement is made."

"But there's a lot of activity in the stock. Someone knows something and rumour has it a Brisbane broker is pushing it to his clients."

Winton pulled a wry face. Mike Robinson was beginning to manipulate by off-loading his own stock to his clients for a certain profit."

"I wouldn't worry about that Miles. They'll only be moving in small numbers, nothing that will excite the market. Listen, leave it to me for an hour or so. I'll get back to you. In the meantime you can stop panicking about McIlwraith and Jardine. They're not going to announce anything until they've got all their ducks in a row."

"You seem to be very sure of yourself?"

"I am."

There was an instant change in Morgan's attitude and tone of voice. From the disturbed state of insecurity he bounced right back to one of overbearing confidence. "For a moment there I thought I'd have to call my ten mill. I had the impression you might be up to something when I couldn't get through to you. You weren't answering your mobile."

"I'll phone you back within the hour Miles." It was only a few days before the Australco meeting. He smiled inwardly. He had set put and call option positions through a network of brokers. The method was slow and systematic. Buy and drop the word out something was about to happen. Sell on the upswing and then cover the short position on the way down. It was a slow, but controlled process. Do it too quickly and the smart money knew it was someone manipulating the market. Do it slowly and the smart money picked up the underlying strength of the purchasing. The task was then to guess or find out who were the large volume buyers. The sellers were easy as they were invariably small investors who had been locked into an apparent dormant stock. Get rid of them first and the real buying strength began to emerge. The hint foreign money was involved added more momentum to the upward movement in the stock price. The smart money sold enough to cover their positions and let the rest ride. It was a game of dog-eat-dog. The best of friends socially, but when it came to money it was everyman for himself.

Winton had learned long ago the market was all front and appearances. Ooze confidence from every pore during the day. Never drop the veil of success, no matter how much you were hurting. At night you could beat your wife and make love to your mistress to relieve the tension. He picked up the phone and got through to Perth. The conversation was short, but its effect would be almost immediate. Next a call to Melbourne with similar instructions. The two brokers would be in the market for the same stock, one buying and one selling. He sat back with a smug smile waiting for the reaction to be noticed. He waited five minutes and then phoned Mike Robinson.

"Hi Winton, what can I do for you?"

"I've been watching Australco Mike, what's going on?"

"I thought you might be able to tell me?"

"Don't hand me that Mike. Aren't you watching your screen? The stock's very strong. It's up ten points this morning. This is not your doing is it?"

"In confidence Winton, I've been selling as I think this run will soon break and I want to take a profit while I can."

"You're making a big mistake Mike. You'll be left at the bus stop unless you get back in. Get all your discretionary accounts in as well. To show you my complete faith, buy me another two hundred thousand."

The excitement in Winton's voice was not lost on the broker. "You really think it's going to be that good?"

"Have I ever put you on a bum horse before?"

"No, Winton you haven't. I've never had inside information as good as this before. Jim bought another large parcel this morning, but I suppose you know about that?"

"I hope you're not also broadcasting my dealings are you?"

Robinson caught the steely note in Winton's voice.

"No, no. I just thought that seeing you two plan your deals together, it was no secret me telling you what Jim's up to."

Winton lowered the tone of his voice and gave a disarming laugh. "Of course I know about the purchase, but you've got to be more discreet. Bain and I do deals he doesn't necessarily tell his friends about. This is one of the times where the information is for a very exclusive circle."

"I'm sorry about that Winton. I got carried away I guess."

"Forget it Mike. Get yourself set. You've got a few days in which to load up on the stock and fill my order. Just take your time and don't push the market any further. Have you bought that plane yet?"

"I've ordered it. A single engine...."

Winton cut him off. "Go for a twin. You can afford it when this comes off."

"My only concern is that McIlwraith and Jardine don't appear to be buyers from what I gather."

"Do you know if Morgan is buying?"

"I've heard nothing on the grapevine."

"Well, wouldn't you say that's a good sign. If Morgan was in on it he'd be shouting from the rooftops now. The mere fact he's quiet confirms our security is still very tight."

26

McIlwraith was studying the bundle of proxies Morgan handed him while considering his demands. The spectacles were poised on the end of the thin nose. He was a small fragile man almost hidden behind the antique partner's desk. The shelves of law books lined one wall of the room, the mildew of ages having crept in a thin green film from volume to volume. His teeth were yellow as was his wispy nicotine-stained moustache. The paintings and framed certificates of his qualifications were coated with a residual film of tobacco smoke. He was studying the proxies as he occasionally flicked cigarette ash into an already overflowing ashtray. Embalming would not be required on his death as it looked as though the process was already complete. Jardine still had the build of a once imposing figure, but advancing age like his accomplice was catching up on him.

Winton noted the two men were in complete contrast. One was a lawyer of the old establishment, courteous and learned, but way out of his class when it came to dealing with men like Miles Morgan. Jardine was the scion of grazing aristocracy, the right schools and the right university, followed by the compulsory year of carousing and partying on the London scene. The frayed collar and loose button on the tweed jacket told Winton the family money was no longer holding out too well. The years of drought, poor prices and declining returns were beginning to show. The years flashed back as he studied the man. The typical despot squattocracy strutting into the shearing shed giving orders of how he wanted the job done. Wool was king then, but no longer. His gaze went back to McIlwraith as he drew a mental picture of how the two meshed together.

The lawyer slowly continued to check the proxies off against the register. He finally pushed the bundle back across his desk.

"Your proxies are in order of course Mr Morgan, but I don't see how they constitute control, or anywhere near control."

"Don't fence with me McIlwraith. You two will do as I tell you."

McIlwraith waved his hand spreading ash over the papers. "What is the purpose of this show of force? Why do you feel it necessary to turn up now and attempt to assert control with these proxies. Furthermore, you are not a director so you're not in the position to demand anything."

"I started this company and I intend to maintain control. You and Jardine have been paid handsomely until now, but I'm now aware certain things have been happening behind my back."

"To what are you referring?"

"There's a lot of interest in Australco at present. There's something going on which I'm not party to, and I want to know what it is?"

"I really don't know what you're getting at. You'd be the first to know if anything was happening wouldn't you Mr Morgan? After all, you're the one who uses this company as your personal plaything."

Morgan nodded as he turned to Jardine. "What do you think all the sudden buying activity in the stock is all about Dudley?"

Jardine had not expected the question and was lost. The imploring look of *'rescue me'* was written all over his face as he looked to the lawyer for help.

"Stuck for an answer Dudley?" The tone in Morgan's question was sarcastic. "I take it you two know the penalties for misleading the market and shareholders of a company?"

"What are you implying?"

"I'm implying Mr Struan McIlwraith that you and your fellow board member are a couple of liars."

Winton waited for the outburst of indignation, but there was none. McIlwraith picked up his fountain pen and tapped it on the desk, each time letting his fingers slip to the bottom before flipping it over to repeat the action. He slowly shifted his gaze from Jardine to Winton and finally Morgan. "You know?"

Morgan nodded without moving a facial muscle.

"And you're going to stop us issuing the shares?"

"On the contrary," Morgan smiled. "I'm going to assist you in every way I can."

The flicker of a smile crossed the lawyer's face, but then hardened as it dawned on him what was coming. "But you want a slice of the action, is that it?"

"Yes, you are quite right. However, I want the major slice. I want fifty percent. You two can share the remainder with Yong and your fat friend in parliament."

"I don't think Stillmore will accept that proposal at all Morgan." The courtesies had been dropped. It was now just plain Morgan. The battle lines had been declared. "As you know our Premier has a certain earthy eloquence and I believe he will express it in no uncertain terms by telling you to get fucked."

"What your crooked Premier thinks or doesn't think has no real bearing on what this company is going to do under my direction. Wake up to yourselves gentlemen, the game has been blown. You either go along with me or lose out completely. You remind your friend who runs this State that it won't be too long before he steps aside and there'll be no more juicy deals such as this coming his way, and that goes for you two as well. The message won't be lost on Stillmore. He's not going to throw away a couple of million just because I start calling the shots. He should be delighted it's me as he knows my reputation for promoting companies. Sure, he's going to get a smaller allocation, but that's more than offset with the profit he's going to make if he accepts my proposal."

"I'll have to discuss it with Arthur in private. You will have to excuse me."

Neither Morgan nor Winton moved. "You discuss it with him now. Get him on the phone now so I can hear what he decides," Morgan directed. "I'm not leaving this room until I know Stillmore's decision and have agreement from you two."

McIlwraith picked up the phone and dialled a private direct number. It was an automatic action which he had done countless times before as Stillmore's lawyer and confidant. They trusted one another to a degree, but Stillmore never let him get too far ahead as to obtain a financial advantage. Just the odd fat bone here and there to keep him loyal and happy, was the limit of his largesse.

McIlwraith knew he was dealing with two dangerous associates. Secretly he admired Morgan more. The man had always delivered and if there was the promise of a kickback he would always receive it. With Stillmore there was always the promise, but as with any politician the promise could be conveniently forgotten. A reminder would only bring a token payment compared with the original magnanimous gesture. He had long ago learned the only way to keep abreast with Stillmore was to present his government with a fat legal bill every month for some obscure advice and consulting work.

"Arthur, Struan speaking. Look, as you know the Australco meeting's tomorrow, but we've got a slight problem in the form of Miles Morgan. He's here with me now."

The whole room heard the uncomplimentary expletives bounce back through the phone.

"Keep your shirt on Arthur, he knows you're in on it." Another unintelligible outburst echoed as McIlwraith held the phone away from his ear. "Don't ask me where he got the information from, but he's got it and he wants in."

The lawyer was cut off as the voice on the other end grew louder. "Before you hang up Arthur, the whole thing will go down the drain if you don't listen. You'll still make millions, but not as much as you've planned."

The other end of the line went quiet as McIlwraith knew it would at the mention of money. "He's guaranteeing you half a million shares, credited to your offshore company in Bermuda. They won't cost you a cent. He'll email you the details to your home computer."

Morgan started to say something, but went quiet when the lawyer glared at him. He knew he had been out manoeuvred. He could not argue the terms now that the lawyer had offered them.

"Just a minute Arthur." McIlwraith put his hand over the mouthpiece. "He says make it a million and you've got yourself a deal."

Morgan nodded his head fractionally while inwardly he was rejoicing at how easy it had been.

"That's agreed Arthur. Yes, one million issued to your Bermuda company. What's that account number again? No strings attached as to when you can sell them." The voice on the other end droned on as the lawyer listened in silence and then hung up as he was abruptly cut off.

Winton noted all the while he had been talking, McIlwraith had been scratching notes on a pad.

"If any of this leaks out before he receives his shares, the deal's off. I can assure you Stillmore is very touchy about press comment these days. He's about to retire and he wants to go out with a clean slate and all the perks that go with it."

"Typical politician," Morgan commented acidly. "Wants all the rewards and recognition, but none of the shit that may stick if it all goes tits up."

"Protest all you like Morgan," McIlwraith replied. "But I can assure you he means what he says. Any market rumours or comments in the press and you can kiss this project goodbye. I don't relish being left with a bundle of shares I can't afford. I think you're in the same boat."

Morgan smiled thinly. "Well, it looks in the bag to me, so why don't we have a little stiffener to celebrate? Are you going to break out your best malt Struan?"

McIlwraith signalled for them to follow him into the boardroom. Morgan and Jardine turned and followed. As they disappeared, Winton leaned over the desk and tore the sheet off McLlwaith's pad. McIlwraith would realise who'd taken it, but there was little he could not about it.

McIlwraith filled four shot glasses and handed them out. "To your continued good health gentlemen." He raised his glass and downed the liquor in a single gulp. "I'll announce the placement of two hundred million shares to sophisticated investors and large shareholders after the board meeting if you're agreeable Morgan?"

"Excellent, that will have the effect of driving the price of the stock down a few points. The excuse for the placement is we need the money for working capital and future exploration programs. We can then buy in on the falling market. Then on Friday afternoon we'll make the announcement regarding the seismic work on the edge of the Barrier Reef, and watch the stock go for a ride in London overnight and here next week. The following week a rumour will surface a site has been selected and drilling is about to commence. That will really set the market alight."

None of the others noticed Winton's dry hollow laugh in contrast to their mirth. Morgan turned to Jardine. "I'll bet you two have being getting yourselves set over the past month or so. You've got a stack of them tucked away in some nominee account, haven't you?"

"We've got a few hundred thousand......" Jardine's voice trailed off as he caught the lawyer's withering glance. "Oh, what does it matter now Struan? He dismissed the admonishment. "Yes, I've got every penny riding on it. It had better come off, otherwise I'll be back trying to make a buck out of sheep again, and we all know how hard that is these days."

"Only gamble if you can afford it," Winton chipped in.

"But, it's a no-lose situation, don't you think?" Jardine suddenly adopted a worried look.

"What if Stillmore suddenly gets cold feet and pulls out?"

"That's not going to happen." Morgan poured himself another shot and held the glass up to study the texture of the scotch. "If my guess is correct, Stillmore will have already been quietly loading up, so he's fully committed. "

"What the hell have you been doing Winton? You never told me you were getting friendly with Morgan. I know you were with him at the Australco meeting. I think it may be about time you joined him permanently."

"I don't back losers Sam."

"Why then are you holding hands with him?"

"I'm not Sam, but I won't discuss it with you over the phone."

"You and I had better have a serious discussion. You're not going to sell my company down the drain to the likes of Morgan."

Winton made no reply.

"Are you still there Springer?"

"Yes Sam."

"And another thing. What have you done to upset my daughter? One moment she's walking around the place like a moonstruck cow, and the next she could kill you for laughs."

"Wouldn't have a clue Sam. Why don't you ask her?"

"I have, but she won't tell me a thing. That last statement proves to me you're holding out on me. You know what's been going on at Australco and you know why. Marty's got the hots for you. You can't glibly lie to me you don't know what's ailing her. I'm too old not to recognise the signs."

"What signs? That's news to me."

"Is it? Well, here's some more news for you. I want your resignation on my desk by the time I get in Monday morning. I can't work with people I can't trust."

"You'll have it Sam." Winton put down the phone without waiting for a reply. He was certain Sam would withdraw his demand. However, the die was cast. He had to move quickly if he was going to destroy Morgan, Bain and Robinson. He reflected it was probably for the good Sam had phoned him. He had intended to hang on until the last moment to spring his surprise, but now his hand had been tipped. He already stood to make a substantial profit out of the Australco derivatives he had bought on the market. The real money was in short selling. Selling stock he did not own and then buying back in at the lower price when the bottom dropped out of the market. Short selling was the area of trading that sorted the men from the boys. You had to have the gonads of a bull to stand the strain of waiting for the share price to crash under selling pressure. He knew he was clear in his thinking so far. There was only one weak link to overcome, but he was sure his quarry would take the bait. It would be too irresistible. He dialled the number.

"Peter O'Grady please."

It was another minute before the heavy voice answered. "O'Grady."

"Winton Springer speaking O'Grady. I thought you might appreciate a story that will break your dismal rate of front page articles of late."

The chesty wheeze was broken by a sudden smoker's hack. "Not about Morgan is it? It would appear McIlwraith and Jardine blind-sided him with that placement of Australco stock. Looks as though he's lost control, but my bet he's taken a huge junk of that placement and hidden it in some offshore account. He'll make a fortune if it continues to run, but on the other hand he'll go down the tubes if the rumours I've heard turn out to be false. No story for me there Springer."

"Listen O'Grady, I'm offering you a story that will not only make the front page of your rag, but will be a major item on every newspaper nationwide."

"What's the guts of it?"

"Make a time and place on Sunday morning and I'll give you the whole box and dice."

"Too late then. I don't work Sundays. I want it now."

"Then, you've just lost the story of your career to the opposition."

"If it's that good, there's got to be something in it for me. You want my help because I've got the readership and influence, and that's what you're after, isn't it?"

The journalist's brain hurried on, excited at the thought of something really big in the way of news. "This is an exclusive isn't it? You can jam it if you're intending to give it to other papers."

"It's yours O'Grady, and yours alone."

"I repeat then, there's got to be a slice in it for me."

Winton whistled softy through his teeth. "You certainly have gone the full circle O'Grady. I can remember when you portrayed yourself as being squeaky clean. At least you were never brazen enough to ask for a backhander."

"I've got older and wiser about cunts like you Springer. The crusading spirit left me years ago when another kind of spirit took control. No one's going to look after me in my old age except myself and that's what I intend to do from now on."

"We'll come to a satisfactory arrangement. It all depends on how much enthusiasm you want to put into writing this exposé."

"You must stand to make a bundle out of whatever it is?"

"Not really. Let's just say I want to see a few people hurt. One of them you'll be delighted to inflict considerable pain on."

"I'm starting to get interested. Make it Sunday morning at my place."

Winton jotted down the address. Not the most desirable of suburbs but close to all O'Grady's haunts.

"I warn you Springer, this had better be good. I hear you and Morgan have been getting really close of late and I bet I won't have to dig too deep to find some shit."

"As I said O'Grady, the story will warp your tiny mind. See you Sunday."

27

The next call took a little longer to get through. It was early evening in Sydney and two hours before the market opened in London. Harvey Roach came on the line, his polished English always appeared to adopt an effeminate tone. However, he was an astute, hard-nosed broker not to be taken lightly. Winton had made money on some of his recommendations and lost on others. A brief mention of gratitude may be exchanged when it came to the gains, but as to the losses there was no compassion or expressions of regret. It was business with no liability implied or accepted. Both understood the rules.

"Winton, good to hear from you. I say, that's interesting news about Australco. The stock took a hit after the placement, but it's bounced back. What's going on? Rumour has it something big's in the offing."

"Yes, it's very interesting Harvey, but I'm not altogether comfortable with anything that has the smell of Miles Morgan about it."

Roach laughed. "I've already spoken to Miles. He told me to get set and he's never let me down to date. There's going to be a major announcement next week."

"Sell ten million for me Harvey. I've had them a long time and they owe me money."

"Delighted. I say, you don't know something you should be telling me, do you? I don't want to get caught up in something a little suspect."

"I thought you were a broker, not a trader Harvey?"

"I'm a jobber Winton. I make markets and I think I'll do very well in making the Australco market today. Your line of stock will certainly cover many of the orders I have already. You don't have anymore, do you?"

"Let's see how you do with the first line. I'll hunt around in the meantime and see if I can get you some more. Phone me back when you've got rid of the first lot."

"Sell at best?"

"Yes Harvey. I don't need to tell you how to play the game. It's running market so I know you'll get me the best price."

"I'll try. I'll phone you back when the market opens."

Roach was one of the best jobbing brokers in the City. Winton knew he would not wait for the market to open, but would be on the line offering tranches to his best customers.

Winton had laid the plan carefully. Sell a line and get the broker excited about handling more. Selling the whole line at once would alert suspicion in the broker's mind. Who was selling? Why was he selling? Did he have the physical scrip to cover the stock he was selling, or rather short selling? Winton knew he had the advantage. The stock was in strong demand and he calculated Roach would be phoning for more after he had quickly offloaded the first order.

The strains of Puccini's immortal Madame Butterfly drifted through the apartment. He did not enjoy cooking for himself and the steak had been tough and overdone. However, the bottle of red was in contrast. It was smooth, with a fine bouquet and the translucent ruby red which was the trademark of the particular vintner. He glanced at his watch. London had been open for ten minutes. If Roach did not phone back within the half hour his plan would have failed. He would be forced to phone another broker. The move would lose its edge however, as the news a parcel was being offered through another broker would create instant suspicion. There were no secrets in the share trading game.

The strains of the music were interrupted by the foyer intercom chime. Annoyed at being disturbed he got up to answer the door.

She looked beautiful. The hair, the makeup and the outfit were stunning.

"Are you going to invite me in?"

"Marty Carlin, you are beautiful. It's my delight and pleasure to see you."

"I'm not disturbing anything, am I?"

"No, not now. I just threw the girl I had in here over the balcony, so it's okay for you to come in."

"You really are the biggest bastard I've ever met. You've completely ignored me. Why should I have to come crawling back to you?"

"The door is still open my dear. You may walk straight back out and nothing more will be mentioned about you crawling in here."

The blood rose in Marty's face, but Winton smiled as he took her arm. "If on the other hand you'd like to listen to Puccini and join me in a glass of wine I would be absolutely delighted." He pulled her towards him and kissed her full on the lips. "You're gorgeous, but I think I've said that already."

Marty threw her arms around his neck and passionately returned the kiss. He realised his feelings for her had not diminished. He was in love with her despite his efforts to resist. The phone broke the moment.

"Do you mind Marty, I'm expecting this call?"

"Let it ring. It's after working hours anyway."

"Can't do that. It could be another of my girlfriends. I'll put her off until tomorrow night," he mocked as he strode towards his office. Underneath he was annoyed she had turned up without warning. Tonight of all nights. It would not take her long to get the drift of what he was up to.

"Pour yourself a drink. I won't be a minute." He closed the door and picked up the desk phone. It was Roach. He felt a surge of elation.

"I've moved that line Winton. I'll take as many as you've got left." Winton could sense the excitement in the broker's voice. Gone was the humourless approach to business.

"I can let you have another ten mill."

"That's one hell of a line Winton. You're not shorting are you? I mean, you have the stock to cover the trade don't you?"

"No, I'm not short selling Australco." He raised his voice without realising it. "And yes, I can deliver the ten million shares."

"Steady on old chap. I just wanted to make sure everything was on the level. No problem moving the line, but it's just that I'm putting a lot of my clients into the stock, and I don't want to find out on Monday morning there's something damaging I should know about."

"Have I ever let you down in the past Harvey? Isn't my word as chief executive of Roma Oil good enough? If you don't want to handle the business, or any other business I put your way, I'll go elsewhere."

"No need to raise your voice at me. The stock is as good as sold. I'm taking them firm as of this moment."

Winton hung up and smiled as he pounded one hand into the other. The mock anger had worked.

"What are you looking so supercilious about?" Winton was looking at Marty's expression as he entered the lounge again.

"That was a bit of heavy short selling, wasn't it?"

"How do you know I was doing that?"

"Those walls are a lot thinner than you think, and you have a habit of raising your voice without being aware. Come off it Winton, I know short selling when I hear it."

"Well, what of it?" Winton adopted an offensive stance as he refilled his glass.

"Nothing normally, but you used your title to whoever you were talking to and we both know you've been fired."

"News travels fast."

"It certainly does when you're standing in the doorway listening to it. Dad didn't realise I was there."

"How is he?"

"Okay, but Louise had to calm him down. I thought he was going to have another stroke, he was so worked up. You took it too calmly. He expected you to fight back."

"I'll choose the terms and grounds on which I fight. I wasn't going to pick an argument with a sick man."

"He means it you know," Marty said with a shocked look. "About you being finished."

"I've got no doubt about that. I've been with Sam long enough to know he means what he says. On the other hand he could have just been blowing off steam."

"Why are you short selling Australco?"

"That's my business. I don't have to account for what I do in my own time."

"You're a deep and devious person Winton. I know you're up to something with Miles Morgan. I don't really know what it is, but I have my suspicions. As long as it doesn't hurt Dad or reflect on Roma Oil, I won't mention the subject again. Now, can we forget I ever challenged you? I came over here for some pleasant company."

"And for some loving?"

"Particularly for some loving. I do love you Winton."

"You know, I was thinking the same about you. Why don't we get married?"

She jerked up straight and looked into his eyes. She was pleading he was not being flippant again. Satisfied, she nestled back into his arms.

"I would like that more than anything."

"On one condition." He felt her stiffen slightly.

"And what might that be?"

"That you become a wife and mother. You resign your position from Roma. I don't want you bringing home work or discussing the company with me over dinner."

"I just can't leave Dad high and dry. He depends on me," she protested.

"Rubbish, the company operated fine when you weren't here, and it will operate just as efficiently without you."

"Do you mind if I don't tell him for a few days? I want to break it gently."

Winton shrugged off-handedly. "Suit yourself, but don't leave it too long or I might change my mind."

"I just can't walk out on Dad like that. Be reasonable."

"You said you loved me."

"You know I do."

"Well, the choice is yours. Either you're married to Roma and your father, or you're married to me."

"What if Dad offers you your job back?"

"I don't need the job or your father. We'll have plenty of money to start afresh somewhere."

Marty nervously played with the dress ring on her finger. "You've stunned me Winton. It's all happened so fast. You know I'll do as you ask."

The phone rang and Winton did not bother to take it in the study. It was Harvey Roach confirming the sale of the entire line.

"You look like the cat that's swallowed the canary as well as the cage," Marty remarked as he put down the phone.

"I feel very happy Miss Carlin. I've made a very good trade in London. I'm about to settle a few old scores and make a pile of money."

"Is money and revenge all you think about?"

"When you've never had money Marty, it gives you the warm glow of security when you do have it and as for revenge, yes it does give me satisfaction."

"You realise Dad can't do without you Winton. He's often said that to me. I bet he tears up your resignation on Monday."

"I've been fired and won't be in the office on Monday. Instead you and I are going to be married. I don't like the thought of long engagements. How does that suit you?"

Marty threw her arms around his neck.

"Steady on. Let's plan the honeymoon. Why don't we go up to the Barrier Reef. I've got a feeling it will be in the news next week. I've got a place at Shute Harbour in the Whitsunday's so we'll go there. Have you ever been scuba diving?"

Marty was not really listening. The tears of surprise and delight were still flooding her emotions.

"We'll look at the outer reef, do a bit of sailing and fishing and diving from my cruiser."

"I'll have to tell Dad."

"Like hell you will. On Monday we get married and in the afternoon we leave on our honeymoon. Scribble your father a note and tell him you've eloped with one of his former employees."

Marty skipped around the apartment, lost in the world of excitement. "This place isn't big enough, and besides it will be dangerous for the children. It's too high up."

Winton laughed. "We've only been engaged two minutes and already you're organising my life. This apartment will do nicely for at least a year. Besides, I'm attached to it. Why don't you just bring the kids home on weekends?" He ducked as the cushion flew over his head.

"Winton Springer you're a chauvinist and completely self-centred. I love you desperately and I hope I've made the right decision."

"Never thought I'd wind up married to the boss's daughter, let alone being married."

"Now you've proposed it's too late to back out."

"We'd better celebrate then." Winton fetched a bottle of champagne and crystal flutes.

"How am I going to keep this from Dad? I can't possibly go home and play dumb all weekend."

"Stay here. Go back on Sunday night and pack your bikini. That's all you'll need on your honeymoon. Come to think of it you won't even have that on most of the time."

Marty took the champagne and curled up on the sofa beside him. She felt warm and secure and intensely happy.

28

Winton slowly cruised looking for the address. It was one of the oldest and shabbiest neighbourhoods in Sydney. Rows of small terrace houses, the hang-out of prostitutes, pimps, addicts and pushers and myriad petty criminals who clung to the city fringes. He found the address and parked. A couple of grubby and morose looking kids were sitting on the front step.

"O'Grady live here?"

One of the kids leaned out of the way and pointed up the flight of stairs behind him. All that remained of the carpet was the threadbare backing. The smell was of any old house suffering from decay and pollution. He climbed the stairs and moved along the corridor looking for the numbers on the doors. O'Grady's was the last. He knocked and waited for an answer. There was no sound as he tried again. He put his ear to the door and could hear belaboured snoring. He knocked louder and a head poked out from an adjacent doorway.

"Go in, the door's never locked. He's drunk again." The head disappeared just as quickly as it had emerged.

Winton twisted the handle and pushed it open. The stench of stale air, alcohol and cigarettes was overpowering. He followed the sound of the snoring. O'Grady was cast diagonally across the bed clad only in boxer shorts. Some humans certainly lose their dignity, Winton reflected as he shook the sleeping figure. O'Grady grunted and resumed snoring. Winton picked up a half empty bottle of beer and poured the contents into the sleeping man's mouth. The liquid was sucked into his lungs as he came awake with an explosive coughing fit and struggled to sit upright. The next instant he was wide awake staring malevolently at his aggressor.

"Oh, it's you." O'Grady heaved himself off the bed and walked into the tiny kitchen. The fridge door opened and closed and he appeared again with a bottle of beer in his hand.

"Okay, you've got a story to tell me Springer, so let's get on with it."

"Aren't you going to take notes?"

"Listen." O'Grady pointed the neck of the bottle towards him. "I've been in this game for more than thirty years now. I could quote you verbatim next week what you're going to tell me now. The body mightn't be too healthy, but the brain's still okay. However, in this instance I suppose I'd better be careful." He reached into a drawer and pulled out a small voice-activated recorder.

"Not on your life O'Grady," Winton protested. "I'm not going to speak into that thing."

"No problem, I'll make notes in shorthand." O'Grady picked up a notebook and rummaged for a pencil.

Winton began to relate the story as the journalist prowled around the room grunting now and again. He became increasingly agitated with excitement as he listened. The foul smoke of the cigar he had lit pervaded the room. He giggled now and then and rung his hands in glee.

"Arthur Stillmore. That greedy old sod has been on the take for years, but no one's been able to pin anything on him. And you say this is the name of his company and bank account off-shore?" Winton had handed him a copy of McIlwraith's notes.

"That's Stillmore's lawyer's writing. Neither will be able to deny it."

"This is dynamite. He'll have to resign and it could even land the old thief in jail. I'll bet the tax investigators will start crawling all over his returns when they read this. He's busted, that's for sure. And you say Morgan subscribed for half of the placement through various nominee accounts? He's awash with the stock. When this hits the streets in the morning he'll be down at the pawn shop hocking the family silver. Tell me how C.T.Yong's connected with this?"

O'Grady listened intently as Winton relayed the details. He laughed like an excited child. He could see O'Grady had bought the story. It was the scoop of his career, the story every press-man dreamed about.

"You've set them all up, haven't you Springer? I'll bet you've sold a shit load of Australco stock, and you're going to short it all the way down. You stand to make a fortune and watch as a few enemies and past friends go down the gurgler."

The smile on Winton's face was all the confirmation O'Grady needed. "Jesus, they're going to do their shirts when this hits the fan." O'Grady began to hurriedly dress. "There's just one vital matter to address Springer and that's my fee. As you can see from my surroundings, my needs are rather simple, but they are constant. Shall we say ten thousand for the job?"

"You rank yourself very highly don't you? I could get the story run for nothing at any of the morning papers."

"You could Springer, but then you would be deeply involved, wouldn't you? You'd be quoted as the source and that wouldn't do at all. Okay, it's such a mind blowing story I'll do it for half that."

"No," Winton replied flatly.

O'Grady looked at him with anguish. He was torn. He had to print the story. It was just too good to miss. His mind was churning. "Fuck you Springer, I'll do the job for nothing. I should've realised I couldn't trust you."

The facts of the story were whirling around in his brain. Already the opening paragraphs were complete as the whole damning treatise unfolded on the yet unprinted page.

"I'll give you twenty thousand to do the job."

O'Grady let go of his trousers and clutched the end of the bed as he studied Winton's deadpan expression for any deceit.

"I'll give you half now and the rest on Monday. Meet me at the Piano bar in the Wentworth."

O'Grady was transfixed as Winton took the bundle of notes out of his satchel and tossed it on the bed. He only looked up when he heard the door close. Gingerly, he reached out and picking up the money, flicked it with his thumb to ensure it was in fact all banknotes. He stripped off and laid his best clothes on the bed. He placed the money on the hand basin shelf and watched it as he showered and shaved. By the time he had dressed and tied his shoe laces the story was written and complete in his mind. He combed his thinning hair and studied himself in the mirror before picking up his laptop. He slung a small carryall bag over his shoulder containing the bulk of the money and the few possessions he had decided to retain. With a final glance around the room he quietly opened the door with a smile on his face. He knew what was about to happen. Generally he dreaded it, but now he was relishing the moment.

Immediately, a door further down the corridor opened and a woman stood with her hands on her hips.

"Ah, Mrs Ryan, the top of the morning to you."

"Shove your top of the morning baloney O'Grady. Where's my rent?" The cigarette hung out the corner of her mouth. A red scarf was tied over the top of the head to hide the thinning red hair. Her apron covered a simple faded floral shift. The ensemble was completed with worn lambs-wool slippers on here scrawny legs. Pay up or be tossed out in the street was written all over her face.

O'Grady pulled a bundle of notes out of his pocket and peeled off a few. "There's your rent Mrs Ryan and a generous tip to cover the cost of cleaning my room. I'll not be returning to these charming surroundings."

She stood open mouthed as he patted her on the cheek. "Goodbye, you charming dear sweet lady." The smile disappeared off his face as he reached the top of the stairs. "I shall miss looking at your raddled old dial." O'Grady was gone before she could recover to answer the insult.

They were married late on the Monday morning. There were no family or friends present, just the celebrant and a couple of registry office staff as witnesses. The ceremony was short and devoid of any onlooker emotion. The couple were finally pronounced man and wife and they signed the register.

"Winton I'm so happy. If only Dad and Alex could have been here."

He put a finger on her lips. "That was part of the deal, remember? No relations."

She nodded and took out a handkerchief. Winton took it from her and gently wiped away the tears of joy.

"Shall we go?" He offered his arm and led her out of the dingy surroundings and into the brilliant sunshine of the busy square. The Moreton Bay fig trees were alive with the sound of birds. It was as though they had just burst into song for the happy couple. Winton took a deep breath and took in the air. It was a magnificent day in a magnificent city. He had been up since dawn studying the early editions of the Financial Daily, and O'Grady's syndicated column in other newspapers.

The journalist had excelled himself. It was not the usual expose' guardedly written with the thought of possible defamation actions that might follow. It was a masterful vivisection carried out by a professional pathologist. The corpse was putrid, but this inspired rather than deterred the brilliance of the investigation. It was surmounted by a clear file photo of the whole Australco board plus Miles Morgan clearly featured. Alongside was an archive photo of a somewhat furtive looking Arthur Stillmore being heckled at some obscure political rally. Rage and frustration was clearly evident. A damning account of his offshore banking details bore witness to his corruption. The financial pages were equally as startling with photos of C.T.Yong complete with graphs and charts of his octopus-like corporate holdings. Nothing had been left out with the allegations being specific and not implied. O'Grady had obviously received complete editorial and management support for his scoop. Winton searched rapidly for any mention of his name, but there was none. O'Grady would be collecting the remainder of his money.

"Let's walk." Winton took Marty by the arm. "I have something important to do."

Marty could not help but notice the first edition newspaper billboards, or Winton's smug expression as he furtively glanced at them as they walked past.

They were already screaming the headlines. *"Stillmore resigns. Secret bank accounts. Financier in trouble. Investigation into Australco. Stock suspended from trading."*

"I've a strange feeling you had something to do with that. Did you?"

Winton dodged the question. "It's all of their own making and greed and it couldn't have happened to a nicer bunch of people."

"Do you always get up at one in the morning to get the early editions?"

"I thought you were asleep."

"On my wedding day?"

"You'll just have to get used to my habits. I do strange things at strange times."

"I intend to change that."

"I think not." He guided her into a store and purchased a small carry bag.

"What do you want that for?"

"It's for my toothbrush and budgie smugglers. I told you we'd be travelling light on our honeymoon."

"What are budgie smugglers?"

"That will be revealed, but they match your bikini when we go swimming."

Marty was puzzled by the remark as Winton steered her into a bank and told her to wait while he got some cash for their holiday. He handed over a cheque to a familiar teller who looked closer at the amount and then up at Winton. "I take it you want this in cash Mr Springer?"

"Yes please." He did not bother checking each bundle before stuffing it into his bag. Finally, with a nod and smile he slung it over his shoulder and casually walked out of the bank with Marty on his arm.

"Are you intending to take that on our honeymoon?"

"No." Winton laughed. "I've got to pay a debt before leaving town. Let's go to the Wentworth and have a drink to celebrate. I feel like the best bottle of champagne they have."

The piano bar was busy. He glanced around and saw O'Grady sitting at one end of the bar with what looked like a glass of orange juice, obviously a vodka and orange. He immediately saw Winton and began to move, but the imperceptible shake of Winton's head checked him.

Winton guided Marty to a lounge table. "While I order the champagne my love, why don't you phone Sam. Don't tell him why you're here unless you have to. Just tell him to come. I think it will be a real surprise for the old boy."

The look of joy spread over her face. Winton went over to the bar and placed the bag in front of O'Grady. The man was immaculate. He was brand new right down to his shoes.

"The new O'Grady I see."

The journalist beamed. "Yes Springer, the completely new reformed being, and off the booze. However, the fags I can't do without."

"I'm impressed. I hope you keep it up." Winton noticed O'Grady's eyes tracing the rectangular impressions of bundles of cash in the bag.

"It's all there, ten thousand as promised, plus another ten as a bonus. Can I buy you a drink?"

"No thanks Springer. The contract is complete, so I'll be on my way."

"I'd like to thank you for a marvellous job. I regret I played the dirty trick on you all those years ago. I hope this makes up for some of the pain."

O'Grady shook his head as he took hold of the bag. "I never forget things Springer. This was just a business arrangement and nothing personal, but if I ever have the opportunity to get you in my sights, I'll not hesitate to take you apart as well."

He slapped the journalist on the shoulder. "I'll remember that, and now I really think you should put that money in the bank. It's a lot to be carrying around in the street."

O'Grady did not answer as he slid down off the bar stool and walked away.

Winton was lost in thought when he saw Sam walk in and wave to Marty. He stopped dead when he saw Winton walking towards him with a bottle of champagne and three glasses.

"What's going on here?"

"Come on Dad, sit down and have a glass of bubbly with us."

"And what are we celebrating?"

Sam was confused. Marty had told him about a meeting she was having with a very important person, someone she wanted him to meet. It was a matter of great urgency she had said, because he was about to leave town.

Winton carefully poured the three flutes and raised his in salute. "We're celebrating our marriage this morning Sam." He waited for the explosion, but it never came.

Instead Sam broke into a broad smile as all their glasses met. He reached over and pulled his daughter to him. "You secretive devils. I wish you every happiness, but why didn't you tell me?"

"We thought there might have been some opposition. You see my husband got fired last week and I'm about to resign from Roma as part of our wedding agreement. And those factors don't add up to making a good impression on a new father-in-law, do they?"

Sam gripped Winton's hand in a crushing shake. "Congratulations. I couldn't be more happy for you both." Sam was looking right into Winton's mind. "By the way, wasn't that O'Grady leaving as I walked in. Odd that you two should be in the same bar. I thought it would have been too up-market for that disreputable soak to be drinking at."

"If you've got the price Sam, you can drink anywhere you choose."

"I want you to reconsider your resignation." Sam abruptly changed the subject. "I acted hastily and irrationally. I just can't let you go Winton."

"I'll give it some thought, but I think it's about time I made the break."

Sam held up his hand. "Don't make that decision now. Leave it until you get back from your honeymoon and we'll talk it over then."

"We're going up to the Whitsunday's for a week or two. I want to show Marty the splendours of the Barrier Reef."

"And the reef is certainly in the news today. Did you hear Stillmore's resigned in disgrace?"

Winton nodded. "It was inevitable from what I saw in the papers."

"O'Grady really did a number on him. Someone really gave him the inside track running."

Winton met the gaze of the knowing eyes. "And Morgan?"

"Right in the hole in a big way from what he was screaming at me when he phoned looking for you this morning. I told him you no longer worked for Roma and it was none of my business, whatever it was he wanted to discuss with me. Do you know what he could have been on about? Hasn't he phoned you?"

Winton shrugged as he topped up their glasses. "My phone's off and will be for the next couple of weeks."

"Australco stock tanked on the market this morning. It's already down to a quarter of its closing price here on Friday and still falling. It will fall through the floor when London opens tonight. Apparently the Federal Government has put the heavies on New Guinea and the licence areas have been cancelled. There'll be no drilling anywhere near the reef, that's for certain. I made a few enquiries and I've no doubt Morgan is about to go belly-up. He apparently bought a big line of Australco through London on Friday night. He must have gambled every penny he could beg, borrow or steal to take up the placement as well as buying in the market. He's got to be down the drain for at least a couple of hundred million, probably more."

Sam missed the glance Marty flashed at her husband who was trying to keep a straight face. The exercise was almost complete.

Marty had listened in fascination when Winton had picked up the phone again after talking to Roach. He had sold twenty million shares he didn't own through Roach. He then sold and another ten through another London broker. He was comfortable Morgan had bought both trades. He would cover his short position by buying back the plunging stock to cover his short position when the news broke. He calculated he would make at least two dollars a share, possibly more like three if his plan went without a hitch.

She was about to confront him with it when he put down the phone, and cut her off with a cold look. It was none of her business and she did not pursue it, but it left her with an uneasy feeling about Winton. Did she really know him that well?

"Marty won't be going back to work." Winton watched as the remark sank in.

Sam's mouth hung open in pain and shock "What do you mean, won't be coming back? Marty you've practically taken over financial control of the company. I can't do without you."

Marty took her father's arm. "Winton thinks it a good idea if we both make a clean break, and I agree with him."

"I'll make you an offer you can't refuse," Sam blustered. "Oh, what's the sense in talking to you now. Just go on your honeymoon and we'll discuss it when you get back."

Sam raised his glass to them and drained it. He kissed his daughter and shook Winton's hand once again.

"You look after my girl," he said as he got up and walked away. The slight lean to one side was the only visible legacy of the stroke. To them he suddenly seemed an old man. They sat in silence lost in thought.

"Shall we fly commercial or would you prefer to take your chances with me as pilot?"

"I like living dangerously, so I'll go with you."

"Settled then. We'll take my plane and do a little sight seeing along the way. I'll show you the north."

"I don't care where we go darling, just as long as I'm with you. Just don't take me where there are too many people."

They made to leave. Marty looked around. "What happened to your bag?"

"I paid a debt."

"You gave it to O'Grady. It was a payoff, wasn't it?"

"It's none of your business Marty," he replied icily. "It doesn't affect you, Sam or Roma Oil, so don't ask me about it."

Her look of shock was only momentary. "Of course dear. I don't care what happened to the money. This is the happiest day of my life and I don't want anything to spoil it."

29

The flight to Brisbane took a leisurely two days with an overnight stop in between. "We could have done that in an hour by commercial jet." Winton banked gently as he lined up for the final approach to landing. Marty did not reply as she leaned back in her seat and closed her eyes in contentment as the aircraft touched down. He taxied to the small aircraft apron and pulled up in front of the fuel pumps. Marty sat in the shade and watched him as he fuelled the wing tanks.

"I'm going back to work for a week or two when I get back Winton. There's one job I have to finish before leaving."

"What's so important?"

"I've got to investigate the manager who runs the Roma operation up here. Unless I miss my guess he's been systematically milking the company for a number of years. It could run into very big money."

Marty did not notice Winton's involuntary jolt as he let go the trigger of the pump and the metallic clang made her look up. The sun was in her eyes and she did not see the fleeting stunned look on his face.

"What's his name? I keep forgetting it."

"Who are you talking about?"

"The fellow who runs the equipment supply and purchasing department here?"

"Reed. Burt Reed. You suspect he's been up to something and stealing from the company? I don't believe it. He's been with us since the beginning."

"I haven't really pinned it down to him yet, but he must know something about it if he's been with Dad that long. Something really smells about Mr Reed."

"Have you spoken to him?"

"No, at the moment I'm just putting together the pieces of what I think he's been up to. When I have enough evidence I'll surprise him and run a snap audit. However, I want to be absolutely sure of my facts before I front him."

"What do you think he's been doing?"

"I suspect Roma has been invoiced for goods and services never received."

"Do you think he's acting alone?"

"Could be. Maybe I should be investigating you," Marty laughed. "After all, you're the person directly responsible for him."

Winton glanced at her as he screwed the cap back on the tank. He could see it was not an accusation, but a throwaway line. A casual remark made in jest.

"And what are you going to do about Reed if he has got his hand in the piggy bank?"

"I'll leave that to Dad. I know he'll come down hard on whoever's involved. He'll bring in the police. It will take another week of checking back through old invoices and bank records to find what I'm looking for."

"And what are you looking for?"

"Phantom companies darling. I suspect large amounts of money have been paid to non-existent companies. First I want to check the status of the companies and directors and then I want to match the invoices to the bank accounts where the payments ended up."

"I certainly haven't suspected a thing. I just can't believe Reed would be involved."

"You probably wouldn't. You're not trained to forensically audit books like I've been. I know all the lurks, because I trained in the home of cooked books, the good old US of A."

"How long have you been working on this?"

"Only a week or so. At first I thought it was just a clerical error, but when I started to check back I found the errors were rather constant. Very clever mind you, but nothing can remain hidden if you start to pick up the threads of a trail. Have you ever heard of a company called Harriman Equipment Supplies?"

"Sure, that's one of the main suppliers of our drilling and support equipment."

"Only half right. There's only one Harriman company on our books, but we've received and paid a string of invoices submitted in the name of Harriman Equipment Consolidated. An apparent simple clerical error overlooked and compounded by the accounts department, and somehow it got past the auditors. Maybe they are one and the same company, but I've got to check."

"As long as we got the goods I can't see the problem. It probably is just a clerical error."

"That's what I've already set in motion. I'm tracking as to whether we did actually receive the goods invoiced. It shouldn't be too hard. And another thing I found strange when I started to delve into it was that Harriman Equipment Supplies operates out of Western Australia but Harriman Equipment Consolidated has an office in the same building as Reed. Indeed on the same floor. The odd thing is, no one answers the phone and there's no email address listed."

"That is odd," Winton replied as he commenced draining a little fuel into a jar checking the fuel for water. "I can see why you want to follow it up. Perhaps it would be best if Reed was fired and the office up there closed. I personally would like to see a lid kept on it. It certainly reflects on me, but I don't think Sam would be impressed to see it in print the company had been ripped off for years by a trusted employee."

"No, that's not good enough. I want to nail this guy and any-one else in this scam with him."

Winton gave her a quick glance, but she was not looking at him. "I can't just walk away from it. I calculate the crime runs into the millions of dollars. You can't just sweep that under the carpet. As a director you're bound by law to bring it to the attention of the authorities."

Winton was wiping his hands on a piece of cloth as he bent down and kissed her. "You're getting uptight honey. We're on our honeymoon, so promise me you'll forget about it for now."

It was late afternoon as they approached Shute Harbour and the Whitsunday Islands. The thick palls of black smoke and dense orange fires dotted the landscape. The ferocity of the fires formed a false sunset as the licking tongues of flame and smoke haze cast an eerie light on the horizon.

"They're burning off the sugar cane before harvesting it," Winton replied in answer to Marty's look of wonderment. "It gets rid of the top foliage, leaves and rubbish. We may have to dodge some of the smoke and strong updrafts as we approach the airfield, but there's no danger."

"I'm not worried darling. It's so beautiful and breathtaking. It's like another world up here."

"I can see you're a country girl at heart." Winton cut back the power and lowered some flap for the approach. "You like the wide open spaces?"

"I love the country, but I can't stay away from the city life for long. I miss the crowds, the smells and hustle of the city."

Winton pointed to north-east and out to sea. "Those are the Whitsunday Islands. Captain Cook named them because he arrived here on Whitsunday 1769. He noted in his log how beautiful they were. It's a beauty that hasn't faded."

The islands dropped from view as he set the plane down smoothly and taxied towards the solitary airport building.

"That's Jimmy Bruce the local taxi driver and the man who looks after my house." Winton indicated the big red-headed figure leaning on the bonnet of his car.

Marty laughed when Winton introduced them. "What are you laughing at lass?"

"That beautiful accent of yours Jimmy."

The Scot's eyes twinkled as he picked up their bags and put them into the boot of the car. "I think you've got a lovely accent too lass. Irish isn't it?"

"No, of course not. I'm American," Marty replied in mock horror.

"That's what I mean lass. I've noticed Americans sound just like the Irish when they're in a crowd. An Australian or Scot will always stand out, no matter how long he's been away from home, but put an Irishman and American together and you begin to realise where the American accent originated from. It's all those Irish immigrants who flooded into America during the potato famine. It's a fact."

"And you think it's rubbed off on me?"

"Aye, I think that's for sure," Jimmy said as he opened the door for her.

"I've been keeping the place in good order Winton. You haven't been up for a fair while. Are you just on a fleeting visit, or are you going to stay for a few days?"

"We're on our honeymoon Jimmy, so I don't know how long we'll be staying."

The Scotsman nearly drove off the road in his excitement and profuse congratulations. "Well, I knew she would always be a beauty, the one who finally got you I mean."

"She didn't catch me Jimmy. I caught her."

"Och man, that's what they all say, but you forget laddie, that's the female way. You chase them until they finally catch you."

They laughed and continued to joke as they drove away from the airfield. Marty studied the lush countryside. The burnt sugar cane emitted a sweet sickly smell. It was an all pervading aroma.

"Why are the houses all up on stilts?"

"They're too lazy to mow their lawns up here lass. They build the houses on stilts so they can get a view."

"I thought that was sugarcane?"

Winton suppressed a laugh and pretended to look out the window while Jimmy's face showed no sign of emotion.

Marty grinned. "I can see I'll have to keep my mouth closed and try and work things out for myself."

"That's right lass. Just remember that everything is twice as big up here. The toads grow the size of dinner plates. The lizards grow a couple of metres long and the snakes are deadly. Just get into bed at night and stay there lass. Hold onto your husband and don't let him go."

"You're full of it Jimmy Bruce."

The Scot emitted a rumbling belly laugh. "That's what I like to see, a woman with a bit of spirit and not afraid to answer back. You picked a good one Winton. Where did you find her?"

"I wanted to keep it all in the family Jimmy. I married the boss's daughter."

The taxi swerved as Jimmy looked around in surprise. "Well I never. You're Sam Carlin's daughter?"

"You seem surprised?"

"Yes, I am lass. I didn't know Sam had a daughter. I worked for Sam for years and he never let on."

The house was set in lush tropical gardens. Palms dotted the carefully tended lawns. Clinging bougainvillea draped from the forest surrounds, spilling the grandeur of a purple and red mantle of colour. The immense Poinciana trees spread their giant umbrellas of dazzling red flowers. The native Kauri pine thrust its glistening bulk skywards as if the richness of the earth was hurrying it on. The view was spectacular with the complete vista of the Whitsunday's stretching across the horizon before them. Jimmy Bruce quickly said his goodbyes, ignoring their pleas for him to stay for a drink.

"Oh, this place is beautiful." Marty gazed out over the panorama from the veranda.

"Yes it is, but I don't come up here as often as I should. I always think it's too far, but when I do make the effort I wonder why I don't make the break more often."

The moon bathed the sea in a vivid, but necromantic beauty.

"Is it yours?"

"No, it's ours." Winton put his arm around her shoulders. "I bought it years ago. I hardly ever use it now, but I'd never sell it."

"It's an absolute paradise. I could happily live here."

"Paradise is an ephemeral dream." Winton leaned on the rail and vacantly stared out to sea. "We all long for paradise and when we achieve it, we realise it's only fleeting. It becomes boring very quickly and the brain atrophies after a while in paradise. Great place for a short holiday to get away from it all, but it lacks any continuing stimulation whatsoever."

Marty caught the edge of dullness in his voice. "You don't sound happy darling. Something's on your mind, isn't it?"

Winton laughed it off. "You stay here and take in the view while I make us a couple of drinks."

Marty jumped as a crash of thunder followed by a flash of lightning lit up the sky. The dark clouds blotted out the moon and the cool rain began to fall. Ten minutes later it had stopped and as if on cue the moonlight glistened from the patina of moisture covering everything. A gentle breeze sprang up.

"Air conditioning works well, doesn't it?" Winton handed her a tall cocktail glass. "It rains every evening at this time of the year and then the breeze springs up immediately after, cooling the whole place down."

"I still think it's paradise."

"Oh, I didn't say it isn't. I just observed paradise can be boring. Cheers, and to us," Winton said as they touched their glasses.

Marty gagged as she sipped the drink. "What's in this?"

"Fine local proof rum. Only just a dash though, to give it flavour and strength. Do you like it?"

"What else is in it?"

"That my darling is a closely guarded secret that's been in my family for generations."

"Rubbish. You just grabbed anything handy and threw in a twist of lime and a cherry, didn't you?"

"My lips are sealed."

"I think too much of this and both our lips will be sealed. I must say, it's quite nice though," Marty giggled.

"It's just the first nip that takes your breath away. After that it becomes completely painless. Anyway, enough about the drink.

What would you like to do tomorrow? There's fishing, sailing, walking, swimming, scuba diving, bird watching or just plain relaxing."

"Let's take it as it comes. I would like to do a bit of everything including scuba diving. Will you teach me?"

"It's easy. Just a matter of common sense and learning not to panic. Know your limits and no harm will come to you."

"No sharks I hope?"

"Don't even think about them. They're too well fed in these waters to bother anyone. It's only in the colder southern waters where people get taken. There are more deadly things up here like crocodiles, stone fish, and box and irukandji jelly fish."

"Stone fish?"

"One of the deadliest creatures known. Looks exactly like a piece of dead coral until you step on it. Excruciating pain and an agonising death."

Marty shuddered at the thought. "What were the other things you mentioned?"

"Crocodiles, but they're mainly around rivers mouths and estuaries. The box jelly fish is deadly with tentacles twenty and thirty metres long and likewise the smaller but equally as deadly irukandji. They shoot thousand of tiny poison barbs into you if you brush against them. You don't swim on the beaches during summer. It's just too dangerous. It's okay to swim out on the reef, because there are no stingers out there. The danger is along the shoreline of the beaches. I saw a child stung by an irukundji once. It was as though someone had given him a savage hiding with a whip. Great welts all over his body. Even in death his face was a rictus of torment and agony. It is an everlasting memory. This place is beautiful, but death lurks everywhere if you ignore the warnings. Despite all the nasty things, including deadly brown and taipan snakes, it's still a place of unparalleled beauty."

"I can see you love it."

The breeze rustled the tops of the palm trees. It was a call for the myriad of night life to break into a gentle hum of activity.

"Yes, it's so peaceful. We must come here more often."

Marty leaned against him and he put his arm around her as they both looked out at the sea.

"You don't know how happy I am darling. I hope it lasts forever."

Winton kissed her behind the ear. He took her hand and led her into the cool moonlit bedroom.

The days drifted by. They swam and frolicked in a large natural waterhole fed by the permanent fast flowing stream on the property. They took it in turns to rub sun screen oil on their naked bodies as the sun turned their skin into a soft golden brown. Some days Marty would wander off by herself while Winton engrossed himself in a book. She spent hours walking along the shore line in her sneakers to avoid the sharp coral detritus scattered over the beaches. She was never bored by the repetition of marine life. The tiny fish trapped in rock pools by the outgoing tide, flashed a kaleidoscope of colours as they dashed under the ledges to escape the shadow of danger she cast over their habitat. The writhing sea snakes revolted her, but they had a natural beauty in all their various bandings and shades.

"I've just about seen everything along the shoreline and in the rock pools. I would like to do something different tomorrow? Aren't you sick of reading?"

"We'll do just that." Winton shut his book. "But we'll need an extra hand for what I have in mind. We'll go into town tonight and catch up with Jimmy Bruce as I want him to stock up and drive the boat. Do you feel like a steak while we're in there?"

"Big, thick and rare," Marty replied licking her lips. "I would like a change from fish and lobster and more fish."

Winton was quiet as they drove into town.

"You're thinking about business aren't you?"

"Why do you say that?"

"Because whenever I walked in and you weren't reading, you had a frown on your face just staring vacantly into the distance."

"I plead guilty. Although I've been sacked, I never stop thinking about the company. After you, Roma is everything to me."

"It's Reed isn't it?" Marty knew she was right. Several times when she came back from walking she heard Winton on the phone. He broke it off hurriedly when he heard her footsteps on the veranda. "Why are you so concerned about him?"

"I can't come to grips with the fact Reed may have been stealing from the company all these years right under my nose. You're right. I am responsible. How many years do you think it's been going on for?"

Marty shrugged. "I suspect for some considerable time."

"In that case I think it would be better if I just fired him. We don't really want our dirty laundry hung out for the whole financial world to see. It would not be a good look. If the losses haven't been picked up by the auditors before now I suggest we get rid of Reed and sweep it under the carpet. Have you mentioned anything to Sam about this?"

"No, I don't have all the evidence yet. No use upsetting him until I have all the facts."

"Are you really sure Reed's been up to no good, or is it just an educated guess?"

"I'm almost positive and I believe my audit will reveal it. The whole scheme is just not that clever, but it would need someone higher up to be also involved to....." Marty trailed off lost in thought.

"I could even be suspect?"

Marty laughed. "I can't imagine you being involved darling, but I suppose you'll have to explain as to how it's escaped your attention for so long."

"Who else knows about this? Have you discussed it with anyone else in accounts?"

"No, I've kept it to myself." She suddenly gave him a penetrating look. "You know something about this don't you?"

Winton shook his head. "No, I don't, but I want it wrapped up quickly for the sake of the company and for my reputation."

Marty nodded in silent agreement. It had suddenly burst on her like a bomb Winton could be involved. After all, all the major purchasing contracts would have certainly crossed his desk for approval. This crime didn't involve petty service invoices. It involved heavy machinery and equipment all tied to supply contracts. He had to know about it. He had to be in it with Reed. Her emotions bubbled uncontrollably to the surface as the look of horror crossed her face.

"You are involved Winton. My God, I've been too blind to see it until now." She did not have to look at his face to confirm she had guessed the truth.

He slowly turned towards her. "What are you going to do about it?"

"I, I don't know. What will this do to Dad? He trusts and loves you like a son. This will kill him. What else are you hiding from me?"

"I don't have any other secrets Marty. The business with Reed was like all crime. It starts small and then grows bigger. Let me explain. Sam never gave me more than wages when I first started and I guess I thought I was entitled to more."

"My father gave you everything you ever wanted. He told me he picked you out of nowhere on an outback road."

"Sam gave me very little in the early days.

"Did you always steal from him?"

"Sam gave me a small wage to start. He doesn't know to this day it was I who was responsible for getting the company off the ground. If I hadn't pulled off something behind the scenes he would have been broke within a couple of weeks. He was in serious trouble."

Marty flared in indignation. "What are you talking about? Dad found the oil and gas and floated the company."

"That's only partially correct." Marty remained silent while Winton related the story of their meeting and his links with O'Grady and Bain and the background of those early days.

"You father didn't even give me a single share to say thank you when Roma joined the stock exchange lists. I got a job, but I felt I was worth much more than that. It was my initiative that got the whole ball rolling. I do have a stack of share options and an excellent salary, but I've made the bulk of my money from share trading."

"And theft."

"That hurts Marty, but yes you are correct. I'm a thief. However, I want you to forget it ever occurred. Neither of us works for Roma any longer and it will never come to light. I retired Reed last week so the circle has closed."

"What am I to do? You are my husband and I love you dearly." Marty leaned back in her seat. "Oh, what a way to start a marriage."

"I could give it all back."

"How? You can't just make a bank transfer and say here's the money I stole. Winton, what have you done? As you say, the only way out is for me to drop the investigation. I don't think anyone will ever uncover it and I could make sure it remains that way." She trailed off as the realisation struck her. "That's why you wanted me to resign wasn't it? You knew your crime was about to be uncovered?"

"No, that's not true. I had no idea you were investigating Reed until you mentioned it while we were refuelling in Brisbane. I do love you Marty. You must believe me."

"And I love you, but I simply don't know what to do."

The back of his hands were cold and prickly. "Why don't we go to Europe for a few years? I've always wanted to travel. I made millions on that Australco deal so we have no worries about money."

He did not see the kangaroo until it was too late. Marty screamed and threw up her arms in front of her face as the animal hit the bonnet with a sickening thud and smashed through the windscreen. Glass showered all over them as Winton fought to bring the car under control. It was pure guesswork as he could not see the road as he pulled up in a screech of tortured rubber. The roo was half in the vehicle and he threw himself across Marty to save her face and upper body being torn apart by the powerful hind legs of the thrashing animal. He opened the door and pushed her out onto the verge. The lifeblood of the kangaroo pumped from severed arteries as he threw open his door and pulled the animal clear of the bonnet. Marty watched stunned in shock.

"That animal could have killed us."

"We're certainly lucky." They watched the death throes of the roo. Its beautiful soft brown eyes gradually went opaque as the life disappeared. "Plenty of people have died hitting roos. I'm sorry Marty, I just wasn't paying attention."

Marty was still in shock long after he had cleaned away glass and wiped the blood from the inside of the car. They slowly made their way into town and parked alongside Jimmy Bruce's taxi outside the hotel.

"Come on, I can see you need a brandy." Winton helped her out of the car. A stiff brandy took the shake out of her hands and a steak settled her stomach. She began to join in the conversation with the other drinkers. A new face in town meant someone to talk to and Jimmy Bruce introduced her to all his friends. However, Winton could see her focus was not really on making new acquaintances and he did not feel like it either. Jimmy Bruce had been watching them.

"Come on you two, I'll drive you home. I'll put your car into the repair shop in the morning."

Hardly a word was spoken as Jimmy pulled into the driveway of the house. "I'll be down at the boat early to check it out and then I'll be back to pick you up." He had tried to strike up a conversation, but could see neither Marty nor Winton were connecting. They had other things on their minds and went silent himself.

"Thanks Jimmy, we'll see you in the morning."

Jimmy Bruce nodded and drove off. They slowly walked up the driveway bathed in the light of the full moon. "You engineered that whole business with Australco the other day, didn't you? You know, Dad knew about your meetings with Morgan. He wondered whether you were selling out on him?"

"Morgan is the last person on earth I'd sell out to."

"But he did have something over you, didn't he?"

"Yes, he did."

"What was it?"

"I don't want to go into that tonight. Just let it alone for awhile. I will tell you another time."

Marty flared. "I'm your wife Winton, and I want to know now."

"That's correct, you're my wife and not my bloody confessor."

The remark stung as she swung around and faced him. "You'd sell my father down the drain too, wouldn't you? Nothing stands in your way if you want something. You're a confessed thief, and probably a couple of other epithets of liar and cheat also fit the profile."

Winton gave her a mocking smile that infuriated her. She lashed out delivering a slap that hit his eye as well as his cheek. The pain in his eye was excruciating as he lashed out with a backhand delivered with its full force. She skidded along the moist grass and lay there in a daze as he stood over her.

"That's the last time you ever do that, do you hear me?"

Marty did not answer as he dragged her to her feet and shook her violently. "Do you understand?"

"Stop it please Winton," she pleaded bursting into tears.

"Do you understand?" Winton pushed his face hard into hers as she felt powerless in the grip of his iron hard hands.

"Yes, yes, yes." Marty sobbed as all the defiance receded. He was too strong. She was repulsed, but completely within his physical and mental domination. Her subconscious told her to run now and get as far away as she could. She looked into his eyes searching for some compassion. His face had softened, but the penetrating blue eyes had an unwavering look of purpose. She resigned herself to the meaning, the message uncanny. Winton realised she was reading his thoughts and let her go.

Winton felt her get into bed. Her naked body curled up next to him, but he made no move to respond. Finally, he turned and began to stroke her face. She took his hand and kissed it. "Have you ever killed anyone Winton?"

"That's a crazy question. Go to sleep."

Their arousal was slow, but mutual some time later. Neither had been asleep, just drifting in the twilight between full consciousness and disturbed awareness. The communication was electric. He touched her satin soft thigh and ran his hand gently over the base of her flat stomach and into the moist cleft between her thighs. In an instant she was in his arms moaning softly with desire. He gently entered her, as she thrust her thighs hard into him to accentuate the rhythm.

"Please don't kill me darling," she moaned softly. "I love you, I love you. I'll do anything you say."

Winton realised the voice was unconscious, a cry from the depths of her mind. They parted and she was immediately asleep. He rested on his elbow and studied her naked form in the moonlight flooding the room. Beautiful and exquisite. He leaned over and gently kissed her on the neck. The skin glistened with perspiration. He lay back and stared at the moon through the open French doors.

30

The next instant he was wide awake, every nerve taught as he searched for the unseen danger. There was no danger, only the morning sunlight beaming across the bed. Marty was gone.

"Good morning darling," Marty beamed as she bounced into the room holding a breakfast tray. "I've brought you freshly ground coffee, orange juice, toast and marmalade. You really do have a well stocked fridge and pantry. I could have chosen from four marmalades. Do you have a fetish for them?"

The previous evening had been forgotten. It was as though it had never happened. Winton pulled up the sheet to cover his nakedness.

"Yes, it's about time you put that thing away." Marty laughed at his sudden show of modesty.

Winton felt haggard as he ran his hand through his hair and over his stubbly growth of beard. "Just let me have a quick shower and shave. We'll have it out on the balcony."

The shower was refreshing, although not cold due to the ambient temperature. A shave and the imagined muzziness began to disappear. He threw on a robe, walked out onto the balcony, and drew in lung-fulls of tropical air. Marty looked and smelled radiant as he leaned down and kissed her.

"You must have got up early?" Winton slowly sipped his orange drink and studied her face for any sign of strain, but there was none, just the complete look of serenity.

"I've been up for hours. We're going diving today or had you forgotten?"

"I must say I had, but Jimmy isn't here yet?"

"Jimmy was here an hour ago. He left his car for us and said he would walk down."

Winton took a sip of coffee. "Why didn't you wake me? We could have been out on the reef by now. That man costs me money to hang around."

"Is that all you think about? Money?"

"Is there anything else?" His brain tried to stop his mouth from uttering the question, but the words spilled out. He quickly rounded the table and embraced her. "I'm sorry darling, I didn't mean to say that. I'm sorry. Please forgive me."

"You meant exactly what you said Winton. I understand you completely now. Remember though, I do love you and nothing will ever change that, no matter what happens."

Her eyes were soft and penetrating as he tried to avert the truth they elicited, but there was no hiding it. His expression of guilt was only momentary, but she had seen it.

"We'd better go then," she said bouncing to her feet. "It's a beautiful day and I don't want to miss a moment of it."

They parked the car in the shade and she held onto his arm as they walked down towards the jetty. The lorikeets in their brilliant green, yellow and blue livery chattered and darted from tree to tree in their loving pairs. Small multi-coloured finches flitted across the forest floor searching for tiny insects. The leaves of the palms looked as though they had been polished with oil.

"I know why you bought this place. It's so beautiful and peaceful."

"It certainly is a beautiful part of the world, but I've been thinking, perhaps I should sell it."

"No chance of that now. I own part of it and it's not for sale," Marty laughed in banter.

"Yes, that's correct. Everything I have is ours now. It's just that it's hard for a single man who's used to thinking singular, adapting to the plural."

"I know. However, I don't know how I'll ever get used to signing my name Martine Springer. It's been Carlin for so long."

The shout from the jetty brought them back to the present.

"C'mon you two love birds, the day is almost over."

The twin diesels throbbed away in harmonic balance as they stepped aboard. The tone of the exhausts burbled and died as the boat gently rose and fell with each swell. Jimmy Bruce manoeuvred away from the jetty and slowly pushed the controls to half. Once clear of the other pleasure craft he opened to full throttle. The craft quickly rose to the plane, and headed out between Hook and South Molle islands. They all sat across the comfortable settee on the flybridge.

"Where do you want to go?"

"You're going to show my wife something really spectacular Jimmy, so lead on."

The Scot cast a sidelong glance at Winton and grinned as he swung the wheel a few points to port. "I was hoping you would say that. You're in for a real surprise Marty."

"Is this something new and unique you're going to show me?"

"Certainly is lass. The very edge of the reef on the ocean side. Absolutely beautiful. Five fathoms on the inside dropping away to three hundred on the outside. Untouched and as yet undiscovered by other divers. The marine life has never been disturbed. You'll see red coral and fish the colour of which you can't even imagine. You might even see Old Bob."

Winton nodded. "And the prostitute as well."

"Did I hear right? Who or what is the prostitute?" Winton's eyes twinkled with merriment. "You'll see, you'll see."

"Tell me what it is, please?"

Winton shook his head. "No, it wouldn't be an adventure then. Anticipation is nine tenths of any adventure. Take that away and there's nothing left."

"And Old Bob?"

"Put it this way," Winton went on. "The prostitute is on one side of the reef and Old Bob is on the other, but I don't think she's the reason he's been hanging around there for the past hundred years."

"Sounds frightening." Marty shuddered as she imagined the unknown.

"Yes, when I first saw him he scared the daylights out of me lass. Absolutely huge, but docile although I imagine he could swallow you in a single gulp."

Marty tingled with excitement and fear. The danger enticed her.

"Have you dived with tanks before lass?"

"Not deep, but Winton has been giving me lessons, and I've been down to fifteen metres."

"Old Bob is around that depth, but Winton is an experienced diver so you'll be safe if you stick close to him."

"I feel I could dive deeper Jimmy."

"That would be very foolish. You can get overcome by narcosis very easily. You confuse up with down and before you realise it, you're in serious trouble. And never tempt the bends. If you go too deep you can get nitrogen in the blood coming up again in a hurry. Play it safe lass and don't leave Winton's side."

Winton stood up to climb down from the bridge. "I'll leave you two to talk. I want to go and check the gear, and put my head down for half an hour."

Marty closed her eyes and let the wind play on her face. She was shaded by the canopy of the bridge.

"Have you known Winton long Jimmy?"

"I suppose I have lass. I worked on rigs with him and your father and then I retired. Winton bought the place a year or so after I moved here."

"But do you know him very well? There's a difference between an acquaintance and really knowing someone, isn't there?"

"Yes, there is lass. I can see what you're getting at, but I really can't comment. Winton is a very solitary character. Keeps very much to himself, but then so do I. We've had some great times together, great times, but I can't say I've ever got into his mind, if that's what you're getting at?"

Marty did not reply immediately. Jimmy went back to studying the sea.

"But you seem to be very friendly?"

"You make very few friends in life lass, but you make a lot of acquaintances. However, I would class Winton as a real friend."

"Would you trust him with your life?"

Jimmy Bruce slowly turned with a querulous look, but she was leaning back with her eyes closed, and he could not read any meaning into the question.

"Yes, I would lass."

"That's very interesting," Marty replied without opening her eyes. "Would you do something for me?"

"Certainly lass, if it's within my capabilities."

Marty handed him an addressed envelope. "Would you put this in the post for me tonight?"

"Certainly, but you know if you leave it in the letterbox at the front gate it will get picked up in the morning. Just remember to raise the flag on the box so the mailman knows there's something for him to collect."

"I know that Jimmy, but I would like you to post it for me when you get back into town. It's just a business matter I forgot to attend to, and please don't mention it in front of Winton. I promised I would not think or talk shop while on our honeymoon."

"You can count on me lass. I'll make sure it goes in tonight's mail."

Jimmy thrust the letter into the folds of a map and caught Marty's look of concern. "Don't worry, I'll not forget it. I've got a brain like an elephant when it comes to detail. I never forget anything people tell me, or ask me to do. It's a hobby of mine, recalling people's names and subjects they're interested in."

Marty laughed. "You sound as though you're going to offer to read my palm next."

"There's no need to read palms lass. People carry all their expressions and thoughts in their faces. I don't have any trouble working out what people are thinking."

Marty raised an eyebrow and studied the man's serious face for any sign of duplicity.

"And what am I thinking Jimmy?"

"You're wondering whether you've married the right person. You're worried about something and you're hiding something. Although you're unaware of it, I've been watching and studying you closely."

"I think you're seeing things when there's nothing to be seen," she replied with a twinge of uncertainty.

"Am I?" Jimmy watched as the nervous twinge turned into a fleeting look of annoyance. "I'm sorry lass, I've gone too far. Please forgive me."

An hour passed before Jimmy broke the silence. "We're almost there lass."

Marty followed the pointing finger and could just make out the break in the continuity of the almost calm water. She was excited as she watched the ribbon of breaking water grow larger and longer as they drew nearer.

Jimmy Bruce throttled back and slowly motored to within metres of the coral outcrops. He followed it for a distance, intently watching the various shapes of the formation glide by before pulling the motors back to idle and climbing down to let go the anchor. There was nothing to suggest the position was any different to the kilometres of coral they had already travelled along.

"How do you know where you are?"

"Instinct I guess lass." Jimmy stood looking down into the clear water making sure the anchor was not dragging. Satisfied, he cut the motors. The silence after the vibrating hum of the engines was complete. Not a sound. Not even a gull broke the complete silence. The vessel sat in a sea of tranquillity. Small ripples generated by the occasional zephyr disturbed the surface momentarily before it settled back down again to its oil-like appearance. The heat of the morning sun beat down.

Winton emerged from the cabin and scanned the horizon. Finally, he looked at the reef and at Jimmy to confirm they were at the right spot.

"Do you want to dive now Marty?"

"That's what we came for darling. I can't wait to see what you have in store for me."

Half an hour later they were both standing on the marlin board as Winton gave a thumbs-up and leaned back into the water. The next instant Marty appeared beside him. The sound of their own breathing was all they could hear. Winton checked his watch and depth metre and kicked for the bottom. Marty noticed the stark contrast to the inshore reefs. The coral heads were a bewildering contrast in formation and shape. The marine life was more plentiful and spectacular in design, shape, size and contrast in colours as the fish appeared to ignore the intrusion into their domain. The parrot fish in its brilliant blue and green hues sucked here and there at a coral head before passing on with a flick of its mantel-like fins. The large coral trout appeared and looked inquisitively before slowly swimming off without further interest or fear. The tropical crayfish could only be distinguished because of its long feelers waving around the entrance to its hiding place. The green and yellow moray eels drifted back and forth in front of their lairs as if bending to some rhythmic tidal force. Each had a cave or well guarded crevice from which it evilly watched for any small morsel that should venture too close. The indescribable array of life danced before Marty's eyes as they slowly swam through the forest of coral heads. The giant anemones opened like enormous flowers, only more beautiful, their colours ranging from dark hues to the most delicate of gossamer shades. The tiny yellow-faced anemone fish darted in and out of the refuge of the flowing tentacles, impervious to the poison barbs which immediately immobilised an unsuspecting pursuing prey. It was a contrast in complete harmony. In return for safety the tiny fish lured larger prey into the tentacles of the rapacious anemone.

Marty felt a tug on her arm and uttered an unheard cry of fear as she saw the giant cod at her side, its body covered in potato size discoloured blotches in contrast to its silvery skin.

It had plucked at her arm with its huge lips. It backed off gently with its pectoral fins slowly beating in reverse. She looked around for Winton who was only metres away grinning from ear to ear. She struck out for him with a strong kick with the inquisitive cod keeping pace. Marty swam straight into his arms, the look of fright clearly visible through her mask. The giant fish swam up to Winton and gently nudged him. Marty shuddered. Its mouth was enormous. It looked as though it could swallow her in a single gulp.

Winton ran his gloved hand along its back and slowly pushed it away. Satisfied it was not going to be offered any food, it gave an idle flick of its tail and drifted off. He signalled Marty to follow him. She could see by his look and gesture she was about to be shown one of the star attractions of the dive. They were descending through two crevices in the coral when Winton suddenly stopped and let himself drift down. Marty laughed as it became clear as to what she was being shown. It was the prostitute, a giant clam more than two metres in length. The usual rich green and blue hues of its flesh were replaced by the most delicate pink as they melded towards the centre of the animal. The outer lips were a delicate red. The single valve in the centre of the pink flesh opened and closed rhythmically as it filtered the micro organisms of marine life and the outer lips synchronised with the movement. Marty was in no doubt what she was being shown. It was the female form with genitals fully exposed. Elongated growths of coral spread out from underneath the shell to form legs. The mutant trunk was an illusory creation of darker corals with gently flowing masses of seaweed partially obscuring the large brain coral that formed the head of the prostitute.

Winton touched her arm, pointed at his watch and then to the surface. It was all too short an experience for Marty, but nearly forty five minutes had elapsed. She was lost in wonder at the alien world she had just experienced, the ultimate beauty created by an unseen hand and, as yet unspoiled by the trampling of predatory man. They broke surface and Jimmy Bruce helped them aboard.

"What did you think of her lass?"

"She looked beautiful, but very lonely. I don't think she's getting too much business."

Jimmy Bruce looked bewildered for a few moments and then broke into a loud guffaw.

"How old would you say she is?"

"I'd say anything from two to three hundred years lass. Could even be older. Some of the smaller ones closer inshore have been around since James Cook named this area and that was more than two hundred years ago."

"I'd like to go down again this afternoon. It's so beautiful I could spend all day down there."

"You should see as much of it as you can lass. If they ever let those bloody oil companies in here they would stuff the place up with one good spill."

Winton realised the comment was aimed at him. "There are pros and cons to that argument Jimmy. Oil spills do have a short term effect on the ecology, but nature is all conquering in the end. If it came to economic necessity and this was the last place on earth likely to contain oil, it would be drilled without hesitation."

"That really would disturb me if it was ever proposed," Marty chipped in.

Winton shook his head. "You're already involved in the business of oil exploration. It wouldn't matter if we were drilling in the middle of the Simpson desert, we'd be destroying some of the ecology."

"Don't talk rubbish. There's nothing out there but spinifex and sand."

"You're so wrong Marty. The deserts team with life just as the sea does. The deserts are beautiful places and in a way I prefer them to the ocean, but if world population and demand keeps growing like it is, I believe this place with be eventually targeted. It would be a tragedy of course, but it's inevitable."

"You know darling, that's the first time I've heard you express concern about the environment."

"Don't get me wrong. I'm a pragmatist. I care to the extent I think it's a pity man would be driven to such desecration, but if the demand arises I'd be just like the next man. It's akin to tempting a confirmed socialist with an easy fortune and watching him change instantly into a confirmed capitalist."

"Would you like to dive with me lass?" As if on cue Jimmy Bruce stepped into interrupt the deepening philosophical conversation. He had seen the look of adoration in Marty's eyes when it appeared her husband might have a soft spot after all, but the look was turning into one of disappointment as she began to understand his true philosophy on life.

"I'd like that Jimmy." She looked to Winton for approval, but he was already smiling broadly at her happiness.

"You go my dear. I'll prepare lunch while you two are down there, but don't make it more than half an hour. I don't want you too tired to look at Old Bob."

He sat watching as the rippling concentric rings of spent air slowly rose and burst on the surface above the descending couple. The trail of exhaled bubbles diminished and then disappeared as they swam down and away from the boat. He started the compressor and refilled the bottles he and Marty had used. The two-way radio on the bridge broke into life to disturb the serenity of his surroundings. He climbed to the fly-bridge to turn it off. As he reached over his arm knocked against a bundle of maps which fell to the floor. He bent down to pick them up when the protruding envelope caught his eye. The name of the addressee was familiar as was Marty's handwriting. The letter was addressed to her father. Winton pushed it back into the folds of the map and dropped it on the console. Probably a letter she had written recently and forgotten to post. He searched his memory, but could not recall her sitting down to write anything since the start of their honeymoon. The letter had to have been written last night. She had obviously given it to Jimmy Bruce to post, but why? Winton pulled it out and turned it over in his hand. He held it up to the light, but the writing was obscured. Premonition told him exactly what it contained and in anger he hooked his finger under the flap and savagely tore it open. The shock struck him as he read the four pages of close handwriting. It was a complete indictment of both Reed and himself. It pinpointed him as the brains in the fraud. It gave estimates of the theft and the progress of her investigation. It was obvious she had not discussed the matter with anyone. He felt the blood pounding through his head as he sat down heavily on the skipper's seat and re-read the letter again and again. The opening and closing paragraphs chilled him as his mind raced back over the past few weeks and then over his entire life span. He felt the presence of acute danger, his life was about to disintegrate, but as yet it was only pieces of paper in his hands. No one knew the contents except the writer and himself. He looked at his watch as he stuffed the letter into his back pocket. It was only ten minutes before they were due back. He hurriedly looked at the piles of maps and sounding charts scattered around the bridge and shuffled them as though a gust of wind had dislodged them. He threw the paper map that contained the letter overboard and prayed it would quickly sink or drift away. He hurried down to the galley and began setting lunch. It was the usual Jimmy Bruce gourmet spread for hungry divers, right down to a chilled bottle of champagne which was purely for effect as they would not drink it while diving. It was to be opened back at the jetty when they sat around discussing the day's highlights. Marty was laughing with excitement as she pulled herself up onto the marlin board. She looked at the smorgasbord in surprise.

"Is this another of your talents darling? I didn't know you were such at artist with food."

"Not me, it's all Jimmy's doing. I merely laid it out."

31

The early afternoon drifted on as they lay about and slept off the effects of the meal. It was Marty who finally decided she had relaxed enough and wanted to see the other side of the reef. "Is it as scary as you make out?"

"No," Winton replied. "It's merely the fact you can't see the bottom. There's no floor to reflect the light so the water looks black."

Winton helped her on with her bottles and weights and Jimmy Bruce checked them both before they went over the side. Winton led a circuitous route through the reef before eventually going over the ocean side. He peered down into the darkness. The sound of his breathing completed the monochrome of dread he felt. Marty was close to his side and he could see from the constant heavy stream of bubbles she was breathing heavier and deeper. The morning dives and the lunch were beginning to exact their toll. Fatigue was obvious and he should not have let her dive any more today, but he had no choice. He accelerated down and then levelled off. The object he was looking for would be lurking very close to a rock ledge, almost concealed in the total darkness by the overhang of the outcrop. He saw it and grabbed Marty's arm. It was several seconds before her eyes adjusted and she saw what he was pointing at. She realised she was looking at a fish about five metres long with a girth to match. The huge ugly mouth opened and closed slowly as it warily eyed the two intruders. Either of them could fit into its giant maw. Marty felt panic rising as she watched mesmerised as the fish began to move slowly towards her. Its size became more evident as its enormous bulk approached. She reached out and gripped Winton tightly as he slowly backed away. The groper sensed the filtered light falling on it from above and backed under the ledge again for safety. This giant of the fish world had survived for so long because of extreme caution.

Winton sensed the effects of narcosis taking over as Marty's hand slowly released. He watched fascinated as she drifted down and away from him. The narcosis had set in within seconds as she fell into unconsciousness. She was swallowed by the blackness as the lead weights took her down. The air in her tanks was sufficient, but it was already too late. He waited five minutes, unhooked his weights and kicked for the light above. The cruiser was a hundred metres away when he broke surface in the brilliant sunshine, shouting and waving at Jimmy Bruce. He saw him jump into the tender and come speeding towards him. Winton felt Jimmy's strong arms pulling him over the side as he retched sea water out of his lungs.

"Where's you wife man?" Jimmy Bruce had a wild and frantic look on his face.

"I lost her. She was beside me one minute and when I looked around again she was gone."

Jimmy did not answer as he swung the tender around and headed back to the cruiser at maximum throttle.

Winton scrambled aboard and quickly strapped on a new set of bottles, as Jimmy did likewise.

"You look exhausted man and you've taken in some salt water. Don't do it. If she's anywhere near Old Bob, I'll find her."

Winton ignored the plea as they both went over the side together. An hour later they surfaced, realising it was fruitless. Her tanks would be empty and she was gone. They sat without talking as they studied the surrounding sea in the hope she had released her weights and her body would float to the surface. They both knew there was no point in radioing for help. They were not looking for a living soul, they were looking for a corpse.

"I can't understand why you let her do that dive Winton. It was plain to see she was tired. What were you thinking man?"

Winton just shook his head without answering. He was relying on his look of despair. The sun was dipping when Jimmy Bruce fired the engines into life and ran for home. Winton said nothing as he went below and poured himself a tumbler of brandy. He read the letter again, crumpled it and went out onto the stern. He turned and looked up, but Jimmy Bruce had his gaze fixed straight at the oncoming shoreline. Slowly Winton let his fingers loosen and the wind plucked the pages away in a second. He watched them settle on the foaming wake before being enveloped in its tumbling embrace and disappear. He stood looking back at the reef as he remembered the look of serenity on her face. It had been so simple.

The two police were standing on the pier as they tied up. Jimmy Bruce had radioed details of the accident. The older was a sergeant, lean and weather beaten with the laconic attitude of nothing fazed him. The younger was a constable with an eager look of achievement written all over him. They stepped aboard and the sergeant pulled out his notebook and began writing down the details of what had occurred. An hour later he was finished.

"I'll have to get signed statements from you both. There will be a coronial enquiry. We'll have to make a search at first light in the morning so we'll need your boat."

Winton nodded his silent approval. The young constable had been watching him intently the whole time without speaking, but suddenly broke in. "You're an experienced diver, aren't you Mr Springer?"

"Yes, I've been diving for a number of years."

"And yet you failed to notice your wife was suffering the effects of narcosis?"

"I don't know if she was suffering from narcosis. I only assumed that was the case because I started to sense the early warning signs. I turned to take her to the surface, but she had simply disappeared."

"Wouldn't you agree it was negligent for such an experienced diver as yourself to subject a novice to such a potentially lethal condition, as has obviously proven to be the case?"

"Nothing's been proven constable," Winton snapped. "Narcosis is symptomless to the person who's unaware, because the brain is switched off. It's akin to dying of the cold. You just simply fall asleep. It's only an experienced person who can read the danger signs fast enough."

"You've just told me you were experienced, and yet you failed to protect your wife from the danger."

Winton felt his muscles tighten as his brain snapped back into focus. The constable was sharp. He would have to be careful with his answers. He was about to reply when the sergeant stepped in.

"I think we'll leave that line of questioning for the coroner, constable. I don't suspect any foul play. I believe it's a case of death by misadventure, and a degree of incompetence on Mr Springer's part. What do you think Mr Bruce?"

The Scot answered quietly, but firmly. "If I thought there had been any foul play Winton wouldn't be sitting here now. He'd be sharing the sea with that wonderful girl I had the pleasure of knowing for such a short period of time." There was no mistaking the look in his eyes as they bored into Winton's psyche.

The returned gaze was hard and resolute. Winton did not avert his eyes for an instant. He knew three people were watching him for the slightest sign of guilt. A nervous twitch of the eye or hand would have immediately signalled doubt.

Jimmy Bruce finally shook his head. "No, I'm sure it was an accident, but I feel guilty as I should never have let her get back in the water."

"I note the champagne. Had she been drinking?"

"No sergeant. As you can see the bottle is unopened. It was purely for effect until we got back here."

"We'll start a search in the morning and then we'll need statements from you both." The sergeant started to walk back up the pier accompanied by the constable.

"I'll stay and fuel up for the morning. Take my car, I can pick it up later."

"No thanks Jimmy, I'll walk. I want to think before I break the news to Sam. He recently had a stroke and this news is going to devastate him. Might even trigger another one."

Winton walked slowly along the pier in the falling light and watched as the tail lights of the police car receded. The night was overcast and clouds hid the moon. The dark form of a snake slid across his path. Winton picked up a rock and hurled it with blind fury at the disappearing reptile. Snakes gave him the shivers. So silent and so deadly.

The house was in darkness as he moved slowly through the rooms without turning on the lights. He picked up the brandy decanter and a balloon and placed them beside the phone. A thought struck him as he went into the den and began turning on the lights. It was not there and he searched through the drawers.

"What the hell did she do with it?" He was muttering to himself as looked out on the veranda table and then in the bedroom. He felt an eerie presence as he searched through her things. The bile rose in his throat as he smelt her perfume rise from the case he had just opened. He finally found what he was looking for in the kitchen. The pen and pad were on the table where she had left them. She had obviously written the letter while preparing his breakfast. She must have been up for hours as it was not a hastily penned letter. It was studied and careful. He held the pad up to the light at an angle and could clearly read the impression of the last page of the letter. He tore the pad into shreds and flushed it down the toilet, ensuring every segment disappeared.

The brandy slid down smoothly as he sat back and reflected on the whole day and particularly what he had told the police. His story could not vary. Satisfied, he finally picked up the phone and called Sam. It was Louise who answered. She was bright, but the tone in Winton's voice told her something was wrong.

"Get me Sam please Louise."

"He's been in bed for an hour Winton. He didn't feel well after dinner. What's the matter? Has something happened?"

Winton ignored the questions. "Get him now Louise. I don't care how sick he feels, just get him immediately."

It was several minutes before Sam came on the line. He sounded drowsy. "Hello my boy, what's the problem?"

"Marty is missing Sam. We went out diving and she just disappeared."

Winton let the silence endure until it was interrupted by the voice of a broken man. "When did this happen?"

"Early this afternoon."

"Is there any hope?" It was a plea, not a question.

"No Sam. We're going out early in the morning to try and recover the body if we can."

"She phoned this morning, you know."

Winton fought to contain the surprise in his voice. "She spoke to you?"

"No, I was in the shower and it wasn't until an hour or so later Alex remembered she'd called. I phoned back immediately, but there was no answer. I guess you'd left for the day."

"Did Alex say what she was phoning about?"

"He didn't take much notice, but apparently it was about a letter she was posting to me. Oh, my God ..."

Winton heard the phone clatter to the floor as the shock took effect. He heard Sam break into long heart rendering sobs.

He put the receiver down quietly and phoned Jimmy Bruce, telling him he would not join them on the boat, but would make an aerial search. The thought of being on the boat with the two policemen was not what he wanted to endure. It would be an entirely pointless search, but he had to go through the motions. The lead weights would ensure the body stayed on the bottom and the marine life completed their allotted task of cleaning up the remains.

The engine of his plane drummed in his ears as he flew up and down the reef a couple of hundred metres above the water. It was late morning when he noticed the cruiser turn for home and he did likewise. He landed and tied down the aircraft. He was about to drive through the town and home when he decided he needed a drink. He sat in an isolated corner just watching, but unseeing the replays of football games on the television.

The bar was almost empty except for the usual bar-flies crouching over their beers mumbling incoherently to one another when Jimmy Bruce entered, followed by the two policemen.

"Why didn't you come in and make the statement? We've been waiting for you." It was the young policeman, and he looked more accusatory than the previous day. "Mr Bruce has already completed his."

"I'm sorry. I've had other things on my mind. I'll drop in first thing tomorrow."

"Make sure you do. We'd like to ask you some more questions."

The sergeant nodded. "I'm sorry about your wife Mr Springer. I don't think there's any point in continuing the search, and obviously you didn't see anything from the air."

"Thanks for your concern sergeant. No, I didn't see anything and I agree with you, there's not much point in continuing. Can I buy you fellows a drink?"

The two policeman nodded, but remained silent as the barmaid pulled the beers and sat them down. She pretended to retreat out of earshot. It was general news there had been a death on the reef, but no one knew the full details.

"Did you happen to see a letter on the boat yesterday?" The sergeant did not look at him as he took a mouthful of beer.

"A letter?"

"Yes, your wife wrote a letter to her father and gave it to Jimmy here to post. He only remembered it this morning, but it wasn't where he left it."

"No, I haven't seen any letter. Why do you ask?"

"Are you sure you haven't seen it, or rather should I ask whether you have it, or have had it in your possession? Your wife gave it to Jimmy and you were the only other person on the boat." It was the constable who asked the question.

Winton realised the sergeant was not as benign as he looked. It was the old one-two trick played by policemen the world over. Patently obvious to some, but to most it was a game that went right over their heads. One would pretend to be ugly with the blunt questions and veiled accusations, then his partner would step in with the helpful advice and gentle manner in the hope of extracting the truth.

"I said I haven't seen it. Isn't that enough?"

"You've answered the first part of the question Mr Springer, but you haven't answered whether you have it or had it?"

Winton shook his head and looked angrily at Jimmy Bruce. "What the hell's this about Jimmy. What's so special about this letter?"

"I'm sorry Winton, but the sergeant wanted me to go over everything that happened yesterday. I'd forgotten about the letter until I recalled Marty had asked me to post it. She said she didn't want you to see it."

Winton laughed as he drained his glass and placed it back on the bar. "That's Marty. She was always thinking about business. I forbade her to even think about it while we were here, but obviously she thought something was very important."

"Jimmy says your wife appeared to be very agitated when she gave it to him. It would appear there was a bit more than business she was worried about. Would you have any idea of what she may have had on her mind?"

Before Winton could consider his answer, Jimmy Bruce joined in. "I did tell the sergeant she was extremely concerned I should post the letter and not tell you about it."

Winton held up his hand. "Don't worry about it Jimmy. I've nothing to hide. I didn't see the letter and I can assure you I had no knowledge of its contents. Let me buy you another drink." He reached into his shirt pocket and pulled out some notes. It was not enough and he reached into his hip pocket for more. He froze as his fingers closed around the money and the envelope of Marty's letter. He felt a cold bead of fear and sweat break out on his brow. He had disposed of the letter, but forgotten the envelope. Jimmy would instantly recognise the envelope and writing if he produced it out now.

"Would you lend me some money Jimmy? I haven't got enough."

Jimmy nodded and dropped a twenty on the bar.

"How long are you staying around for Mr Springer?"

"I'll take the boat out in the morning, do a final search and drop some flowers. I'll fly out for Sydney straight after sergeant."

The policeman downed his drink. "You'll be informed of the coroner's inquest. Don't forget to drop in and sign that statement before you head home."

Winton felt the inner tensions and danger ease as he watched the two policemen leave.

32

Winton sat in the huge lounge nursing the glass of scotch. He rolled the ice cubes around and chinked them against the crystal surface. The memorial service had been brief and Sam had asked everyone to come back to Roma. It was to be a quick drink to thank everyone for coming and to also lift the gloom. His outward grief was over and complete. He wanted to share the joyous moments of his daughter's life. He did not want pity.

Throughout the service Louise had felt his hand unconsciously grip her arm as his grief surfaced in spasms. After the service he took control again and moved away from her to demonstrate his independence.

Alex had not spoken to Winton since his sister's death. He had not even offered his condolences and Winton could sense something was stewing inside him. Now he was suddenly aware Alex was standing over him. He was drunk as he wavered on his feet.

"Well big man, did it go according to plan?" Winton looked shocked, but ignored he remark.

"You heard me you murdering bastard. I asked you a plain enough question."

"Go away Alex." Winton was trying to stifle his anger. "You're drunk."

"I may be drunk, but I'm not as drunk as I want to be." He staggered forward and grabbed both arms of Winton's chair for support. His glass shattered on the polished parquet flooring. Winton leaned back as the face stinking of liquor was thrust into his.

"You know how my sister died Rupert bloody Springer. You murdered her."

"Yes, she drowned." Winton was shocked by the sound of his Christian name after all these years. "That's already been established by the coroner and yes, I am to blame for my negligence in letting her make that final dive when she was already so tired."

"Well, the coroner didn't know all the facts, did he?"

Winton pushed Alex away forcefully. "Please go away Alex. You're drunk and I find your accusation particularly offensive."

Alex began to froth at the mouth as he staggered back. "Of course I'm being offensive. You were offensive to my sister. You murdered her."

Winton remained motionless as he fought for self control and smiled thinly as Alex pointed an accusing finger.

"Alex." The whole room froze as Sam shouted at his son. He was shaking with rage. Louise went to support him, but he shook her off as he advanced.

Alex looked around with a leer of pleasure and delight as he gained the attention he sought. All eyes were focused as he raised his accusing hand again and pointed at Winton. "You murdered my sister Winton Springer," Alex screamed at him. "I know it and you know it, but you've escaped because there were no witnesses other than yourself. You committed the perfect crime."

Winton bunched his fists and rose to his feet. Alex broke into a hideous laugh when he saw the look on Winton's face. "What, are you going to murder me now?"

Winton stopped and regained his composure. "I did not murder Marty. She was my wife and I loved her dearly. It was an accident and grief I'll have to endure for the rest of my life."

"You're lying. She phoned the morning she died. I took the call, but she wouldn't tell me what it was about. She said she was very worried something could happen to her. She said she had written a letter to Dad which would explain everything. She was right Springer, wasn't she? Something did happen to her. You murdered her. I don't know exactly how you did it, but I heard enough in the coroner's court to understand what happened. And what happened to the letter she wrote? It never turned up and yet the boatman said she had given him a letter to post, but then it simply disappeared."

"I'm quite aware of what Jimmy Bruce said at the inquest, but I saw no letter. And he did state it could have been blown overboard with some other maps which he had not secured properly." Winton replied quietly as he stood and took Alex's arm in an attempt to guide him out of the room.

Alex flung his arm away and moved towards the centre of the room again. "You're a liar Springer. We all know what Bruce testified to, but he was not asked to speculate on what might have happened. The coroner wasn't interested in hearing hypothetical theories. I've since talked to Bruce and he's of the opinion the only time the letter could have disappeared was when he took Marty diving and left you on the boat by yourself. That's when you found the letter, read the contents and decided you had to murder my sister."

Winton felt naked standing centre stage in the huge room with dozens of pairs of eyes fixed on him. It was an inquisition witnessed in silence by a stunned audience.

"I'm going to tell you one last time Alex. I did not murder my wife. I loved her. We'd only been married for two weeks. What possible threat could she have been to me to commit the crime you're accusing me of? What motive did I have?"

Alex hissed in his face. "You had a motive and it was contained in that letter. We'll never know the truth, but we both know you're guilty."

"The coroner made no such finding. It was recorded as death by misadventure. Now go away and sober up."

Sam Carlin had been watching the scene in horror and disgust. "Alex, stop this nonsense. Apologise or get out of my house now."

Alex swung on his father and grabbed the back of a chair to stop himself from falling. "Don't worry Pop, I'm going and I won't be returning. I realise I've been a hindrance ever since I arrived, someone to be tolerated, but given no responsibility and all because of him."

"You know that's not true." Sam was shocked by the accusation.

"It's true alright, but you're just too bloody screwed up with business to see it. You did the same to mother. You totally ignored her. She didn't die of a disease, she died of a broken heart."

Alex did not see the cane coming. Winton tried to block it, but it was too late. The heavy ebony stick caught Alex on the temple and he collapsed without a sound. Blood began to flow from the broken skin of the wound. One of Sam's doctors broke away from the crowd and knelt down to look at the wound. He rolled back an eyelid. The pupil was already dilating as concussion and shock set in. He felt for a pulse and then quickly loosened the tie to ease the pressure.

Sam stood over his prostrate son still shaking with rage and guilt as to what he had just inflicted. "What have I done Max?"

"Call an ambulance immediately. You could have quite easily killed him with that blow Sam. He's heavily concussed and his pulse is weak. With the amount of alcohol he's consumed he could quite easily die."

Sam let the cane drop to the floor with a grief stricken expression as he looked to Louise for support. He said nothing as the guests made their excuses and quickly faded away.

The siren of the ambulance grew louder as it approached up the rise and swung into the driveway. The two paramedics quickly took control and after checking the vital signs lifted him onto a gurney and into the ambulance.

"Will he be alright? He's my son."

"I don't know sir, but it looks as though he could have a fractured skull."

Winton stood by Sam's side as the ambulance sped away.

33

The plane rolled gently to the right as he watched the stark sandstone cliffs appearing to drift upwards. Five years ago he had watched them recede on an equally as bright day. The chain reaction of memories was vivid as the coastline came into clearer focus.

Why had he returned? The question had gone over and over in his mind during the long flight from Los Angeles. What force was dragging him back to see a man who had never really existed, a man to whom he owed nothing, who owed him nothing and was already dead?

At least he had been dead in his mind for the past five years and yet he was drawn by a timeless natural instinct to witness the final scene in the multi-act play called life.

Death was no stranger to Alexander Carlin, the dry scorched earth of Afghanistan would never dim from his memory. His father was now acting in that final scene. He could feel no compassion, but some of the bitterness of the years was fading.

The jet settled in on its final approach, the engines alternating between a high pitched whine and a dull murmur as the pilot maintained his flight path. The touchdown was the gentle thump as the weight of the aircraft settled onto its tires and the hydraulic rams took the full weight. As they taxied towards the

316

terminal Alex could feel the inner tension mounting. Thirteen hours ago it was a millennium separating them. Now it was less than an hour before he confronted his father again.

He followed the rest of the jet-lagged passengers as they walked the long corridors to Customs, the tedium of baggage claim and then finally out through the packed arrivals hall. He started to step around the faceless person blocking his way.

"Mr Carlin," he said as he reached for Alex's bag. "It's nice to see you again."

Alex's mind snapped back to the present and then back through the subconscious file to put a name to the face. He could vaguely remember the man as being one of his father's drivers. He started to reply, but the driver just nodded acknowledgement as he strode ahead through the automatic doors. The door of the Mercedes was open by the time he caught up.

"Mr Springer would like to see you right away sir." The driver glanced across at Alex as the car silently moved away from the kerb.

"Take me to the hospital."

"Mr Springer said your father is unable to speak, and he would like to see you first."

"Take me to the hospital now." The hard and flat monotone of the command was sufficient instruction to demand compliance.

Alex recognised nothing familiar about the surroundings, nor attempted to until the vehicle pulled up in front of the hospital half an hour later. The sudden jolt he was about to confront the last member of his immediate family opened a chasm of guilt and recrimination.

The foyer was full of flowers and the staff talked quietly. Their bright smiles and cheery nature belied the true nature of the place. It was a hospice for the dying.

"I'm here to see my father, Sam Carlin."

The nurse beckoned him to follow her down the hallway, her rubber soled shoes making the usual squeaking sound on the highly polished floor. She opened a door and peered inside.

"He's asleep Mr Carlin. He lapses in and out of consciousness, but he's in no pain. You can stay as long as you like." She departed without another word.

Alex pulled up a chair and studied the face of the man who was his father. He reached out and took the enfeebled hand. The skin cancers stood out clearly on the translucent skin, the dark purple whorls and blotches and angry proud scaliness signifying the legacy of years exposed to the sun.

The signs of the stroke were clearly visible with the left side of the face contorted and the mouth open to that bias. A constant dribble of saliva glistened to one side of his chin and down his neck where it disappeared into the open top of his pyjamas, the irreversible destruction of a once vital person clearly evident. Alex looked up to see the eyes open and staring at him. One was vacant and dead, while the other had a barely perceptible flicker of recognition.

"Can you hear me Sam?" He gently squeezed the hand as he searched for further life. There was no reply, but the slight movement of the decaying hand wrapped itself in a feeble movement around his. The eye went blank.

"It's no use, he'll never be able to talk to you again."

Alex did not have to turn to recognise the speaker. He knew the voice. It was as though she had only got out of his bed yesterday. He could smell the aroma of her as she moved into his line of vision on the opposite side of the bed. She was still a magnificent woman, and he knew she was one of the reasons why he had left.

"Hello Louise, you're still a stunner." He studied her beautiful form. Her fine aquiline looks had not changed. A little of the youthful suppleness had faded, but only a fraction. She was lithe and stunning, a magnificent throw-off of Mediterranean blood with enough power of presence to command the instant attention of any man. Every movement had poise and purpose. She was one lady who knew what she wanted and graduated summa cum laude from the university of carnal attraction.

"Thank you Alex." She studied him intensely. "Still the Alex Carlin I used to know visually, but I can see you've changed." Her eyes fell on the skin grafts on his hands as he made an involuntary movement to pull them away. Louise tossed her jacket over the back of a chair and casually studied the figure in the bed.

"How long has he been like this?"

"About two weeks. It's his third stroke in less than a month. The doctors say there's no hope, and it's only a matter of time before an aneurism in the brain bursts and it's all over."

He caught sight of the large solitaire diamond and wedding ring. "As his adoring wife you don't seem too concerned."

"Don't be a hypocrite Alex. I don't accept you can just blow in after all these years and pass judgement, or make any adverse comment on my conduct. You didn't expect me to pass up the opportunity did you?"

Louise noted the look of irritation on his face and intercepted his reply. "Everyone has to die Alex and don't give me any rubbish about suddenly feeling remorse. You came into his life for an instant, and then ran when he gave you your first hiding. Are you planning to stick around or are you leaving on the next plane?" She was in complete control of the situation and dismissed his obvious annoyance at her cutting remarks.

"Grow up Alex. Can't you see he's dead. He's breathing, but only just. His vital organs are shutting down, or are in the final moments of total failure. Sam always believed life is a survival of the fittest. He was not a charitable man who worried about his less fortunate human equals."

Louise was blunt, but she made sense. He was clouded by compassion looking for all his father's good points, but now Louise had opened the wound, he agreed his father was one of the most intolerant and driven men who ever walked. An achiever who let no one and nothing stand in the way of his goals. He was convinced Winton Springer was from the same mould, but there the similarity ended. Sam was a tough, honest and ethical businessman, while Springer represented pure greed and danger.

Louise could see she had struck a nerve. She smiled and her soft brown eyes danced with sensuality. The years had not diminished the magnetism he felt for her. She moved her hand across the bed towards where he was holding his father's lifeless limb. At that moment he felt the faintest flicker of strength in his father's hand and glanced up into his eyes. They were still and lifeless, but the corner of his mouth twitched. Alex made to move his hand away from Louise's reach in a guilty reaction brought on by the subconscious thought he was reaching out to her.

"Still scared of him, aren't you?"

It was a taunt he could not deny. It was obvious the power and charisma of the broken shell lying in the bed dominated the son. Even on his death bed the father was in control. Alex made no reply as he stared impassively into the stricken face looking neither for forgiveness, nor seeking it. The eyes were almost closed but he sensed life within the tormented frame would instantly regenerate if it sensed any further contact between himself and Louise. He gently released the entwined grip of his father's hand. The fingers were unresisting and fell limply. Alex slowly pushed the chair back and stood up.

"Where are you staying?"

"I don't know yet Louise."

"There's plenty of room at Roma."

"I think I'll give it a miss thanks Louise."

"Don't worry, I won't attack you. You'll be perfectly safe."

"And how long do you think that would last for?"

Louise laughed as she stood up and threw her jacket over her shoulders. "You're right. Some other time perhaps. Does Winton know you're here?"

Alex nodded. "One of his drivers picked me up at the airport."

Louise looked thoughtful. "I wonder how he knew you were coming. I most certainly didn't."

"Maria Stenner probably told him."

Louise shook her head. "No, I don't think so. Winton didn't want you to know about it. He maintained there was nothing between you and Sam and had given Maria clear instructions she was not to contact you."

"But she did."

"I realise that now, but she certainly would not have told Winton. He's been looking for an excuse to fire her."

"Then why hasn't he? Isn't he the chief executive of Roma Oil?"

"In name only. Sam has complete control over the company and Winton would not make a move to red-card one of Sam's oldest and most trusted employees while he's still breathing. But by the look of it he won't have to wait much longer. The moment Sam dies, Maria Stenner will be shown the door. Winton is just as scared of your father as you are."

Alex did not reply as they slowly walked out in silence and down the front steps of the hospital.

"Can I drop you somewhere?"

"No thanks Louise. I've been summoned by Winton Springer." Alex motioned towards the waiting Mercedes.

"Well, if you change your mind about the accommodation, you know the address."

Alex did not signify he had heard as he got into the Benz. He watched as Louise crossed the road and slid fluidly into the Aston Martin. The woman matched the image and standing to the letter, as with not so much as a casual glance or acknowledgement she swung the powerful machine out into the traffic and accelerated away.

Roma House was in the broker belt of the city. An imposing modern structure representing the success of the company and the billions in shareholder funds. Property; the silent appreciating asset.

The security guard showed Alex to the lift, keyed it for the top floor and stood silently to one side. The doors opened onto an olive green carpet which blended perfectly with the rich blackbean wooden panelling of the foyer walls. The expense was silent, but all pervading. The receptionist projected an aura of confidence and maturity. She was not what he expected. From what he could see of the top half, she was a head-turner. Winton Springer certainly had taste. It was apparent Maria Stenner had already been shown the door.

"Mr Carlin. Mr Springer is expecting you. He will be a few minutes. Can I get you a coffee or something to drink?"

"No thank you." Alex sank back into one of the lounge chairs, comfortable and opulent, the touch of soft leather with its instant appeal and aroma. The secretary smiled and busied herself with some undefined task.

"How long have you been here?"

The big brown eyes focused on him. She squinted slightly and he judged she normally wore glasses. The tinted contact lenses gave her eyes the intense caramel colour.

"I've only been here a week sir."

"What happened to Maria Stenner?"

"I don't know sir."

Alex noted a slight hesitation in her reply. Surely, she had to know who she had replaced after a week in the job. Any new employee would certainly make discrete or indiscrete enquiries about whose shoes they were replacing.

"Maria Stenner sat at that desk for nearly fifteen years and you mean to tell me you haven't heard of her. Surely someone around here has mentioned her name?"

The brown eyes remained calm, the smile firmly attached. "No Mr Carlin, I don't know anything about her. I can assure you no one has mentioned her name to me."

She either had not heard of Maria Stenner or was a good actress, a professional secretary who observed everything, knew everybody's business but remained loyal and reported only to her direct superior. A fifteen year record would have invariably left an indelible mark on the minds and actions of her associates, and yet this person claimed complete ignorance of the existence of Maria Stenner. It was as though she never existed.

His train of thought was interrupted when one panel of the floor to ceiling double doors to his office opened and Winton Springer appeared and walked swiftly towards him with a wide grin and hand out thrust. The animation was false along with the fixed expression which had obviously been practiced before opening the door. Alex's hand was enveloped in a bone-crushing grip. The only thing different about the stereotype of the man fixed in his mind was the thin silver hairline and the slight upturn at the corner of the eyelids which had obviously been subjected to cosmetic surgery. Other than that, he was still the Winton Springer who was responsible for the death of his sister and whom he despised.

"Well, well it's great to see you Alex. Come in, come in. I want to hear about what you've been doing these past years." Winton ushered him into his office, his hand planted paternally on his back.

"I'm not in to anyone Kim," he directed to his secretary as he turned and closed the door.

"What can I get you?" Winton did not wait for a reply as he picked up a crystal glass and poured a measure of fine bourbon, dropped in two ice cubes and handed it to Alex. He had style and a good memory. After five years he still remembered Alex's preference in alcohol.

Winton raised his glass. "Here's to the future. You've been to see the old man?"

Alex sampled the liquor, looked at him levelly and nodded.

"How is he?"

"Winton, you know full well the exact state of his condition. He will die at any minute and I believe you'll be informed the very moment he breathes his last. Let's cut to the chase. What do you want?"

The last meeting with Winton Springer was still very clear in his memory. In fact, the expression was identical, the lips drawn back in a thin clinical smile with the penetrating expressionless blue eyes looking straight into his mind.

Winton slowly put down his glass and leaned back in his leather-bound captain's chair. "I don't want anything. I would just like to offer the hand of friendship and ask you to forget about anything that happened between us in the past. I hope you are back for good and we can work together. After all, you will no doubt become a major shareholder in the company when Sam goes."

Winton was appraising the identical die-mould of Sam Carlin sitting before him. He was mature and assured, and completely in command compared with when he had last seen him.

"I know you have serious doubts, but I did not murder your sister. I was in love with her, deeply in love with her. It was an accident."

Alex nodded. He had been utterly convinced Winton had murdered Marty, but over the years and the passing of time, and lack of real motive had somewhat turned the previous monochrome of guilt into the melded colours of doubt. However, now he was facing the man again, he had no doubt.

"Can we work together?"

"I don't know Winton. I doubt whether I have any ties here at all. I know very little about the company because I've never been involved with it. I will have to think about it. By the way, where's Maria? I thought she was part of the furniture?"

Winton turned to look out the window and across the harbour. "That was the trouble. She was part of the furniture and had the view she was indispensable. I've learned when someone believes they cannot be replaced, it is the exact time to fire them. She was Sam's secretary and she knew she was immune. I don't know if they had something going, but they were sure glued to one another."

"He's not dead yet. Why didn't you wait and allow her to resign with dignity?"

Winton snorted with derision. "Dignity be dammed. She was a conniving, scheming individual who reported directly to Sam, and I mean reported everything. She even controlled my secretary and all the secretaries in this company. She knew exactly what everyone was up to. I couldn't fart in private without Sam knowing about it. She had to go, but I wanted to beat her to it. I wasn't going to let her resign."

"Did she have something on you?"

Winton swung back to front his accuser. "What the hell do you mean by that?"

Alex shrugged, but inwardly he was delighted at the reaction. He could see he had struck an exposed nerve. The thin veneer and pretence of being delighted to see Alex, was cracking.

Alex held up his hands in submission. "I didn't mean anything by it, but there must have been some underlying reason why you obviously despised the woman?"

"I've already made it very clear why I got rid of her."

"Fair enough Winton. It was your call and I can hardly walk in here and question your motives. My apologies."

Winton nodded and leaned back in his chair. The shoes of Sam Carlin fitted him well. Both were ruthless men who took what they wanted and he could see he was not wanted. Alex realised then, the business was not his life. It was alien to him and in any case he seriously doubted whether he had the desire to deal with Springer on his own ground.

"Why didn't you call me about Sam's condition?"

"I had no idea where to reach you," Winton lied smoothly. "You've been incommunicado for a number of years. I know you went back to the States and Sam apparently traced you to Afghanistan, but could never confirm it. No one had a clue where you were."

"Maria knew."

"That maybe so, but she never communicated that to Sam or me."

"How long ago did he have the first stroke? I'm referring to the present series."

Winton appeared to not hear the question as he got up and moved back to the liquor cabinet. He casually dropped ice cubes in and poured himself another drink. Alex shook his head at Winton's silent gesture with the decanter as to whether he wanted a top up.

"I would say about a month ago. It happened in this very room. I can assure you it came as a complete shock to me. One moment the usual aggressive demanding Sam and then the next, a complete basket case. Horrible to see a person deteriorate so quickly. On reflection though, I can't say I was really surprised. He really burnt the candle at both ends. Always working at top speed with his mind churning over the next deal or project. I'd been telling him for years to let go the reins a little, to slow down and occasionally smell the roses."

Alex nodded and studied what was left of the ice cube in his glass. "You say it happened in this office, and you were with him at the time?"

"Correct."

"Were you having an argument?" Alex noted the instant change in attitude. The voice turned icy although the facial expression remained impassive.

"Are you implying something?"

"No. I just asked whether you and my father were having an argument at the time he suffered the stroke. It's a simple question really."

"We were not arguing, although I admit we'd had plenty of disagreements which are common in any business. Sam was not an easy man to get along with at the best of times. We were actually discussing a new drilling program. He stood up suddenly and just pitched forward onto his desk."

"How's the company fairing?"

The sudden change of tack took Winton by surprise. He was unprepared for it and answered a little too quickly. "Fine, fine. Overall, it couldn't be better, but that's not to say there haven't been some hiccups now and then. It's a risky business as you know."

The quick nervous movement of the glass to his lips did not escape Alex's attention. It was as though the man had expected to be questioned at length about the circumstances of his father's stroke. The answers were well prepared. The sudden change of focus was unexpected.

"We've had a very profitable year and the current expansion programs are really going well. The shareholders should be well pleased with management as they've had years of improving profits and healthy dividends."

Alex sat motionless and studied the chief executive of his father's company. The shades of doubt recurred and drifted in and out of his mind, but he could not dispel the belief this man was responsible for his sister's death. Alex knew he was the rough product of the Australian outback who had acquired style and manners which masked his innate guile, cunning and ruthless manner. He was not the product of a defined seat of learning, but rather the polished and articulate graduate of the university of experience. Just below the surface lurked the menacing danger of the deadly taipan. Keep well clear and you were safe, but threaten the reptile's space and it would strike without warning.

"Don't worry about your father Alex. If you don't want to wait around I'll ensure he gets the best of attention. My understanding is stroke victims can linger for some time. You've got to face hard facts; he can't talk and doesn't recognise anyone. He's a vegetable. He is your biological father, but you must admit that did not extend to natural love and affection. There was a chasm between you, two distinctly different personalities with divergent interests. It's pointless just hanging around waiting for the end. I'll keep you fully informed if you leave me with contact details."

Alex nodded. There was nothing here for him. He did not want to step into his father's shoes, and he had no interest in the company.

"What happened to your hands? Did you have an accident?"

Alex had his hands casually draped over each side of the armchair, the scar tissue clearly visible. "Yes, it happened in Afghanistan, but it wasn't an accident."

"Do you want to tell me about it?"

"Not really Winton. It's a memory I'd prefer to forget."

"My apologies. I didn't mean to be inquisitive. Please remember Sam was a father to me. I deeply respect and revere the man for all his faults." Winton rose from his chair and walked around to prop on the corner of his desk. "I owe him everything. Without him I would have still been a shearer doing the rounds of sheep stations and getting drunk in the local pub. I've everything to be thankful for Alex, and your father is the one person to whom I owe the most. There is nothing he will want for."

The voice was modulated to an attitude of complete compassion and understanding. Alex could sense the sincerity and the deep bond that existed between Winton and Sam. They had been together from the very beginning and although the world knew Roma Oil belonged to Sam Carlin, there were those who believed Winton Springer was a compliant, but driving force behind the entity. He was paid exceedingly generously, maintained an expensive apartment and houses and never showed the slightest inclination he wanted more, or he was anything more than Sam Carlin's trusted employee.

Alex had always been suspicious of Winton and his motives. At first he had just passed it off as natural filial jealousy, but realised that theory did not fit as he never wanted to take over the reins of his father's empire. He had long given up thinking there could ever have been a deep bond in their relationship. Sam was his natural father, but that's where the association ended, or appeared to end in his opinion.

Winton had never given the slightest hint he was annoyed by the sudden appearance of Alex out of the blue all those years before, or his arrival on the scene now. In the short time he had known his father there had been the occasional attempt at conversation and contact. Sam was totally engrossed in the company and lost interest when Alex tried to discuss business opportunities unrelated to oil.

"You're dreaming boy," Sam would say before he had been given a minute to explain his idea or view. "I'm not interested in anything but oil and gas, and neither should you be."

Sam's unrelenting attitude had resulted in heated arguments. Alex was not annoyed his idea had been canned, only distressed he had not been given the time of day to outline his thinking. He came back to the present and looked up from his glass to see Winton studying him intensely.

"Something wrong?"

"No Winton, just ebb of memories at something you said. I'll be on my way I think."

"I want you to think seriously about joining the company. After all, I would say a large part of it is going to be yours very soon. On the other hand if you wish to sell your holding, I'll buy it. I'll make you a very generous offer."

"I'll give it some thought Winton, but I don't feel the slightest inclination to stay. You indicated I stand to inherit a part of the company. I don't expect anything and don't know anything about it, but if so I'll certainly give you the first right of refusal." He did not notice Winton's expression change fleetingly to a look of triumph in those ice-blue eyes.

"I'd appreciate that. Roma Oil is my complete existence. There are plenty of sharks out there who would love to control this company. It's asset rich with plenty of backing, very liquid and very stable. It has taken years longer than I would have liked, but Sam has been proved correct and taught me the lessons of accumulating wealth slowly. If you are genuine about selling I could get my lawyers to draw up an agreement. We'll have an independent valuation and pay you whatever the bottom line arrives at, plus a premium of ten percent."

"I'll give it consideration Winton. Let me think about it and I'll come back to you in a couple of days."

34

Alex was watching television when the phone went.

"Mr Carlin?"

"Yes."

"This is St Vincent's hospice. Your father is asking for you."

"Are you sure? I thought he was in a coma."

"Normally he is Mr Carlin, but occasionally he comes out of it and has brief spells of lucidity. I suggest if you want to speak to him, you had better come immediately."

Fifteen minutes later Alex was striding down the corridor towards his father's room. Sam turned his head slowly at the sound of the door opening and a faint smile crossed his tortured features. He gripped his son's hand with all the strength his enfeebled fingers would allow. A nurse came into the room and began to fuss over her patient.

"Can he talk?"

"He can, but you will have to be patient as it may take a few minutes for him to form what he wants to say. He's so excited. He's aware you were here earlier and he wants to tell you something." She gently lifted Sam's head and propped the pillows up. "There you are. I'll leave you two alone now for a few minutes."

Sam's eyes closed like a slowly descending curtain. Alex made to disengage his hand, but immediately felt the grip return in an attempt to pull him closer. The lips moved. A mumbled sound emanated, but he could not understand what his father was attempting to say.

"Nurse."

The nurse turned as she was opening the door and hurried back.

"I can't understand what he's saying. Can you help me please?"

The nurse leaned closer to listen and slowly shook her head. "Stroke victims rarely talk again how you remember them Mr Carlin. One moment you can understand every word and the next its just mumbo jumbo. Don't be fazed by what he may say. His mind has been wandering all over the place. He was mumbling about someone killing someone yesterday. Poor dear, his mind does wander a lot. It's quite normal."

Winton looked up to see Sam's eyes open again and his hand release its grip and point to the bedside cabinet. He opened it, but there was nothing there except a pair of glasses, a book and a pen, the final few possessions of a dying man. He began to shut the cabinet when his father became agitated and attempted to roll on his side to reach into the cabinet. His actions bordered on the frantic. Alex reached in and removed the book and then saw the small voice recorder. He held it up and Sam nodded, mumbling and beckoning him to lean closer. He caught the name Maria Stenner, but the rest was unintelligible.

"Winton said she had retired and moved to the Gold Coast," he replied in an attempt to humour and guess what his father was trying to impart. The words were hardly out of his mouth before Sam became extremely agitated.

"Springer has killed her as well."

Alex was shocked. The words had come out crystal clear as the motor function of the brain and speech synchronised momentarily. The stricken man sank back on the pillows as he reached out for Alex's hand again. The grip tightened and then suddenly relaxed. He looked up to see the eyes staring vacantly back at him. His father was dead.

As if notified by a hidden alarm the nurse came back into the room. She closed the eyes and gently laid the arms by his side. Without a word she left the room, closing the door gently behind her.

Alex sat studying the face and tracing the lines of torture and age. Each line conjured up a year of life. However much he tried he could not establish any grief at his father's death. It was just another death and he had seen more than his fair share of the dead and dying. He wondered if it was because he had absolutely no compassion or love for his father, or he had become hardened to the sight of death. He felt a slight tinge of remorse for not answering his father's letters, but it was too late for that now. He had often thought about the confrontation with Winton the day Sam hit him. The days in hospital lingering between life and death as the clot within his skull slowly diminished and the pressure on his brain subsided. In his moments of consciousness he was aware of his father sitting beside his bed, but made no move to acknowledge him. He became intensely irritated with doctors flashing penlights into his eyes. They were worried he was not talking when his other vital signs were showing clear improvement. The blow had affected the right side of his body. He had heard the neurologist talking to Sam as to whether they would surgically remove the clot or administer drugs. Surgery was dangerous. It was a delicate path to the left frontal lobe then inserting the drain into the damaged tissue. Sam shook his head and opted for the safer course of letting nature do the healing, a slow and painstaking process of physiotherapy and rest. If there was no improvement Sam agreed to the surgeon resorting to opening his skull. The risk of infection was possible and an infection in that area would lead to only one conclusion.

Winton had come to see him, but one look from the smouldering hatred of the bedridden patient sent him away without saying a word. Sam sat by the bed for hours talking quietly to him. The contrition was sincere, but Alex remained within his cone of silence despite the fact his mind and body were co-ordinating again. Finally a police sergeant appeared at his bedside and attempted to question him about the incident. Alex just stared blankly at him.

"If you want to lay a complaint we can charge your father with assault and grievous bodily harm. All we need is for you to sign a statement and we can get on with it." The cop waited for him to answer. "The doctors assure me you can speak. You may not speak to your father and I can understand why."

Alex raised his hands and motioned for him to move closer. The words "fuck off" were clear and distinct. The policeman jerked back in anger and walked out. A week later he checked himself out, bought a ticket to the States and flew out without telling anyone. It was a year before his father caught up with him again. His commanding officer called him in and handed him a letter.

"I don't know what gives between you and your old man Carlin, but why don't you patch it up and get on with life?" He flicked the envelope over his desk. "No, I haven't opened it son. Your father sent me a covering letter so I do have a bit of the background."

"Is that all sir?" The officer tapped a pencil in the palm of his hand and nodded his assent. Alex snapped a salute and swung out of the room. As he passed the reception desk he tore the envelope into quarters and dropped it into the waste bin. The door of the inner office was open and the officer had clearly seen what had happened. He shook his head slowly. Carlin was a first class helicopter pilot with an ice-cold personality. No point in trying to psychoanalyse people now. The war of attrition in Afghanistan was a conflict of never ending hell. The officer called for his orderly and snapped out a command. Five minutes later Alex had been assigned to Afghanistan.

Alex leaned over and kissed his father's forehead before walking out without a backward glance. It was not until he was at the front door of the hospice he realised he had forgotten to pick up the recorder. Retracing his steps he quietly opened the door. The bed was empty. The workings of the hospice were swift and efficient. The bed had been stripped and about to be made ready for another dying admittance. The shock finally hit him as he leaned against the wall and tried to stifle the grief. It would have been such a small effort to forgive and come to terms with his father years before. Why did he let his anger of retribution fester for so long? Who was the ancient Chinese philosopher who said: *if you seek revenge, dig two graves.* He picked up the recorder from the side table and switched it on. The battery was flat. Whatever it contained, it had something to do with his father's stroke, he was sure of that. The nurse entered the room with fresh linen as he pocketed the recorder, smiled at her and made to leave.

"Normally we have to make an inventory of all possessions before handing them over to the next of kin sir."

"I am the next of kin, and there's nothing but his glasses and a book which I don't want."

He slowly walked out of the hospice and into the evening air. The Mina birds were intent on their cacophony of sound in the nearby Moreton Bay fig trees. The prostitutes plied their trade in the doorways and openly solicited him as he strolled through

Darlinghurst and into Kings Cross. How insignificant human life really was. The cheapest and yet the most expensive commodity known to man. Cheap when it came to war. Human life meant nothing until the enormity of the crime caused a ground swell of public indignation and outcry. The flower of youth was being killed and maimed. The politicians swore it would never be allowed to happen again. A few years passed before the regeneration process healed the scars and the murmurings of conflict were heard again. The conflict would have to be dealt with as the hawks fanned the still warm embers. Life was a never ending series of crises blown out of all proportion to their importance, or effect on fellow human beings. His father was dead. The mourners would turn up and listen to the unctuous and meaningless eulogies. Condolences would be offered constantly over the next few weeks until finally they subsided as the memory and significance of the man faded. Sam Carlin was just an ordinary man, but driven and self-centred to the cost of his family. Alex leaned against the post waiting for the lights to change.

"You looking for some company, love?" It was the prostitute's beat and she sauntered towards him chewing her gum.

He ignored her as he crossed and continued walking lost in thought. His life unravelled before him as he tried to place his father in roles of importance at various stages of his growing up. He could not remember him. Only his mother came to mind. She was vivid in his memory. His father was a faceless person who managed now and then to send presents for his birthday or at Christmas. They were perfunctory with no meaning or love attached to them. He tried to hide his disappointment, but on one occasion he threw the unwrapped gift and smashed it on the floor. He was twelve at the time and the present was that for a ten year old. His mother had admonished him as she picked up the present and put it back in the box.

"Your father is a very busy man Alexander. He just forgot how old you are today."

"That's not right mother, and you know it. The present was bought by his secretary. He treats you the same way. We just don't exist."

It was his mother's only loss of control he could remember when she lashed out and slapped him across the face. "He may not be much of a father, but he is your father and one day you will learn to love him, as he will you."

The words had stuck in his memory. He had loved his father and his father had loved him. Why had he not returned more quickly after Afghanistan and his discharge? They would have shared some time together. Deep down he knew Winton Springer was eating at him. He was like the dark shadow of the night that frightened a child. Turn on the light and the evil immediately disappeared. He was convinced Springer had murdered Marty. He wondered if he had also killed his father. He started to briskly walk the last kilometre to his hotel. He felt suddenly he had arrived home. It was as though he had been waiting for years for someone to tell him where home was. The words of his aunt rang in his ears.

"You're a misfit here Alex," she said as she dropped him off at Los Angeles airport. "You belong with your father, so don't come back."

Alex had leaned across and given her a bear hug and walked away without looking back. She was the one who had slowly put his broken mind and body back together. He vividly remembered the flights to recover the dead and dying, legs and bodies shattered by hidden explosive devices. There his memory stopped. He remembered nothing about the day his chopper was brought down. He remembered the orange ball of flame as it exploded before his eyes, but from there it was a blank.

35

The clerk at the check-in recognised him. "Good evening Mr Carlin. How can I assist you?"

"Would you have a couple of batteries I can put in this recorder?"

"I don't have any batteries I can give you, but I'm sure I can find a couple in the manager's office if you just want to listen to it."

"I just want to listen to what's on it and then you can have the batteries back."

He could hear clerk rummaging through drawers before reappearing with two batteries. "Try these sir."

Alex uttered his thanks as he replaced the batteries, switched it on and held it up to his ear. The sound was clear and the voices were immediately recognisable as that of his father and Winton. Sam's voice was the clearer of the two and he was electrified by what his father was saying and the answers being given. It was obvious Sam had set up the meeting and was secretly recording the conversation. The answers to his questions flowed easily, but with a rising and gloating arrogance. Alex was suddenly in the room with them. He could clearly picture Winton standing over his sick father pressing home a violent verbal attack. The old man was on the verge of another seizure as he tried to discard the truth of what Winton was telling him. It was too monstrous to contemplate. The final act was preceded by the crash of a fist on the desktop as Winton drove home his final confession. He listened in horror as he heard his sister's name mentioned. The tape went silent until a low howl of anguish emitted from a tortured being. It stopped suddenly and Alex heard the sound of objects falling to the floor followed by a heavy thump. He realised it was his father collapsing onto his desk and then onto the floor. He heard Winton yell for Maria Stenner to call an ambulance and then the tape dissolved into a jumble of voices. He had heard all he needed to as he stopped the machine and removed the batteries. His blood was boiling as the anger and revenge rushed to his brain. He picked up the phone to dial the police, but then put it back down again.

"No, Winton Springer, I'll deal with you on my terms," he muttered to himself.

"Everything to your satisfaction Mr Carlin?" The desk clerk noted Alex's expression as he placed the batteries on the counter.

"Yes, thank you. Would you have an envelope please? I would like to lodge this in your safe if I may."

The clerk locked the recorder away and wrote out a receipt. "Don't lose it sir. Without that you'll have to wait until I come on duty to identify you."

Alex's mind was crystal clear as he caught the elevator to his floor. All his suspicions about Springer had proved correct. He opened the door and was about to reach for the light when he was violently pushed from behind. He stumbled forward and attempted to spin around, but the blow caught him across the back of the head. He had taken no notice of the person who stepped into the lift at the last moment, and did not realise he had followed him out of the lift on his floor.

Blinding light erupted and then flashes of total darkness as he felt his knees give away. It seemed only seconds later when the same lighting display began to erupt again. He pushed himself up on his elbow and looked around for the danger. The blinds were open and the light from a building opposite flooded the room with a dull glow. He picked himself up and stumbled onto the bed. Nothing synchronised as the depth of field of his sight wavered in and out. He was looking through a zoom lens camera as his eyes fought to adjust and focus. Nausea overcame him as he lay back staring at the ceiling. Any attempt to close his eyes sent the room into a gentle swaying motion. He did not hear the door open.

"Mr Carlin, I'm the duty manager. Are you okay? Your phone's been off the hook for some time." The manager walked in and looked at Alex. "You don't look so good Mr Carlin. I'll get a doctor." He clucked as he looked at the disarray of the room. Nothing had been left untouched in frantic search for whatever his assailant was after.

"Do you have any idea who did this sir? There's considerable damage that will have to be paid for."

"Well, don't put it on my bill. If you allow unsavoury types to wander around in your hotel, what do you expect?"

The doctor appeared and shone a pen torch into each eye. "You've got a mild concussion. I think you should stay in bed for the rest of the day. I certainly wouldn't walk around the streets. You could easily black out." He flicked off the torch and slipped it into his breast pocket in a deft movement before pulling out a prescription pad. He scribbled on it and handed it to the manager. "Would you mind getting someone to attend to that please?"

The manager picked up the phone and within minutes a porter appeared and took the prescription. Maids appeared and began to tidy the room.

"Had a little trouble here, have we?"

Alex opened an eye to study the questioner. There were two of them, both overweight, expressionless and in suits. He knew they were police.

"You could say that officer."

"Got any idea who roughed you up?" Alex shook his head as they looked around the room.

"Lose anything?"

"No, I don't think so."

"Not even your wallet?"

"I've still got that."

"Strange isn't it that someone biffed you over the head, tears the room to pieces, and doesn't relieve you of your money. There's no such thing as a motiveless crime. Your accent tells me you're American. Can I see your passport?"

The cop flipped it open and studied the details. He made some notes on his pad as his offsider suddenly became interested, and took the passport out of his associate's hand.

"What are you doing in Australia Mr Carlin?"

"I came out to see my father. He died last night."

"Where did your father die?"

Alex told him. The cop picked up the phone. "What else have you been doing here?"

Alex was becoming annoyed by the questions that followed. His head was splitting with pain. However, there was no point in telling these two to shove off as it looked as though they had a low tolerance threshold. Courteous, but stone faced.

"Not mixed up in anything we should know about? Drugs or shit like that?"

Alex shook his head as the cop flipped the passport back on the bed. He looked at his colleague as he put down the phone.

"It checks."

"Okay, Mr Carlin that's us done. If you have any more trouble or would like to discuss this further, just give me a call." He handed Alex his card. "As I said, there's no such thing as a motiveless crime. You were attacked for a reason, and I've a feeling you know something about it."

Winton was on the verge of stopping them as they walked out, but decided against it. He had not had time to think through the implications of what he had heard on the cassette. He winced as he got up and checked his jacket. He checked every pocket again, but the receipt was gone. He cursed himself as he grabbed for the phone. It was not the voice of the duty manager he'd spoken to the previous evening. After a minute the reply came back as he knew it would.

"The envelope was picked up early this morning Mr Carlin. I have the receipt in front of me. Do you want me to call the police again?"

"No, there's no need." Alex replaced the handpiece and reached for the phone directory. Whoever, had mugged him had waited until the morning when they knew there would be a change of shift, and they could simply present the receipt. The desk would have been busy, and the envelope handed over without query.

Maria Stenner's number was listed, but there was no answer. The cold shower invigorated him as he let the cool jets play on his head to relieve the pain. The manager was in the lobby when he came down.

"How are you feeling Mr Carlin? Not taking the doctor's advice I see. Are you sure you don't want to report the stolen envelope to the police. The duty manager from last night told me it contained a recorder. Was it something of value?"

"No, it was nothing to worry about." Alex moved away to avert further questions. He winced inwardly as each footstep seemed to jar his brain. The doorman hailed a cab, and five minutes later he was crossing the harbour bridge to the north shore. Maria lived in an imposing block of apartments tiered up and back from the road to take advantage of the magnificent view across the harbour. The street-front foyer door was security locked and there was no answer to her intercom. He walked around to the entrance of the internal car park and waited until finally a car pulled out and drove off. He quickly stepped in as the automatic door started to close. He caught the lift and pushed the bell on Maria's door. There was no response so he knocked loudly.

"I don't think Maria's home. Can I help you?" Alex gave a start and turned around. He had not heard the door to the next apartment open. The old man had a paper and glasses in his hand.

"Could you tell me where she might be or how I can contact her?"

The old man shook his head. "Can't be too far away. I'd say she'll be home sometime today. If she goes away for more than a day she always gets me to water her balcony plants. Sorry I can't help you."

"Does Maria have a unit on the Gold Coast?"

The old man chuckled. "No, Maria is a nature lover. Just about every weekend she's off bushwalking or bird watching. She wouldn't go near such an artificial place as the Gold Coast. You obviously don't know Maria that well then."

"She worked for my father for many years."

"Is your father Sam Carlin?"

"Yes, I'm Alex Carlin."

The old man's eyes lit up. "I know Sam well. He's been to dinner at Maria's often, and they've invited me to join them on many occasions. Tell him Stan Morris sends his regards. Say, how is he? I haven't seen him for quite some time."

"He died last night."

"Oh, I'm sorry to hear that." He turned to shuffle back inside. "Please, please come in. I'll just sit down and collect myself." He slumped back into a chair. "This is indeed a shock. Sorry, bad manners." He pushed himself to his feet. "I'm going to have a brandy. Would you like to join me?"

"Certainly. I've got a splitting headache so I'll take you up on that. When did you last see Maria?"

"Yesterday morning." Stan suddenly put down the decanter. "Say, you don't think something's happened to her do you? C'mon boy, I've got a key."

The scene that greeted them was reminiscent of his hotel room, only worse. Complete chaos with everything torn open, cupboards, closets and even the fridge contents were strewn over the floor. The bookshelves had been emptied.

"Who could have done this?" Stan wandered through the wreckage. "I'd better phone the police."

Alex had seen enough. Stan did not notice him leave. He was watching television in his room when the expected knock came at the door several hours later. He opened it and stood back without a word to let the two policemen in.

"We meet again Mr Carlin. It's obvious you were expecting us."

"I didn't know if it would be you two, but I knew it would be the police." He indicated for them to sit down.

"What were you doing at Maria Stenner's apartment?"

"I wanted to see her."

"About what?"

"Maria Stenner was my father's secretary for many years. She phoned me in the States to tell me my father had suffered a terminal stroke, but when I got here she had left the company. I wanted to see her to thank her."

The senior cop jotted down some notes before looking up. "When did you last see her?"

"It would have been about five years ago."

"Would you be able to identify her again if you saw her?" Alex laughed. "I'm sure I could."

"Okay then." The cop folded his notebook and stood up. "Come with us, and you can positively identify her."

Alex frowned. "I take it she's dead?"

"From the photos we've found in her apartment I think we fished her out of the sea at the base of North Head Gap this morning. She's been bashed around by the surf pushing her up on the rocks, but most of her features are still there."

"Why me? I haven't seen her in years. Why not get Winton Springer at Roma Oil, or Stan Morris her next door neighbour?"

"Springer is out of town and there's no point in shocking hell out of the old fellow. He'll be dead soon enough without speeding up the process. What's wrong, are you scared of stiffs?"

"No officer, I'm not scared of stiffs as you put it. I've seen more corpses than you'll see in a lifetime."

The cop laughed. "What line of work were you in?"

"I flew choppers in Afghanistan. I've seen more than my share of the dead."

A look of respect crossed the policeman's face. "Pretty rough scene over there?"

"Yes, it was an experience I don't want to live through again."

An ambulance was backed up and unloading into a bay. They brushed past the covered gurney, a blood soaked shroud partially covering the head of the cadaver.

"Car accident?"

"Nope detective, just a garden variety homicide. A bullet to the head," the attendant replied laconically as he began to push the gurney inside.

The rendered walls were painted a dull green to match the atmosphere of the place. An attendant came out of an office when he saw the two policemen and without a word signified for them to follow. A swinging door led straight into the brightly lit room with a number of stainless steel draining trays. Two of them were occupied by naked forms. The only thing different was their obvious sex.

"That her?" The cop was watching the expression on Alex's face as he moved closer and stood right over the corpse. There was no mistaking Maria Stenner.

"Yes, that's Maria."

The air outside was humid in contrast to the morbid and cold atmosphere he had just left.

"Do you think there's a connection between her death and you getting roughed up last night?"

"I really don't know. We were both burgled and she's dead and I'm alive. I only got mugged while she was obviously murdered."

"How do you know she was murdered?"

"I don't, but Maria was not the sort of person who would go leaping off a cliff-top to her death. She was full of life. A bubbly irrepressible personality. I just can't believe she took her own life."

"You're right Carlin. She was strangled and already dead before she was tossed over the cliff. I've got a strange feeling there's a connection between the two incidents. Whoever clouted you and murdered Stenner was looking for something, hence the ransacking. I hope you're not mixed up in something sinister Carlin, because if I find you're into drugs or the like, I'll stick it right up you." The cruiser pulled into the entrance to the hotel. Alex got out without answering.

36

He buried two people that week. First Maria Stenner, then his father. He had wanted Sam's funeral to be a quiet affair, but Winton Springer turned it into a grand opera. Springer was the new chairman of Roma Oil and he revelled in the limelight.

Alex wryly studied the face of the killer as Winton stood in the doorway of the chapel greeting everyone as they entered. He had adopted a sombre devastated look, but it was only an act. Deep down Alex new he was gloating at finally gaining control of Roma.

A minister read the meaningless eulogy over the bier. Did they actually believe the nonsense they pretended to read from the book? They could recite it in their sleep, they had repeated it so many times. The piped music started as the casket began to roll towards a curtained entrance. It moved silently on its nylon tracks towards its final destination. Such was life. Everyone moved down the same track to the same inevitable end. The coffin moved through the curtain and disappeared.

He felt a terrible loneliness as he realised the last person on earth close to him had gone. The music went up a few decibels as the mourners filed out in silence, only to break out in animated conversation when they perceived they were clear of the chapel and its terminal message. Alex was the last to leave. The minister held out his hand automatically and muttered a meaningless condolence. There was no life and no compassion in the handshake. It was the detached action of a man bored with his job.

Alex stood in the sunlight and looked up at the sky. It was a beautiful day, but the air was dead, not a breath of a breeze or sound of a bird, just the overall hum of traffic as it pounded its myriad ways. It was the perfume he smelt first. There was no mistaking it as Louise Carlin positioned herself beside him. The black veil hid nothing. The eyes were dry although she carried the required lace handkerchief. She looked radiant as she always did. However, she now had the radiance of a very rich widow.

"Well, you certainly made it this time Louise."

She was momentarily taken aback at the stinging remark. "I loved him Alex. You may not believe it, but you are wrong."

"I thought you loved me once?"

"I did, but you ran away."

Alex studied her eyes. They were soft and inviting and without malice. "You are right Louise. I did, but it would never have worked out."

"Can I talk to you about Roma, it's very important?"

"Could it wait until we get clear of this place? Nothing's going to happen to the company in the next few hours. Why don't we leave it until tomorrow sometime?"

"Why not come out for dinner this evening?"

"Just you and I and a couple of mood candles." Alex mocked. "Really Louise, can't it wait until tomorrow?"

She gripped his arm tightly. He could feel her long fingernails digging into his flesh. "No candles Alex and no music, just dinner. I've got to talk to you. Please?"

It was the imploring note in her voice he could not resist. "Okay, I'll be there at eight."

She squeezed his arm and was gone. He felt a tightening in his groin as he watched her get into the waiting limo. She spelt danger, but what man could resist her? If there was some secret hormone that inexorably attracted the opposite sex, then she had more than her fair share, she had the market cornered.

"Beautiful, and particularly beautiful in the trappings of death, don't you think?"

Alex went cold, but controlled himself as he turned to face the voice. "Yes, she's certainly that Winton."

"You had something going with her once, didn't you?"

"I think we've both been guilty of that. I know you've denied you'd ever met her before she became Sam's nurse, but we both know otherwise, don't we?"

Winton ignored the accusation. "What did she want? She seemed desperate to talk to you."

"She wanted to talk about Roma Oil."

"Did she now?" Winton replied with a knowing smirk. "I say, you haven't forgotten our discussion about selling your Roma holding to me, have you?"

"No, I haven't. I think I'll go back to the States soon, so I'll let you know my decision in due course."

"It was bad news about Maria Stenner."

"I thought you said she moved to the Gold Coast?"

"I did. She was always going on about wanting to retire there. I hear you had a nasty experience the other day?"

"How do you know about it?"

"A couple of cops came to see me about Maria's death. They were very curious about you and your background. Mind you, I can understand why. You were roughed up and then you were seen at Maria's apartment. And then the old girl is found floating off the Gap. She did start to go a little cuckoo when Sam had his last stroke."

Alex realised it was a test. Winton was waiting for a reaction, an outburst of accusation which would signify he was aware of the recorder and its contents.

"I didn't see you at her funeral Winton. I thought you would have turned up seeing she was such a loyal and longstanding employee."

"The loyalty I would question, but the truth is I never liked her. She was your father's secretary and that's why I dispensed with her services. I'm not hypocritical. I just couldn't be bothered going to someone's funeral I had no regard for. You obviously attended?"

Alex nodded. Yes, he had been to her funeral. There were about twenty mourners, the difference between hers and his father's was that all her mourners had been genuine friends. In contrast, his father's funeral had been the total circus complete with jackals and vultures to fight over the legacy. Mourners jockeying for position as they calculated the benefits and disadvantages Sam Carlin's death would have on them and their fiscal interest. The usual politicians and aspiring politicians, barristers, solicitors, stockbrokers, commodity market dealers, bank managers, finance company directors, merchant bankers and of course, the media recording the big-top event.

Sam's life had directly and indirectly touched them all. He was vital to their very existence. Not one of them had any real grief. It was an hour to take off from the pursuit of wealth to bury the man who had contributed to their prosperity. It was a compulsory, but begrudged hour. Wasting it on the dead was one of their occupational duties. What effect would the death of one of their benefactor's have on their financial future was the only question they mulled over.

It was clear to all Winton Springer had assumed control of the corporate empire. He was the man to pay homage to now. The son was evident, but no threat as it was strongly rumoured he would sell out and return to America. Winton Springer was recognised as the driving force behind the company. His tactics worked as Roma continued to go from strength to strength on the guidelines laid down by Sam. It was an active company, always in the news. It had been noted over the past year Springer was making more and more of the commercial decisions, and was the man to be courted. They had noticed Sam's grief at the loss of his daughter, which was compounded when his son went back to the States. He became a changed person in both his personality and the appearance of age. Obviously, he was losing control, but would not recognise it.

Winton Springer had shown grief at the loss of his wife, but overcame it outwardly through his increasing aggression in the business world. His destruction of Miles Morgan had been ruthless, but a brilliant financial coup. Australco stock shot up to dizzying heights when a newspaper article revealed the company was about to commence drilling on the edge of the Barrier Reef. Then came the crash into oblivion as those involved were named. The disclosure of his secret bank account and offshore company lead to Stillmore's immediate resignation as Premier of Queensland. The Federal Government pressuring New Guinea to rescind the exploration permits the following week was the final straw that collapsed the whole conspiracy and the company along with it.

It was common knowledge Springer was involved in the destruction of Stillmore and Morgan as well as the board of Australco and others. He had been selling the stock as it sky-rocketed and covered his short positions by buying in as the market crashed, making millions in the exercise. The final humiliation for Morgan had come when he stormed into Luciano's demanding the millions he had apparently loaned Springer, making veiled threats about exposing offshore bank accounts and the tax implications. Springer had taken him by the arm and gently led him to his table all the while talking quietly to him.

Luciano had rushed up. "Mr Morgan you cannot have your usual table. It is booked. You are three months in arrears with your account."

"I will settle Mr Morgan's account before I leave Luciano." Winton smiled at the restaurateur. "Mr Morgan and I will be dining at his table, so you can change the reservation."

Luciano stood open-mouthed, but he was mindful of Morgan's outstanding account and the promise of payment today. Better to keep his mouth closed, change the reservation and wait an hour.

"I don't feel like eating anything Springer. I just want my money."

"And you shall have it today Miles. But, join me in a drink and let's walk out of here without showing any acrimony."

Winton signalled to Luciano. "A bottle of good red and Mr Morgan's bill please." Winton glanced at the bill, dropped his credit card on top and handed it to Luciano who had poured two glasses of St Henri with a shaking hand. "Now that's taken care of Miles, why don't I meet you at your apartment around eight this evening to settle up."

It was two days later before the smell from the Mercedes became obvious and the police were called to the underground car park in Morgan's unit block. Morgan had been shot twice in the head with a small calibre weapon at point-blank range. It was a professional hit.

"Have you got a car here?"

"I caught a cab."

"Well, ride with me then. There's something I want to discuss with you."

The chauffeur held the door open. The smell of rich leather of the Bentley wafted out.

"Given up on the Porsche, have you?"

"No, but the car has got to fit the image when image is the order of the day. The first lesson in making money Alex, is that to attract money, you've got to smell like money."

Alex sank into the Connolly hide as the car glided away without a murmur.

"You're probably wondering what you inherited from your father. I'm the executor of his estate, and in addition inherited twenty five percent of his holding in Roma Oil. Louise, gets a similar share with Sam's house, and a living allowance thrown in while she remains unmarried. If she marries again she loses the house. You inherit twenty five percent. It's that shareholding I would like to buy."

It was obvious to Alex that Sam had not had time to change his Will before his terminal stroke. The contents of the recorder would have terminated Springer's inheritance and his position if Sam had survived. Springer must have somehow found about the recorder. In retaliation, had Maria unwisely said something, or threatened him with the existence of the recording, which led to her murder?

"What happened to the remaining quarter?"

"That belonged to Marty, and on her death as her husband, I inherited her entire estate. We made a Will in each others favour the night before we married."

"And through those holdings you almost control the company?"

"Not, almost Alex. I do control Roma Oil. I've been slowly buying stock over the years and I'm by far the largest shareholder."

"I hear what you're saying. I can see there's no chance of me ever assuming control of what my father built."

"No Alex. I'll be blunt about it. I control the corporation and would like you to sell me your interest. You can keep it of course and live off the dividends, but if you cash in now, you'll have all the money you need to do what you want. You and I both know your heart is not in the company or the country."

The Bentley glided to a stop in the driveway of the hotel and the doorman stepped forward to open the door.

"Why don't you think about it overnight and call me in the morning. I'll pay you a twenty percent premium to the last closing price if you sell to me tomorrow. I can have the funds in your hand by tomorrow afternoon."

Alex nodded, but ignored the extended hand.

Louise greeted him at the door. Alex made to resist her, but she leaned forward, taking his head in both hands and kissing him. The lips were sensuous and full of meaning. The latent desire was irresistible.

"You really are a slut Louise."

Louise laughed as she pulled him inside. "I'm a slut in bed Alex, but you know that. I'm a lady out of it. Don't all men crave for women like that?"

"Obviously my father did?"

She clucked her tongue in mock horror. "You shouldn't talk to your stepmother like that Alex. Don't I command some respect?"

"You would if you'd earned it."

"Oh, let's stop it. Can't we call a truce for one night. I've cooked something special."

Alex followed her into the house. For a woman who had just buried her husband there was not the slightest sign of mourning. Every light was blazing and floodlights bathed the lawn leading down to the jetty. There was no staff, just the two of them.

Alex picked at his food, but claimed the bottle of Merlot. It had been a long day. He felt like releasing some of the tensions as he poured a glass of wine.

"What do you want Louise?"

"What makes you think I want something? I merely said I wanted to talk to you."

"I know you too well. You invited me here for a specific purpose. Now how about coming clean and tell me what you're really after."

"It's Winton. I want to discuss Winton Springer with you."

"Go ahead."

"What do you think of Winton?"

Alex pushed his plate to one side. The question was loaded. He felt he was back in Afghanistan picking his way through ground fire. "To sum up, I would say ambitious."

"Nothing more?"

"There is more, but I won't go into it. I know what he wants, and that's complete control of Roma."

"Are you going to let him have your father's company without a fight?"

"He has complete control of it now. There's nothing I can do."

"You're not concerned about what's going to happen to the company then?"

"Nothing is going to happen Louise. You seem worried Winton is in control, but I'm not, and I don't think the stockholders are either."

"You're a stockholder."

"I know that, although I only found out today from Winton. Apparently, I own twenty five percent. I intend to sell out to him."

Louise looked horrified. "You, sell out to Winton? You would walk away from it all?"

"Yes, that's my intention Louise."

She looked into her wineglass as if reading the dregs. "You're thinking this dinner is a setup don't you? You think Winton is in the background?"

Alex threw his hands up in resignation. "I don't know what to think."

"I'm scared for my life Alex. Will you help me?"

"Of course I'll help you, but don't you think you're being a bit melodramatic about this. Why are you so scared?"

"Winton is a killer. Don't ask me how I know, but I know."

"You two go way back don't you? You just didn't meet Winton when you came to work for Sam, did you?"

Louise did not answer, but he could see from the way she was averting his gaze he knew he was correct. "He has killed someone in the past, and you're aware of it aren't you?"

Louise nodded. "Yes, but it wasn't murder. It was self defence, and that's all I'm prepared to tell you at this stage. However, in the case of Marty I agree with you, it was murder and he as good as murdered Sam."

"My father died of a stroke. Winton had no part in his death."

"I don't know about that. I believe he died of a stroke brought on by something Winton disclosed to him. Sam told me as much in a lucid moment, although it was very difficult to understand what he was getting at. He said you would sort it out when you came. Did he by any chance give you something in hospital?"

"He gave me a voice recorder, but I never got to listen to it. It was stolen from my hotel room."

"Ah, now the pieces are starting to fall into place. He gave you a recorder and now you don't have it and haven't listened to it? I wonder who has it now?"

"I don't know Louise, Sam is dead so it doesn't really interest me."

"That maybe the case, but whatever is on the recorder would have shone some light on why Sam collapsed in his office in Winton's presence. Maria told me there had been a heated exchange. Thinking about it, I wonder if Sam set up the meeting with Winton and secretly recorded it with Maria's assistance? He never told me what it was, but he did mention on several occasions he had his doubts about Winton. She didn't jump off a cliff and both you and I know that."

"What did my father say about Marty's death?"

"At first he accepted Winton's explanation and was strongly against your accusations. However, over time he began to wonder how such an experienced diver as Winton would let an amateur such as his new wife out of his sight. He was always remorseful about what he did to you. He just didn't know how to communicate or discuss anything with you. He called it the chasm of time, but he didn't know how to approach you to heal the wounds."

"He didn't try too hard, but I can understand how he felt. Why did he begin to suspect Winton may have murdered Marty?"

"Sometime later someone in the library let it drop Marty had apparently discovered something going on within the company. She suspected someone very high up in the company was skimming off using a system of phoney invoices from phoney companies. She never named Winton, but Sam had his suspicions."

"Why did he begin to suspect Winton?"

"Because Winton apparently convinced Sam audits over the years had not shown any evidence of wrongdoing, but agreed to undertake a thorough investigation. Nothing came of the investigation, because it never commenced, and I don't think Sam wanted to be confronted with the truth. I feel he went into denial."

"Okay, in your opinion he murdered Marty and was responsible for Sam's death, and you think you're next?"

"Yes, I do. Two down and one to go. You're proposing to sell out to him so you're not in the firing line. That only leaves me. Sam left this place to me, but it's far too big. If I move out or get married again I lose all title, and the company until now has been paying the running costs. Winton has already hinted to me the company can no longer maintain that position. I know he wants me out so he can move in. As for my twenty five percent, I can't sell the stock. I can only live off the dividends as the trustee has control, and if I die my interest reverts to the trust. Are you beginning to get the picture? Can you see now why I believe I'm in danger."

"Sell out to him while you can."

"I probably have a bit more pride than you Alex. I'm not selling to Winton Springer. Why did you run out on your father? Why didn't you stay and take over?"

"We were two very alike persons Louise. I doubt whether I could have worked for him and I don't think he really wanted me involved."

Louise shook her head. "That's not true. He desperately wanted you to work with him. It was all he ever talked about. It was his dream."

"I probably was a disappointment to him, but then you were a disappointment to me."

"In what way?"

"You gave me the flick and targeted Sam."

"That's not true. You left the country without as much as a goodbye."

"I was laid up in a hospital bed with a broken skull and bleeding on the brain and you never came near me. You were well aware I could have died at any moment. You knew where your next meal was coming from, and that's why you decided to target my father. He suited you just fine. You had money and position. On the other hand if you'd made the break with me, you couldn't predict the future."

"I loved you Alex and still love you," Louise got up and moved towards him. He felt her soft hands begin to slowly massage his neck. He reached up and held them. The sensuous touch conveyed an electrifying signal through his body. The old desire was still there.

"It's all over Louise," he said without turning. He could not trust himself to look.

"Don't say that Alex. I love you. Please tell me it's not finished." She leaned down and kissed him on the cheek. The reek of perfume sent the blood pounding through his brain.

He twisted away and stood up. She threw her arms around his neck in a fluid movement, but he did not react. She pulled back and looked into his eyes. "Is it really over?"

"Thanks for the invite and the fine meal Louise. I apologise for not doing it justice. As for the house I really can't give you any advice. I believe you'll just have to rely on Winton's charitable disposition."

"I'm not going to give Winton the pleasure of taking it away from me."

"Do you really think he aspires to this mausoleum?"

"Winton wants all the trappings that go with Roma Oil, and that includes this house."

"You two would make a cosy pair you know. Why don't you marry him and wrap the whole fortune up?"

"You can be as cruel as Winton when you want to be Alex."

"I think everyone has their fair share of cruelty Louise." He moved out into the foyer to where Sam had struck him.

She was reading his mind. "He did love you Alex."

"You are probably right Louise, but unfortunately it was far too late. I could have loved him too, if only he'd put his hand out a little earlier in my life."

"Can I call you a cab?"

"No, I'll just walk for awhile. It's such a beautiful night."

The driveway gravel crunched underfoot. It was a colonial touch in keeping with the imposing sandstone house constructed in colonial times. It kept a gardener busy sweeping and grooming it to give the appearance nothing drove over it. The street was almost in total darkness as he sauntered down the footpath to kill time for half an hour. He calculated it would be ample time to prove his theory. He was standing in the shadows of a property next to Roma when he saw the oncoming headlights swing into the street and slow down. He pulled back into the shadows and watched the Bentley turn and glide into the driveway. The front door of the manor opened as the car slid to a stop and Winton got out. They kissed as Louise led him inside.

Alex whistled softly to himself as he thought how close he had come to confiding everything to the one person who he felt he could trust. He had the feeling he would have wound up like Morgan if he had done so. Louise had been fishing all along as to the extent of his knowledge, and in particular whether he had listened to that voice recorder.

37

It was early. The receptionist had not arrived when Alex knocked on Winton's door and pushed it open. Winton looked up puzzled and then bounded from behind his desk holding out his hand, his face wreathed in a broad grin.

"It's good to see you Alex." The grip was firm as though confirming his sincerity. "And what have you decided?"

"I'll give you an option to purchase my stock on the condition if at the end of three months I'm still of the same opinion I am now, the stock is yours at a twenty percent premium to the closing price on that day."

"Done." Winton picked up the phone. "I'll have the agreement drawn up and we can get it signed this afternoon."

"There's just one other thing."

Winton hesitated. "And what's that?"

"I want to be elected a director of the company in the meantime. I'll resign of course, on exercise of the option." He could almost hear Winton's inward sigh of relief.

"I've no objection to that Alex. In fact, I think it's a very fair proposal. It's only a formality and I can arrange that this morning. We have a board meeting at ten."

His election to the board was waved through after he was introduced to each member. A polite hand clapping signalled his formal acceptance. He studied the faces around the polished mahogany table. They represented the cream of city financial power and influence. Winton Springer had them firmly in his grasp as he chaired the meeting. Financial reports, production reports, drilling reports and a variety of other intelligence flowed over the table in prepared manila folders. Each divisional head was called in to give an overall rundown on the report being tabled. A few questions were asked by various board members to justify their existence and heavy fees. Alex quickly grasped the reasoning. By adopting this approach Winton was keeping any written material from leaving the room. The reports were expansive and complete, but far too detailed for any board member to digest, let alone read within the time of the meeting. By calling in the various department heads the reports were delivered in précis. It was all staged as the various managers had been through it with Winton previously and had anticipated any questions. Alex could see it was democracy at work through the eyes of a dictator. The reports were quickly gathered up after each presentation. The directors did not require copies. The company was running smoothly under the direction of the new chairman. Why should they change the established protocol?

"And now gentlemen, we come to the final item on the agenda, that of the North Rowley Shoals project. Unfortunately, there's only one copy of this report so you will have to accept my interpretation and that of the department head. It appears we're not having any luck in the area and I move we abandon it. I can secure a two year option to sell it to Delco Oil for what we've outlaid. It will cost them a million for the option, plus we retain a ten percent carried interest. I accept it's not the greatest deal, but it could pay off if they find what we couldn't, if you ask me we should jump at the deal."

One board member raised his hand. "We've spent twenty million bucks there Winton. Why the sudden haste to toss in the towel?"

Winton fixed the man with an icy stare. "That's precisely the reason we should abandon it now. It's way over budget and I want to stop the haemorrhaging."

The director nodded his assent as he averted his gaze. The displeasure of Winton Springer had cost many a director his cosy position.

"All those in favour........"

He was cut off abruptly by Alex. "Aren't we going to hear from the head of exploration before abandoning it? If you will pardon me Mr Chairman, I realise I might be talking out of turn, but I've noticed the various heads have all addressed this meeting. Why not now? I would have thought this is a very important decision we're being asked to vote on."

"I don't think it necessary Alex. I have the report here that shows we're blowing money. We cannot continue to sustain losses on projects not showing any promise."

"Could I have a look at that file?"

Winton slid the folder across the table without comment. Alex opened it and began to flick through. It was a financial report and not a technical report as he had expected. He was conscious all eyes were fixed on him, but he deliberately took his time.

"Are you satisfied?"

"No, Winton I'm not. Could we hear from the head of this department?" Outwardly, he remained calm without the slightest look of concern, but he was worried about his approach. Was he taking the man on too early?

"I've already told you it's not necessary, the project is a dead loss."

"That's your opinion, but as a member of the board I would like to hear from whoever it is, so I can make up my own mind."

"I would remind you I'm the chairman and chief executive of this company and I will determine what projects are to be terminated. I've taken the stance on advice of my experts, and we're pulling out of North Rowley as of today. I've already agreed to the terms with Delco and the contract is being prepared."

"I'm not saying I don't accept your decision Mr Chairman, but it would appear to me every department head has been invited to give a presentation, except in this case. Why can't the formula continue?"

"Okay, you can discuss it with John Colenso after the board meeting. Now, how about we vote on it and wrap this meeting up?"

"What are you not telling the board Winton?"

An icy silence enveloped the room. "Are you suggesting I'm hiding something? I take grave exception to the insinuation."

"What else can I assume?"

The only sound was the drumming of Alex's fingers on the table as he waited for an answer. All eyes were fixed on Winton as they waited for the explosion. Winton's expression was like cold marble as he got up from his chair and strode out of the room. The door was left open signifying he would return. No one moved or spoke. The displeasure was not of their making. Why get dragged into something they wanted nothing to do with? It was nearly five minutes before Winton re-entered. The anger had left his face, but it was clear he was seething just below the surface.

"You shall have your report Mr Carlin. Colenso will be in directly to answer any of your questions. Following that I demand an apology or your resignation."

"I won't be apologising Winton, and as for my resignation you may recall we have an agreement. I will stick to the terms of that agreement."

Winton was stung by the riposte, and was about to make a reply when Colenso strode into the room.

"John, Mr Carlin would like to know why we're pulling out of North Rowley?"

"Simple Mr Carlin. It's because the results don't justify continued expenditure."

"How many holes have we drilled and what has it cost to date?"

"Two exploratory in shallow water near the shoreline at three million a hole."

"That's six million. What happened to the other fourteen million?"

"Drilling is not the only thing that costs money Mr Carlin. There are the preliminary costs such as seismic and the pure logistics of mounting the program in these remote locations."

"Add another three mill for that and we've spent nine million. We've got eleven million to account for."

"There was the cost of acquiring the licence areas." Colenso was hesitant and looked to Winton for assistance.

"You mean to tell me we are paying the government for the concessions. I was under the impression any fees were only initial licence payments. Isn't that correct?" Alex looked around at the other directors for an explanation, but there was complete silence.

"In this case Alex we had to buy an option over the the concession from a party who had been granted the original licence."

Winton hurriedly broke in when he noticed Colenso was stumbling for an answer.

"How much did we pay them?"

"We paid five million. The board approved the agreement as it looked an excellent deal at the time. I don't believe we need to discuss this any further."

"Who did we pay the money to?"

"To Delco of Canada. Your father approved it."

"Did he? Was that before or after his stroke?"

"I don't like where this is leading Alex. I'd be careful if I were you."

"I don't like it either Winton, but I can tell you it's got a certain smell about it. And where is this Delco registered? It's not in some tax haven such as Bermuda is it?"

"The finance department will be able to furnish you with a full account, now....."

Alex cut him off. "Very good Winton. I'll expect an audited financial statement by the next board meeting, and I mean audited. I want to know where every cent has gone. Have you got that Mr Colenso?"

"It's not my department Mr Carlin."

"I don't care if it's your department or not. I'm making you responsible for a full report and I also want to know who Delco is. I want the names of the directors and whether it's a private or public company. I want a full rundown on its operations."

"Just a bloody minute Carlin." Winton exploded as he listened to the hard line being taken by Alex. "I make the management decisions in this company. Colenso will report what I tell him to, not you."

Alex grinned slowly as he realised he had Winton rattled. "I've no doubt Mr Colenso will report exactly what you tell him to report Winton. I want to know more about these people we paid five million to. We gave them five to buy-in and now they're getting it back for a million after we've spent twenty. Something doesn't add up. What do they know we don't? As no one else on the board appears perturbed by the payment of such a large sum of money we're about to write off, I think it's up to me to get some clear answers."

There was a sudden change of mood in the room as the directors felt the weight and implications of the questions shifting directly onto their shoulders. Their director's liability insurance would not cover them if they had overlooked malfeasance on the part of management. Their legal liability for damages could be massive. Alex knew he had hit the target as they squirmed in their chairs and looked to Winton for assurance.

"You'll have your audited figures by the next board meeting Alex." Winton looked around gauging the mood in the room. "Is there anything else?"

"Yes, I want to see all the data on North Rowley. Can you get it for me please Mr Colenso?"

Colenso was about to answer when Winton cut him off. "It's out on the rig. We don't carry any of it here at all."

"Did you make the recommendation to pull out of the project?"

Colenso hesitated. "It was a pure commercial decision Mr Carlin, made here in head office. I simply report on the drilling and offer my opinions. Mr Springer makes the final decisions."

"Then you must have filed a report. I note you have nothing with you now. Would you ensure I have a copy of it by this afternoon."

"Check whether you have a copy now Colenso," Winton broke in. "If not, arrange for one to be sent over will you? It may take a day or two before you get it Alex."

Alex could see Winton was giving his subordinate the clear message, nothing was to be produced that afternoon.

"Now, I would like to put this to the vote again. Those in favour please signify by a show of hands."

The majority were clearly uneasy. Everything had been cut and dried in the past. This was the first time anyone had ever queried a Winton Springer decision.

"Have we dropped any other ground in the area?"

The question stopped the meeting dead. One director who had partially raised his hand in support of the motion, hastily scratched his ear in a nervous cover up.

"We dropped the South Rowley a year ago." Winton gavelled the table with his pen in frustration.

"Did we drill it?"

"Yes we did." Winton could not contain his anger at the interjections. "Seismic pointed to good entrapments, but a hole disproved the theory. We had a lot of trouble keeping the rig on station. The water was a bit too deep. We did appear to be getting something interesting when the rig moved in a cyclone and we lost the whole drill string. Once again no positive results and mounting costs forced us to pull the plug."

Alex was watching Colenso closely as Winton gave the explanation. The geologist was not good at covering up his true feelings and falling in behind his boss.

"And as regards North Rowley you say all information is out on the rig?"

"It is. The drill ship has plenty of room on board. We don't have to bring the data ashore to interpret it as we've got all the facilities we need out there."

"Well, how about we adjoin this meeting until I've had a look at the data?"

Winton laughed mockingly. "You haven't got the numbers for that Alex. I want a decision now."

Alex ignored the sarcasm. "If you attempt to drop the North Rowley before I've had time to look at the data and obtain advice, I shall obtain a court injunction restraining the board of this company. I'm a major shareholder in case you've forgotten."

"I don't take directions or threats from you Alex. Your boots are not as big as your father's, and I'll be damned if you can just walk in here and give orders."

"You are only one man Winton. You have a board here of very professional people who have reputations to protect. They might think otherwise."

One of the board members cleared his throat. He was speaking out of turn, but the mere mention of litigation had him worried. "We have nothing to lose by his request Mr Chairman. We're not spending money while Mr Carlin looks at the data he wants. I move we make the decision at the next meeting."

Alex could see Winton was about to assert his authority and cause a board split which would be disastrous for market appearances.

"Can I suggest a compromise gentlemen?" He studied the concerned faces around the table. "We vote to drop the area in principle now. If after reading the reports I make no objections, then the area can be dropped without reference to the board."

Winton realised he was trapped and shrugged his shoulders in resignation. "That's okay with me. Now can we have a vote on that?"

Alex watched as all hands went up. A thought suddenly occurred to him.

"Do we own our own drill ship?"

"No," Winton replied in a relieved tone now the proposal had passed. "No one owns their own drill ships or platforms. They're all on contract hire."

"Do we hire from C.T.Yong?"

"Yes we do, but why do you ask?"

"Nothing really Winton, but I do recall Dad mentioning the name when he met me in the States. Does Yong have any connection to Delco, I wonder?"

Winton's cold eyes bored into Alex. "I wouldn't know, but Yong has a spider web of connections and he could be involved in Delco. There's nothing suspicious about that."

"Isn't there?" Alex let the question hang as Winton closed the meeting.

"Can I help you Mr Carlin?" Alex was taken aback as studied the strange looking woman. She wore a severe grey suit, and thick soled shoes. The fringe of the severe haircut finished a centimetre above the black horn-rimmed glasses. She was short with no neck, and an incongruous little face stuck on top of square shoulders.

"Yes, I think you can," Alex replied with a disarming smile. "I'm looking for any reference to C.T.Yong. I would like to know who and what he is?"

"And in particular his connection with Roma Oil, or persons in control of Roma?"

"You mind read as well I see?"

The small woman beamed. "Yes, and I'm also a very good librarian. Yong is the head of C.T.Yong of Hong Kong, and a thousand other Asian companies. Everything from fish meal to shipping, property, banking, oil and gambling. You name it, he's in it."

"Where have I heard the name in connection with oil in Australia?"

"One of his companies ran the seismic studies for Australco when it proposed drilling on the edge of the Barrier Reef. As you probably know, that's all history now. Australco lost the concession, and the Premier of Queensland along with the board of Australco lost their jobs."

"Have you ever heard of a company named Delco Oil out of Canada?"

"Yes, Delco is the company Roma purchased the North Rowley Shoals option project from. Strange don't you think, that an unknown Canadian shelf company should beat an Australian producer to a prime piece of real estate? Springer made millions when he did a double deal on South Rowley also. He's in it up to his neck with Yong."

Alex looked at her in surprise. "What is your name?"

"Doris Cluff."

"Please call me Alex. Now Doris, why are you venturing this information? I'm intrigued at your accusations."

"I know what you're thinking, but you can relax. Winton Springer has been playing a double game for years. I've already read yesterday's board minutes so I know why you're here looking for answers. Correct?"

She was amused by Alex's look of puzzlement. "How could you have possibly read the minutes? They are strictly confidential."

"Alex, I'm the librarian. I'm aware of every bit of information that flows within this company. However, I do regard all information as being strictly confidential. What would you like to know about Mr Springer? I've known for years he's a crook on a grand scale. How your father didn't wake up to him years ago, I'll never know."

"Why didn't you say something to him?"

"I value my job. It was not my business to be a whistleblower at the expense of my livelihood. I did float a rumour once, but it got nowhere."

"Why don't you just tell me what you know? It doesn't have to follow any pattern. I'll try and piece it together."

Doris laughed. "You won't have to piece it together. I can make it flow like a book."

Doris talked for an hour. Alex was incredulous. It was like listening to a carefully edited tape recording of the entire history of the company and its personalities.

"Do you think he had anything to do with my sister's death?"

"I don't know about that. I know you accused him of murdering her and of the row with your father. Is that why you left?"

Alex nodded as the memory of that day flooded back. "Yes, it was. I was convinced Springer was responsible, but had no proof. Now I know he did, but still can't prove it."

It was Doris' turn to look puzzled. "How do you know that?"

"My father gave me a recording of his last meeting with Springer. He must have been trying to gain evidence about something Springer was up to for him to have a recorder running. Anyway there was a violent argument. Springer could obviously see Sam was having a stroke or was on the verge of it, when he as much as admitted he'd let Marty drown. I believe that admission was the trigger that ultimately killed my father. There was a lot more on the recorder. Winton was boasting about fake companies, but I really didn't take too much notice. My mind was focussed on Marty. It proved what I'd always suspected, that he'd murdered her. The recorder was stolen from me so I don't have a shred of hard evidence other than my word against Springer's."

"Maybe I can supply the key to the fake companies he referred to. It will take an expert to unravel though."

"Tell me what you've got."

"Marty was working on something just before she got married. It was something to do with the Brisbane office and a man named Albert Reed. She spent hours and hours going through old files of accounting data. She worked here because there was plenty of room to spread documents out on these big tables. At the time I thought she was a pest as I could never get my work done because she was always calling for files.

"Please Doris." Alex grabbed her hand in excitement. "Tell me what my sister found?" He followed her gaze and realised he was gripping her hand tightly. "I'm sorry Doris, I didn't mean to be personal."

"Don't apologise. You're the only person in this company who's ever held my hand and meant it. Yes, now what was I saying? Oh yes, Marty told me late one day she thought she'd discovered a massive fraud, but needed more time to unravel it completely. It concerned Reed and someone very high up in the company. She remarked it had to go all the way to the top. I remember joking it had to be your father or Springer. It was a spur of the moment remark I made without thinking. I can tell you, it was not well received. I could see she thought I was referring to her father. That was a week before she married Springer. When she drowned I wrote a memo to the chief accountant asking what to do with the files she'd been working on. The next day I got an abrupt phone call from Springer telling me to bundle them all up and deliver them to his secretary."

"And you did?"

"Oh yes, I bundled up a lot of old accounting files and delivered them. You see, it occurred to me the person responsible for the fraud had to be Springer. Why would you want old files years out of date? I confirmed my suspicions a week or so later when I phoned Springer's secretary to see if he'd viewed the files as I would like them deposited back in the archives. She said Springer had sent them out for destruction as they were no longer relevant. The files Marty was working on I still have."

She turned and beckoned him to follow her to a row of flat map-filing cabinets. "This cabinet contains everything she was working on at the time. It is practically how she left it."

"And nothing is missing?"

"Nothing goes missing in my library. That's exactly how she left it."

Alex looked down at the neat layers of carefully pencilled spread sheets and financial data. He could feel his sister's presence.

"It's all there, layer by layer and it goes back years prior to Marty's death. I knew I could never throw it away. I had a premonition something like this would happen one day. Your sister was a very warm person like yourself. I warmed to her from the first moment we met. She was never pushy or overbearing like many of the executives are here. She was a live human being and I admired her immensely."

"Do you know someone in the company you can trust to look at this?"

"Yes there is, Alex."

"Who is this person?"

"Can we leave it by saying I trust him completely. When he's unravelled all this and confirms your sister was right, I'll introduce you. He will have to work on it away from the premises. Can you give me permission to do that?"

"I can and it's a deal. You tell who ever it is, I want Marty's suspicions confirmed or discounted as soon as possible. I don't care what it costs."

"Some things don't require payment. I would do anything for your father. Let's just say I'm doing it for him."

"Is this fellow Reed still around?"

Doris shook her head. "He's been spread over a memorial garden for some years now. They fished him out of the river. Cops knew he was a homosexual and believe he was tossed in by a group out gay bashing. I don't buy that story."

"It would appear you know the truth?"

"I do. You see we people are really a close knit group. We have an underground. Reed was picked up outside a gay bar by a couple of unknowns and twelve hours later he's found floating in the Brisbane river."

"Was there any link with Springer, do you think?"

"Doesn't appear to be, other than a strong coincidence. It happened less than a week after Marty's death. Springer went to Brisbane. I could even retrieve the exact flight number and time if you like. He had fired Reed. I heard on the grapevine there was an argument over money Springer is supposed to have owed him. Reed died sometime that night. People have a habit of dying around Winton Springer, don't they?"

"And that's another reason you've left these drawers untouched?"

"I believe the wheel always goes the full circle. People don't get away with anything they're trying to hide. They think they do, but the indiscretions and dirty secrets eventually always catch up."

"Do I detect a big serve of revenge in there somewhere Doris?"

She laughed and slid the drawer closed. "Yes, you do. Springer treats people like dirt. I've had to take it because it would be impossible to get another job at my age, and my appearance doesn't exactly attract me to would-be employers. I know he refers to me as the ugly butch-bitch behind my back. He would never say that to my face. I would bust him one."

Alex burst out laughing, but cut it short when he noticed the look on her face. "I'm not laughing at you Doris. I just find it hilarious. The thought of two black eyes or a busted nose on Winton Springer is just too much to visualise."

Doris grinned beneath the heavy glasses. "What if I just kick him in the nuts then?" They laughed together, their bond of friendship complete.

"Okay, I'll take these home tonight and get my trusted friend onto them tomorrow. You'll have your answer within the week. I promise you that. Now, is there anything else I can help you with?"

"Would you by any chance have any of the seismic or drilling data from the North Rowley Shoals program?"

"No, that's all kept aboard the drill platform until the completion of the program. The project was abandoned yesterday so it should find its way into my hands for filing within the next month or so."

"Your infallible system is falling down Doris. The project is not being abandoned until I've had time to look at the data." He trailed off when he saw Doris shaking her head.

"Springer ordered the program stopped immediately after yesterday's board meeting. All emails and phone calls in and out are recorded. One of my staff prints all emails off our mainframe every day to ensure we have a hardcopy record."

Doris walked out and came back with a file which she was flicking through. "Here it is. The order was given by Springer."

Alex read the email in dismay. "That deceitful bastard. I'm going to take this up with him immediately."

"You're wasting your time. He's already left for Western Australia and the drill ship."

Alex sat down heavily in exasperation. "What was my father doing while this was going on."

"He wasn't a well man. He never got over Marty's death and you were obviously on his mind. The company appeared to be running smoothly with Springer at the helm, so I guess he felt he could leave all the decisions to him."

"Did my father have anything to do with giving away South Rowley?"

"When the helicopter went down I don't think he had the board support to oppose it. Springer pushed it through. Roma didn't exactly give it away, but optioned it off to Delco of Canada, as now they're proposing with North Rowley, for a couple of million. They've got two years to come up with a drilling program and complete two holes, otherwise the area reverts to Roma. Of course, if they hit it they'll on-sell it to one of the majors for millions in excess of what they would get if Delco simply exercises its option to purchase."

Alex looked thoughtful as he tried to recall something he should know about or been informed of by now. Why wasn't it mentioned at yesterday's board meeting? "What helicopter? Where did it go down?"

Doris studied him in surprise. "You mean to tell me you don't know about that?"

"Of course not," Alex snapped. "Doris I'm sorry, it's just that I'm ignorant of a lot of things going on around here. Tell me about this accident."

"It was about a year ago. Just a moment." Doris disappeared behind a row of tracked file cabinets and returned with a green bound ledger. She dumped it on the table and began to thumb through. "This is a board meeting minute ledger. Ah, here we are. I'll start at the beginning to put the accident in sequence of events. Springer moved the South Rowley be optioned off because of the difficulties with drilling. The drill ship moved suddenly late at night and snapped off the drill stem. Springer claimed the water was too deep for the existing technology. However, I know something about that particular accident. You see I know someone of impeccable integrity who maintains they appeared to be drilling into oil bearing strata when suddenly the rig went crazy. It happened while the engineer on watch was in the galley making himself a coffee. Somehow the computer controlling the positioning of the ship went down and the backup failed to activate. It wasn't a normal computer crash. Someone had tampered with it and it wasn't the work of an amateur. The engineer was fired and the program shut down."

"You mean you can produce the person to verify what you're telling me?"

"I certainly can, but I'll come back to that later. Let's just follow this chopper accident though. According to the minutes your father opposed the dropping of the program. He wanted to redrill the hole as the seismic profiles looked exciting. Your father proposed he would study all the information before such a decision to abandon it was passed at board level."

"Where have I heard that suggestion before?"

"What do you mean by that?"

"Nothing Doris. I was just thinking aloud. Please go on."

"Two days later the chopper with all the data plus the pilot and four staff disappeared between South Rowley and Onslow. I've got press clippings on file if you would care to look at them."

"Thanks Doris. I would."

Alex read the clippings glued into another folder Doris produced. Highly experienced pilot, perfect weather conditions, no radio calls and no debris found despite a widespread search.

"Springer has a lot to answer for."

"You really think he had something to do with this Doris? You're talking about five deaths. You're suggesting murder on a grand scale."

"The motive is money Alex. Five or five hundred souls wouldn't make any difference to Springer."

"I think we need a bit more evidence than that. Suspicion is not evidence."

"Find the wreckage of the helicopter and you might find part of the truth."

"Why is the chopper so vital?"

"Springer was out on the rig at the time of the accident to gather up all the information Sam had requested. He could have had it sent over but no, he decided he would go get it personally. A row broke out between Springer and Max Brown the chief geophysicist on the ship. Brown caught Springer and Colenso running data through the computer late one night. Brown spotted they were altering data. Springer tried to pull rank, but Brown got his way and ordered them out of the area."

"How do you know this took place Doris?" Alex was sceptical.

"That person of impeccable integrity I referred to before told me."

"What's the person's name?"

Doris ignored the question. "Brown viewed what they'd been attempting to do and sat up all night writing a report to Sam. He told my informant he was going to deliver a full submission to Sam personally. He also recommended the board fire Springer. The basis of the report was that it was crazy to abandon the project. When Brown finished the report he told Springer about the contents. Springer fired him on the spot and ordered him to hand over the hardcopy and his computer. Brown was a big powerful man and more than a match for Springer. Finally Springer backed down and said rather than go back with Brown he would follow the day after so Brown could discuss his findings with Sam without his presence. Brown fell for it. His helicopter disappeared an hour after leaving the ship. Springer delivered a report prepared by Colenso ruling out continuing the program due to lack of encouraging results and technical difficulties. Sam had complete faith in Colenso and it was agreed to. I wonder how much Springer paid Colenso?"

"I can't come to grips with what his real motive was. He's a multi millionaire and is paid millions every year."

"Greed, absolute greed Alex, is the way I read it. You would naturally think he would be comfortable with what he already has, but that's not what makes Winton Springer tick. He plans to move to absolute control of Roma. Now Springer is planning to abandon North Rowley and Delco will then consolidate both blocks and start drilling. According to my confidant they can't miss an oil or major gas strike. They'll flog it to a major for millions. Springer's thinking is, why work for salary and a few stock options when you can make millions without the shareholders becoming aware of the crime being committed."

"Unbelievable, but I can now understand what Springer was saying on the recorder. Where do I find this impeccable source of yours Doris? I must speak to him. Why didn't you just front with him at the time? I'm sure my father would have listened. If your source is as good as you say, he would have been a key witness in any action against Springer. I take it we have a report from Springer giving his reasons for the South Rowley being dropped?"

"Yes, that's on file along with all the altered drilling data."

"How do you know that?"

Doris smiled. "Because my source has checked it, and it's completely opposite to what Brown was carrying with him when he disappeared."

Alex became irritated. "Who the hell is this person Doris? Why didn't he step forward? The world is full of gutless people who stand on the sidelines because of fear of reprisal."

"You are correct of course, but whistle-blowing seldom happens in the real world," she replied calmly. "You can't blame him. He could not level accusations at the managing director of a company he'd only been employed by for a short time. He only wanted to do his job. He didn't want to get mixed up in the politics, and if you're going to attack him I won't tell you who he is."

"I'm sorry Doris. I don't suppose it matters much now anyway. Without the chopper records being recovered there's no way it can be proved Springer's report is false. The fraud cannot be matched with the original so to speak, and I daresay Brown and his report would have been devoured by marine life long ago."

"Not so. Any data transported between ship and shore was always carried in water tight cylinders. My source said Brown sealed his reports and technical information into four of those tubes. Brown would have also been carrying his computer, which I've no doubt would have been in a waterproof container."

"Okay Doris, I promise I won't bring any pressure to bear on your informant. I will not implicate him in anyway, but you must tell me who he is."

"He's my son. He's an oil geologist with Roma although I've never told anyone of our relationship, and neither has he. He's now here in head office."

Alex could not hide his shock.

"You can take that look off your face Alex. I'm still human despite my appearance and looks. I did love someone once."

"Can I meet your son?"

"Why don't you come around for dinner this evening? You can judge for yourself whether he knows what he's talking about."

38

Peter Masterman was the complete professional, quietly spoken and venturing nothing during dinner. Even his answers to small talk were carefully considered.

"Let's go into the lounge and talk Mr Carlin. My mother said you wanted to know about the South Rowley. I will help you if I can."

They went in and sat down. Alex could clearly see that Masterman was uncomfortable with what he was about to disclose. "You ask the questions Mr Carlin and I'll see if I can answer them."

"Can you confirm before the drill-ship moved and broke the drill stem you were drilling into oil bearing sediments?"

"In my opinion we were onto something very significant."

"Who besides yourself knew that?"

"Besides myself, Brown and Colenso were the only other people technically qualified, and I was junior to both of them."

"Come on Peter," Doris chipped in. "Don't be reticent. Why don't you open up and tell Alex everything you've told me? It's high time Springer got what's coming to him."

Masterman gave his mother a sharp look of disapproval. "I don't want to get mixed up in this mother. Springer has never been a threat to me. Of course he didn't realise I witnessed the

383

argument when Brown caught him and Colenso tampering with the computers. I certainly don't know if he had anything to do with the loss of the helicopter. What have I got to gain by accusing Springer of something that cannot be proved? I know the reports on South Rowley were falsified, but until someone produces the originals there is no way I can reconstruct them as the computer hard drive on the drill ship was totally corrupted by someone. Of course the hole could have been re-drilled, but Roma no longer has the area."

"Do you think the North Rowley is as prospective as the South?"

Masterman's face lit up. "Mr Carlin, South Rowley should never have been relinquished. It was a ludicrous decision."

"Then why did my father agree?"

"Simple really. It was obvious he was not aware he was victim of a fraud."

"And North Rowley?"

"North Rowley is even more prospective than the South. From what I've seen there appear to be some large gas and oil entrapments. I wish I was working on the program out there rather than being stuck here in head office."

"Then you haven't heard the company is proposing to option it off to some small Canadian outfit?"

Masterman sat bolt upright. "Is it what? Are the directors out of their minds? You've got to stop this folly."

"I intend to Peter, but I'm pushing it up hill at the moment. I would like to call a board meeting, but it will have to wait until Springer gets back from the west."

"He's probably gone to confirm whether it's Brown's helicopter they've apparently found."

"What did you say?"

"I was chatting to a friend of mine in Onslow this afternoon. He's on shore leave from the rig for a few days. He mentioned part of a rotor blade had been dredged up by a fishing trawler to the south-east of Rowley Shoals near a little outcrop called Zeenuis. It's a tiny cay only marked on marine maps. If it is Brown's chopper, it was well outside the area searched at the time it went missing."

Alex was trying to control his excitement. "Are you sure the wreckage was a chopper blade?"

"I can only relate what my friend told me, but if you want confirmation you could phone the Onslow police. He did say Springer had apparently been informed."

"Thank you Peter. I'd better get going."

"What are you going to do at this hour?"

"Roma has two company jets. Springer has obviously got one, so I'll see if I can't use some influence and commandeer the other. I want to be there when they pull that chopper out of the water."

It was late morning when the Cessna Citation touched down in Onslow. Alex looked out from the right hand seat as it slowly taxied back down the runway. The ramp was empty except for a company helicopter in its blue and gold livery beside a hangar.

He knew Winton was grounded in Perth while a technical fault in his plane was being fixed.

"Tango, Sierra, Gulf calling Charlie, Alfa, Romeo. Please respond?" Alex had heard the call sign and saw the pilot begin to respond. He quickly leaned over to restrain him.

"Don't answer that."

"But that's our call sign and that's John Chance the pilot of Mr Springer's plane."

"I said don't answer it. I know who it is, but I repeat, don't answer it."

"I can't comply with that request Mr Carlin. He could be in trouble and I must respond."

Alex nodded in resignation.

"Charlie, Alfa, Romeo. What can I do for you John?"

"We're in Perth with a tech problem. We know you're headed for Onslow, but Mr Springer wants you to divert to pick him up. We understand you have Mr Carlin on board?"

The pilot looked at his panel. "I can't divert John. I'm about half an hour out of Onslow and don't have the fuel to divert. Confirming Mr Carlin is aboard. I'll refuel and then come on down."

Alex unbuckled himself as the jet came to a standstill. "Thanks for the lift." The heat was stifling the moment the stairway was dropped and he stepped down onto the tarmac. There was a solitary taxi outside the terminal. He opened the door and woke the dozing driver.

"You available?"

"Sure am. Ly Chan at your service. Where you wanna go?"

"Someone fished part of a helicopter blade out of the water a day or so ago. Do you know where I can find him?"

"Sure, that's Rocco, Mad Rocco. He a good friend of mine." Ly pointed at his chest. "What you want of him?"

"I want him to show me where he found it."

"You must have money eh? Cost you plenty to get Rocco to show you."

"Haven't you got air conditioning in this car?"

"Fully airnishinned," Ly laughed. "Just keep window open."

They approached the jetty with its assortment of small trawlers in various stages of repair and decay, all tied up securely waiting for the next high tide to refloat them. Ly drove onto the first few boards of the wharf and pulled up sharply.

"Better not drive any further. Forty bucks please. Rocco on his boat for sure."

"Which one is his?"

"Go down until smell get too bad. That Rocco's boat."

"You wait for me please?"

Alex picked his way down the wharf stepping gingerly over holes in the decking. Ly was right. The stench of rotting fish was overpowering as he came abreast of a battered trawler. A solitary figure was leaning over the engine.

"Hi there, are you Rocco?"

The figure lifted his head and grunted. "If you can fix a fuel pump you're welcome. If you can't, piss off."

Alex swung down onto the deck and looked at the dismantled pump. "Looks beyond repair to me."

"I agree with you. What do you want?"

"You found part of a chopper a few days ago?"

"I did, but the cops took it away."

"Do you know where you found it?"

Rocco nodded as he wiped his filthy hands on a piece of cotton waste. "Yep, I do."

"Could you take me out to it?"

"It will cost you. I have to make up for lost catches, the cost of fuel and expenses………"

"I'll give you two grand plus expenses. I'm assuming you know exactly where it is?"

"Like an Italian knows where the pleasure of a woman is," Rocco replied laughing. "However, my boat will be out of action until I get a new pump. That's the boat you need."

Rocco pointed to a pearling lugger standing upright in a mud berth carved into a clump of mangroves.

"Where do I find the owner?"

"Ma Chan. She owns the pub. That's her son Ly driving the taxi. The old girl owns just about everything in town and Ly is just waiting for her to kick the bucket so he can gamble it all away. I wish my Momma had been so hardworking, God rest her sainted soul." Rocco crossed himself while momentarily raising his eyes to the heavens.

"You are sure you can find the site again? I don't want any bullshit."

"I tell you what. You look like a gambling man, so let's make it double or nothing. I know the sea as you know your own street. I'll take you straight to it."

"You're on."

They shook on the deal, but Alex had the uncomfortable feeling he was already on the wrong end of the bargain.

"What's in the wreck that you so badly want to find?"

"Information I hope."

"That's what the other person said too."

"What other person?"

"A Dr Coulson. You know this person? Mama Mia, she's one good looking lady."

Alex shook his head. He had never heard of the name before. "No. Do you know where she staying?"

"At Ma Chan's pub. Now let's get down to business. High tide's at two in the morning. You'll have no problem getting Ly to skipper the boat. Just watch it though. That thieving little slant will try and get you for every penny. Better still, I'll come back and negotiate for you now."

They walked back along the jetty to Rocco's pickup. It was as bad as his boat with the stench just as unbearable. Alex hung his head half out of the window to get some relief. Rocco swung the pickup into the yard of the hotel closely followed by Ly.

"Must clean that out one of these days." Rocco got out, slammed the door and looked in the tray. "Phew, that stinks. I must have missed a few prawns."

The oriental woman behind the bar was skinny and toothless. It was impossible to guess at her age as her actions and speech were firm and decisive as she chatted to other patrons. Without being asked she propped two schooners of beer on the counter and held out her hand for the money. Rocco pretended not to notice as Alex grinned to himself and handed over a twenty.

"I've got a customer who wants to hire your boat Ma, along with that lying son of yours."

"Grand a day plus fuel." Ma shouted from the other end of the bar.

"And diving gear if you've got it and a diver if possible."

Ly was suddenly at his elbow. "How much this thieving wog charge you to show you where wreck is?" He stabbed his gnarled finger into Rocco's chest.

"Five hundred," Alex replied with a deadpan expression.

"Eeeh, you bigger liar than me. Cost you grand a day for boat, an five hundred for me as skipper an diver. I'm expert," he said giving himself the familiar stab in the chest.

"Best diver on coast."

"Lying bastard, but he'll have to do." Rocco sank the remains of his beer and signalled for Ma to refill it. "Only thing he's expert at is diving on pussy and then he's got to pay for it. Can't get it otherwise."

Ly looked furious at the insult before breaking into peels of laughter. "You only jealous you stinking dago. No woman let you touch her, you stink so much."

Rocco twisted Ly's shirtfront in his massive fist and lifted him off his feet, the thin arms and legs flailing in all directions.

"You put me down you dirty wop. I kill you."

"What shall I do with him Ma. Shall I send him to his forefathers?"

Ma did not look up as she busily pulled more beers. "Don't exterminate him just yet, useless son though he is."

Rocco let go and Ly dropped silently to the floor. Alex was astounded with the speed with which he moved. The next instant Rocco was flat on his back on the floor with Ly's foot planted firmly in his throat. He had hold of one of Rocco's hands and was bending it slowly back as he watched the pain increase on his face. Rocco finally thumped the floor with his other hand in submission. Ly laughed as he let him get up.

Alex had not seen the policeman enter the bar. The uniform topped by a broad brimmed hat just appeared beside him.

"Excuse me. Are you Alex Carlin?"

"Yes, that's correct."

"I've been told you may be here to locate the wreck of the helicopter Rocco found."

Alex nodded uneasily. He had the distinct feeling he was about to be told something he did not want to hear.

"I've had a call from Mr Springer. He's informed me no one's allowed near that wreck until he gets here. Mr Springer said it contains important company records which he wants to recover. Also there are probably human remains and the wreckage will have to be hauled out to determine how the crash occurred. Mr Springer is personally taking charge of the whole operation. "

"My father was the founder of Roma Oil. I'm a director of the company and I think I've got every right to go out there."

The cop stiffened and his voice took on a hard edge. "I knew Sam Carlin and I know Mr Springer, but I don't know you although I've got no doubt you are who you say you are. However, I'm telling you you're not to go near that wreck. You can sort it out with Mr Springer when he gets here. I've told the lady also."

"Lady?"

"Yes, Dr Coulson. She's also staying in the hotel. Mr Springer will be here sometime tomorrow. In the meantime you are not to go near the wreck. Do I make myself clear?"

"Certainly officer," Alex replied affably. "I'll wait for Springer."

"What you going to do now?" Ly could see his charter fee disappearing as he watched the cop walk out of the bar.

"Why don't we just go fishing. How long will it take to get out to a decent fishing ground?"

Rocco raised a questioning brow and then broke into a broad grin. "About six hours if we catch the tide in the morning."

"Okay. I'll see you down at the boat. In the meantime Ly, can you give me a room?"

"I put you in room next to lady. You will be awake all night dreaming about her."

"Is she that good looking?"

"Eeeh, you wait till you see. I give anything to get knickers off." Ly picked up Alex's bag and darted off up the stairs.

The room opened onto a broad balcony overlooking the street. A huge ceiling fan slowly turned, gently stirring the becalmed air.

"I wake you in morning. Pleasant dleams." Ly giggled as he disappeared closing the door behind him.

Alex walked out onto the balcony and flopped into a wicker chair. He propped his feet up on the low table and closed his eyes. He felt tired. He did not hear her sit down. It was the perfume that aroused his senses as it overcame the lingering odour of Rocco's pickup.

"I didn't mean to wake you."

Alex slowly opened and eye and studied her. "Yes you did, but I don't mind at all. You must be Dr Coulson?" He took his feet off the table and held out his hand to introduce himself. "Alex Carlin."

"Peta Coulson. I work for Roma as a geophysicist."

"And you were sent here by Winton Springer to intercept me I suppose?"

"No, that couldn't be further from the truth."

Alex studied her face. It was sincere and the eyes remained steady with none of the flickering unease or averted gaze of someone trying to hide a lie.

"Well, why are you here?"

"I want to go out to that wreck with you."

"I'm not going. The local constabulary has squashed the idea. I can't do a thing until Springer gets here sometime tomorrow."

"You don't expect me to believe that, do you?"

"You don't have to," Alex replied curtly. "But that's the truth of it."

"You make a very unconvincing liar."

Alex pulled himself up straight in the chair, jolted by her remark. "Look, I'm not very fond of being called a liar."

"Well, why don't you tell the truth then? We both know you'll be catching the high tide in the morning. Why don't we talk about this? After all, we're both after the same thing."

"And what's that?"

"The containers of technical data, and computer that must be down there."

"Does Springer know you're here?"

"I'm sure he does by now. I commandeered a company chopper to bring me ashore this morning on the pretence I was sick and needed to see a doctor. The onboard medic had to accept it without query when I told him it was a women's problem."

Alex chuckled at her explanation. "But why do you want to go out to the wreck. Why's the data so important to you?"

"The very same reason you want it Alex. You see, Max Brown was my husband and I want to prove he was murdered."

Alex slumped back in the chair and gave a low whistle. "Did Springer know about your relationship?"

"No, he didn't. Roma had a strict policy of not employing married professional couples. The explanation was drilling rigs were not the place for husband and wife teams as too many complications could occur. We kept a strict professional relationship which was very difficult, but it worked. I believe Max was murdered because of the report he intended to deliver to your father."

"Murder is a very finite accusation."

"Nevertheless, I'm convinced the helicopter was sabotaged, but I can prove nothing at this stage. You see, I helped my husband prepare those reports and I know exactly what they contained. After he died I made a request to see the report recommending abandonment of the concession and the name of the person who submitted it. I was eventually taken aside and quietly informed if I wished to continue my employment with the company, I should forget about my request and devote my time to my specific tasks."

"You'll certainly get the chop if you come with me then."

"I don't really care about that now. In fact, I know my cover will be blown eventually, so I've decided to resign. We received a message on the rig yesterday that North Rowley was to be abandoned. I don't want to work for a company that won't listen to its technical staff's advice."

"You're quite a witness. Powerful testimony, but whether it would convict Springer without the actual data to back it up is a grey area."

"I know, and that's why I'm pleading with you to take me along. You see, within half an hour of Max leaving the rig, Springer had closed it down. He called in support helicopters to remove the entire technical crew to shore. All that was left were the necessary crew to pack up the ship and return to port. By the time the last helicopter had taken off, my husband was dead and there was not a scrap of technical evidence, including the hard discs aboard that ship."

Alex drummed his fingers on the arms of the chair. Here was the confirmation of what Masterman had already told him. "I don't think you should come with me in the morning. I think you should wait here."

"No, I'm coming with you. I'm an accomplished diver and it will make the search a lot quicker."

"I've hired Ly Chan also, so there will be three of us," Alex replied slowly as though lost in thought. He could see it was no use arguing with her. She was one of the most strikingly vivacious women he had ever laid eyes on.

"Why are you grinning?" Her sparkling hazel eyes were penetrating as they danced with intensity and light. Her breasts thrust through the blue Roma Oil monogrammed shirt tucked into form-fitting slacks. Her nipples stood erect as she asserted her bearing. Her body moved in unison with her voice; vibrant and demanding.

"I was just thinking how lovely you are."

"I've been told that before by every loved-starved individual with lust in his eyes."

"I've no doubt you have, but you are the most attractive person I've ever met, and I don't mean only in the physical sense. I think I'm already in love with you."

She gave him an exasperated look. "Don't shoot that line of bulldust at me Alex Carlin. Just because you're the only decent looking man I've seen in months, doesn't mean I'm going to believe your baloney. How many times have you tried that line on?"

"Never."

It was the finality in his voice which confirmed he was telling the truth. His eyes did not waver, and his expression remained completely deadpan. She could see he meant it.

"Would you like a drink Peta?"

"Yes, thank you. Just a small gin and tonic. Alcohol and the sea don't mix with me."

Ly Chan started giggling as he mixed the gin and tonic and scotch for Alex. "You makin out eh? She just like fresh plawn, beautiful and succulent isn't she? She be very sweet to eat."

Alex ignored the lurid slurping sound Ly made between his teeth as he picked up the two drinks and went back upstairs. They sat in silence and watched the brilliant red ball of sunset as it covered half the horizon.

"It's beautiful, isn't it?"

Alex nodded, but said nothing as the nuclear fire dipped away below the horizon. The nightlife immediately commenced a low overtone of nocturnal sound. The heat of the day began to diminish slowly at the zephyrs of cooler katabatic air sprang up.

39

He awoke with a start as the hand shook him. It was Ly grinning from ear to ear. "No have much success with sweet plawn eh? Time to go. Half and hour to catch tide."

The light was already on in Peta's room and he could hear movement as he slowly pulled himself out of the cramped confines of the chair he had dozed off in.

The diesel was already ticking over when the three of them walked down the jetty. "That wog sleep on board last night an check all gear. We ready to go. Eeh, I forgot waiting time for my cab when I quote you. Have to negotiate again when get back."

Alex pretended not to hear the remark as Ly scuttled aboard laughing at his own joke.

Rocco was at the helm when he noticed the approaching headlights. "Cast off you yellow heathen," he shouted.

Ly had seen the lights first and moved with the speed of a cat. The mooring lines were gone by the time Rocco had finished the sentence. The diesel roared into life as he pushed the throttle full ahead.

The vehicle skidded to a halt fifty metres back along the jetty as the policeman sprang out and shouted. He dared not drive any further on the ailing structure.

"You come back here Rocco. I'll have your arse for this Ly Chan. Go near that wreck Carlin and you're under arrest." The threats tumbled out as his closing strides did not match the gathering speed of the departing vessel. He drew his pistol, pointed it at the boat, then thrust it back in its holster with a bellow of rage. Rocco doffed his fisherman's hat in a mocking farewell.

The moon was at their backs as the powerful diesel thrust the vessel through the gentle swell. Alex was intrigued by the immaculate appearance of the boat compared with its owner and his battered taxi.

"He keeps it in top condition," he remarked to Rocco.

"It's his mother's boat. It's really a pearler which she used to dive off and finally bought. She takes it out by herself and disappears for days at a time. She buried her husband from its decks and I'm sure she goes out to the spot and just anchors and talks to him. She's a fine old girl really. Ly gives the appearance he's a fool, but don't be taken in by that. He's a first rate person, absolutely reliable and trustworthy, but a bit of a gambler. All Chinese gamble."

Alex gave him a look of surprise. "I thought you two could barely stand the sight of each other."

"It's an act," Rocco replied with a grin. "Why don't you go below and take it easy. We've got a good six hours ahead so there's no point in all of us standing around."

"Call me if you want me," Alex remarked as he and Peta clambered down the short stairway. The long cabin was all exposed Jarrah, the rich red giant timber of the southern forests. It was oiled and polished to bring out the vibrant natural colour. The thick ribs were of the same timber as the hulls thick planking. It was a hull built to withstand any conditions, particularly the cyclones that swept through this region every wet season.

Alex suddenly felt exhausted as he lay down on a bunk. He and Peta had talked long into the night and she must have quietly left him when he eventually drifted off. His eyes were still heavy, but his mind remained strangely clear. He watched Peta as she methodically inspected the diving gear. Everything she did had the mark of a professional about it. Nothing was overlooked. Every last item was checked and re-checked and then put carefully to one side. Finally, she lay down on a bunk and within minutes was asleep. They had hardly spoken a word since the previous evening, each lost in their own world and thoughts. The gentle rhythm of the engine finally lulled him into a troubled sleep.

It was the aroma of food cooking that awakened him. Ly was humming as he watched the bacon and eggs sizzle in the large frying pan. He noticed Alex swing his feet down from the bunk.

"Eeh, thought smell would wake you. Sweet plawn already above." He pointed above his head with the spatula.

It was cool in the cabin, fanned by a breeze created by the air being funnelled through a large open hatch in the forepeak. The sea had a turgid oily appearance as Alex thrust his head above deck. Rocco was like a figure transfixed as he looked ahead, his gaze unwavering.

"Is the bet still on, double or nothing?" Alex asked the question to break the silence.

"Sure is," Rocco replied with a broad grin.

"What's the bet about?" It was Peta who asked the question. She was sitting back under an awning shading the stern from the heat of the sun.

"Just a little bet he wouldn't be able to find the site again without going around in circles searching for it."

"I think you're going to lose that one. I can see it from here." He followed her pointing finger. It took him a few moments to make out the brilliant orange marker flag attached to a float. "Is that it Rocco?"

"Certainly is miss." He broke into laughter as he turned to Alex. "I told you I could sail right up to it."

"But I wrongly assumed you were using compass bearings and seafaring skills." Alex was shaking his head at his own folly. "It just shows how befuddled my mind is at the moment."

"I flagged its position. You owe me double the charter fee. Agreed?"

"Yes, agreed Rocco." He was delighted it had been so easy. A quarter of an hour later they were anchored over the spot. The water was an intense azure. Alex was securing his single tank when Peta came on deck, the single piece bathing suit revealing all. She took no notice of the three men as they stopped what they were doing. They suddenly broke into a babble of proffered help, but she ignored them as she began to pull on a wet suit. The interest died as the flesh disappeared and she strapped on her tank and weights.

Alex stood on the stern and cast a final look around. He could see a small outcrop of an island to the north. It was part of the Zeeius group. There was nothing visible to seaward. To the east he could make out the vague outline of the coast, a smudgy line dancing in the shimmering haze. He adjusted his mask and stepped backwards with Peta following him along with Ly, a few seconds later. Visibility was excellent as they sank towards the seabed. Half an hour later their earlier expectations were in total disarray. They had found nothing. The small coral outcrops stretched endlessly with their teeming marine life taking no notice of the intruders.

"I think we may have to re-think that bet Rocco," he said as he pulled himself aboard.

"This is where I pulled up the trawl and the blade was in it," Rocco replied indignantly. "However, the flag could have been dragged by the tide."

"We're too far to the south I think," Peta replied as she studied a chart Rocco had spread out. "I noticed the current down there had a southerly set, so I think we should move a couple of kilometres to the north-east and drift back to here and then repeat the exercise."

"Yes, I was trawling from the north-east, so that theory makes sense." Rocco fired up the engine and winched in the anchors.

It was half an hour later when Alex spotted a flash of gold and blue in the distance. They had been swimming in ever widening circles with each dive. Peta, who had been swimming off to his right, saw it at the same time and quickened her pace towards it.

The wreckage was lying on its side, the scorched fuselage open to a gaping hole where the twin turbines were housed. One or both of them had exploded taking out all power and communication in a split second. The pilot had no chance of controlling the aircraft as the complete tail assembly was gone. It would have spun into the sea at full speed, exploding the doors open and killing all occupants on impact, a terrifying descent, but a quick end. Alex expected to see skeletal remains, but there was nothing. The cabin was empty except for the remains of the seats and attached debris. The expected report canisters were not there. He attached a cord and inflated a marker buoy, letting it go to the surface so Rocco could reposition over the site. They searched out and away from the wreck in the hope what they were looking for had been thrown out by the force of the crash. They searched methodically, but there was nothing. Finally, on the point of exhaustion Alex gave the signal and they surfaced, where Rocco helped them aboard.

"It's strange there's no sign of any canisters. They would have been heavy with the weight of those reports and I don't believe they've just drifted off," Peta said as they sat around gathering their thoughts. "And there were no human remains."

"I wouldn't have expected to find any Peta," Alex replied softly as he realised what she was thinking. "The marine life would have taken care of that very quickly."

Peta did not reply as she looked vacantly out to sea lost in her personal thoughts.

"Perhaps someone made it to that island." Rocco was pointing at the tiny coral cay nearby.

"No chance of that Rocco, judging by what happened. No one would have survived the impact," Alex replied.

Peta shook her head. "No, Zeeius was searched thoroughly and supplies and a radio were left just in case someone had made it. A check was made a month or so later. The food was untouched and the radio battery flat." She stood up and began to pull on another tank. "I'm going down again. I've just remembered, there's an enclosed cargo pod built into the bulkhead behind the rear seats. You didn't see it did you."

"I didn't notice it, but let's rest for awhile. You must be exhausted?" He could see she was not to be dissuaded as she strapped on her tanks. He reached out for his and began to strap them on.

They all heard the sound at the same time. The creaming bow of the oncoming drill rig support vessel was only metres from the centre of the pearler. The noise of its approach had been drowned out by the steady thud of the compressor filling scuba tanks and the fact they were below the surrounding noise level in the well of the stern. A yell rose in Alex's throat as he sprang to his feet. It was too late as the vessel hit at full speed. Ly disappeared in a splintering mess of shattered deck as Rocco was thrown and sucked down through the maelstrom. He was already dead, his chest impaled by a length of Jarrah decking.

Alex threw himself backwards and sideways over the low railing. The harness of the tank was caught around one arm as he felt the sea close around him. He was thrown violently against the hull of the oncoming vessel. The impact drove the air out of his lungs. He felt himself falling into total darkness as he struck out to clear the thrashing twin propellers he realised would cut him to pieces on contact. His world went strangely quiet and then he felt a mouthpiece being forced between his teeth as he gulped the life-giving air. Peta was dragging him down and away from the danger before helping him pull on his tank and secure it. He had no face mask and his eyes stung as he followed her. He was disorientated and made to swim for the surface, but she dragged him down and away from the receding propellers. They had been swimming for about fifteen minutes when the supercharged shock waves from the explosion of the seismic charges reached them.

Alex felt the excruciating pain hit him and watched as Peta clapped her hands to her ears and lost her mouthpiece in a gurgling scream of pain. A second shockwave from a following explosion knocked her senseless as she went limp and began to sink. Alex roughly pushed her mouthpiece back between the rictus of her lips and pulled her towards the surface. He knew the danger, but it was their only hope. She began clawing at the water with paralysed actions, her co-ordination gone as she tried hopelessly to move her arms and legs. The streams of bubbles from her mouthpiece ranged from spasmodic and irregular, to great sheets of bubbles as she fought to survive.

Alex was at the limit of his endurance as they surfaced. He supported her head and gently took out her mouthpiece. It was late morning with the sun already dipping past its zenith. Alex could see the vessel in the distance and watched as it slowly started to move in a wide circle. They were between the vessel and the glaring sun at their backs and he realised it would be near impossible for anyone spot them while looking directly into that fireball. They were bobbing up and down in the gentle swell, but his heart sank when he saw a helicopter rise from the decks and make a low sweep to the north towards the cay. On the return pass he calculated it would fly directly over them. Suddenly, it diverted further to the north, appeared to hover for a short time and then return to the ship. Obviously, it had been dispatched to check on some floating debris or survivor.

"C'mon Peta. We have to swim for that cay. It's our only chance." He stripped off his tanks and weights and helped her out of hers. She slowly began to stroke and kick as he remained at her side all the time encouraging and cajoling her to keep going. Neither spoke as they fought their private battle for survival. Each knew they could not rely on the other if they cramped up or simply stopped, exhausted. Alex could feel every muscle screaming in pain as he drew close to the ultimate threshold where either the body simply collapsed or the brain adjusted to the agony and allowed the fight to continue. He looked at his watch. They had been swimming for almost an hour and appeared to be barely making headway. He then began to feel the tidal pull and his ears picked up the sound of waves breaking on the rocky outcrop of the cay. He surged on and felt Peta responding as she had also recognised the sound. The cay crept closer and then within a few hundred metres of the shore they felt themselves being checked and could feel the pull of the tide as it began to suck them back out.

"One last effort Peta," he shouted. "We've got to really swim for it."

He struck out with all his remaining strength without waiting for a reply. There was no point in looking around to see if she was following him. She was either with him, or she was as good as dead. Within seconds she was at his side stroking blindly, driven on by fear and the pursuit of life. He felt the roller begin to surge up behind them and they both fought hard to keep on its crest. It finally broke and dumped them in a spinning twirl of arms and legs. He felt the litter of shells and broken coral under his feet, but was knocked over as the undertow fought to reclaim him. The oyster encrusted rocks tore at his wet suit as he was tumbled along the bottom, the air driven from his lungs as breaker after breaker relentlessly burst on top of him. Blind panic made him thrash out for something to hold onto. His hand brushed something soft. It was Peta's unconscious form being tossed around in the maelstrom of the pounding surf. The surf suddenly delivered the spent beings onto the beach before once again tormenting them as it clutched at their exhausted forms. Alex staggered to his feet and pulled Peta further up the beach, out of reach of the demanding sea. Coral debris and rocks tore at the soles of his diving boots, but he was oblivious to the pain as death receded with every step he took as he helped her stagger up the beach. Finally, they collapsed behind a scrub-covered rise, his tortured body overtaken by his exhausted senses. It was dark when he stirred and staggered to his feet driven on by the fear of imminent danger. He looked out to sea. The vessel was clearly visible with all its deck lights blazing where it was riding directly over the top of the wreck.

He knew the cay would be searched at first light as there was no doubt in his mind Springer was out there. It was one of

Roma's supply vessels, immensely powerful and able to tackle any sea with its reinforced hull and bows that would withstand the hardest crunch against the side of a drill rig. It was purpose built with high bow and bridge perched well forward of the usual centreline so the afterdeck could carry a large helicopter and heavy equipment. The immense power generated by the turbo-charged diesels had crushed Ly's boat to matchwood.

He became alarmed at their barely concealed position. They would be easily discovered when Springer came ashore. He shook Peta violently. "For God's sake Peta, wake up. We've got to move now."

She gradually opened her eyes. "I can't move Alex. I'm exhausted."

"You've got to, and now." He pulled her savagely to her feet and threw her over his shoulder in a fireman's lift. Every muscle screamed in agony as he began to climb slowly away from the shore. Spasms of pain began to wrack his aching back as he picked his way through the clumps of stunted saltbush. Realising he would be perfectly silhouetted against the skyline, he walked just below the ridge line as he put distance between them and the beach. Exhaustion forced him to stop every so often and rest. With a final glance backwards as he began to walk up a gully largely concealed from the vessel, he saw the inflatable detach itself and begin to make for shore. He believed they had not been spotted otherwise Springer would have surely used the helicopter. He hurried on, the sharp terrain tearing at his feet. He was moving blindly while trying to find somewhere to hide. Peta was a dead weight as he stumbled up and over a crest and sat down under a ledge from where he could see the extent of the cay. It would only take an hour to walk around and any search would quickly find them.

He smelt the smoke long before he saw it. It suddenly came bursting up over the ridge behind them as the wind fanned the blaze. There has been no sign of wildlife previously, but native rats and lizards began to scurry around them driven by the natural fear of fire.

Alex pulled Peta to her feet again and leaned forward to bend her over his shoulders. He stumbled and pitched forward as his ankle twisted and gave out beneath him. The flash of pain seared up his leg. He swore loudly as he ignored the pain and picked her up again. They were now on the opposite side of the tiny cay and out of sight of their pursuers. The fire had given them time, because whoever was pursuing them would have to wait until the fires died down before re-commencing their search. Each step sent a searing pain from ankle to brain. He froze as the deadly snake flashed across his path. It was more intent on escaping the fire than striking anything that moved. It ignored its natural prey of rats as it slithered amongst them in its bid to escape. Soon the crest of the island was enveloped in smoke as the fire took hold. He knew it was only a matter of time before they were discovered if they did not quickly find a hiding place. If they had been seen, their fate was sealed. The island was a perfect grave, uninhabited and so isolated only the most dedicated of naturalists would visit. Hide the remains in a shallow grave and nothing would ever be found. Alex stumbled onto the rocky foreshore and blindly moved towards the sea again, away from the fire and the vessel on the opposite side. His subconscious knew what he was looking for. From where he was standing the shore looked as though it just sloped gently out to where it met the sea. However, the extreme tidal surges commonly gouged out ledges and caverns in a terraced formation which were not visible unless approached to within a few metres. He calculated the tide was still on the ebb as he ventured as far out as he dared looking for a concealed position under one of the ledges. They were completely exposed and he expected to hear a shout from behind him at any moment. He eased over a terrace and then saw it, a cavern right back under an overhanging ledge. He leaned down as he walked in and dropped Peta onto the wet floor. They were safe for a few hours until the tide turned and drowned them. Alex sat back and studied the relentless surge of the Indian Ocean. Even if Springer did not find them, their chances of survival were extremely slim. Who was going to mount a search? He looked at Peta and toyed with the idea of giving themselves up. It would provide a little time and maybe a chance of survival. Maybe Springer was out to rescue them rather than intent on murder. The image of the supply ship and its lethal bow loomed back into his mind and he immediately dismissed the thought of any compassion from Springer. The shattered hull and Rocco's impaled body were still vivid. Winton Springer wanted them dead.

His wandering mind snapped back, galvanised by the sound of voices. They were close, probably standing right on top of the ledge above. He looked across at Peta, but she was completely out to it. The swells had already begun to lap at the shelf below with the occasional rogue wave sending a giant spume into the air before dropping back. He could hear someone scrambling around the rocks. It was only a matter of minutes before their position was discovered.

"Nothing down here." The shout came from right on top of them. Alex withdrew further as loose rocks fell inches from his face. "I'm not going any further," the voice yelled again. "If anyone's out there, they're as good as dead anyway."

There was a muffled reply and then he heard footsteps as someone jumped from rock to rock as they retreated up the terrace. He waited and listened for voices, but the crash of the encroaching sea was dominant. He slowly moved out from under the ledge and cautiously looked over the top. Two figures were hundreds of metres away studying the stunted growth of the landscape. The fire had burnt out when it reached the ridge on the eastern side. The prevailing westerly wind had prevented the fire from spreading down onto windward side but he knew the moment the wind abated they would set fires to complete the total destruction of the vegetation.

Alex shook Peta awake. He half dragged her up over the ledge and away from the sea which was now within metres of their concealment. They were still partially hidden as he scanned the beach and skyline for any movement. He froze as he caught a flash of colour and saw a solitary figure sitting on a rock well above the waterline, staring directly at him. Alex looked around at the advancing tide. They could not move anywhere, but forward towards higher ground. Their escape was blocked. Retreat into the sea meant death as their exhausted bodies could not take another beating. Gradually, the incoming waves began to clutch at them until the boiling foam hit with a pounding rush and lingered as it endeavoured to suck them back into its grip. He held onto Peta tightly as he clung to a handhold above with his free hand. He raised his head again, but the figure was still there, staring directly at their position as though mocking them in their predicament. Desperately, he looked back at the sea. Ten more minutes. That would be the limit before the sea reclaimed them completely. Another rogue wave suddenly smashed into their backs and dislodged them. They floated for a few moments before being dragged back by the surging water. His fingers dug into a crevice and he cried out in pain as he felt his fingernails tearing. Peta was a dead weight and unable to offer any assistance. The wave burst forward again and flung them back onto the ledge. The next wave would be their last as he used the last of his strength to shove Peta up and drag himself clear. His breath came in exhausted gasps as he waited for the shout of discovery. He waited, but the only sound was the crashing of the surf as it persistently pounded to crest the terrace in its relentless rush towards the high water mark. He rolled over and focussed. The person had disappeared.

He pulled Peta to her feet and staggered up the pebbly shore and into the dense dry undergrowth. It completely enveloped them as they pushed further into the centre of the grove of stunted bush. They were safe for the moment, the slender thread holding their lives in balance was still intact. The sun beat down mercilessly. The low scrub and their tattered wet suits shielded them from its scorching rays. His blood ran cold when he noticed the figure walking slowly back along the beach, his upraised arms draped over the pump-action shotgun held across the nape of his neck. Suddenly he swung the gun down and looked directly up at them. Alex crouched lower.

"Nothing down here boss. I don't think anyone's on this place."

A voice replied barely twenty metres from their position. "You could be right. There were four people on that boat and we've only seen one body. The other three are probably at the bottom, but I want to make sure. Two of you can stay here tonight. I want this side of the island burnt off as soon as the wind swings."

Alex did not have to look to identify the speaker. He knew he could lay in wait for Springer and surprise him if he came closer. However, his reflexes and body were tired and one slip or hesitation and Springer could blow him away at such short range. The effect of a shotgun blast so close would be devastating and final. Alex held his breath and pushed Peta into the ground as Springer walked past only metres from his head. He was scanning the rise above and away from where they were concealed. He bent down and attempted to light the grass but the prevailing wind would not let it run in the intended direction. In another hour the wind would swing and that side of the island would be reduced to ash within minutes as the fire raced through the undergrowth. Alex watched as the two men strolled back along the beach and disappeared around a low headland. He was deep in thought as to their predicament when Peta slowly sat up.

"How do you feel?"

"A lot better than you I believe." She was looking at his torn feet and hands. "I'm sorry I'm such a burden, but I've had everything knocked out of me. You saved my life."

"I haven't saved it yet. If we don't find a way of getting off this cay we're as good as dead. Springer means business and he's going to set fire to this side as soon as the wind changes."

"I can't imagine how I look." She tossed her head and instinctively pushed her hand through her hair. She grimaced as she felt the cloying salt, matted vegetation and sand.

"You're still beautiful, but you could do with a makeover." Alex grinned at her dishevelled appearance.

"Has Springer gone?"

"I didn't know you realised it was him. I thought you were out to it."

"It's a voice I'll never forget," Peta shuddered. "But I thought he was stranded in Perth?"

"Obviously, the problem was fixed and he got into Onslow before we left. The chopper ferried him out to the support vessel and they got here well before we did. Rocco must have given the cops the position so Springer would have had no trouble in finding it."

"What are we going to do now?"

"We've got to find a place to hide for the rest of the day and move as soon as it becomes dark. They're coming back to fire this side of the island. We'll be barbecued if we stay here."

"Have you any ideas?"

"I was hoping you wouldn't ask me that. I just don't know yet."

"Can we make a raft? There looks to be a lot of loose wood on the shore."

"We've got nothing to tie it all together with and if we did, we certainly wouldn't make it to the mainland. The huge tides would just keep us going backwards and forwards forever. Without some means of propulsion we would be doomed."

"How long can we last?"

"No trouble in surviving. I've seen a couple of springs with water seeping out and there's plenty of animal, birdlife, oysters and crabs. A bit of roasted rat or snake would supplement a diet of bird's eggs and shellfish. We'd certainly survive in that sense, but we'd probably never be found as there are hundreds of these isolated cays that no one ever comes near. You read jokes about people being stranded on desert islands, but I don't want to actually experience it."

They heard the sound of the outboard motor. Alex crawled through the scrub and up to ridgeline looking out over the burned side of the cay. He could see the inflatable with three people on board heading towards the support vessel. He turned and retreated down the slope.

"We're safe for now," he said as he slumped down beside Peta. "I don't think they'll come back until late this afternoon when the offshore wind arises."

"We're in real trouble, aren't we? Now I know what a condemned man feels like before he faces the executioner."

Alex nodded. They hardly spoke as they watched the day roll through its cycle, each lost in their own thoughts. The sun gradually sank and then disappeared leaving an afterglow followed by a moonless night. The wind had died to nothing. They heard the sound of the approaching outboard motor.

"We're lucky there's no wind to fan the fire otherwise they would have been here earlier. We'd better move."

"Where are we going to hide now?"

"With the enemy."

Peta gave him a puzzled look.

"It's just occurred to me we do have a slim chance of getting away," Alex said as he looked down at the beach and out to the brightly lit vessel.

"And how's that?"

Alex did not reply as he took her arm and led her quietly down the slope making sure they kept in the shadows of the rocky terrain. He pointed as he rounded a large outcrop. She saw the inflatable runabout pulled up on the beach.

A small camp fire further up the rise of the beach signified the presence of the hunters and he could hear voices. Alex squatted and watched for any movement. The night air grew cooler and Peta shivered. Alex drew her towards him and she was suddenly in his arms and quietly sobbing. The last vestige of self control was being stripped away and she felt incredibly scared. The enormity of their precarious hold on life suddenly hit her.

"We're going to die here Alex. I know it. I don't want to die in this place."

He kissed her gently.

"I was in love with you the moment I first saw you."

"I as much told you the same thing, but you brushed me off," Alex replied with a low chuckle.

"I've never been propositioned like that before. So direct, I thought you must be joking. I thought you were Alex Carlin, the wealthy playboy who could do what he liked and take what he wanted. And I wasn't interested in being just another conquest."

"No, Peta I'm not a playboy and I'd like to marry you if we get out of this mess in one piece."

She grasped his head between her hands and pulled him to her. "I accept."

"You'll have to wait for the engagement ring," he said as he broke away and held her hands. "And now Mrs Carlin, we've got work to do. We're going to take their boat. They've started the fires so they'll be looking to see if they flush us out. The last thing they'll be looking at is the inflatable."

A look of fear crossed her face. "But they have guns. We'll have no chance if they see us."

"We have no chance if we stay here." She followed him as he slowly picked his way ahead carefully until they were the shortest distance from the craft.

"Come on, run as hard as you can. It's now or never and don't stop or look around."

Minutes later they had the craft launched and were paddling as hard as their energy and lungs would allow. They dared not start the outboard.

"We're going in the wrong direction. We're headed for Springer's boat," Peta became alarmed when she took note of where they were heading.

"We can't survive in this thing for long. We've got to take the chance and see if we can't get aboard without being seen."

"Do you always live dangerously?"

"I did once."

"Is that where you got those burns from?" Peta was looking at his hands and wrists as they became exposed with each thrust of the paddle. The replaced tissue on the burned flesh stood out against the darker skin of his forearms. She had also previously noted the thin but faint scar line around the forehead and cheeks that had marked the edges of his flying helmet.

"Yes, I was in Afghanistan. My chopper was brought down and my hands and face needed resurfacing. I don't remember a lot about it."

She stopped paddling for a moment and touched him on the cheek. "There are deeper scars there Alex, not visible, but clearly there. I have a complete picture of the man I've fallen in love with and I don't want the canvas re-touched."

Neither spoke as they paddled quietly towards the ship. In contrast to what they had seen earlier, the vessel was only lit by its riding lights, a single white beam on the masthead and the port and starboard red and green lamps.

Something seemed odd to Alex, but the thought was gone in a split second. He approached the bow head-on and slowly dropped down the starboard side. The stern of the vessel was only a metre above the waterline, the after-deck a broad flat expanse. The powerful twin-turbine Agusta helicopter was squatting in the middle of another platform above.

Alex clung onto the stern for several minutes listening for any sound, but all he could hear above the lapping of the water on the hull was the dull hum of the ship's generator. He pulled himself up until his eyes were level with the deck. It was clear. He slowly studied the superstructure for any signs of life and then bent down to Peta.

"I'm going to try for the chopper. It's our only hope. You stay here until I signal it's okay and then come running."

"They'll hear you the moment you start the engines," she replied anxiously.

"Not necessarily. It's a turbine and it may take a minute or two for anyone to register if they're sleeping or watching a movie below. Springer is most probably on the island."

"I'm coming with you."

"Let's go then." He pulled himself up on the deck and then reached down for her. They ran painfully across the deck on their bleeding feet and began to climb the short stairway to the helipad. He scanned the deck below for danger as he opened the cockpit door and helped her up and in.

His actions were automatic as he scanned the cockpit instruments, switching on all operating switches before turning the master on. He hit the starter and watched and silently cajoled the blades to commence to turn. The turbines began to run up with a low rumbling whistle as he watched the revs mount towards the minimum lift-off position. Finally, it came with a rush as he prepared to raise the collective. Five seconds and the danger would be gone.

Something hard was pushed into the base of his neck. He could feel the cold spears of fear shoot to his brain. He froze and twisted around to see Winton Springer grinning broadly as he moved the Glock level with his right eye.

"You really thought you could get away with it, didn't you Carlin? Now shut it down and climb out. If you attempt to take off I shall shoot Dr Coulson."

Springer stood at the top of the platform as they descended. He indicated them to move to the side of the ship before he backed down the ladder. He was not going to take any chances Alex would rush him.

"Well, that accounts for three of you. It only leaves one to account for, but he must be dead if he's not with you. I don't know how you avoided our search of the island, but I knew you had to be there somewhere. I was on the bridge watching through night glasses when I saw you take the inflatable so I thought I'd give you a real surprise."

"And now you're going to murder us?"

"Yes, I want you gone before my crew gets back. I don't want any witnesses. I want a clean boat by the morning so I can tell the crew to head for port."

"You really are a psychopath Springer. How many people have you killed now?"

"Two. One was self-defence and the other unavoidable; Marty knew too much and was about to expose me."

"You're also responsible for Sam's death. I heard the recording of you taunting him. And what about Reed and Maria Stenner?"

"I started this company with your father," Springer sneered. "It was half mine by right. I did fall in love with your sister, but then she discovered something she shouldn't have, and now you two are the only impediments remaining. I'm sorry Dr Coulson, but you shouldn't have got involved."

"You murdered my husband along with others on that helicopter." Peta shouted as she lurched at him. Alex grabbed and restrained her.

"That was unfortunate, but he would have exposed me and the others were just collateral damage. A seismic detonator with a timer was all it took. And yes Dr Coulson, I was aware Max Brown was your husband. I managed to get to the helicopter first and remove the data you were after, but then I realised I would also have to get rid of any pointing fingers of accusation. This way it is clean and no one will be the wiser. I want you to strip out of those wet suits so the reef sharks will quickly remove all evidence of your existence when they smell the blood in the water."

Alex caught a movement in the shadows behind Springer. "You've still got one final impediment you haven't thought about Springer, and that's Louise."

"Oh, I'm about to cover that base. She's sleeping below, but as soon as I've dealt with you, I'm afraid the beautiful Louise will suffer the same fate."

Louise stepped out of the shadows with the shotgun clutched awkwardly. "You bastard Winton. Now I understand why you insisted I come with you. All your talk about love and marriage was just a front. If you didn't kill me here, you would have killed me somewhere in the near future."

She started to raise the gun, but Springer spun sideways and fired twice. The heavy slugs tore into her body. In a compulsive reaction, she pulled both triggers of the double-barrelled weapon as she crumpled to the deck. Winton Springer took the full force of the two twelve-gauge barrages of lead pellets at such close range. His chest exploded in a showering burst of blood and shattered bone as he was thrown backwards over the side.

Alex knelt down beside Louise and gently closed her staring eyes before turning to Peta and taking her by the arm.

"Come on. Let's get out of here. The police can come back and clean up this mess."

As the helicopter lifted off he looked down and could see the foaming mass of flashing silver and black-tipped fins tearing at the remains of Winton Springer.

9 781925 477542